PRAISE FOR *27 DAYS*

"Moore skillfully delivers in the rat-a-tat style of Hammett and Spillane, daring you to turn the page and see what happens next."
—Charles Salzberg, two-time Shamus Award nominee for *Swann's Last Song* and *Second Story Man.*

"PI Nick Crane, hard on the outside, compassionate within, is truly a justice warrior and is brilliantly suited for these uncertain times. Can't wait to see this as a TV series or movie."
—Max Myers, award-winning author of *Boysie Blake: Problem Solver*

"Patrick H. Moore delivers a dark masterpiece here, a brawling, gunfire symphony dripping with ominous overtones. A contemporary western, a compelling and intricate mystery, a social allegory of the oldest sins of humankind—this book has it all."
—John Nardizzi, Shamus Award finalist for *The Burden of Innocence*

"Readers looking for unrelenting suspense and fascinating, well-developed characters will find it all here, as the bodies pile up and the action cascades in unanticipated twists that will keep you riveted until the final page."
—John Brown, Los Angeles private investigator

"Patrick H. Moore has done it again with *27 Days,* his latest offering in the explosively entertaining Nick Crane series. This time Moore's complicated tough-guy PI Crane finds himself in the crosshairs of a domestic terrorist organization whose motto is *Make America Safe Again.* What follows is a blisteringly taut page turner with loads of engaging attitude plus blind-side twists that Moore delivers with the authority of a pro investigator that he is."

—Michael D. Sellers, award-winning director of
Eye of the Dolphin

"A searing cocktail of Dennis Lehane and James Lee Burke, with a double-shot chaser of Dashiell Hammett. This red-hot page-turner careens through the underworld of a divided America, sparing no one as Nick Crane races the clock against domestic terrorists. Wall-to-wall heart-pounding action, riveting dialogue, and a dark vision of our country, you'll be left breathless when you finish."

—Kirk Sanders, Silicon Valley technologist

"Nick Crane may not be looking for trouble, but trouble finds him in the form of a cabal of domestic terrorists who want him dead. In the face of impossible odds, Crane fights back, embarking on an audacious tour of the American heartland in the process. What follows is the gripping tale of one imperturbable PI taking on powerful forces that will leave the reader on the edge of their seat."

—Daisy Swan, reader of great fiction

27 DAYS

BOOKS BY
PATRICK H. MOORE

The Nick Crane Thrillers
Cicero's Dead
27 Days
Rogues and Patriots (coming soon)

PATRICK H. MOORE

27 DAYS

A Nick Crane Thriller

DOWN&OUT

BOOKS

Down & Out Books
3959 Van Dyke Road, Suite 265
Lutz, FL 33558
DownAndOutBooks.com

Cover design by Margo Nauert

ISBN: 1-64396-298-1
ISBN-13: 978-1-64396-298-6

To *Warren Larry Foster, Vietnam veteran,*
American hero, and friend unto death.
May he find the peace that
every Vietnam veteran longs for.

And to BJW Nashe, my good friend and unflinching
literary advisor, without whom this book
may have never seen the light of day.

PART ONE
Chapter One

I was just about to settle down with *The Zebra-Striped Hearse* by Ross MacDonald when the brick shattered the cabin window. I ducked for cover and reached for the gun I did not have. Heart pounding. A sickness deep in my gut. It was a few days before Easter, but I wasn't in the mood. The brick lay on the floor at the foot of the bed in a Ziploc freezer bag. I got down on my hands and knees. The envelope inside was addressed to me in large letters. *Mr. Nick Crane, I am your friend. You and your cabin will be bombed in five minutes. You must leave right now. My driver Mars, a tall black man with burn marks on his face, is next door at The Gourd waiting for you. Enter by the back door.* Underneath it was signed in longhand, *Yours faithfully, Willem Spahn.*

Since escaping from Marguerite Ferguson and Thomas Quincey and their gang of traitorous aristocrats, I never go to sleep without being prepared. For moments like this. I threw on jeans and a denim shirt and peered out front. No one. Picked up my grip and stepped out onto the back patio. Hopped the low back fence and stopped. If I turned right, and if I got away, I would plunge back into the void where I'd been wandering. Other than random attacks like this, it wasn't a bad place. Plenty of good books, reasonable daily alcohol intake, the gym every

1

other day. And the occasional futile night in some obscure watering hole. And to what end? Only the nothingness that loomed large late at night and clung to me like a miasma in the morning.

If I turned left, it would start all over again. With no guarantee I could weather another campaign. I don't remember deciding. Just turned left. Down past the cabins and through a break in the chain-link fence into The Gourd's parking lot. Carrying everything I owned in my compact leather traveling bag. A few clothes, my books, half-a-dozen burners, my shaving kit, a pair of night vision binoculars, and an aftermarket Taser-X2 that I had picked up in a Portland pawnshop. My wallet was in my left front pants pocket and my drop point hunting knife was strapped to the inside of my left ankle.

The parking lot was half full, the usual collection of late-model pickups, SUVs, and domestic and imported sedans. Nothing alarming until just as I was nearing the back door, a brace of flat-black Chrysler 300s with deeply tinted windows came into focus.

I stepped back into the shadows between a black SVAutobiography Range Rover and a blue Hyundai Santa Fe. Took out my binoculars and trained it on the driver's side of the closest Chrysler. Both side windows were halfway down. Dark bulky shapes inside.

Hmm. I waited. Two drunken cowboys came outside. One tried and failed to square his Cattleman; the other announced that he had to piss. Cattleman put his arm around Pissman. Together, they did a one-eighty and headed back into the bar.

No movement inside the Chryslers. I didn't like it. Their plan was to either jack me here in the parking lot or follow me to a lonelier spot and jack me there. Dirty business either way. I turned and walked back to the break in the chain-link fence. Stepped through and cut between the cabins. Came out on the main road. Waited thirty seconds, took a deep breath, and edged my way quickly to the front door of The Gourd.

It was a small bar. Greeted by the satisfying crack of a cue ball striking true. Hank Williams, Jr. singing in the background. I was no more than three steps in the door when a tall black man, wearing a leather jacket over black jeans and a black point collar dress shirt, walked up to me. Prominent burn marks on his right cheek and forehead gave him the look of an infidel.

"Nick Crane, I believe."

I nodded. "Look, Mars, we've got a problem." I grabbed him by the arm and steered him back toward the pool tables. He didn't resist. The last booth was empty. Motioned for him to sit down. Sat down next to him.

"Take it easy, Mr. Crane." Voice a low, calm rumble.

"There are two black Chryslers parked near the back door. Marguerite's people, I assume. Waiting for you and me to walk out. Unless you're actually with them."

"Does the name Desmond Cole mean anything to you?" Same low, calm voice.

Indeed. Desmond Cole and Marguerite Ferguson and Thomas Quincey. The full Monty. The total wrecking crew.

"My boss, Willem Spahn, is helping Mr. Cole on a number of matters. One of which is to get you out of here. You can either come with me, or Marguerite's people are going to scorch your ass. Your choice. Here." An M1911 was cradled in his big hands. Then it was cradled in mine.

Handsome gun. Stainless steel. Seven-round magazine. I looked at Mars. His blue-black lips curved into a smile. "I'm sure this isn't what you were expecting tonight, but it's better than the alternative."

He was right. We put our heads together and came up with a plan. Then we stood up and walked out the front door. I showed Mars how to cut through the cabins to the hole in the chain-link fence. He would walk casually to his SUV, get in, and drive out as unobtrusively as possible. In the meantime, I would walk north on the main road. He would swing by and pick me up.

Only one problem. One of the Chryslers got there first.

Maybe Marguerite's crew had a plant in the bar. Or out on the street. Or maybe Mars was in cahoots with them. I had a choice. Duck or run? Couldn't run. That way you get shot in the back. I ducked into a stairwell leading up to second-story apartments. A Thai take-out joint on one side, a life insurance company on the other.

Too late. The Chrysler was parked in a loading zone. No sign of its twin. Three men got out. Dark suits. Bulky look. Guns in their hands. The driver seemed to stay put. The stairwell was narrow, and I stopped halfway up, immersed in shadows.

"Nick Crane." The voice was high, whiny, and came from one of the suits. "We know you're up there. We need to talk to you. We can do this the easy way, or we can do this the hard way. So drop your weapons, put your hands on your head, and get your ass down here. You have sixty seconds. Then we're going to come up after you."

The Range Rover pulled up behind the Chrysler. Mars got out. I studied him and the suits through the binoculars. Mars produced a gun, stared at it, and put it away. Some guys don't like shooting people...Two of the suits were thick-trunked and didn't look worried at all, which pissed me off. The other, his hair slicked back in a Pat Riley pompadour, kept checking his watch.

Sixty seconds turned into ninety, then one hundred twenty. Fear? Hesitation? Maybe.

"Time's up!" said Pompadour suddenly, his voice rising. "We warned you, you dumb fuck." The two thick-trunked guys sprinted toward the stairwell, keeping low to the ground. Pompadour followed suit. It was over fast. The screaming of men in pain is a sound I never get used to. Wish I could say I only shot one of them. Or two. But I shot all three. Three clean hits—two gut shots, one to the chest—two misses, and one shoulder shot. Saved one bullet for dire circumstances...

"C'mon!" shouted Mars.

Left them there lying on the ground. Dead? Maybe. Unless

they got help, they soon would be.

Tossed my bag into the back of the Range Rover and sat up front next to Mars who guided us expertly out of Burns, Oregon and onto Highway 20—two hundred miles to the Idaho border. I fought off the urge to call 911 to report the wounded men. Their driver or the fools in the other Chrysler could take care of that. Or maybe they were "cleaners" and would take care of it themselves. I leaned back into the plush leather upholstery.

The nausea came over me in waves. I rolled down the window and stuck my head out. Didn't vomit. Haven't since I was a kid. Took a couple of deep breaths. Cold mountain air. Pulled my head back inside. Whatever this play was, it was better than being stripped naked, chained to a chair in a Black Site interrogation room, which was how my recent adventure with Marguerite Ferguson and Thomas Quincey had begun back in September.

I insisted Mars pull off the highway and kill the lights at the next cattle crossing. In case we were being followed. Let them get ahead of us. If Mars was shaken by the mayhem, he didn't show it.

"So, what the hell was that about?" I asked. "Who were those fuckers?"

Mars looked at me, his burn marks black against the bronze of his cheek and forehead. Then he shrugged. "Just like I said back in the bar, Marguerite's people were going to scorch your ass."

My turn to shrug. I knew they didn't want to kill me. Orders were to take me alive. So that Marguerite could deliver the coup de grâce personally. Which in this case had worked to my advantage. I decided to take another tack.

"So who the hell is Willem Spahn?"

Mars grinned. "You mean Sir Willem Spahn. He's my wealthy boss. Says he's descended from German Burgraves, who, it turns out, are one step up from barons. But that's jive. He talks like an ordinary American with a Midwestern accent."

"Is that so?" Obnoxious Crane. "So spill, baby. What's going on? I suppose you threw the brick through my window?"

Mars looked me over. White teeth visible in the dim interior. "That was me. Based on Willem's orders. The idea was to get your attention before Marguerite's people caught up with you." He emitted a low, sonorous chuckle. "That was a crazy scene back there on the street, Mr. Crane. I thought you were toast…" He paused, pondered, and ran his fingers across his burn marks. "Just in case you're wondering, we're on our way to Willem's estate in Vail, Colorado. He wants to meet you. We may not stay there long. He likes to keep moving. He's been that way ever since Desmond Cole showed up one cold November morning."

Then as if he'd said too much, he ran a finger across his lips, the old zip-it gesture, and reached into the center console for his dab pipe. A big lunger. Another. Offered it to me. I declined. Ran my hands up and down my legs and across my chest. Took a deep breath. I was alive and that was a good thing.

Chapter Two

We waited for an hour and got back on the road. Mars did all the driving and most of the talking. But stayed away from why Desmond Cole, with Willem Spahn as his proxy, had chosen to rescue me. Didn't push him. He expounded on his Jamaican roots while demonstrating his love of ganja by periodic dabbing. Sometime after midnight, he told me his hard-luck tale about a London gas heater that exploded when he was nineteen and left him scarred but unbroken. We were the perfect team. Mars could really talk, and I excelled at riding point with the reloaded M1911 at ease in the glove compartment.

Between catnaps, I tried to suss this play. What was Cole's game? Six months ago, he had looked the other way when Marguerite's gun moll had gut-shot me on the Charles River Esplanade in iconic old Boston. Was he trying to make up for it? Not necessarily. Cole was a hard man to pin down. And where did Spahn come in? Cole's moneyman, I would assume. For all his savoir faire and brilliance in the art of manipulation, Dee Cole had a problem. He'd never recovered from going belly-up in the tech crash of 2000.

Marguerite's current dark passion was to detain pending deportation all Latinos who had been in the U.S. less than five years and all Muslims who had been here less than ten. New legislation was afoot that would permit Homeland Security to detain targeted individuals for extended periods without actual deportation...which meant scores of new private prisons that Marguerite's consortium would bankroll. The private sector jailers would put the "prisoners" to work building whatever the market demanded for twenty-three cents an hour.

It was diabolical—a flat-out money grab. With some of the seed money to break ground sent over from foreign lands, washed by compliant banks, and then handed off to our new super-class of private prison CEOs. With Marguerite waving the conductor's wand.

I understood her endgame. Or thought I did. What I didn't understand was the nature of her relationship with Desmond Cole and the other principals. Or their relationship to the traditional avenues of power. Based on the little I knew, the principals appeared to be a ring of aristocratic criminals and power mongers, twenty in number. Not to be confused with certain high-ranking government officials, also sometimes referred to as the principals.

Now, I had two choices. I could cooperate—dirty word— and see what Cole's plans were, or I could force Mars to let me out of the car at two a.m. at some godforsaken intersection in the next mountain hamlet. I decided to cooperate.

We pulled into a rest stop near Twin Falls, Idaho around four a.m. and slept for a few hours. Then a straight ten-hour pull south through Salt Lake City and the heart of Utah. Then east on I-70. It was snowing steadily, thick warm flakes, when we arrived at Willem Spahn's mountain estate on the southern edge of Vail.

Mars led me to the guest cottage, which was high-end rustic, bigger than some folks' houses. A second M1911, holstered, lay on the night table next to the bed. On his way out, Mars told me dinner was at seven and asked me how I liked my London broil. I told him whatever way the cook had in mind.

Got on Amazon and ordered biographies of Nureyev and Baryshnikov for my daughter Maleah for her upcoming birthday. After devouring the London broil and toying with the side dishes,

I poured myself a second cup of coffee and hunkered down with *The Zebra-Striped Hearse*. Although PI Lew Archer was having a tough time keeping his client, the irascible Colonel Blackwell, happy, he was in little danger of being shot, abducted, or tortured. Lucky fella. When I finally slept, I dreamt about flat-black Chryslers and thick-trunked men bleeding out on sidewalks.

When I pried my eyes open the next morning, I stumbled to the Jacuzzi and washed off my travel grime. Then I toweled off, shaved, and pulled on fresh jeans and a clean denim shirt. Checked the refrigerator. High-end water and not much else. German thrift.

My problems began in 2011 when my team and I liquidated Frank Constantine. Quite a guy! A military psychiatrist and serial killer of women, he was highly regarded by the principals, Thomas Quincey in particular, for his cutting-edge research in "gentler, kinder torture techniques."

The night before Constantine died, my LAPD friend Tony Bott and I had confiscated and cached his "torture records." This was a mistake. Two weeks later agents of an unidentified agency parked their brown panel trucks at the curb and retrieved the records. Matter-of-fact manner. Case closed. Or so I thought. What I didn't know till recently was that Constantine had been a member of Marguerite's cabal. She and Cole and Quincey. They did not forgive, and they did not forget.

Fast forward seven years to September 2018. I was abducted by Marguerite and her goons. Given two choices. I could work for them as a hired gun and operations manager in charge of organizing false flag terrorist operations, or they would have me arrested for stealing Frank Constatine's torture records so long ago. With timely help from Bobby Moore, I had escaped. Round Two in a dizzying welter of events.

By that point, I had been secretly retained by Thomas Quincey's wife, a beautiful Iraqi American named Adara Ghaffari, to find and liberate her father Mohammad Ghaffari who was being held under house arrest by Quincey.

Counting forward from the night of my first abduction and escape, the next five weeks were a monstrous ordeal. I was ambushed repeatedly. Survived through luck and native wit. And, perhaps, a modicum of courage.

The good news was I finally did succeed in liberating Moham-mad from Quincey's control. Spent an unforgettable night with Adara in a Boston hotel room. The next morning, under leaden skies, I was gut-shot and nearly killed by Marguerite's gun moll on the shore of the Charles River.

Spent two weeks in a Boston hospital recovering, Marguerite's people lying in wait. Escaped through a bit of subterfuge staged by Bobby Moore, my partner at Nick Crane & Associates, our LA PI firm. I left Bobby in charge and wandered the Pacific Northwest, lying low, for the next six months. Which brings us up to date.

A knock on the door. A soft-featured woman with mahogany-colored skin stood there holding a stainless-steel chafing dish. "I'm Angelica. May I come in?" A Caribbean lilt to her voice. I waved her in, and she set the dish down on the breakfast table. Then she set the table and unveiled a full English breakfast: sausage, bacon, baked beans, tomatoes, fried eggs, fried bread, and hash browns.

An hour later, the staff masseuse Tina arrived. She was strictly business—strong hands, thorough knowledge of human anatomy. She worked in silence except for occasional barely audible gasps when she came to my bullet holes. Hot stones and cupping along with the massage. It all felt good…in a painful kind of way. After she left, I thumbed through the books in the cottage library. Mostly historical fiction and contemporary thrillers.

Forty-five minutes later another knock on the door. This time a white man, old, with thinning white hair and peculiar pink eyes, deep lines cross-hatching his sunken cheeks, and an air of nervous authority. "Sir Willem awaits you in the great room."

No handshake. Hmm. Just to fuck with him, I picked up the holstered M1911 and attached it to my belt. "Sir, that won't be necessary."

"Sorry, it is necessary."

"Now hold on just a minute, young fellow!"

"No, you hold on." Some people have no sense of humor. He actually gritted his dentures. "Look," I said, "I don't plan on using this firearm. I believe, however, that Colorado is an open-carry state."

"Sir, that is beyond my province."

"It's not beyond mine. Let's go. We mustn't keep Sir Willem waiting."

He wouldn't budge. I sat down on the bed, and he sent a text. Received one back. I won.

The day was sparkling. Colorado Rockies in the near distance, the whole world heaped with fresh white snow. Felt like paradise but I knew better.

Chapter Three

A log fire was blazing in the great room. A china tea set and an antique sterling silver coffee pot sat on a rosewood coffee table. With a leather-bound King James Bible close at hand. Van Gogh reproductions on the wall. I sat down and waited. Five minutes passed. Ten. I picked up the Bible and was casually riffling through the whisper-thin pages when Willem Spahn walked into the room.

Pressed khakis and a polo shirt. Short and compact with broad shoulders and a deep chest. Thick hairy forearms and big hands with square-cut, manicured nails. Deep lines etched into his forehead. Age, perhaps late fifties. Dark complexion and curious dark brown eyes behind black-rimmed glasses.

We shook hands. He sat down across from me, frowned, adjusted his glasses on the bridge of his nose, and smiled. Powerful men and women project their power in different ways. With Spahn, it was his incandescent smile. Let him make his play.

"I'm pleased to meet you, Mr. Crane." I nodded. "I trust you found Mars an amiable companion." A second nod. "Very well, then. Since fate has brought us together, I'm going to speak frankly." No trace of a German accent. If anything, he sounded like he came from somewhere in Wisconsin up near the Canadian border. "I brought you here because Dee Cole asked me to help keep you alive, and because I believe he has plans for you." Here we go again. Make Crane useful to advance someone else's agenda. Of course, were it not for Cole, my occasional ally, I might be in even worse straits. Weariness washed over me. I exhaled and forced myself to sit up straight. Spoke.

"Excuse me for being blunt, but what exactly is your relationship with Cole?"

Willem hesitated. Wrinkled his furrowed brow further. The wheels at work. Spoke. "We've been friends for a long time. Recently, I've been helping him out. I believe Dee thought our association would fly under the radar because I'm a businessman, and I'm not politically connected. Sadly, he was wrong. About flying under the radar, I mean. The truth is this whole thing is making me nervous. And according to Mars, you came within a hair's breadth of getting whacked not five minutes after he met you in Oregon." He took off his glasses, shot me another smile, this one rueful, and put them back on. "I'm glad to see you appreciate my little handgun. Even better, you actually know how to use it."

Didn't bother to respond.

"I met Dee thirty years ago. He was impressed by my financial acumen, and I was impressed by his old Yankee pedigree." He paused as if rummaging through an ancient memory bank.

"How did you make your money?"

For a moment, something feral flashed in his eyes. "Securities. I borrowed my seed money and got into the market. Buying long, selling short. I was fearless then, which is no longer the case." He paused. "Would you mind pouring me a cup of coffee? I have shaky hands. And please help yourself." After I'd poured us both cups, he picked up his with both hands and sipped carefully. I had just raised mine to my lips when his cell phone trilled. "Spahn." He listened for a moment. "*Scheisse.*" Said firmly, little emotion. "Okay, Milton. Listen closely. Phone the sheriff's department. Tell them I need an escort to the airport. Armored cars. And tell them we have no time to lose."

On the way to the airport, which was ten miles down the road in a picturesque hollow, we drew double coverage. A fleet of police vehicles and a brace of—oh, so familiar—Dodge cargo vans accompanied by a single Humvee. I looked at Spahn.

"Don't worry, my friend. This has happened a few times. Fortunately, I'm tight with the police 'cause I donate generously to our local civic causes. We're in good hands."

Sixty minutes later we were in the air, heading for Santa Fe in a Hawker 400XP. Spahn and I sat facing the tail, sipping Pellegrinos and eating cashews. I was carrying two of the M1911s and eight extra clips. And my night binoculars and Taser X2 and drop point hunting knife. Mars was listening to African trance music on a headset. Spahn was perfectly calm. At forty-five thousand feet, it would take a small, guided missile to knock us out of the air. After a pause in the conversation, Spahn told me that Marguerite was now holding rallies at small venues throughout the Midwest. "To fire up the base. Wake up the sleeping giant. Dee said she's in the Michigan area working the mid-sized towns...But I digress. I just received new orders from Dee. He wants me to walk you through what's going on."

"Please do." Agreeable Crane. Willem filled me in, reaching out from time to time, placing his warm thick fingers on my forearm for emphasis. After Cole learned that Marguerite had decided to track me down to execute me on the spot, he hired a D.C. investigative firm with national tentacles to locate and monitor me. It was expensive and Cole had turned to Spahn. "I owed him one. He got me out of a bind when he found me a fixer back in '96 when two of my brokers—I was running a hedge fund at the time—got linked to a male prostitution ring." Spahn grimaced. "Plus, I like the guy. I don't know why. Maybe because he doesn't give a damn. If you know what I mean? There's something to be said for not taking yourself too seriously."

I had thought the same thing about Cole. But found it disturbing. With Marguerite and Quincey, I knew where I stood. At least I thought I did. They wanted to use me, torture me, and kill me. In that order. Cole was different. He wanted to sit back and watch the spectacle, not unlike a cruel child slowly tearing the wings off a fly while watching it squirm.

I looked at Spahn and shook my head slowly. Though the devil may have all the best lines, I had no desire to join his team. And here I was high in the air, yet still so far from heaven. Spahn then explained that Marguerite had used her pros to locate me, then had given her personal militia orders to kill me at the first good opportunity. Which had turned out to be at the motel-bar complex in Burns, Oregon.

At times during my 180 days on the road, I'd sensed a tail. Could have been Cole's men, could have been Marguerite's. I'd shaken them with rudimentary counter-surveillance. Or so I'd thought. But they find you in the end. If they are professional and determined. But if Marguerite's people had found me, they would *not* have killed me. They would have abducted me and turned me over to Marguerite.

Spahn stuck to his story. "Dee tells me his people picked you up in Portland. From then on, they watched you and they watched Marguerite's people watching you. Cat-and-mouse, my friend. Almost like a movie, and it took a lot of manpower."

I decided to play along. "Damn, man, I don't think I deserve that much attention. But why does Cole think it's time," I raked a horizontal hand across my throat, "for me to, shall we say, come in from the cold?"

"That's where it gets interesting. And please call me Willem." Again, he placed his warm fingers on my forearm and moved closer. Lowered his voice. "One of Dee's people infiltrated Marguerite's team and reported back to Dee."

"And?" I lowered my voice to match Spahn's and firmly removed his hand.

Spahn's thick lips curved into a smile. "Don't worry. I'm not gay. I'm just a friendly guy."

"Well, I'm not."

"I'll remember that...But to answer your question, Cole thought that rescuing you would be a good way to bring us all together."

"But why?" As soon as I said it, I knew the answer. Back in October, I'd been shot and nearly killed by Marguerite's boot woman, a hit that Cole had known was coming but had not tried to stop. Now, six months later, he was trying to make me believe that with Spahn's help, he had repented and saved my life. A lot depended on whether the suits I'd left bleeding on the sidewalk were really Marguerite's people *or* simply Cole's people working the other side of the fence to make the danger seem authentic. Or Cole's people working with Marguerite's people, which was too depressing to contemplate.

"Cole can be slippery." Stating a fact.

Spahn shrugged his beefy shoulders. "You must understand that Dee is under tremendous pressure. He tells me that now that the country has taken a hard turn to the right, the principals have increasingly looked to Marguerite for guidance."

I stayed quiet. Tried to invoke the rational Crane. Not easy. For all his treachery, Cole was my only ersatz ally among the principals. His loss of influence, political or otherwise, was Marguerite's gain. Still, my sense was that she was in no hurry to deliver her grisly brand of justice...to me personally. Better to prolong the agony. A spasm of disgust. Hunted by Marguerite, here I was, flying in Willem Spahn's private jet, in the shadow of Desmond Cole, bound for I knew not where.

Decided to probe. "I understand what you're saying. And I appreciate your help." I offered him my hand which he shook solemnly. "But I need you to bring me up to date. What's the status of Quincey's case? The last time I talked to Cole, he told me Quincey was getting a sweetheart deal. And singing off-key."

Spahn took off his glasses. Scratched his right cheek with a blunt index finger. "Somebody likes his song. I don't know the details, but Dee tells me he's on the verge of being released. Something they call time-served with supervised release. Are you familiar with that?"

Barely suppressed a snort of derision. My five narrow escapes from Quincey and Marguerite, all in the course of five weeks.

The Black Site on Motor Avenue; the old Nazi encampment in the hills above Pacific Palisades; the river prison; the Dodge van on I-5; and, finally, the Boston hospital room. And all the bodies stacked in cool rooms...or buried anonymously in unsanctified ground. Meanwhile, Thomas Quincey would serve a mere six months for trafficking hundreds of kilos of cocaine to finance false flag domestic terrorist operations...Which meant I now had at least two active, potentially lethal threats—Marguerite and Thomas Quincey—and possibly three, depending on Desmond Cole's game.

Quincey, who at that time had reinvented himself as Miles Amsterdam, was the reason I was approached by Adara in the first place. Adara, femme fatale, looking like a Middle Eastern Lana Del Rey, quoting the great poets...and a bunch of female rappers I'd never heard of. The night with her meant more to me than it should have. It was eight years since my ex-wife Cassady and I had separated. The danger of the Frank Constantine affair had been the last straw.

A few casual girlfriends since then but no one who moved me like Adara. Such uncharacteristic yearning.

"It may not be as bad as it sounds." Soothing voice. Where had I heard that before? Spahn channeling Quincey's soothing whimsy. Like warm shit before the stench hits. "According to Dee, Quincey has come around. He now realizes that Marguerite is the real clear and present danger to him and to everything we hold holy."

Everything we hold holy? What was it about these folks? Betray, repent, forgive. Betray, repent, forgive. While claiming to be patriots...As if he'd read my mind, Spahn said, "You must understand that Dee didn't make this decision lightly."

"What decision?"

"To bring you into the fold. He could have just left you hung out to dry and saved a lot of money in the process. My money."

I sighed. Money, money, money. Same old refrain. "If it makes you feel any better, I'm very grateful."

"And we're grateful too. You see, Mr. Crane, Dee tells me that in addition to being a highly competent badass, you have integrity, something that's in short supply these days. And you're good in the ring. What's not to like? Unlike you, I learned the twin arts of dissembling and compromise while I was still sucking on my wet nurse's nipples."

I started laughing. Some kind of nervous reaction. No idea if my vagrant mother had offered me her breast. Knocked over my Pellegrino. Bad form. Hoisted the bottle upright. Spahn chuckled. I grimaced. Reached for another bottle.

Chapter Four

A Hummer with *Spahn Investments, Ltd.* stenciled across its door panels met us at the Santa Fe Regional Airport. The driver, a leathery-faced Latino, said his name was Luis. Grudgingly. Only after I'd asked him. When in strange company, always find out who the strangers are. Decided to watch him.

We headed southeast on I-25 through the national forest and then northeast across the tableland. Not much conversation. Spahn texting and occasionally cursing softly when the signals got lost. I closed my eyes, catnapped for a while, and woke up feeling glum. Wherever the fuck we were going, it wasn't where I wanted to go. Which got me thinking about LA. Philippe's. The Third Street Bar & Grill. Japantown with its quiet Buddhist shrines. Even MDC and its depraved cousin, Men's Central County Jail. The ocean breezes that soothe the wounded spirit. Venice. Santa Monica. LAX. Even the fucking traffic. My partner Bobby Moore, who's been running Nick Crane & Associates during my absence, and my junior associate Greg Thurston, paraplegic database expert extraordinaire. And Audrey, who handles our adultery stakeouts.

Then I stopped thinking and went back to sleep.

Cold and nearly dark when we got to Wagon Mound, New Mexico, an old trading post on the Santa Fe Trail. A thin dusting of rare April snow covered the surrounding pastureland and the wagon-shaped butte outside of town was barely visible in the lowering sky. Mars said Spahn's ranch was half a mile off a picturesque road ten miles west of town. Before going there, however, he had his spiritual health to look after. We came to the local Catholic Church. Luis parked and honked, two short blasts. A few minutes later a priest appeared in a cassock and clerical collar, followed by two tall slim Latinos wearing white shirts and black jeans.

"Listen, Luis," said Mars to the driver. "This'll take about thirty minutes. You can wait or meet us back here in half an hour, whichever you prefer."

He thought it over. Scowled. Spoke. "That'll work, boss. I'll go grab some coffee."

We got out of the Hummer. I kept my bag with me. "Care to join me for confession?" said Willem. "Father Antonio won't mind." I declined but to my surprise Mars accepted. I was in no mood for absolution. Never am. Unless it comes from within. Sat in a pew behind the transept. One white shirt nearby. It was cool and dark and peaceful, and I closed my eyes for a while. Then I got up and wandered over to examine the Stations of the Cross. According to the legend, Christ fell three times before they stripped him and nailed him to the cross.

The confessions were taking a long time. I went outside. One of the white shirts followed. Two men stood at the corner under a streetlight about one hundred feet from the church steps. Dark suits. Bulky with short hair. Where had I seen this before? I told White Shirt to go back inside. When he declined, I got in his face. He listened. There are times when a man needs privacy. I transferred my taser from my bag to my right jacket pocket. My pistol was secure in its holster. Bag in hand, I walked casually over to the two men. Big necks. Beefy faces. Too old for football, boys. Distinct feeling they weren't there to show iron. Not this time.

"Hello, I'm Ned. I need some information. Maybe you can help me?" They stared at me. Never give an inch. All right. We can play that way. "Who's calling the shots, boys? You can save me a lot of time and aggravation by just spitting it out." Silence. Not unexpected. One set of beefy jowls clenched; the other set stopped chewing its gum. "C'mon boys, spill. Is it Spahn, is it Cole, or is it Marguerite? You know—the small woman with the big personality who wears the bomber jackets. I don't care which, I just want to know." Faint flicker of recognition when I said bomber jackets. In the eyes or viscera. Could mean something. But maybe not. Lots of people know people who wear bomber jackets...I pulled out my wallet and started counting out Franklins. Stopped at three. "Well?" The gum chewer slowly held up five fingers. Two more Franklins. Dangled them in their direction.

"Okay," said Jowls. "We work for a man named Tommy. That's all I know."

I handed over one Franklin. "So, who is this Tommy guy?"

"Wish I could tell you. I've barely met the man."

"What's his last name?"

Jowls looked at Gum. Then he spoke. "His last name is Blank. B-L-A-N-K." They thought that was funny. Cracked up. Unpleasant fellows. I handed over another Franklin.

A chill passed over me. How many of these workaday thugs were under contract with these domestic para firms and the rich right-wing creeps who run them? I nodded pleasantly. "Where can I find Mr. Blank?"

Again, Jowls looked at Gum. "Where can you find him?" said Gum.

"You don't find him," said Jowls, "he finds you. Tommy doesn't really stay in any one place. He keeps moving." Stopped. Expectant look. I handed him a Franklin.

"Where does he go?"

"Where does he go?" said Gum triumphantly, "He goes wherever the four winds take him. Seattle, Portland, Denver, San Francisco. Anywhere out west from Canada to Mexico."

"Thank you," I said. This was news. I handed him a Franklin. "Okay, last question. What does Mr. Blank look like?"

Gum looked at Jowls. Jowls bit his lip and Gum spat out his gum. "That's hard to say," said Jowls. "Most of the time, he looks pretty normal. Average height, dark hair, babe-magnet kind of a guy. Except for the big scar on his cheek. But other times, it's different. It's hard to look at the man."

"There's something about him," said Gum, moistening a fresh piece of gum. "So look out, baby." He held out his hand.

I gave him a Franklin. "And where's his headquarters?"

Jowls gave the faintest of shrugs. "My partner told you. He moves around. But if I had to guess, I'd say it might be Los Angeles or maybe San Diego. Somewhere around there." He held out his hand and I gave him the last Franklin.

"Thanks. You guys are all right. Why don't you go have a cup of coffee? I'll collect my crew and make like the breeze. Give me fifteen minutes." I produced one more Franklin, handed it to Gum, turned, and walked slowly back toward the church. Knew they could shoot me in the back. Knew they wouldn't. It's a wonderful thing to have money. I met Spahn and Mars coming out of the church. No white shirts or Father Antonio. I turned and looked back toward the corner. Gum and Jowls were walking slowly away...

I told Spahn I'd join them in a few minutes and ducked back into the church. Sat down in the same pew and thought things over. The stiffs I'd just dispatched shouldn't have been there on the corner. Sun Tzu said where there's smoke there's fire. At least he should have. After three or four minutes, I got up and walked back outside. The Hummer had just pulled up in front of the church. Spahn and Mars were heading toward it. A different driver, a lanky white boy with bright red hair tucked under his chauffeur's cap, had gotten out to greet them. Something about his body language...

Proceed with caution...when things don't feel right. I circled around the other side of the Hummer, past the blacked-out windows, and ducked down behind the hood, perhaps ten feet from the redhead who now held an S&W .40 in his left hand.

Which was pointed at Spahn. "Get in the car, Mr. Spahn. Now."
"What on earth?" Spahn was shocked.
"I said GET IN THE CAR, Mr. Spahn. Just you. Your black boy stays here." The kid's gun hand was wobbly, not a good sign. Spahn, in utter shock, moved toward the Hummer in little cat steps like someone who doesn't want to get his feet wet. Almost subconsciously, I heard the rear passenger door open. I crouched down low behind the hood and waited. The second man, who turned out to be Luis, came around the front of the vehicle, a big nasty Colt .45 dangling from his right hand. I tased him before he knew what hit him. The X2 dart delivers a nasty wallop. Luis fell to the ground, spasming like an alley cat that's just bounced off somebody's bumper. He dropped his gun and I picked it up.

Unnerved, the redhead whirled around to face me as Mars launched an awkward but effective dive hitting the kid somewhere between his ass and knees. Would've been a ten-yard penalty on the gridiron but life is not a football game. The kid hit the ground, furious Mars on top. Mars spat on his hands, grabbed the kid by his hair and began smashing his face into the asphalt.

The redhead dropped his gun. I picked it up and used the grip end to tap Mars on the shoulder. "Okay Mars, that's enough." I set the Smith & Wesson back down on the pavement. Turned back toward Luis. By now he was contracted into a ball. Back to Mars who smashed the kid's face into the pavement, one more time for good luck. Then he turned the kid over and straddled him. The kid was bleeding badly from his nose. Mars took a long look. Slapped him three times across the face—left, right, left. Spoke. "Sheeit! Fuck you, white boy!" Then he pushed off hard and stood up.

I was caught off guard watching the drama while the back door on the driver's side of the Hummer opened and the Monster appeared, a pistol in each hand, one trained on me, one trained on Spahn. I faced him Dirty Harry style, Luis's .45 rock-steady in my right hand. The Monster moved closer. So did I. He appeared to be a white man though I couldn't really tell. It was his lurid face tattoos, purple and blue devils and dragons, along with his bearish physique, that threw me.

"Don't make any sudden moves," I said. "I won't hesitate to kill you." I flipped off the thumb safety. He took a step closer. So did I. We were right on top of each other. I knew he didn't want to die. Knew their mission was not supposed to end in death. But still…"Mars," I barked, "Keep an eye on the redhead and Luis. Spahn, try to do something useful."

Back to the Monster. "One thousand dollars, brother. Cash. I give it to you, and we drive away. Spahn, give me a thousand dollars. Right now." Spahn broke out of his paralysis and gestured to Mars who whipped out an alligator-skinned wallet and counted out ten Franklins. I snapped my fingers and held out my left hand.

Mars surprised me. He walked up to the Monster himself and held out the bills. The Monster, who didn't have three hands, shook his head.

"I got a question for you," I said calmly. "What is it about this Tommy Blank character? How come people are afraid of him? Mars, give him another thousand. Now!" Mars produced a second stack. Monster thought it over. I could feel the wheels turning. I waited. Too slow. Using Mars as a shield, I darted past him and slammed into the Monster, skull first, straight into his solar plexus. He grunted, staggered, and fired both pistols wildly. I drove hard and he staggered backwards. I jerked my head straight up and uppercut him hard in the soft meat under his chin with both forearms. His head snapped back, and he fell. Didn't move. Might have broken his neck. Didn't want to know. The thirty seconds it took to pick up the guns and money and load up the Hummer seemed like eternity. Then we were out of there, Mars behind the wheel, me riding shotgun. Spahn had the back seat all to himself.

We took I-25 toward Santa Fe. I wiped the guns and threw them out the window at five-mile intervals once we were well clear of Wagon Mound. Spahn was in a state. Hunkering down on his ranch, which was ten miles out of town and visible from three directions, was now out of the question. His new plan was to fly to Chicago where he had a penthouse on the Loop. In the back seat, he alternated between hyperventilation and depressed resignation.

"I thought I was dead."

"They weren't going to kill you. They just wanted your money."

"But why?"

"You tell me."

He shook his head, his heavy face ashen, the lines in his forehead like ruts in a washed-out road.

"Hah!" I laughed. "Good thing I paid off the two guys on the corner while you guys were in the church. Cost me five hundred dollars. Five to three would not have been good odds. Really five to two since you, Spahn, are not much of a combatant. Somehow, Marguerite's team knew that you stop in at that church on your way through town. You were sitting pretty. They probably didn't know I was with you. But this is what happens when you swim with piranhas. I should know..." I shook my head. "But I bet Marguerite is gnashing her teeth right about now."

"I don't even know the woman," said Spahn acidly.

"My guess is she knows you're keeping Cole afloat. And she wants a piece of the action. But what I don't know is this: What exactly is Cole's plan?" I leaned back over the seat and stared at him. "This is no time to be coy, my friend." It took a while, but Spahn finally admitted that Cole was scheduled to meet us at his ranch outside of Wagon Mound on Easter Sunday. Two days from now. "For what purpose?"

"To discuss."

"Discuss what?"

"Plans, I guess."

"What kind of plans?"

"I don't know. If I knew, I'd tell you."

"I doubt that."

"All I know is that Dee said it's very serious and that he'll explain everything when the time comes."

I laughed out loud. As if Cole, the master of false leads and misdirection, was ever going to explain anything clearly. All I knew was that I was jumping ship. I told Spahn and he didn't like it. He wanted me to come with them to Chicago. He and Cole had already made plans to play baccarat in the casinos in Joliet. They wanted me to join them. I didn't care. I'd saved his ass and that was the end of it. Spahn was used to getting his way. We argued. It got intense. Mars slowed down. I ordered him to keep driving. Told Spahn that he had two choices. He could drop me off in Santa Fe like a good little billionaire or we could turn off the interstate. Take a local country road out to a quiet spot to talk it over. He didn't like it. Not one bit. But knew he couldn't win. He finally told Mars to keep driving. And to drop me off wherever I wanted.

I don't like making enemies. Told him he didn't want me in his orbit and that he should get out of Cole's world before it was too late. Said I knew he wouldn't listen but that I had to tell him to clear my conscience. He ignored me and started working his phone.

My new game plan? Ease back to LA. Reconnoiter with Bobby Moore and talk to my LAPD detective friend Tony Bott. See if I could snap him out of the funk he'd been in ever since Thomas Quincey's people murdered his prize informant Roberto Diaz back in September. As a prelude to putting our heads together to come up with a battle plan. In the darker reaches of my mind, the suicidal urge to go to war with Marguerite was getting hard to ignore. One thing I was sure of: It was time to fight back.

Just to be ornery, I insisted that Mars drive me to Albuquerque instead of Santa Fe. Sixty miles out of their way. They both grumbled but I was firm. They dropped me off around midnight.

Perfunctory handshakes, Spahn still pissed. But at the last minute he handed me a card with contact information for him and Cole inscribed neatly in ink.

I watched them pull slowly away from the curb. It was raining, more of a mist really, but it did settle the dust. I walked around town till I came to a Super 8 two blocks from the Greyhound station. Economical Crane.

Chapter Five

It was raining in Los Angeles when the Greyhound finally pulled into the downtown bus depot at 7th and Alameda. Easter Sunday, seven p.m. Backside of town.

I pulled a yellow slicker over my denim jacket and started walking north on Alameda. Wasteland of littered streets and abandoned warehouses. Water pooling up on the sidewalk and streaming in the gutters. Grey as far as the eye could see. But so fond of this old place. The unique charm of a town that can laugh at itself.

My destination was the Poseidon Building near Third and Alameda. This is where Bobby Moore and I started Nick Crane & Associates over thirty years ago in a corner cubbyhole funded by Bobby's U.S. Army crazy money.

I ducked out of the rain at the Valero station at Fifth and Alameda. Bought a Heineken. Went outside and stood under the awning. Phoned my daughter Maleah to wish her a happy Easter. She didn't answer.

Finished my beer and trudged onward, one of my recently appropriated M1911s warm and dry in its belt holster, the other stowed in my grip. During our last conversation just before I escaped from the Boston hospital last October, Desmond Cole had warned me to steer clear of LA. Thought I would be too conspicuous there. But it was my office and my agency in my city. Bad enough when they try to kidnap or kill you, almost worse when they try to quarantine you like an infectious disease.

When I got to my block, the rain was letting up. Our homeless friend Elena's small green tent was tucked into the lee between my building and the parking lot. The tent flap was open and her little, wizened face was poking out. I waved and she came out to greet me. Stained drawstring sweatpants and a thin, short-sleeved cotton blouse. Tracks and goosebumps. Her hair back in a bun. Rogue hairs escaping. Lines in her face like the coastline of Maine. A duly registered S&W 9 mm tucked in her waistband. She was trembling.

"Where ya been, *mi papa*? I gotta tell you something." She looked at me strangely, her right hand fingering the scars on the inside of her left elbow. "They took Bobby, *mi papa*. Commandos in a black van."

I stared at her. Eighty-five pounds of two-legged, tough old bird. I took her by the hand and pulled her into the lee of the building. "Okay, Elena. Take your time and tell me what happened."

Words came tumbling out. It was hard to follow. I had to stop her, calm her down. There'd been two Dodge cargo vans, one black, one white. Three men in each. And Mitch, a local homeless crackhead, probably used as bait. Commando gear and sunglasses, even in the rain. They'd trooped into the Poseidon Building sometime after five o'clock. Elena had watched them through the flap of her tent. Three of the men came back out with Bobby ten minutes later, Mitch straggling behind them. All five of them got in the black van and drove away. The other three men were still in the building. Elena pointed across the street. A white Dodge cargo van was parked in front of the Third Street Korean Bar & Grill.

I pulled Elena into her tiny tent and sat down next to her. Barely room for the two of us. Religious tracts, bibles, and comic books stacked up all around us. A bag of syringes in the corner that she didn't bother to hide. I pulled my GPS locator out of my bag. Clicked it on. Traced Bobby to the Tejon Pass halfway across the Grapevine. Then nothing. Captors must have searched him and found it. I sat back. Tried to think. They didn't really want Bobby. He was a bargaining chip. They wanted me. But that didn't mean they would go easy on him. I cursed Marguerite, but quietly. Didn't want to offend Elena. She looked at me with big eyes.

"Have you seen Greg?"

She shook her head. "Who's Greg?"

"You know, the handicapped kid."

"Oh, he's a cutie, that boy is."

"You haven't seen him today, have you?"

"Not today."

I nodded. Phoned him on a burner and he answered on the third ring.

"Hello, Greg."

"Happy Easter, Nick."

"Likewise."

"You haven't talked to Bobby, have you? I sent him a rush surveillance report that he was waiting for a few hours ago, but he hasn't gotten back to me."

"Listen, Greg, I'm right here in town. On Third Street. Bobby's been abducted. The war's back on."

"What? Bobby? You're kidding. It's been so quiet…"

I cut him off. "Listen, Greg, three thugs are still holed up in our office."

"What the fuck! What are they doing there?"

"Ransacking the place, I imagine. You have everything backed up, right?"

"Of course."

"Okay, good. Here's what I need you to do. I need you to get me Marguerite Ferguson's itinerary. You know, little old Marguerite, who would cut your balls off and jam them down your throat? The word is she's holding political rallies in the Midwest. I need to know when and where. Top priority. Find out everything you can. And then try to crack her email. Maybe she still has the same password."

"She doesn't. But I have my ways. I'll get right on it, Nick. Where do you think they took Bobby?"

"Last GPS report had him driving through the Tejon Pass on I-5. In a black cargo van. Then nothing."

"They found his transmitter. What about calling law enforcement?"

"I could, but it probably won't help. The assholes will hand Bobby off to someone else in another vehicle. He might get handed off four or five times. But somebody's calling the shots on the ground. I don't think it's Marguerite. I think it might be a guy named Tommy Blank. Spelled B-L-A-N-K. So get what you can on him, too. But listen, one of their vans is still here. Parked across the street. Do you have any GPS tracking kits on hand?"

"'Course I do. I collect them."

Nothing like sitting on your ass and letting the electronics do the walking. "Okay. Get here fast. Bring me two sets hooked up to a live iPhone. Park down at the corner in front of the sushi place."

"I'm on it."

Greg lived in Altadena thirty minutes away. I sat with Elena for a few more minutes. Then I kissed her on the forehead and gave her some money. She was sad to see me go.

I keep an old Corolla with a full tank of gas parked year-round in the Little Tokyo parking lot across the street on Alameda. For times like this. Audrey drives it around the block once a week to keep the battery charged. I turned the key and it shuddered to life. Pulled out, circled the block, and parked behind the white van facing west in front of the Bar & Grill where Bobby and Tony and I used to hang out in happier times. I called Tony who didn't answer. Left a message. Urgent. Then I called Leo Perez, my Mexican compadre who ran the paint and body shop in East LA where'd I'd barely survived an ambush ordered by one or more of the principals back in October. Leo answered, two and one-half sheets to the wind.

"Nicky. *Felices Pascuas, mi compadre.*"

"Happy Easter, Leo." I told him Bobby had disappeared and would he please make sure that his goats were fed until I found him.

"Oh, Nicky, I am so sorry. Is he all right?"

"I hope so, Leo. I'm on it, but I can't really talk now." I thanked him and signed off.

They might torture Bobby to try and get to me. Or just for the hell of it. Either way, it hit me hard. At my worst, my rage morphs into stone-cold absolute zero that starts in my chest and ends up splitting my skull. I sat there behind the wheel riding it out. This was going to take time. Had to think strategically.

Cole. I sent an email and phoned. He didn't answer. Spahn. Willem picked up on the second ring. Could tell he'd been drinking. "Nick Crane. What an unexpected pleasure. My man Mars hasn't been the same since you gave us the cold shoulder in New Mexico. Happy Easter, my friend."

"Listen, Spahn. I need you to listen to me. I saved your ass. Now I need some help. Where's Cole?"

"Dee? If I'm not mistaken, he's in Monte Carlo."

"Fuck! I thought you met him in Joliet."

"I did. Just long enough for him to lose some of my money. Then he flew to Monte Carlo to try and recoup it. I'm not holding my breath."

"I don't blame you." Permitted myself a brief chuckle. "Now listen closely. I have a partner named Bobby Moore. He's just been abducted by Marguerite's people."

"Oh, shit! That's a lump of coal. How do you know it's her people?"

"It's them. Same people who tried to abduct you. Get me Cole. I don't care how you do it."

"Hang on, my friend," said Spahn. "I got a text from Desmond a little while ago. I haven't read it yet. Let's see what it says…Oh, shit, this is another lump of coal. Here's what it says: *Tell Nick Crane he's got twenty-seven days to turn*

himself in. The clock doesn't start ticking till Friday. We are
generous people. Bobby Moore will be released when he sur-
renders. Crane's got till twelve a.m., May 22nd, to surrender."
Spahn coughed. "Here's Dee's most recent number. Better write
it down: 213-628-3344." I wrote it down and we signed off.

I tried the new number. No answer. I waited.

When Greg arrived in his paraplegic minivan, I got in next to
him and watched carefully as he showed me how to track the
transmitters on the iPhone. Simple. Knew he wanted to ride
with me. Knew that he could not.

"Listen, Greg, you know what's up. I know you want to
help, and I know you can handle a gun. But you're too valuable.
You're the only person I've got left to run the goddamned
company. Deal with the white-shoe boys. Make sure stuff gets
in on time. Keep the equipment up and running. Audrey's good
at what she does, but you and I both know she's no manager." I
stopped. He looked at me. We both knew that when I'd hired
him, I'd made a vow to keep him away from the rough stuff.
This time, he didn't give me a hard time. I was grateful. We
shook hands and I got out and walked back toward my car.
Paused to slap one of the tracking devices on the inside of the
white van's left rear bumper.

Then I got in my car, turned on the engine, plugged in the
iPhone to keep it charged, and waited. It rained off and on till
around ten when the air cleared, and a few stars eased their wary
light through the cloud cover. Finally, around midnight, three
men dressed in black wearing black stocking caps sauntered out
of the Poseidon Building carrying cardboard boxes filled with
my company records. They made three trips in all.

Two choices. Confront them on the street or follow them in
the hope that they'd lead me to Bobby. Chose the latter. There
are certain things you never want to get used to. Like killing
people. I was sick of being described by certain parties as a latter-
day Manchurian Candidate. And sick inside because I was afraid
that on some level, they were probably right.

Gave the creeps a five-minute head start, watching their progress on my readout. Nixed the impulse to check my office. I knew it was trashed. Drove east across the weatherworn Fourth Street Bridge and north on I-5. Traffic was light.

The van drove straight up I-5 across the Grapevine, then took U.S. 99 north toward Bakersfield. East on 223 toward Weedpatch, the old Dust Bowl migrant camp.

I followed at a steady pace, the Corolla chugging its way up the grade. Gassed up in Tejon. The rest was cake. I was almost to the 223 turnoff when my daughter phoned.

"Hi, Maleah. Or should I say Night Owl? You realize it's two a.m."

"Can't sleep, Dad. I'm returning your call. As you know, I'm home for spring break. Mom and her boyfriend are making a tremendous racket."

"Oh, boy! Lovers can get a little rambunctious."

"That I could handle. Not that I know much about that particular topic. The problem is they're fighting again. At least you and Mom kept your problems on the down-low."

"The down-low?" Where does my daughter learn this shit?

"Yeah. The down-low...Anyway, I was thinking that after I graduate in June, I could work for you. I could set up an auxiliary office up here in NorCal to investigate technological fraud, patent infringement, intellectual property rights, Silicon Valley-type stuff."

Seems like half of the powers that be want to steer me into the safe haven of white-collar malfeasance, while the other half want to crush me with violence and corruption. I turned off 223 onto a county road and pulled over to the shoulder.

A little more back-and-forth and I capitulated. Hell, why not? "That's not a bad idea, Sweetheart. I've often thought about going in that direction, but don't have the background. Greg Thurston in my office could help you get started."

"Good. I'm glad to see you're thinking clearly, Dad. 'Cause you're way off base if you think your only daughter is going to work in marketing or human resources for some scumbag, tax-chiseling corporation." Somehow, despite my bad example, Cassady and I raised an idealist.

We talked a while longer. It felt good. Then we signed off and I checked my readout. The white van was now parked next to the black van near a farmhouse a quarter mile up the road from the Weedpatch camp.

Chapter Six

I waited for half an hour and went in on foot. The wind was gusting, the sky a black-and-grey gridiron hanging low over the fields. I had the two pistols, half-a-dozen seven-round clips, and a G700 military flashlight. And my drop point hunting knife. Up the driveway, treading lightly. Installed my second tracking device on the inside rail of the black van's luggage rack. Crouched in the shadows between the two vehicles, thinking. Smoke was pouring out of the chimney of the farmhouse. Nearly three a.m. I stood up and recced the area. Good-sized barn with adjoining silo and small corral. And a scattering of dilapidated outbuildings.

I decided to start with the barn, which was big and airy with an overhead hay loft with chutes leading down to the stalls. A small grey quarter horse and a painted Appaloosa were sleeping on their sides, while a one-eyed roan, knees locked, was out on its feet. Start a stampede to create a diversion? Lure the men out into the night? Pick 'em off, one or two at a time? Tempting, but I didn't want to disturb the horses. They looked so peaceful, their great sides heaving as they breathed. For a long minute, I just stood there watching them. An old-fashioned Dutch door, with glass panes on top, sighted into the mudroom that connected the barn to the silo. On a whim, I unlatched the top half and swung it back. A voice or voices were singing in the silo in what sounded like a foreign language.

I opened the door and started across the mudroom. Stopped. A chunk of the silo wall had been cut away. Workmen had installed a steel door with a barred window. With a hasp and heavy-duty combination lock. As I moved forward, the voices grew louder. I looked through the bars. Two Arabs wearing kaftans and head wraps were praying. Not in the supplicant position. They were sitting with their backs against the wall, their hands folded across their stomachs. First one sang, then the other. I stepped back out of sight and listened for a while. Their voices rose and fell, at times anguished, at times joyful. I looked back through the bars. Two men singing prayers and three men sleeping on the ground. Arabs. Imported by whom? With Thomas Quincey still in custody, I had to put my money on Marguerite...

The rest of the barn was used for storage: tractors, a monstrous self-propelled combine, and—how'd I know—a spare Dodge cargo van. A curtained area veiled a good-sized armory—everything from pistols to AK-47s to bazookas, not to mention ammunition, blow torches, gas grenades and gas masks, stun guns and tasers, and enough plastic explosives to take out several city blocks. And, of course, every true Nazi's favorite toys—heavy-duty Clejuso handcuffs and leg irons.

Left the barn. Was gazing out over the corral thinking about my next step when a bogie jumped on my back and slammed me into the fence. Hit my forehead and fell to the ground but stayed conscious. Just enough strength to slither out from under him. Then we were on our feet squaring off. He was a big man, tall and heavyset with thick lips and a crewcut. "Hang on," I said. "I need to call mother." Crewcut didn't move. Didn't speak. Knew he was formidable. We both started to go for our guns. Both stopped. Would I have gotten the drop on him? Maybe. It didn't matter. He had decided to kick my ass instead of shooting me. He waded in biker-style and launched a booted foot straight for my chest. I side-stepped and leg-whipped his other foot out from under him. He fell hard. Got right back up.

My turn. Tennis shoes are a far cry from work boots, but a

good strong Converse kick with plenty of velocity can knock a man down. F=MA. I feinted left and right, whirling like a California dervish. Delivered a decent kick just below his rib cage. He went down again. Got back up. This time he advanced carefully, hands high, Marquess of Queensberry style. Two choices. Fight on till I could deliver an elbow to the temple, which was probably the only thing that would take this fool out (and might kill him in the process) or stick my gun in his face. I chose the latter. Distance: eighteen inches.

"Hey, I thought we were fighting." He looked genuinely hurt.

"You're too tough for me, big boy. Like you don't hardly even feel pain. So shut up and get moving. Into the barn." He tried to talk me out of it, cajoling and practically begging. I forced the issue and marched him back to the armory where I trussed him up with the Clejusos and gagged him with an old shop rag, which was the only thing handy. "Don't suck on the rag," I said. "Unless you like the taste of oil. I'll send them out to get you once I'm done with them."

Sun Tzu said that the ultimate martial tactic is to subdue the enemy without fighting. That's where gas comes in handy. Problem was Bobby. You don't want to gas your oldest and dearest friend by mistake. In the unlikely event he was in the house. Which left Plan B. The oldest, crustiest PI I've ever known was named Frenchy Lefevre. A short, scrawny fellow with a face like bronzed shoe leather and a mind like a steel trap, his dying request as he coughed his lungs out—courtesy of Gauloises— was that one day, in his honor, I would resort to a certain B&E technique that he said was virtually indefensible...Frenchy, I hope you're watching...

I carried the hayloft ladder out of the barn around to the side of the house and propped it up against the roofline. Back to the barn for handcuffs and leg irons, two tasers, a handful of gas grenades—just in case—and a clip of .45 caliber bullets. No C-4 cartridges. Something downright unsportsmanlike about simply blowing the enemy to kingdom come. I deposited everything near the front porch except for the clip. Walked around to the side of the house and extracted six .45 caliber shells from the clip, which I put in the left side pocket of my jean jacket. Checked the ladder for stability. Once on the roof, I eased my way up the incline to the chimney. Banking on no chimney cap in such an old house and I was right.

Could Frenchy have been blowing smoke? Too late to worry about that now. I dropped the six cartridges down the chimney at three-second intervals. Scrambled down the incline and half-climbed, half-slid down the ladder. The first shell exploded just as I reached the front door. More twang than crack. Followed by the second five seconds later. A loud crash like the fire screen had fallen over.

"Whaddafuck?" High-pitched voice, familiar. It was the jailhouse cook and deviant Emory, former employee of Thomas Quincey. Grinned despite myself. A third explosion. This time Emory screamed. I kicked the door in and fired three warning shots, then stepped back out of the line of fire. A creature holding a handgun came sneaking up the hallway, keeping close to the wall. Waited till he reached me, then stepped out of the shadows and clobbered him. Straight right to the solar plexus. The sneaker's momentum flipped him up into the air and he fell on his face. Not nearly as tough as Crewcut. I had to help him up. Disarmed him and shoved him back down the hallway toward the living room, my gun in the small of his back. Broad and tall, he made an excellent shield. Two more shells went off. We reached the living room where hot coals were spewing across the floor.

My lucky night. Except for Crewcut and Sneaker, everybody was bedded down together like cub scouts on horror night. Or vermin in the book Kafka forgot to write. One piece of crap didn't stir at all. Two sat up in their sleeping bags, rubbing their eyes. I shoved Sneaker in their direction, and he fell on top of one of them. The last shell exploded. More hot coals. The other two men were on their hands and knees in their long johns. I was right. Whaddafuck was Emory, Quincey's former—I guess

39

you gotta make a living somehow—cook, jailbird, and stoolie. The other was his "cousin" Todd, whose jaw I'd cracked with a well-placed elbow back in October, while escaping from Quincey's soldiers.

"On your feet, fellas. Where's Bobby?"

Emory played dumb. Shook his head with a little too much attitude. I took dead aim and fired right past his ear. He blanched and fouled himself front and back. Dawg! Have some dignity. Todd didn't piss his pants. Instead, his legs gave way and he sat down hard.

"All right, everybody up against the wall. 'Cept for you, Todd. You just sit there and don't move." Didn't shout. Kept my voice low, ominous. The look in my eye of someone who's been down this road one too many times. When nobody moved, I fired two shots into the ceiling. A shower of plaster. This did the trick and the men began to move, except for the sleeper who did not stir. One bullet left. Time to switch guns. Once the four men were lined up shoulder to shoulder, I told them to strip down to their shorts and sit on the floor. Great reluctance except for Emory, who couldn't wait to shed his soiled long johns. Another warning shot got the stragglers moving.

"Okay. Todd, is that guy alive?" pointing at the sleeper.

"OD'ed."

"Is he dead?"

"Dunno. If it's heroin, he might wake up. If it's fentanyl, mo'fo is gone."

"How's your face?"

"Pretty good. Why'd you hit me so hard?"

"'Cause I had to. You know that. Where's my partner? Where's Bobby Moore?" Damned if he didn't start to twitch, like a man on heavy psychotropics. "Relax. Where's Bobby?"

Todd looked at Emory, who nodded. "All right, then. You ain't gonna like this. We handed him off to another crew."

The ball of fire started somewhere mid-brain. Filled my skull. Turned black at the base of my skull. Very deliberately, I pointed my gun at Emory. "You're in charge, right?"

He nodded slowly.

"Who'd you hand them off to?"

"Gil, Larry, Vince, and Tommy." Smug voice.

"Where are they going?"

"It's need to know. And I don't need to know."

I wish I could say I didn't try to shoot him, but I did. A good angel pushed my hand to the left. The slug barely grazed his shoulder. But got his attention. "Okay, boys. Now if you can only manage to can your lousy fucking attitudes for a minute, nobody is gonna get hurt. Todd, you collect all the weapons— guns, knives, and cell phones. Separate the clips and phones from the gun and knives. Do not miss a gun or knife or fuck up in any other way, or I'm gonna hurt you. Now get started."

Slowly, with the utmost care, Todd went to work collecting eight handguns, all automatics; four knives, two of them illegal in California; three sets of brass knuckles, a felony under California Penal Code §21810; and half-a-dozen cell phones. He placed the clips and phones in a pillowcase and stacked the weapons up on the kitchen table. Then, at gunpoint, I forced Emory and the three conscious soldiers to walk down the hallway and out to the front porch, where Todd clapped them in irons. Had him bring another set inside for the OD victim. Folks walk slow in leg irons, and it took a while to get everybody back inside. Then I had Todd douse the OD victim with cold water. He grunted and stirred. I told Todd to get dressed and turned to Emory.

"Okay, Emory, one more time, where are they taking Bobby and what are they driving?"

"I told you. I don't know where they're taking him. They're in a dark blue Dodge van. Who do you think I am, a fuckin' lieutenant or something?"

Medium red flash, mid-brain. Suppressed it with effort. "Okay, now I'm going to ask you a question that I know you can answer. How many Arabs are in the silo and where do they come from?"

He thought about it and finally answered. "Five ragheads—three Saudis and two from Fuckistan."

"How'd they get here?" His affect shifted. He smiled, exposing his awful tripwire teeth. Winked. Slithery.

"How do you think? She brought them here."

"Why?"

"You tell me. Our job was just to keep 'em here. Give 'em three squares and haul their shit away."

Well, now. *She.* That was something. "Who's she?"

He shook his head, looking almost thoughtful. "I don't know her name. Just her username on a deleted email account. I only spoke to her once."

"When was that?"

"Just before they brought the ragheads here."

"Who brought them?"

"I don't know. She had me down to LA on a fool's errand 'cause she didn't want me to be here on the day they arrived. That way I wouldn't know who dropped them off."

"What about the rest of your crew?"

He shook his head. Grinned. Nasty. "Those assholes. They stayed in the house like good boys while the delivery fellas locked the ragheads up in the silo. My orders were to keep my boys inside the house. I passed it all on to Todd. And told him to feed the ragheads until I got back. Everybody needs to eat." That was Emory: For all his faults, which were legion, he always made sure everyone got fed.

"What's the combination to the silo lock?"

"Ten, thirty-three, thirty-three. Left, right, left."

"Thank you, friendo. Where was Tommy Blank all this time?"

"Tommy Blank. Hmm..." He held out his hand...Great reluctance. But money talks. And makes people talk. It was nasty to see his fingers clenched around the two Franklins. Emory said that Tommy Blank was in Seattle when the Arabs were dropped off, but that he'd expressed no surprise at finding them here when he returned. Tommy mostly communicated by phone. Made a personal appearance every week or two.

"You said you handed Bobby off to four guys and that one of them is named Tommy. Is that Tommy Blank?"

"Different Tommy," said Emory.

"Where does Tommy Blank live?"

Emory shrugged. "Close by, I think."

"Why do you think that?"

"'Cause he likes those Hollywood women. And 'cause it never takes him long to get here after he phones."

Before we left the house, I had Todd carry enough food—leftover Chinese takeout and loaves of bread and apples and boxes of sweetened cereal and a couple cases of soda—from the kitchen into the living room to tide the bastards over until they were rescued. And plenty of bottled water. Todd would be back by late afternoon. They would survive.

That was it.

Chapter Seven

Outside, dawn was threatening. On our way to the barn, I glanced into the white van. Nine boxes of records. Everything I had on the Frank Constantine case including the subsequent investigation in which Tony and I were exonerated. Tony received a much-deserved LAPD commendation, and I was paid a lot of money by my client, the charming and passionate Caroline Best.

It took some doing but Todd and I managed to escort the Saudis and Pakistanis out of their silo holding cell, which stank to high heaven—fertilizer, silage, piss, shit, sweat, and fear—and into the back of the white van where Todd shackled them. Then back to the barn to escort Crewcut back to the house. Dumped him just inside the front door. Then I removed the bugs from both vans, and Todd and I drove together in the white van, me riding shotgun, back to where I'd parked the Corolla. Transferred my company records from the van into my car. Told Todd he had two choices. He could drive the van to the police station in nearby Arvin with me following in the Corolla. We would leave the van there with the men shackled inside. Law enforcement would discover them before long.

Or Todd could make a run for it with the Arabs in the van, in which case I would shoot out his tires as a prelude to ending his short, unhappy life. Knew he'd make the right call.

We left the van half a block from the police station and started the long haul back to LA. I had Todd drive so I could keep an eye on him. He drove carefully, easing the little beater up the steep Tejon Pass grade. We hit some early morning traffic around Santa Clarita. While we crawled along, Todd pitched himself as a friendly enforcer—lethal when necessary—but able to handle most situations with smarts and willpower. "You need me on your crew, Kid Crane. I'm like you. Tougher than damned near anybody but not a complete asshole. I can get along with people. And keep my mouth shut. I tell you, I'm the whole package, man."

My first thought was that he was out of his mind. But instead of turning him down flat, I looked him over. Spoke. "Listen, Todd. I know you can handle yourself. You did a good job back at the farmhouse. And I got nothing against you personally. The thing is, right now, my focus is on getting my partner back. And maybe you can help. That woman Emory was talking about, the one who gives the orders, her name is Marguerite, right?"

Todd hesitated. Checked the rearview mirror and accelerated past a truck. Felt around inside his mouth up along his right gum line. "Tell you what. You buy me breakfast when we get to LA, and I'll tell you what I know."

Fair enough. I bought him breakfast—hash browns, bacon and eggs, and limitless coffee—at the Novel Café around the corner from my office. Looking none too fresh, we got a few strange looks, but I've had worse. Todd perked up from the food. Said that he and Emory and the rest of their crew used to work for QB Tragg who worked for Thomas Quincey, but now they worked for Tommy Blank who worked for Marguerite. And that Tommy was a good boss, although he had a psycho side that kept everybody on edge. And that Tommy preferred working with him rather than with Emory.

"Why is that?"

"'Cause Emory gets under his skin. He needles Tommy. Calls him a pretty boy and says he's gay 'cause he's so good-looking."

"Is he gay?"

"I don't think so," said Todd. "The dude is killer with the

women. Why would he be a gay?"

"I hear you…So, while we were driving over here, you were talking about working for me. Here's what I propose for now. I put you on retainer. A thousand a month. You just keep on doing what you're doing and keep your eyes and ears open. Once a week you call in to an encrypted phone number connected to our answering service. Just like you were talking to me, you tell the number everything you've learned that week. Then, after I've listened to it, if I have any questions, I'll call you directly."

"You'll put me on retainer?" I could tell the word pleased him. A guy thinks he's got it made when some fool puts him on retainer.

"That's right, Todd, I'll put you on retainer."

He bit his lip, snuffled, pulled at his nose, and took a sip of coffee. "You're not fucking with me, are you, Kid Crane?"

"Of course not. What do you say?"

In the end, it was a no-brainer. I phoned Greg and told him to set up a voice account immediately for our new CI, and to call me back as soon as it was ready. It took Greg less than ten minutes. I'm blessed with the world's most efficient database expert. Todd's call-in ID number was 000778. He'd get paid on the first of every month. I drove him to the Greyhound station at Seventh and Alameda, where he'd catch the bus back to Bakersfield. From there he'd Uber to Weedpatch. To liberate Emory and his crew. Cover story was that he'd spent the last ten hours in a Bakersfield motel room tied up and blindfolded with a gun barrel in his gut, but that he was finally able to escape when I got bored and went out to buy beer.

We exchanged burner numbers, and I handed him three Franklins to cover the rest of April. He was to call in the first of each month and ask for his monthly retainer. I reminded him that the number one order of business was collecting everything he could get on Tommy Blank—who he is, where he goes, what he does, and who he talks to.

A shadow passed over Todd's face. "What's the matter, baby?

Why's everybody so afraid of Tommy Blank?"

"It's not fear," said Todd. "It's something deeper than fear."

"That's deep, baby. I'm listening."

"It's like this. Tommy just spooks people. But not me. So don't worry. I'll get you the goods." That's where we left it.

Chapter Eight

I was driving down Alameda in my Corolla trying to decide where to go next when one of my burners rang. Tony Bott. I've known Tony for over a decade. His children and my daughter Maleah grew up together. This whole nightmare that I can't seem to shake was triggered by the gruesome murder of Tony's prize informant, Roberto Diaz, back in September. By then, Tony and Roberto had bonded in the peculiar manner of a detective and his best informant, and my friend had been carved up by his friend's sudden death. When Tony asked me to ride along to Sinaloa to deliver the "fuck you" money to Roberto's widow, I said *why not*?

Not the best decision. Returning from Mexico, I was abducted at LAX and my little south-of-the-border excursion became the centerpiece of Marguerite and Quincey's outlandish claim that I was conspiring with Tony's *compadre*, a corrupt, retired *federale* captain named Raymundo Ochoa, to smuggle Muslim terrorists across our southern border. Now, nearly seven months later, I was still reeling from the carousel of abuse, death, and disaster that began with Roberto's death.

"Morning, Tony. How's it going?"

"Bad. I think you know that. Why'd you call me last night?"

"Simple, we've got to talk."

"I don't know, Nick. I'm taking it slow." Sick of his *oh poor me* act but not the right time to cross him.

"You're home, right?"

"Yeah."

"Good. I'll be there in an hour." I hung up before he could object.

Wanted to check the damage at my office. Fought off the impulse. Phoned my starchy assistant Audrey instead and told her to report the break-in to LAPD. And that she should work from home until further notice. She was not happy, which didn't surprise me. Not always easy to keep the help happy. No matter how much cash I wave at them. I said nothing about Bobby. Phoned my lawyer friend Jack Snow and left a message telling him there'd been a break-in at my office, and could he please check out the damage and get back to me.

LAPD consists of nine thousand cops. Large, mostly white cop enclaves ring Los Angeles County—Simi Valley and Santa Clarita to the north, Chino Hills to the east. Tony and his wife Esther opted for the latter. When I rang their doorbell, Esther answered, gave me a hug, teared up, wiped her eyes, and told me I'd just missed Tony who was on his way to their local bowling alley. Said I should meet him there.

When I got to the bowling alley, I rented shoes and selected a ball. Met Tony at his lane.

"Put that piece of shit ball away, Nick. I brought a ball for you. And get yourself a beer." I obeyed. "Okay, Nick. Three games, right? Loser pays. Fair enough?"

"Sure, Tony." Felt the nudge of competition.

Three games with little conversation. Tony won two. Then he finally started talking, desolate like a man who's lost his closest *compadre*. Which maybe he had. He said he was sick of being a cop, sick of the hypocrisy, and sick of being a one-man army trying to combat the dope trade. Then he moved on to his three dead informants.

"All killed for rolling?" I asked.

"No. One was killed by a jealous husband. One got depressed and shot himself." Tony shuddered and ran a hand through his thick black hair. "That I never understood. And then Roberto. But you know how it works, Nick. Agents in separate departments compete for collars. Who gets the big convictions? Who gets promoted? Folks get hurt in the process. Sometimes folks get murdered. For no good reason. Make me sick."

Well. Murder is serious business but odd that a veteran narcotics agent would get upset because your rank-and-file career agent wanted to get ahead. Didn't buy it.

The hardest battles are the invisible ones—the ones we fight inside ourselves. It took a while, but I'm a patient man, and Tony finally uttered the words through clenched teeth. "Roberto was bringing me collar after collar. Meth and cocaine. Black tar heroin. Even some fentanyl. Like a fuckin' tsunami." He paused and took a deep breath.

"So that's good."

"Yeah. Real good. But here's the thing. When you've got a good informant, you have to look the other way. Some of the time. You know that."

I nodded.

"Problem is Roberto was still moving weight. Sure, the collars made me look really good. But I should've made him dial it back, but I didn't. 'Cause we were all making out." Tony grimaced and wiped his mouth with his right hand. "Then the damned guy gets murdered. And you get dragged in. Wrecked your life. And how many other poor fools went down? All because I got weak."

This could have shook me. If I'd let it. I decided to dig deeper. 'Cause there's almost always deeper. First, I stood up and rolled a frame. Two shots equaled a shaky spare. I rolled another. Same result. Walked back over and sat down next to Tony. Laid my hand on his shoulder. Gently. "So, you were taking a cut. For your kids' college. Or whatever." Tony brushed my hand away. Bowed his head and mumbled, "So how come you're so damned calm? Like none of this bothers you?"

I glared at him. In dubious battle. "You know me better than that. Everything bothers me. I just don't show it that much 'cause I'm walled off. It's both my strength and my fatal flaw. And it's true: I am good at stonewalling the killings. Most of the time. At least I've never murdered anyone in cold blood. And as you know, that kind of restraint can be a big disadvantage when you've got fools gunning for you." I shook my head. Had the curious thought that if I was really unlucky, I might meet all my dead people again someday. In hell. I took a long pull of my Corona. Tasted good. We looked at each other. Tony got up. Changed his mind. Sat back down.

"So now that I've spilled my guts," he said, "what is this really about? You're not supposed to be back in town."

Shit. Brought it all back. One of my burners rang. Jack Snow. He told me my office had been thoroughly ransacked. The computers were smashed and lying on the floor. Good thing Greg and Bobby had everything backed up. The scoundrels had left a letter addressed to Nick Crane, American Traitor. Inside, there was nothing but a phone number, 859-234-4400.

I thanked him and signed off. Tony was looking at me curiously. "So, like I said, Nick, what is this really about?"

I sighed. And divulged. Told him about Bobby's kidnapping and roughed out what I'd been through so far trying to get him back. Skipped the brick-through-the-window event in Burns, Oregon. Then Greg phoned. I put him on speaker and gestured for Tony to listen in. Greg told me Marguerite was holding recruitment rallies at Leach Hall in Waupun, Wisconsin on Friday, May 3, and at the old Fox Theater in Fond du Lac, twenty miles down the road, the following night. Bingo. I thanked him and told him I'd get back to him. Faced Tony. Could tell that he was still wrestling with something.

"So where do I come in?"

"What do you mean?"

"You heard me. Where do I come in? I got you and Bobby into this...and I'm gonna help get you out. I'm in a good position to help 'cause I've taken a leave of absence from the department."

Interesting. But still. "I'm not here 'cause I want you to do anything." A white lie but felt it was necessary.

"I don't care why you're here. Just answer my goddamned question, Nick. What do you want me to do?"

His savage look was back. The Tony Bott snarl. Good. The mopey Tony I could not abide.

"It's like this, Tony. For about forty-eight hours there, I lost my mind. Started thinking I needed a squadron. Then I realized I just needed a couple more good men. On standby—"

"—on standby for what?"

I stood up. Stretched. Felt the bond that had been growing since Tony had started to divulge. "To bust out Bobby once we find him. Yeah, that's it. We need a small crackerjack crew. They can be former Special Forces or ex-law enforcement, but they can't be too crazy. And there's another problem. If I don't bust Bobby out, I have to turn myself in by May 22. Or else..."

"Or else what?" Tony sat straight up, suddenly completely sober.

"They ship him off to some foreign torture site—Poland or Egypt or Syria."

"Holy fuck."

"At least we have a little bit of time. The clock doesn't start ticking till Friday. It'll take me a week or so to get outfitted. Then I'll drive to Wisconsin in Bobby's van. Go to work. Figure out a way to jack Marguerite and whoever else needs jacking. Her man in the field, Tommy Blank, is my other target. I've got one of Blank's underlings calling in with intel. Everything he can get me on Blank, who's reputed to be a very bad actor."

"Fuck him," said Tony.

I laughed. "The recruits are apparently in awe of him...But anyway, for now, just be ready. In case I need you to hop on a plane to Milwaukee."

"Ten-four, baby. I'll be ready."

Outside, we shook hands and got in our cars. I drove to Highland Park where I rented a one-bedroom suite at the Cradle Rest Motel on Figueroa, the same quasi-dive that Bobby and I lived in for several critical days during the October War with the Ferguson-Quincey cartel. Picked up some Mexican food at an open-air joint down the block. *Agua fresca* and the world's juiciest burrito. Turned the TV on and the volume off. Let the food soothe me. Left part of the burrito for the morning. Lay back on the bed. Slept.

PART TWO
Chapter Nine

Friday, May 3, 2019. Nineteen days till my surrender date...Leach Hall in Waupun, Wisconsin is a posh venue in a small city. Spank in the middle of the great American heartland. But the folks attending Marguerite's rally weren't posh. They were red-blooded, heavily armed Americans who would kick your ass if you accused them of being posh. These are my people. I was raised among them, a bit to the west and north in nearby Minnesota, and although I fled before the ink was dry on my high school diploma, I have a soft spot in my heart for the Midwest as big as Siberia.

The sign out front said it all: *Make America Safe Again! Lend a Hand the Wisconsin Way!* So much as I love to provoke, I kept my mouth shut as my conservative brothers and their ride-hard-until-death girlfriends, daughters, and wives (some of whom were even tougher than the men) sauntered into the hall. If you listened closely, you could hear their hardware clank (open carry state, you know).

Marguerite recognized the importance of publicity. The press was welcome. My press pass, which cost me $750, courtesy of Barry Camus, LA-based forgery expert par excellence, said I was Blaine Greer, political correspondent for the *Fond du Lac Free Press*, a tiny alt-right weekly. My disguise: basic. Blond curly wig, ruddy orange beard.

It was twelve days since Bobby's abduction. Eleven days since Willem Spahn had passed on Marguerite's ultimatum. In a terse phone call just before I rolled out of Los Angeles, Cole had informed me that Marguerite had told him that Bobby was okay. No torture and no more deprivation than what the average convict endures. Cole assured me that Bobby would be released with a pat on the back and a one-way ticket to Argentina if and when I turned myself in. And that he was meeting Marguerite in Wisconsin at one of her rallies to discuss my surrender. If I failed to surrender on time, Bobby would be transported to Scorpion Prison in Cairo.

Marguerite was the keynote speaker, but she didn't come on until after four or five retired cops and agents, along with one or two agency types gone para, had whipped the already excited crowd into a frothy, steaming goulash of aggression. From my perch in Press Row, I lent half an ear to the drivel being spewed by the ex-somebodies on stage. You can only listen to so many folks babble about Manifest Destiny and how God blessed this great land for patriotic white Americans and how it's our job to take it back from the Muslims and the other minorities before hellfire and damnation blanket the land like a cloud of poisonous gas. Amazing thing is some folks either believe this shit or pretend to believe it. Even a hardened cynic like my father Adam would not be cheering on the apocalypse from his perch in Purgatory.

I can sleep anywhere. Took a brief catnap and woke up to cheering. Time for Marguerite? Not quite. First, a local country trio played three songs and exited to considerable applause.

Then Marguerite, dressed soberly in a dark knee-length skirt, a pearl grey blouse, and a brown bomber jacket, launched into her talk, the gist of which was simple. The president was under attack. The enemy was a powerful, well-organized cartel of left-wing socialists and communists. With CNN and MSNBC on the front line, based on orders from the Deep State. To drive her point home, Marguerite described the horror of living in a socialist nation, complete with starving babies in orphanages and bloodthirsty death squads whose job was to round up, incarcerate, and murder innocent, hardworking citizens. Then she described what the good people of Wisconsin and the good people of every other decent, law-abiding state would face if the socialists took over after the next election. It would be the end of freedom as we know it. Abortion would be mandatory for all pregnant unmarried women and a one-child per family policy would be enacted. Families in violation would be treated with utmost severity.

"I'm sure lots of you good people have brothers and sisters who for whatever reason could not be here tonight." The crowd voiced its agreement. "Thank you," said Marguerite, extending her hands in a humble gesture. "Thank you for listening. Now, I'm going to ask you all a question. How many of you are the oldest child in your family?"

She waited. Hands slowly rose. "Don't be shy, my friends. Please raise your hands. Hold them high and proud so that I can see you. Under the new socialist regime, you would be spared. But your brothers and sisters would be raped, euthanized, or sold into sexual slavery...or at the very least, expelled from this country that has always been their home." Marguerite paused. The crowd rumbled its disapproval. Mutterings, groans, growls...

Marguerite waited. Waited some more. Then she spoke. "I can see how pissed off this makes you, my friends. As it should. It should break your hearts. But it should do more than that. It should make you furious. It should make you blind with rage." She wrenched her mouth into the blackest scowl, then placed her right hand across her chest. Tapped it three times. Again, she paused. Waited. Spoke. "Those of you close enough probably saw me tap my chest three times. Why three times? Simple. The first tap is to honor every manly, god-fearing American father who gets up early each morning, turns on Fox News to bring him up to date on what's going on in the world, drinks his second cup of coffee, and heads off to work. The second tap is in honor of all you hardworking mothers who devote your lives to your children, you mothers who work a second job to raise tuition money so that your children can go to a decent Christian school. And the third tap is for all your children, your brave boys and girls who keep their noses clean and their eyes on the prize. What is the prize, you ask? I will tell you. The prize is liberty, the right to thrive and prosper, to live bold and free in this freedom-loving nation. Our nation. The United States of America."

She paused and the crowd burst into sustained applause. Could feel the heavy testosterone. And the estrogen, powerful and dark, all around me. Unleashed humanity.

Would take no great effort to extract my S&W 9 mm from its belt holster, aim and fire, hit this swill-spouting enemy of the people somewhere between her chin and forehead. But even if I did, *cui bono*, who profits? Humanity would be better off with one less Marguerite Ferguson, but Bobby might also be a casualty.

The applause went on for a long time. Marguerite finally gestured for silence. Spoke with great solemnity. "Thank you. Thank you for caring. Now I don't mean to upset anyone with doomsday predictions. It's the last thing I want to do. But there are times when one has no choice other than to tell the truth. Whether or not it makes you popular. Just like our truth-telling leader in Washington, D.C. He and I believe in the truth and believe it is our duty to tell the truth. Always. Every day. There are no vacations from the truth." Another pause. She then launched into an impassioned denunciation of Muslim terrorists, whom she claimed were in every state and every large city hiding in their repulsive sleeper cells, stockpiling weapons and building dirty bombs and bioweapons and getting down on their hands and knees five times a day facing the east while mouthing their satanic prayers. At times during her diatribe, Marguerite seemed to be tearing up. At one point, she wiped her eyes impatiently. As if she were deeply moved by the horror of it all. But that didn't stop her from talking. After another round of denunciation, this time directed at illegal Latino immigrants, whom she claimed were swarming across our southern border, Marguerite stopped. Took a deep breath. Held up her hands. "Enough, my friends. You've been a great audience. Now, I want to leave you with this..." But before speaking, she bowed her head and prayed silently. For a good ten seconds. The crowd waited. Hell, I waited. She finally raised her head. Spoke clearly and simply. "I love God, my friends, I love you, and I love our country. With all my heart. I hope you do too." With that, she waved to the crowd and walked slowly to the back of the stage where she vanished through the drapery.

The country band came back on stage for a quick rendition of John Mellencamp's "Rain on the Scarecrow." I doubt John would have been pleased. But there was still more to come. Marguerite had one more trick up her sleeve.

After the poor scarecrow was relegated back to his wind-blown field, and the musicians, glowing with honest sweat, had left the stage, Marguerite returned to the lectern, smoothed her hair, and announced, "My fellow freedom-loving Americans, I'm sure many of you are itching to grab a drink and get in line to sign up with one of the branches of our political action brigade, but first I want to introduce a very special friend and comrade, a Marine Corps captain and JAG who has fought for our freedom all over the world including Iraq and Afghanistan, the man who single-handedly foiled a Muslim terrorist plot to blow up the main branch of the New York City Public Library, this brilliant friend of mine is a patriot of the first order..." She paused dramatically.

It was like a Dempsey right cross to the temple. As soon as she said "Marine Corps captain." The house lights dimmed, and the crowd hushed. Strangely cavernous steps came marching across the stage. The lights came back on. Wish I could say it was a hallucination. It wasn't. There was Thomas Quincey standing next to Marguerite. At first glance, six months in an off-the-books federal detention center appeared to have had little effect on the man. Same tall, aristocratic bearing. Same pale, flat eyes, knife-cut mouth, well-barbered, dark blond hair. Still feral and deadly, or so I assumed.

But when he spoke, something was different. Hard to put a finger on what it was. Still the same warm, soothing enema of a voice. The same nationalist, isolationist theme. The difference was not one of voice, tone, or carriage. He told the crowd how glad he was to be here in beautiful Waupun and how proud he was of Wisconsin for turning out in such good numbers at this patriotic event. He cheerfully parroted much of what Marguerite had said about the socialist threat and the Muslim threat, how they both had to be neutralized, stopped in their tracks, but it was not the same Thomas Quincey. The passion of the true believer was gone. Instead, something scarier, the passion of the true unbeliever. Or so it seemed. Was he now Marguerite's own personal yes-man, damaged beyond repair from the trauma of his recent arrest and incarceration? Perhaps...

He didn't talk long. Eight or nine minutes, tops, the most banal kind of patriotic drivel. Canned music. I wasn't listening. I was thinking about the night I spent with Adara Ghaffari, his estranged Iraqi American wife. The way her skin glistened after lovemaking. Her lovely smile when we woke in the morning. Even the way she wolfed down her vanilla pancakes at breakfast. Charming. My fear was that she had already forgotten everything we had shared. Because I knew that passion can be like the wind leaving emptiness in its wake.

I was wrenched out of my reverie by everyone standing up and applauding. Were they cheering Quincey? Marguerite? The country trio? Or even themselves for banding together to make America safe again?

Chapter Ten

Found myself face-to-face with Marguerite and Quincey later that night at a political action recruitment meeting in the den of somebody's ranch house on the edge of Waupun. Watched Jimbo Clark explain how we volunteer para guys and gals would not only be issued per diems; we would also be given Glock 17s and M4s. "Free guns," said Jimbo. "It don't get no better than this."

I was drinking slowly. Keeping my wits about me. Marguerite and Quincey had looked right at me, first one, then the other, when I entered the room. Passing glances. Any recognition deep in the viscera only. Jimbo finished talking and Marguerite introduced him to Quincey. Again, the mechanical affect. Neurons off-kilter. Gave me the creeps. I stood up and walked unsteadily out of the room, mumbling something in my best Fargo accent about needing to use the bathroom. "Down the hall to your right," said a voice.

Down the hall to my right turned into out the door into the night. Quick perusal of the cars out front. Only one, a black Lincoln Navigator (how'd I know it would be one of those?), had rental car bar codes on the windows. Moving fast, I slapped a bug under its left rear bumper. Got into Bobby's customized Ford Econoline van and waited. Storage compartments full of firearms, ammunition, stun guns and gas grenades, coma drugs, surveillance equipment, handcuffs, and leg irons. Carted from Los Angeles. Two thousand fifty-three miles, three twelve-hour days behind the wheel. Almost on the stroke of midnight, Marguerite and Quincey walked out of Jimbo's house.

I watched as they pulled away from the curb in the Lincoln Navigator. My readout showed them heading northeast up Highway 151 toward Fond du Lac. I waited. Rolled down my driver's side window and took a deep breath. A light breeze soothing my worried brow. The air already heavy with humidity that would only get worse as the year ground forward. So still. Hush. I pulled away from the curb.

I drove up 151 toward Fond du Lac and started making phone calls. First Greg, my paraplegic assistant. Since I'd been giving him real work, he was uncrippled in so many ways. I had a simple message. Phone every high-end and mid-range motel and hotel in the greater Fond du Lac area and give some sob story about a relative on life support and how Marguerite Ferguson's presence was absolutely necessary because they were about to pull the plug. Find out if either Marguerite Ferguson or Thomas Quincey had reservations. Or Tami Wheat or Miles Amsterdam. Just in case they were registered under their pseudonyms.

Bad karma to cry wolf. Shook it off. Next, I called Tony, who agreed, groggily, to get on the horn.

Five miles from Fond du Lac, it hit me. With Quincey a free man, Adara could once again take him in her arms. I wanted to warn her, spirit her away...but to where? To the life of an exile hiding in rented rooms, waiting for the next brick to shatter the calm? It would never work. My knuckles white on the steering wheel. Which made no sense. I barely knew her.

Turned to Bobby. Even if they weren't torturing him, they could be drugging him, working him, trying to turn him. The big guy wouldn't do well in captivity. Even worse in solitary. The rage in his hooded brown eyes would turn first to fear and then to the madness of absolute midnight. I knew what he would say if I could talk to him. *Worry about me but don't worry about me. Stay clear and figure it out. Be yourself. Don't charge in half-cocked. Until it is time. Incision by misdirection.*

'Cause this is a battle you cannot lose.

When I reached Fond du Lac, I followed the readout to Marguerite's black Navigator, which was parked in front of Fat Billy's all-night diner. Though I could break into and search their vehicle with the help of a portable radio signal booster, I resisted the temptation. Not likely to find much. What I was interested in was their conversation. For that I had a Javelin XQCR, a tried-and-true burst ghost transmitter recording device (with sweeper detection capabilities). But needed to know where to plant it.

I parked near the Navigator. Waited. Ten minutes later, my phone rang. Tony. "I found them, Nick. They're at the Starlight Inn. One hundred N. Pioneer Road, room 302. She's registered under her own name. It's on the west edge of town. I told them you'd wait in the lobby until they arrive. They haven't checked in yet. That's the best I could do."

"Best you could do? That's fantastic." Tony was back, the smooth intimidator, getting the intel we needed. I phoned Greg on the way over and left a message that Tony had found Marguerite's hotel.

When I got to the Starlight, I recced the place and wandered into the lobby casual as hell. Didn't bother to introduce myself. Sat down to watch the news. For maybe sixty seconds. Then I wandered up to the third floor. Now the tough part. Finding and bribing a housekeeper to let me into Marguerite's room. Facing the language barrier, the ethics barrier, and the fear factor. My one positive was spelled c-a-s-h. Almost one a.m. and no one in sight. Went back downstairs. Wandered past the laundry area and the gym. Practicing the art of invisibility. The hallways were empty. About to despair when a housekeeper came out of a supply room pushing a cart loaded with soft drinks and snacks. She looked Hispanic, possibly Filipino. Like an apparition, she got on the elevator. I followed. We rode together to the third floor. She got off first and pushed her cart down the hallway. Stopped at the vending machine alcove.

In this business, take nothing for granted. Or you will not last. It hit me just as I was starting to extract C-notes from my wallet. Something Frenchy Lefevre had told me while staggering out of Philippe's a year or so before his last roundup. A good operative engaged in delicate maneuvers rarely stays at a place where he's made advance reservations. Too easy for someone like me to recce and bug it. I checked my GPS. The Navigator was on the move heading east from Fat Billy's. I took the stairs down to the lobby three at a time, got in the Econoline, and drove east across town.

I caught up with Marguerite and Quincey in the parking lot of a Courtyard by Marriott on the eastside of town. Another black Navigator parked next to theirs. Her palace guard, no doubt. Errant desire to shoot out the windows. Fleeting. Needed Bobby to calm me down. Like I calm him down. I needed to find a way to smuggle the ghost transmitter into Marguerite's suite, which meant I needed the room number.

Thought it over. Time was passing. Got mad. Who were these bastards and where did they get off? Floating on aggression. Dangerous. Hotel bar was packed, patrons little more than shadows in the soft, dark light. Something to be said for a packed to the gills, dimly lit bar full of Midwestern sports fans and gun lovers, including three big-shouldered, short-haired guys...ex-military, I'd bet. Blackwater rejects? Cheerful sadists? Or just regular guys? Ignored them and they ignored me. Ordered a double shot of Jim Beam with a Heineken back. Wished Tony was with me. One of our favorite pastimes, drinking together in convivial watering holes.

Sip the whiskey slowly. Like foreplay before the main event, which brought me back to Adara. Just before our first kiss, I'd looked at her and she'd looked at me and said, "I've been dreaming of this moment. And now here we are..." I've tried to hold on to that image of Adara. To be that lovely and that real and an eternal refugee. As the whiskey began mangling my brain, I tried to segue back into the moment. The goons at the other end of the bar loud and stupid. Marguerite and Quincey upstairs in their suite.

Logic doesn't cut it when there's no right choice. So I let the whiskey talk. Left a tip with the barkeep and walked up to the front desk, two crisp Jacksons conspicuous between my middle and ring fingers. "Merry Christmas, buddy. Been one helluva ride this year. How 'bout you, buddy?" The diminutive Southeast Asian deskman looked at me with some disdain. "Listen, buddy," easing the Jacksons toward him, "I need you to call up to Marguerite Ferguson, the lady in the brown bomber jacket who checked in about an hour ago. She's with a tall thin gentleman. Tell her Dee Cole's down in the lobby and that he wants to have a drink. Ask her to come down and meet me." The twenties seemed to be moving toward him on their own volition. We looked at each other. I went stern. It can scare a man. But not him. I placed the Jacksons down on the counter, took out my wallet, and extracted a C-note which I dangled languidly while scooping up the twenties.

The Franklin did the trick. He made me write out exactly what I wanted him to say. Then he phoned Marguerite. Explained the situation. She said she would be down in five minutes. "What did you say her room number is?"

"Huh?" The Jacksons fluttered down on top of the C-note. He winked and smirked at the same time. "Two fifty-one. At the end of the hall." Go time.

Marguerite never saw me. A rear naked chokehold with both arms. She struggled like crazy, butted me hard in the crotch and flailed around. I stuck a knee in the small of her back and increased the pressure so she couldn't cry out. Pretty funny. This woman worth at least half a billion dollars (and that's just her own money, according to Greg) had an experienced knee centered at the base of her spine while her air was being cut off. I pulled her into the stairwell and applied just enough pressure to keep her quiet. I had to bite my lip to keep from laughing. "Well now, you listen to me, you hear," my best phony Swedish accent. "I'm going to give you a shot of Versed. It won't hurt a bit. Then I'm going to rob you, so just calm down so I don't have to hurt you. I don't like hurting women." To my surprise, she went limp. Aversion to shots? Like me. Unlike Bobby, I hate shots. I yanked off her bomber jacket and delivered the entire syringe of Versed straight into the flesh of her shoulder. Just drunk enough to carry it off.

Once she was borderline unconscious, I went through her purse. Key card in wallet next to her credit cards. It was that or knock on the door and incapacitate Quincey with a taser. Unless he was asleep, which was what I was banking on. I wanded the reader and the green light flashed. The suite had two bedrooms with actual doors, a kitchen with dinette, and a living room with a large, oval-shaped coffee table. Quincey's door ajar. Lying on the bed, his head was turned toward the wall. Didn't stir. I velcroed the ghost transmitter under the coffee table. Took the cash out of Marguerite's purse. And her phone. Left the credit cards and everything else.

Crept into Quincey's room. He stirred, rolled over, seemed to look right at me. Grunted. Dangled a hand over the edge of the bed. Sighed deeply, his dangling fingers pointing toward his wallet, which he'd dropped on the floor. It was stuffed with cash. Though I grabbed most of it (just to keep up appearances), the money was not what interested me. What interested me was a trio of photos. Quincey and Adara reciting their vows in Boston's Old South Church. Adara on the stage reprising her iconic *Bus Stop* scene, legs crossed, perched on a battered old suitcase. Quincey and Adara reclining on deck chairs on a yacht trolling some tropical sea. I slid the photos into my front shirt pocket.

On the way out, I grabbed a bottle of expensive champagne that was airing on the kitchen counter and used it as a doorstop. Found Marguerite on her hands and knees in the stairwell. I grabbed her by the hair and pushed her back down. Treated her to another half dose of Versed. Dragged her back to their suite and dumped her just inside the door. Popped the cork on the champagne and doused her thoroughly. Dropped the empty bottle next to her and walked out, closing the door behind me.

Chapter Eleven

Sixty minutes later. Propped up in bed eating beef jerky in my newly rented room on the second floor of a discount motel across the street from the Marriott. I'd left another message from Desmond Cole (to be delivered in the morning) saying that I had waited for half an hour in the lobby, and that unless something else came up, I'd be attending the Fond du Lac MASA rally tonight.

I'd activated the ghost transmitter but had not yet told it to send. Prolonging the pleasure, you might say. Transmission range up to seven hundred yards, and I was much closer than that. I'd removed my blond wig and ruddy orange beard and had cached Marguerite's cell phone, wrapped in plastic, behind a dumpster in back of a Phillips 66 station near a power plant on the southeast edge of town. Operational security.

Didn't quite finish the jerky. Fell into an uneasy sleep that deepened as the hours passed.

When I finally stirred, I lay still for a long time. Pulled myself together. Sat up. Staggered over to the sink and poured a glass of tap water. Drank it down. Another. Back to the bed. Sat down. Reached for my shirt and fished out the pictures. Merely glanced at the wedding and suitcase photos. Could linger over them later. Instead, I fixated on the yacht photo. Adara, sleek and tan, sipping red wine and sporting a puka-shell necklace. Quincey lean as a young Paul Newsman, with chiseled abs and well-defined biceps, tufts of thick blond hair covering his chest. I slapped myself gently on the cheek. So impossible, our worlds light years apart, brought together briefly by Quincey's lunatic machinations.

The slanting beams of early morning sunlight drove light slivers through the blinds. I took a shower and got dressed. Today's disguise was a dull brown toupee with standard-issue military moustache.

I ordered the ghost transmitter to send but didn't start listening yet. Packed up and went downstairs to pay in advance for another day. The diminutive Southeast Asian deskman (oddly, the same guy from the night shift at the Marriott working his day job) grinned when he saw me. "Why you not stay at the Marriott?"

"Couldn't afford it. I gave you all my money." Then I started laughing. Not sure why. Maybe all the tension of the last two weeks just erupted. Deskman looked at me like I was crazy. Maybe I was. But it felt good to laugh. He knew I was insane when I booked a different room to check into later that afternoon.

Found a spot facing the street in a breakfast joint the deskman recommended.

Ham and eggs and a bowl of oatmeal with walnuts and raisins (hold the milk). And coffee. Attached my ghost transmitter to a set of headphones and plugged in. At first, silence. About to fast forward when the whimpering erupted, female, almost like a child. Marguerite licking her wounds. I almost choked on my oatmeal. Tried to wipe the smirk off my face. The moaning continued for a while. Stopped. Started up again. Then sudden shouting. "Tom, goddamnit, why didn't you help me? The Swede took my phone and money." No answer. "I'm talking to you, Tom. Get your ass out here!"

This time the keep America safe crusader answered. Sort of. "Huh? Whaz-z-z-a-mat-ter?"

"Oh shit! Wake up, Tom! Wake the fuck up!" Damn, this woman was crude. Such a contrast to the sober super-patriot who had beguiled the eager throng at last night's MASA rally.

Sixty seconds of silence. I chewed my food thoughtfully. Maybe she'd gone into Quincey's room to wake him up. I was right.

"Get away from me, you're all wet. I'm trying to sleep."

"Sleep!" This propelled Marguerite into a towering rage. "All you do is sleep, now that you're hooked on that fucking Valium."

"And whose fault is that?" Half awake now.

"Oh, so that's the way you want to play. As you may recall," her voice calmer now, "after your arrest, for the first month you experienced profound anxiety. Remember? I don't know why. That Boron jail was like a three-star hotel. You were so bad off that Dee and I feared for your safety. Thought you might hurt yourself. We had to move you to that private jail in Inglewood where they put you in that padded cell for a week for your own protection."

"Stop," said Quincey sleepily. "I was going through a tough time. All you had to do was get me bail. I would've been okay."

"I've told you a hundred times. We couldn't get you bail, not until Dee and I came up with a persuasive narrative turning you back into a patriot rather than a domestic terrorist selling drugs to support his sicko scheme."

"I am a patriot."

"I certainly hope so. Anyway, Dee and I put our heads together and he said, 'I think we better put the little wuss on Valium. And fast.' So we did."

"The hell with Dee Cole! I never did like that sanctimonious pauper."

Another long silence. The sound of a toilet flushing. Took advantage of the interval. Flagged my server and ordered toast with strawberry jam.

The sound of people moving about the room, Quincey speaking, more slowly than normal, the Valium, perhaps. "So what happened, Marguerite? How come you're all wet and smell like champagne?"

Brief silence. Then she spoke, a bored recital like she was

describing traffic patterns. "Some low-life Swede grabbed me in the hall and put me in a chokehold. I'm lucky to be alive. He would've broken my back if I'd made one wrong move. He dragged me into the stairwell and injected me with something. Said it was Versed. Isn't that like what you're taking?"

"I don't shoot up," said Quincey indignantly.

"Well, that's certainly something to be proud of." Sarcastic thing. "All this to steal my cash and cell phone, which won't do him any good without the password. Which just happens to be my birthday. But he won't know that. The reason I'm wet is the Swede doused me with our champagne while I was knocked out. Some kind of sick ritual."

"Good thing we've got another bottle...But didn't you just have a birthday? I seem to remember we did something that evening."

"Yeah, three days ago. If you call that doing something. We drank champagne after the rally in Des Moines and you started quoting those depressing poets that you're so fond of. Meanwhile, you were trying to get your hands on me. The truth is, Tom, you're starting to remind me of that Nick Crane idiot. When Dee Cole and I debriefed Adara a few days after Crane got shot, she said one of the reasons she liked the bastard was 'cause he knew that famous line from 'The Second Coming,' 'The worst are full of passionate intensity.' Apparently, that's an important consideration in choosing a man these days."

"Crane's right," said Quincey, a bit more spark in his voice. "Very few women can say no to a man who knows his poetry."

"This girl can." Marguerite's laugh was like her smile, a singular flash of light. Her mood darkened. "What is it about you and Crane? You act like you like the SOB. Even though he slept with your wife."

Quincey's laugh was slow and dry. Motherfucker sounded like William F. Buckley, Jr. Smooth, smug, confident. Then he said, "If it wasn't him, it would be someone else. Crane's a tough bastard, like I would be if I were a fucking peasant. I respect that. He wiped out QB Tragg in the ring. That wasn't easy. That's why I never actually wanted to kill him."

"You're a liar." They both laughed. There was a long silence, the sound of shuffling, water pouring, and then Quincey said, "I didn't even know you left our suite. I thought you were in for the night. You shouldn't have gone outside by yourself."

"Damn you, Tom, I wasn't just wandering around. The desk clerk said Dee Cole was down in the lobby and wanted to have a drink. I've been expecting him. He told me he was going to attend one of our rallies as soon as he got back from Europe...But there's something we need to discuss. Although you looked great, you always do, and I mean that sincerely, your talk at the rally was not up to par. You were as bad as those ex-Company guys. They were too strident, and you were too passive. Maybe you don't quite understand. Here we are, the vanguard of the campaign to reelect our leader. We are on a mission to save our country. That's our lodestar, Tom, to save our country. Looking sharp is not enough. You've got to act and sound sharp."

"All right, all right," said Quincey. "I get it."

"I'm not so sure you do. If it wasn't for Dee and me, you'd be doing ten years in federal prison for trafficking a warehouse full of cocaine. I need you to deliver. Powerful, passionate speeches. And there's something else that we need to discuss. I've hesitated to bring this up, but it's been gnawing at me. Why in the world, when we started investigating you, did you not wise up, calm down, and shut down your false flag operation? I don't get it. Do you have a death wish or something?"

I could see her there in the suite, chest heaving, blue eyes filled with an unholy combination of disappointment and glee. "Look," said Quincey, "my vision to save America appeared fully formed in my mind. I thought of it as penance for getting my rifle teams killed in Iraq. Through my own fucking hubris."

He sounded genuinely sad. Did I pity him? Not at all, though I did feel sorry for his dead soldiers.

Another lengthy silence. Then a shout of rage. "Your fucking

Swede took my pictures of Adara. I'll kill him! I'll kill the sonuvabitch!"

Marguerite's turn to rub it in. "What's wrong with that? She's a beautiful woman. If I were a man, I'd steal her pictures too."

This made Quincey laugh. Then he spoke. "Oh, well, she's in the rearview mirror now. So much for trophy wives. Truthfully, I think you're way hotter. 'Cause you've got personality to complement your beauty."

A moment of silence. Then Marguerite softened. "Why, Tom, that's the sweetest thing I've ever heard you say."

"Well, I'm not very sweet most of the time. But it's the truth. I just wanted you to know." Quincey laughed. "Listen, Marguerite. I've got an idea. Why don't you get the other bottle of Dom? It's in the fridge. We should celebrate a very successful rally and an even more successful recruitment meeting."

"You're right," said Marguerite. "It was a great evening until that fuckin' Swede came along and upset my equilibrium. Which is hard to do. But he managed."

"That's okay. You just need a little TLC. Bring the bottle over here. I'll give you a back rub. It'll calm you down."

"N-O," said Marguerite coquettishly. "You just want to get in my pants."

"That's one way of looking at it. But really, you do need to relax."

They went back and forth for a while, Marguerite flirting, Quincey calm. Then I heard a cork pop and the sound of pouring. As the champagne took hold, the giggles began and then their voices trailed off...until Marguerite finally purred throatily, "Tom, you make me feel like such a woman." More sighs, silence, then deeper sighs at which point, chuckling grimly, I turned the volume all the way down. Under the right circumstances, an audio sex tape, while not as powerful as a video, can still destroy the career of anyone from your local P.E. teacher to a head of state.

But I had to hand it to Quincey. The Valium and champagne weren't keeping him from persuading Marguerite to act like a very normal woman. Twinge of jealousy. First his years with Adara, and now this.

I waited ten minutes and turned the volume back up. Back down. Ten more minutes. Volume up. They were finally spent. An occasional rustling or soft, inchoate sigh. It was almost touching.

Sat there thinking. Wisp of a plan. An evil one. Left a nice tip, got in Bobby's Econoline, and drove back to my motel. Did not expect Marguerite to hang around the hotel during the daytime. She'd be out preparing for the rally while Quincey slept in. I set up the ghost to capture come what may and drove soberly and sedately toward the outskirts of town, then southeast on county road V. Passed through Campbellsport, one of those spick-and-span, built-to-last Midwestern villages. Lots of churches and taverns. Passed a tiny hamlet called Elmore and came to the Lake Inn across the road from a pond called Lake Bernice.

Parked next to a row of pickup trucks. The Lake Inn, which I remembered from my teenage years as being little more than a neighborhood dive, was now all marble and sleek hardwood with good mirrors and good liquor. I asked the bartender where Jimmy Sain lived. Met with some resistance but finally a spry, little German guy named Myron with a big nose and a permanent sunburn said he would lead me to Jimmy's place.

Before we left, I bought him a beer for his trouble. Then I followed him out past the lake into the back country. Overcast, the air hung heavy, the humidity high. The freshly plowed fields were brown and the box elder trees in the fencerows were sprouting new buds. Passed a small lake and an abandoned quarry and a trio of tidy farms with red barns and tall grey silos. Finally turned down a long driveway. Passed several black iron metal sculptures and a large poplar tree. Turned into the barnyard and came to rest near an old, dilapidated barn and farmhouse. More metal sculptures and stacks of useable lumber. A late-model Nissan pickup with a sculpture in its bed. A dog stuck its head out from under the rear bumper, barked, yawned, and went back to sleep.

I parked and got out. "Jimmy's in his shop. In the back of the barn where the cows come in." Myron pointed. "Go on, now. He's expecting you."

Chapter Twelve

The barn was built on a shallow incline, the first floor dug into the side of the hill. I entered through the milk house. The beautiful stainless-steel, milk-processing equipment was unused, covered with dust. I stepped into the barn and let my eyes adjust to the light. It was an obstacle course. Discarded farm equipment and chicken cages and feeding troughs piled up to the ceiling. Stacks of pallets and salvaged lumber. Had to change course several times to avoid sheets of moldy insulation that had broken through the tar-papered ceiling.

There was light at the far end, and as I got closer, I could hear a steady, rhythmic hammering. This part of the barn was updated with recessed lighting and spotlights.

I hadn't seen Jimmy Sain in thirty-five years. Wearing a Milwaukee Brewers' cap, grey hair curling behind his ears, he was working a piece of metal in his forge. I walked toward him. "Hey, Jimmy. It's me, Nick." He grunted, put his hammer down on a steel table and grasped the hot metal with a pair of tongs. Quenched it with a hiss in a tub of oily water. Then he set the metal down and spoke, or rather, rasped. "Where the hell you been the last thirty-five years, Nicky?"

"California. You know that." For years, I'd checked in by phone pretty regularly, but that ended when Jimmy drew a ten-year state prison bid in 2007 for sales of methamphetamine. "You got a pretty cool setup here," gesturing toward his metal-working equipment and welding rig.

Jimmy shrugged. "It's a living. A creative monkey could probably do this metal sculpture bullshit if somebody gave him the tools and a bag of meth to get started." Jimmy laughed, his wounded brown eyes sparkling for an instant before reverting to their habitual gloom. "I had a con talk me through the steps before I got out of the joint. I always could draw. You probably remember that. It was the one thing I was good at besides raising hell." He laughed. "But I do have a knack for this. First, I draw it up, and then I build it. And it feels kind of peaceful under the hood." He pointed at his welding hood.

"I saw some of your work driving in. It looks good, Jimmy. I always knew you had talent."

Jimmy looked me over, his hooded brown eyes not unlike Bobby's. Then he stepped forward and offered me his hand, almost shyly. "So, what can I get you? I got three or four different craft brews, some wine, plenty of Scotch and bourbon, and some of those imported waters. Whatever you like."

"A craft beer sounds good. I hear this state has got some great micro-breweries."

"That's what they say." A trace of attitude. Jimmy's way. I let it pass. He moved to the far corner, lean and leathery with a small beer belly. Plucked two brews from a stainless-steel refrigerator, flipped the caps off on the edge of his steel table, and handed me one. Black Jack Porter. In his jeans and black Metallica T-shirt, Jimmy looked like Willem Dafoe playing a bad guy. The old youthful cockiness was now a kind of sad confidence. He grinned—gold-and-silver teeth, one or two missing. "Is it too hot in here, Nicky? I installed all this." He pointed at the ceiling and the heating and air conditioning units attached halfway up the wall. "Pretty cool, eh? This is what I do now. Shit like this. Not that other shit I used to pull..." His voice trailed off, and for a moment he looked completely forlorn, an aging ex-con with bad teeth, grey tendrils where there was once thick black hair, and fading jailhouse tats.

"The temperature's fine. How'd you get this place?" I spoke quietly.

He hesitated for a minute. "Uncle Eugene. The bank foreclosed on the Ohlsen brothers and Eugene lowballed it and walked it right through. You remember the Ohlsen brothers? Roger and Dale? You and I used to kick their asses 'bout once a month every summer." I nodded and Jimmy continued. "Eugene got me this place just before I got out of prison so that I'd have a place to stay, and we wouldn't ever have to see each other except on holidays. Eugene's a very smart man. The older I get, the more I respect his intelligence. We can't argue as long as we don't see each other." He grinned broadly, then sneered. "I know, Nicky. I look like shit. But don't get your ass in a sling. I'm on an upward trajectory."

He put his beer down on the table. Two long strides and he was almost in my face. But not hostile. Worn-out look in his eyes as if something had been lost. We stared at each other. Jimmy's one year older and I'm three or four inches taller.

"What is it, Jimmy? I'm listening."

"I know. You always were good at that, while I never listened to a single, living soul..." He broke off, scowled, and retrieved his beer. "Yeah, the truth is I never listened to a single motherfucker until I met this old con named Draymon in Waupun. He talked like just another swinging dick but actually had something to say. He's the old boy who explained how easy it is to build metal sculptures. He knew I could draw 'cause that's all I did in the cell. One day he heard me telling another con that I was thinking about getting a welding gig when I got out."

Jimmy took a big slug of his porter. "So that night, this old guy, he's a lifer, you understand, tells me he's got a good way for me to make it on the outside when I get paroled. *Surefire*, he says. Then he explains about metal sculptures—how towns and schools and libraries eat that shit up...It was like this little light went on in my brain, but a clean light, Nicky, nothing artificial about it."

I swallowed hard. Jimmy knew. He laughed. Then we were hugging, pounding each other on the back. Then Jimmy brought two more porters and we sat down together, drinking and talking.

He explained that he had medical insurance under the Affordable Care Act and that he was prescribed Adderall for his ADHD. That he hardly felt it but that it kept him focused, which was why he was selling sculptures. "I bust some serious sweat, baby, twelve-hour stretches, four or five days a week. Building these bastards is like putting big gnarly erector sets together. My penance, I guess. But it's all right. Sometimes I tell myself it really is art. My agent Buzz says it is."

"Buzz should know."

Jimmy shrugged. "It's fairly lucrative. I churn 'em out and we give our customers a good deal. Buzz says he could charge more, but he doesn't. Says it would give him heartburn. I'm just the artist. Buzz says I need to get my teeth fixed because we're going to tour Europe in the fall."

Flat-out amazing. Jimmy Sain. The kid everyone knew was headed straight for the joint. So I asked him something I'd always wondered about. "What I've never understood is why did you love to call out bigger, older, tougher guys? We were fighting for our lives. Constantly."

Jimmy stood up, tested his balance. Lined up our empties on his welding table. Came back over. Sat down. "'Cause you needed that, Nicky. You were a good boxer, can't take that away from you, but you didn't know how to fight. I mean fight like a man. Kicking and scraping and gouging. I figured my job was to teach you..."

Jesus Christ. Pretty much the same thing Adam used to say. Only he was talking about boxing, not street fighting. "And my job was to protect you. Just like I promised Eugene."

Jimmy wound up and chucked a beer bottle toward a garbage can near his welding table. Perfect shot. "Eugene loved you for some fuckin' reason. He kept insisting you were a good boy. 'I see good in Nicky. I see good in him...Listen to Nicky, Jimmy. That kid's got something on the ball.' I hated him for it. But I didn't hold against you. 'Cause you were such a badass. Even though you didn't know how to fight like a real man until I trained you."

He laughed and we both shook our heads. It had been a long time.

Tonight's event started at seven thirty. Local and national "patriots" of every stripe would turn out and spew Nazi drivel, which was now fashionable. How could it not be with patriots such as Marguerite Ferguson, Desmond "Turncoat" Cole, and the beleaguered Quincey working to make us ordinary Americans slaves again?

But here was the rub. These guys didn't go down easy. They could take a beating and walk away whistling. I personally witnessed Cole getting severely caned by his dear friend Thomas Quincey. One hour later, tux covered in blood, he was whistling, popping into his Lamborghini on his way to a wedding in Holmby Hills. And now Quincey—disgraced and hooked on benzos—had seduced America's most despicable villainess. As for Marguerite, two hours after being strong-armed, injected with Versed, and doused with Dom Perignon, she was happily flirting with Quincey. There was something disturbingly healthy about these bastards. Even James Franklin Rowe, who barely knew me, and who I had made for the weak one among the principals, had taken a bullet for me as if it were a sporting event, and bled out in my arms. And let us not forget their other dead pal, Frank Constantine, a serial killer of women, resolute to the end and willing to take everyone down with him.

Formidable opponents? Indeed. And they had taken Bobby. And I was working on borrowed time. Again, the rub. I waited until it felt right and eased into politics.

"I suppose most folks around here voted for the president. How do they feel now?"

Jimmy grinned, his old cunning look. "I assume they feel like shit but only a few will admit it. Truth is, a lot of folks around here voted for him just for the hell of it, just a big *fuck you* to the D.C. establishment. They didn't think it through, didn't consider the consequences."

Jimmy looked at me narrowly. Stroked his chin. "You fucker. I can read you like a book. Nicky's here. Way the fuck out here. What's this city boy, this fuckin' Angelino, doing here? What in the name of hell is he up to? And why are you wearing that ugly disguise (my brown toupee and moustache)?" He squinted at me, his right eye half-closed.

"Okay, Jimmy. I'll be straight with you. There's an old saying from Sun Tzu, that Art of War guy. It goes like this: 'Attack him where he is unprepared, appear where you are not expected.' Well, Jimmy, that's what your old friend Nicky will be doing tonight. Truth is, I need a little help. I came here thinking maybe you'd like to run interference for me at the Make America Safe Again rally in Fond du Lac tonight. The people putting it on are these alt-right folks who are trying to kill me and have been for some time. Kind of a slow death where I'm never certain if it's going to be today or tomorrow." I paused. Hesitated. "That's really all I can tell you. For your own protection."

"Like hell. I need to know more than that." Jimmy scratched the side of his nose. "Why the fuck they want to kill you? And what's this slow death bullshit?"

"In my business, there's something called 'need to know.' It protects the innocent and the not-so innocent. In this case, I want to protect you."

"The fuck you say. So, what do you need me to do?"

So wrong. So goddamned wrong. Here this guy was finally doing well, and here I was trying to wreck it. "Sorry, I can't do it. Change of plans. You're doing really good and I'm not going to wreck that. You can't afford to have your parole violated, and if, god forbid, they connect you to me, with your record, you'll be facing serious time in a federal penitentiary on some kind of an aiding and abetting domestic terrorism charge. So, much as I hate to say it, I think it's a terrible idea. But it's been really good seeing you." I put down my bottle and stuck out my hand.

Jimmy wasn't buying it. Narrowed his eyes and told me to sit my ass down. Suddenly very intense. I laughed gently, backed off, and told him to calm down. He got pissed. Came straight at me. Stopped when he saw the gun in my hand. His turn to back off.

"You calm down. And put the gun away. I was just testing you. To see how serious you are."

"And?"

"You're serious."

"Thank you. Don't think I feel good about coming out here and asking for help. I'd much rather be having another beer and talking about the Packers. Anyway, I need to get back to Fond du Lac and figure out my strategy for tonight."

"I get it," said Jimmy. "My friend Nicky, who's always been a little too smart for his own good, is up to his ass in some serious shit. And he doesn't want me to get nailed on a conspiracy to commit terrorism charge. Neither do I."

"Yeah. That's about the size of it. I should never have brought it up. My bad."

"Hmmm…" Jimmy dragged out the sound while chewing on his lower lip. "Hang on just a minute." He wandered down toward the far end of the barn, dodging streamers of wet, moldy insulation. Wandered back. An old habit of his, pacing when he needed to think. "Okay, Nick. Now, just for one cotton-pickin' minute, I want you to listen closely…"

I listened and as he talked the light from one of the spotlights played across his features. He reminded me about the time I'd found him back behind the first-base bleachers during an adult summer league baseball game taking a beating from three seriously nasty twenty-somethings. Blood was pouring from his nose, but he refused to stay down. I stepped in and put an end to it. Can't remember how…and it wasn't easy, but with my help, Jimmy sprang back to life, and we left them lying there in pain.

"I never told you this, Nicky, maybe 'cause I never realized it till one night talking to Draymon. I was playing back that night out loud; Draymon was listening. Then he stops me. He looks at me all serious-like and says, 'You know, they was maybe gonna kill you.' Still gives me a chill." And Jimmy shook, just a little, probably for effect. Then he tells me that since it appears the need is there, he's willing to help by committing a little old potential misdemeanor, if and only if, I get my big-shot ass in gear and retain him a lawyer named Jack Turley out of Milwaukee, who he says is the best in the state.

To my relief, Mr. Turley said that for a mere one thousand dollars he would be delighted to stand by at the MASA rally at the old Fox Theater in Fond du Lac. We agreed to meet at seven p.m. at the Bald Eagle restaurant across the street from the theater. Then Jimmy and I put our heads together. Afterwards, he walked me to Bobby's Econoline. We hugged and shook hands. It had been a long time.

Chapter Thirteen

On the way back to Fond du Lac, I verified Marguerite's birthday with Greg Thurston. Back in town, I gassed up at the Phillips 66 station and retrieved Marguerite's phone from behind the dumpster. Examined it from all angles. No sign of a tracking device. I gave myself two hours to gather what I could before caching it again. For further remote viewing if I decided to turn it over to Greg.

Drove around charging the phone and recceing the backside of town. Walked into a dive called Robbie's Place—no windows, highball glass on an unremarkable neon sign. Place deader than Adam, his bones picked clean by buzzards. Never-ending regret 'cause I could have done more to keep my father alive, but I was young and selfish then, and at that time, staying away from my madman father as he stumbled through the terminal zone had made perfect sense; now, I wish I'd fought harder to save him. Sometimes think my whole life's work rescuing people is just me trying to save my poor drunken father.

One old drunk at one end of the bar, his double at the other end. Husky fellow with jowls and a dirty white apron on duty. Ordered a draft beer and took a table in back. Sixty feet of dim light between me and the door. Wandered over to the jukebox and popped in two quarters. Turned and faced the sad threesome. "What would you guys like to hear?"

"Fuck if I care," said the bartender.

"All right, then." I spun back to the jukebox, hit "Friends in Low Places" and some other country song I'd never heard of. Sat down and took out Marguerite's phone...

...ordinary Samsung smart phone. According to Greg, her birthday was May 1, 1979. The lucky lady had just turned forty. I typed 5-1-7-9. That easy. Went to her Gmail. Hit the compose icon and typed in M-a-r. MargueriteWheatfields@gmail.com came up.

The usual suspects and a new one. Tommy Blank. And other new names that seemed to leap off the screen: Jethro Shimanski, Paul Reardon, Elizabeth Octavia Smith. Who were these people? Even Adara. Her threads—neighborly, apolitical—seemed more pro forma than anything else, a gesture designed to keep Marguerite off her back. That was something. And she never cc'ed Quincey. That was also something.

But no time for lovesick Crane. Needed news of Bobby. Beginning to think the trail might run through Tommy Blank. I read Marguerite's emails to Tommy carefully. Peculiar in their blandness, except for the coded language, which seemed to reference different parts of the country. *I'll phone you* messages at the end of certain emails. The first Tommy thread began about a week before the kidnapping.

Checked Marguerite's contacts. There he was, Tommy Blank, 859-231-7754. Wrote it down and Marguerite's cutesy email address. And Tommy's, which gave pause: tommy-blank&empty@gmail.com.

Checked the *I'll phone you* dates against her actual calls and came up empty. No Tommy Blank calls. None. She could have deleted them or...wait. WhatsApp. Of course. Wiped a hand across my forehead. My surprise at the rally, for which I'd recruited Jimmy Sain, would be my first public act of terrorism. Didn't make me feel good. Shook my head. Walked over to the bar and asked for coffee. Bartender served it up, thick and black from the bottom of the pot. Walked back to my table and brought up Marguerite's WhatsApp contacts. Again. They were all there. The usual suspects and a few of the new ones. Cole. Thomas Quincey. Tommy Blank. James Franklin Rowe, dead for six months now after taking a bullet meant for me. Even the despicable QB Tragg, also worm food. And Shimanski and Reardon and Ms. Octavia Smith. Principals? Possibly. I moved to her chats. The same suspects minus the dead people. I wrote down as many names and numbers as I could in five minutes. Perhaps thirty people.

Knew I had to hurry. Checked April 19 and 20. Tommy Blank's number came up seven times. Opened my Chromebook. Took some searching but I found it. A WhatsApp recording app called Cube ACR. And to my delight, there it was on Marguerite's screen. The peculiar insistence on self-incrimination that is so common among criminals.

It took fifteen minutes to listen to all seven calls. Throughout their exchanges, Marguerite's voice was terse, yet honeyed with pleasure, while Blank's was calm and pleasant, the non-accent of a Californian. It was all there. Same pattern, each call. Marguerite wanted progress reports and Blank delivered, everything but actual names. Said his best men, whom he called the First Wave, would handle the actual taking. Said the First Wave was very professional. Marguerite had nothing to fear. It would be done. It was done.

On impulse, I checked a Cole WhatsApp recording from April 28. Jackpot.

"I spoke to Crane."

"And?"

"I gave him your terms. Made it crystal clear. He turns himself in at a prearranged location on or before May 22 at which time Bobby Moore is driven to the nearest airport with direct flights to Buenos Aires. But if Crane fails to surrender, Moore gets shipped to Cairo the following morning."

"Did you tell Crane what happens to him if he surrenders?"

"I said you and he would meet to discuss what happens next."

"Ah, Dee, it's going to be tasty, old man. You ever see what happens to a man when he starts losing his testicles one at a time?"

"Really, my dear Marguerite. You should keep such sentiments to yourself."

"I bet Crane is shitting his pants. I suppose he asked you where we were holding Moore?"

"He did. I said I had no idea. I got off the line quickly. He was right on the edge. I kid you not, Marguerite, I broke into a sweat. Crane may fit the Noble Warrior mold, but that doesn't make him any less dangerous. Much as it pains me, I'm starting to think that he's got to go."

"Obviously. But Dee, you disappoint me. You started to sweat with him three thousand miles away. That's weak, Dee. What kind of a man are you?"

"I'm a cautious man. I was two thousand miles away in Joliet with Willem Spahn. But I'll tell you what kind of a man Crane is. He's a fucking ninja warrior. That day when he rescued me, he walked right into the cellar where Thomas was caning me. The cellar was full of people. And nobody saw him. And then a few weeks later, he escapes from the hospital in the dead of night."

"Jesus Christ, Dee. He obviously had help."

"That may be, my vindictive friend. But he didn't have any help that afternoon when two SUVs full of QB Tragg's soldiers ambushed him coming out of the auto body shop in East LA. And according to what you told me Tommy Blank told you, just a few days ago Crane single-handedly disarmed and manhandled a whole house full of your employees before turning your Arabs over to law enforcement...But your mistake, my dear, was letting those Arabs hang around too long. I've told you this before. You need to slide them in and out like chess pieces. Bring them in, they do their job. Soon as they're done, you ship them back out. Between missions you keep them in a safe house on Mexican or Canadian soil. But that being said, I have to admit that the way you spun it after the shit came down, that was pure genius.

I nearly creamed when I saw the headline: Roving Gang of Suspected Arab Terrorists Taken into Custody Near Weedpatch, California. It was sweet...But this proves exactly what I've been saying: We've got to stop messing around and get down to brass tacks. This is not a game..."

Gave me a chill. Cole. The master strategist? Brass tacks. Anything smacking of final solution gives me the creeps. He was in some ways the worst. Affable. Avuncular. Treacherous...

"Speaking of which," Cole continued, "what the hell was that fiasco with Willem Spahn in New Mexico?"

"New Mexico? I don't know what you're talking about."

"Don't play dumb, honey. You know exactly what I'm talking about. You dispatched a crew to kidnap Willem Spahn. You scared my meal ticket half to death."

"What in hell are you talking about? I did no such thing. And I have to tell you, Dee, I find your accusations rather offensive."

"Testy? Much!" said Cole in a snotty Valley girl accent.

"Not at all. But listen, old man, I do not have time for this bullshit."

"Whatever. Let's change the subject..."

No time to lose. Right there at the table in the back of Robbie's Place, I sent an email to Tommy Blank courtesy of Marguerite:

Hi there, you roving Boytoy. Where are you? We need to discuss strategy. You're doing a great job out west, but I don't want you to get left behind. I'm in Wisconsin pumping up our base. We're putting on these incredible Make America Safe Again rallies. It's beautiful, Tommy. But I need your help. My security needs beefing up and Thomas Quincey is constantly on my ass about it. And he's right. I wouldn't let some of these clowns watch my dogs back in Memphis. And that's been our problem all along. We need more First Wavers...and I need you, Tommy. We're putting on a rally in Racine, Wisconsin on Wednesday, May 8th, at the Civic Auditorium. It starts at 8:30. I want you to be there, Tommy. If at all possible. Put it on the company card. We'll meet backstage. In fact, maybe you can give a little talk and help with the recruiting. Your handsome face would look great onstage. Afterwards, we'll have some drinks and talk strategy...Text me YES if you are in agreement. And delete this email ASAP.

I waited five minutes. Erased the email and deleted it from trash. Then, a tough call. Sent the key email threads, including the usual suspects and Messrs. Blank and Shimanski, to a cloud-protected database that Greg Thurston checks daily. He would spot them and know his job was to crack their passwords and begin tracking their daily correspondence.

Drank the dregs of my coffee and drew a reasonable likeness of Marguerite standing in a jail cell. Tore it out of my notebook and ripped it into little pieces. Watched as they fluttered to the floor...

Left Robbie's Place and drove back to the Phillips 66 station where I cached Marguerite's phone behind the dumpster.

Back in my discount motel room with the cheap Formica countertops and the ancient square television, the black dog hit me hard. Went out to a liquor store and bought a pint of Jim Beam. Mixed a couple of shots with some tap water. Poison is an acquired taste. Drank it halfway down and logged onto my Chromebook to check an email address that only Greg and I share. Smiled. The kid was already jumping on our newly purloined emails.

Nick, I'm all over the new stuff. And here's a link you should read...

https://www.cdvr.com/2018/09/12/migrant-children-in-federal-shelters-hits-record-high-facilities-near-capacity.html

To click or not to click? I clicked...and nearly threw up my bourbon. Marguerite's plan working to perfection. Already almost thirteen thousand migrant children were separated from their parents and locked up in privately owned "detention shelters." Five times the number of a year or two ago. Children crying in their cells alone at night. Dark-eyed children injected with psychotropics to correct "anti-social behavior."

Not true what I told Tony. That I keep the carnage of this duel to the death with Marguerite and Cole and Quincey buried so deep that I don't feel it much. The truth is every day I plunge deeper into this abyss that is swallowing me whole.

Chapter Fourteen

Attack him where he is unprepared; appear where you are not expected.

Wearing my blond wig and rusty orange beard, a backpack strapped over my left shoulder, I stood at the top of the balcony of the old Fox Theater, suffering through the mind-numbing preliminaries. Cops, creeps, and paras babbled their right-wing nonsense and a noted English capitalist named Vernon Clerkwell blathered about how POTUS's new economic plan would lead us into an era of astounding prosperity. No sign of Quincey, who I assumed would speak after Marguerite had worked the crowd.

A different country band this time, more rocking than the country trio in Waupun. Finally, Marguerite appeared, showing no signs of post-mugging wear and tear. She had just started talking when Jimmy Sain bounded onto the stage wearing torn jeans, a flannel shirt, and a Green Bay Packers cap. He held a megaphone in both hands.

"Lissen up, you fine people. My name's John. John Tischendorf. I work in construction. On Sundays, I sing in my church choir." Marguerite's in-house security team moved in to yank Jimmy off-stage, but she motioned them back. "Lately, in honor of this great land, we've been rehearsing patriotic songs that we're going to sing in our village square during our summer concert series. So, if you don't mind, I'm going to sing you one of my favorite songs." He paused. Placed his hand over his

heart. Grimaced. Began, his voice deep, melodious…
My country, 'tis of thee,
Sweet land of liberty, of thee I sing;
Land where my fathers died,
Land of the pilgrims' pride,
From every mountainside let freedom ring!
Enough. I unloaded. A white phosphorus smoke grenade burns with a yellow flame followed by dense white smoke. Three shots, three loud metallic pops, followed by three eerie whooshings. Sprinted down the stairs to the main level. By now, the whole theater was enshrouded in smoke. Shouted, "SMOKE GRENADE. DON'T PANIC. SMOKE GRENADE. DON'T PANIC." Knew I was dead wrong. People could be killed. But Marguerite and her team of sycophants were messing with the wrong man. I raced for the exit, shoving a few security guards out of my way. Stuck my .38 in the gut of a few others. Seemed like a soft lot. Don't fuck with an Angelino.

Plan was for Jimmy, shielded by smoke and confusion, to slink away from the stage. He would take the back exit and I would meet him in the parking lot. We would jump into a black Cadillac CT4, courtesy of the Southeast Asian deskman.

I eased through the main entrance and calmly walked down Water Street. Rounded the corner and circled around to the back of the theater. Black Cadillac present for duty. Driver female, mysterious looking, black leather jacket with matching shades. I waved to her and started toward the back entrance to meet Jimmy.

The back door flew open and half-a-dozen men came flailing out onto the asphalt. Two bearded bikers wearing their colors squared off against four blue-jeaned, flannel-shirted guys. Two of the flannel boys were lantern-jawed with that inbred look that makes the short hairs stand up. The other two had soft, round faces, which meant nothing. Soft-looking guys are often the toughest. Potential for a real street fight with plenty of knees to the chest and boots to the groin. Could not fathom what this had to do with Making America Safe Again, but I must admit, if you've never seen a bad hombre wade into a street fight, you haven't really lived. Truth is, I feared for the flannel boys and for half a crazy second, I considered going to their aid.

"Motherfucker," said the taller of the two bikers, speaking, it seemed, to all four flannel boys. "I heard what your bitch ass said to my woman. I guess you think you're a real tough guy. Well, c'mon, motherfucker. I'll show you, tough guy."

One of the lantern-jawed boys spoke. Softly. "What'd you say?"

"He said," said one of the round-faced boys, "that your mother ain't really your mother. She's your sister."

Everything stopped. Bikers rocked forward on the balls of their feet.

Rare to welcome an onslaught of loud, drunken women, but this was one of those times. Two stout, one angular, one short with bristling red hair. The stout ones were aligned with the bikers, the other two with the flannel boys. Foul-mouthed and sloppy, they went at it, shouting insults—their own female version of street fighting. But still works in progress. Kicks were missed and kickers fell flat.

By now the crowd had swelled, upwards of fifty people. Maybe it was the shock of missing their kicks and kissing the hard asphalt. Two of the women suddenly wanted no more part of this and scrambled back to their men who grudgingly made room for them. But the last two, one stocky, the other with the bristling red hair, got serious. Toe-to-toe, they began trading punches like seasoned warhorses. Little Red had a formidable short right and her opponent started to falter. Now, the crowd was all mobbed up. It could only get worse…

…And where the fuck was Jimmy? Horrible vision of him being beaten by Marguerite's security goons, whom I'd spotted during the prelims.

Little Red's opponent went down, the crowd roared, and the bikers and the flannel boys charged into the fray and began trading punches. I fired off my last two smoke grenades at five-second intervals. The smoke cloud spread, and my phone dinged. Text from Jimmy: *I'm walking north on Water Street. Pick me up. Please!*

As I'd hoped, the smoke had a calming effect on the crowd. The men gradually stopped banging on each other and folks began to disperse in clusters. Tomorrow was another day, and with luck, everyone would live to tell their story. Walked over to the CT4 and got in on the passenger side. The driver had a black cloak around her shoulders and smelled like citrus. Said her name was JC. She spun the car around expertly. We scrammed. Found Jimmy walking rapidly up Water Street. He jumped in back.

Jimmy directed JC to drive to a Starbucks out near Highway 151 where we met Jack Turley. I gave JC a Franklin for a job well done, and we got in Turley's black Mercedes. I asked Jimmy why he hadn't met me in the parking lot.

"Right after I got off-stage, my PTSD kicked in. Knew I had to get out of there."

"Well, you did a great job."

"I guess this means that my work is over, then," said Jack Turley.

"I hope so," I said. "One stack. Not your usual rate but it was for a good cause."

"Hell, I almost feel like I should give you back half the retainer."

I shook my head. "Not a good idea. They could still bring Jimmy in for questioning. He'll call you if he needs you. And in the oft-chance they bring a case, even a misdemeanor, I want you to pull out all the stops to get it dismissed. I don't care how much it costs. Jimmy will call me, and I'll retain you. This man cannot go back to prison. And this whole thing had nothing to do with me because I don't exist."

That was it. Turley dropped Jimmy off at his Nissan pickup and drove me to my motel.

I went upstairs and lay down on the bed. Twitchy. Got back up. Took off my disguise and got in the shower. Feeling vaguely triumphant. First, I'd mugged Marguerite and stolen her phone. Smooth execution. And less than twenty-four hours later, I'd shut down her rally. Pretty sure no one had been killed. That part made me uneasy. But shook it off. Jimmy could hold his mud if questioned. But doubted law enforcement would even approach him. Next step was the hard one: detaining Tommy Blank before the Racine rally on Wednesday.

Toweled off and shaved. Presentable. Strong jaw. Capacious forehead.

No need to shadow Marguerite and Quincey for the next few days. It would probably be fruitless, anyway. Meanwhile, Greg would devour the endless email threads and tell me where to look...A single dislodged thread can unravel an entire tapestry. If Sun Tzu didn't say it, he should have.

Dicey to just lay low in this fleabag. Though I'd been trading off disguises, it wouldn't take a genius to cast a rancid eye in the direction of Bobby's brown Econoline with the California plates. Connect it to the tall blond guy with the press pass who'd been seen hanging around various Fond du Lac hotels. If I wanted to continue the ghost transmitter surveillance—and tonight's episode should be sweet—I had to stay put or move to the Motel 6 next door (still within range).

I lay down on the bed. Long sigh. Another. Opened *The Zebra-Striped Hearse*. Although his wife seemed reasonable, Colonel Blackwell was one jealous father. No boy good enough for his daughter. Next thing I knew, Lew Archer catches the Colonel pointing a gun at the boyfriend. A mistake. I sighed and rubbed my eyes. Must have dozed off. The front desk rang. I lurched and fumbled. "Hello, sir. Please check your room phone. Your message blinker has been on for over an hour."

Greg. Said to call him immediately. Still early in California. He answered on the second ring.

"Nick, I got this crazy email on our everyday company

account. Hang on while I bring it up." I waited. "Okay, see if this rings a bell...*The Bird of Time has but a little way to fly—and Lo! The bird is on the Wing.*

"Remind you of anything, or should I say, anyone?" He knew perfectly well who it reminded me of. "Here's the strange thing. She gives a phone number but doesn't say to call her. Says you should meet her in room 207 at the La Quinta Inn in Oshkosh. That's thirty minutes up Highway 41 from Fond du Lac."

Trust Greg to figure everything out ahead of time. "When am I supposed to meet her?"

"When do you think? Tonight. Whenever you can get there. And then she says, *if you want to?* You lucky sonuvabitch!" Our bad language was wearing off on the boy.

Both thinking the same thing. Deferred to Greg. "She knows you're in Wisconsin. How does she know that? You're being surveilled, that's how."

"Hmm. Gotta make the right call here."

"Yeah. But there's another part. This is sweet. *Do not worry, Nick. This has nothing to do with Marguerite. You need to believe that. I have a new ally. I am not putting you in any more danger. Please come.* Jesus, Nick, this is killing me. She wants you, man. Either that or she's setting you up to be tortured and killed."

"I might not mind if she does it herself." A moment's silence. "What would you do, Greg?"

"You're asking me? C'mon, Nick. I can't answer that."

"Sure, you can. You're no different from me. What would you do?"

Silence. Then Greg spoke. "I'd knock on the door of room 207."

PART THREE
Chapter Fifteen

Half past eleven when I reached La Quinta Inn. A note taped to her door. *The door is unlocked. Come in. If you like, you may wake me...*Smiling, I quietly turned the knob and walked inside.

Stopped smiling. Light from a bedside lamp revealed Adara and another woman sitting side by side on a queen-size bed. Adara wore a red-and-gold University of Wisconsin sweatshirt with nondescript sweats and little makeup. Her lustrous rose-brown hair was straighter than I remembered. Her companion was buttoned down and zipped up in a blue dress shirt and thick purple sweater. Pixie hair with a side part. Gamin face, ski-slope nose, bright blue eyes. And a strong, determined mouth.

Both women clutching near-empty wineglasses. Made Adara's friend for a fellow thespian. Or maybe a Sunday school teacher. Her name was Carrie North. We shook hands. "Took you long enough," said Carrie with a straight face. "We were placing bets on your ETA, or if you'd even show up at all. But you're here now and since it's late, I'll just leave you two lovebirds alone." Looked me up and down on her way out. "I'll be damned, Mr. Crane. Adara's right. You are a rugged kind of fellow." The women exchanged a look and Carrie walked to the door. Tipsy but under control.

Adara smelled of orange and lemon and something dry and

musky, a heady scent that filled my nostrils. Unaccountably shy. Me, not her. "Vino?" she said. "Stranger."

"Please." Gestured toward the wine bottle.

"Sit down, Nick." Adara crossed to the sink. Rinsed out Carrie North's glass. Poured and handed me the glass. Finished hers and poured another, which she hardly touched.

"Well," she said, "I'm glad you're here. We've got a lot to talk about." But then instead of talking, she sat down across from me and smiled. Eyes, nose, and mouth—her entire face. Then she laughed, like cool, dark wind chimes. Her mood changed. "But I really wonder about you, Nick." She frowned. "Remember when I told you your lifeline says you're going to live a very long time?"

"Sure. And I remember how good it felt when you were touching my hand." Sentimental Crane. Amazed to be in the same room with this woman. But wary. Afraid it wouldn't be like when we flew to Boston in October. With reservations at a discreet and elegant hotel. Could not forget that night of passion or the strangely tender feelings that had filled me. Or the fact I'd been shot and almost killed the next morning. And now? I had no idea...She was thirty-one, a talented thespian with a handsome guaranteed income. Cole was now her minder. A pushover. Perhaps. Pretty sure he had no idea she was here in Oshkosh. He had other things on his mind.

"Yes, Nick, darling, that's what your lifeline said. But you're going to prove it wrong if you keep this up."

Keep what up? Of course, I wanted to escape from Marguerite's orbit. From this ordeal in which surrender or capture meant torture and execution. The wine began to jumble my thoughts. I looked at Adara, her elegant cheekbones, her hair falling across her shoulders. Don't remember deciding what to say. The words just came out.

"I agree. Completely. I'm in the middle of a dangerous game. Bad odds. Very bad odds. The only way out is to leave the country. And I sometimes lean in that direction. But even then,

Marguerite might find me." Stayed away from Bobby. Didn't think she knew. Not yet.

She nodded, tapping an index finger against her wineglass. "I think you'd find a way to disappear without too much difficulty. I really do. But that's a drastic step for an American like you." She shook her head. "I've got some other ideas, but they can wait until tomorrow. As for now, I've got a little request." She paused. Treated me to a brilliant smile. "I would be honored if you would escort me on a country drive under the moonlight in my carriage. It's only right. You look like a country squire. Of the decadent variety."

Which was why I found myself riding shotgun in a Mercedes S-class sedan at one thirty a.m. Sunday, May 6. Said I hoped she wasn't too tipsy to drive. She shot me a look. Daggers. Then she laughed. Said she had packed six years of living into the last six months. Which included driving home after having a glass or two of wine.

We drove north and west on Highway 45. I rolled down my window and she put in a CD. Lana Del Rey, *Lust for Life*. The singer's voice was high, sweet, and distant. I looked over at Adara who sang along with the choruses. Adara's voice was different—lower, strong and clear, her cheekbones flashing darkly against her lightly tanned skin. Hands on the wheel. Hands I remembered. Slim and strong.

"I hate to even ask, but what are you and your friend, Ms. Carrie North, doing here in Oshkosh?"

"Ah, the PI pops the big question. Don't worry. We'll get to that. Soon enough. First, let me explain something. It will make us both feel a lot better." She looked at me. "Capiche?"

"Capiche."

"Thank you. This is about Marguerite. I loathe and despise the bitch. As you know, she and Desmond Cole abducted me two days after you were shot. They threatened to charge me with conspiracy. They said you and I had conspired together to bring illegals into the country. I knew Desmond knew it was pure crap. Marguerite wanted to play games with me, and he wanted to watch...

"Here's what led up to it. I checked up on you in the hospital two days after you were shot. You were unconscious but at least you were out of ICU. So, I was feeling hopeful. Then I ran into Marguerite near the elevator. We were both surprised. She knew right away. Because there was no reason for me to be there unless I had feelings for you."

Adara paused. Turned left off the highway onto a country road. We crested a hill and she let up on the accelerator. No other cars in sight. Not at this hour. Deep in the heartland. Coasted to the bottom of the hill. She stepped lightly on the gas. "I was wringing my hands, Nick. I wasn't in love with you, but I certainly liked you. Fate had brought us together for that special night and then decreed that we must part. But then when you were shot, I felt responsible. You were in very bad shape. Your doctors said it was sixty-forty."

She reached out and put her hand on my shoulder. For a moment.

"When I ran into Marguerite, I acted like I hadn't yet visited you. Because I didn't trust her to be alone with you. So we went in together, which made her all the more suspicious. As in *what the hell was I doing there*? Then she acted so relieved to see that you were doing better. It was so phony. She's a terrible actor." A scornful laugh, then silence. And then, "There's a place up ahead where we can turn off. Carrie and I were here earlier this afternoon. It belongs to friends of her family." Again, her hand on my shoulder. Longer this time. She turned off onto a well-maintained dirt road that sloped down a hillside to a clearing in the trees, space enough for four or five cars.

We parked and got out of the car. Flicked on our flashlights. It was a beautiful setting. Spruce and pine. A star-scattered sky. We trooped down to a locked gate made of unfinished one-by-sixes. Adara produced a key. We locked it behind us. She moved nimbly down the well-worn trail. I followed. Clusters of stately bald cypresses sheathed the path. We came to a rocky beach with patches of black, pebbled sand. Adara said the water was a tributary of Lake Winneconne, which led clear to Lake Michigan, with numerous stops along the way. She said she was fascinated by watersheds because water was scarce and ever so precious in her native Iraq.

We picked our way through the rocks. Came to the water's edge. The wind wafting off the river blew her hair back off her shoulders. She was wearing a simple, sand-colored, waist-length zip-up corduroy jacket. She smiled at me. Her lips were trembling. The cold. And something ancient. I wrapped my arms around her. Encased by hers. Her lips. At last. Nipping. Nibbling. Biting. I found her throat. Lost myself. Warm flesh, deep kisses. Body and soul taking flight. Wind freshening. Beside myself with desire. But knew. Foreplay. Slow love. Patient Crane.

Later we hunkered down on the rocks trying to stay out of the wind. "That wasn't supposed to happen," she said quietly.

"I disagree. I think it had to happen."

She smiled quizzically, the cold moon her watchman. "Why's that?"

Smiled back at her. Most innocent and spontaneous. "I'm not sure. Something eternal. The sort of thing I don't really believe in."

"What do you believe in?"

"That's a good question. I guess I believe in people. People like you and me."

"That's a good answer. You know what I'm afraid of?"

"No. What?"

She didn't answer. Not at first. Instead, she looked out over the water. Finally spoke. Quietly. "I'm afraid of your dangerous side, but more for your own sake than mine. And at the same time, I rather like it. I've got way too many pretend bad boys who want to go out with me. There's something to be said for the real thing." She laughed. "But listen, Nick, I have to explain something. This is important. You even asked me about this once, but I wasn't ready to answer."

She then told me the story of her escape from Baghdad. In January 1997, she and her genteel father, Mohammad Ghaffari— a courtly, urbane man, a banker by day and historian by night— had escaped from Iraq across the border into Saudi Arabia, where a group of shadowy, hooded men drove them to Riyadh. From there, they boarded a plane to Boston.

She and Mohammad had spent the night wrapped up in quilts and buried under straw in a covered pickup truck. With breathing tubes to poke up through the straw. Mohammad had chosen January because the colder temperatures would bring less scrutiny at the checkpoints. "I was so cold, Nick. My father tried to keep me warm and sang to me to keep my spirits up. And made sure I was getting enough air. He was so sweet, like a mother hen...But I was so cold and so scared. Like many Ba'aths, we weren't religious, but I made up prayers to Allah while my father sang me songs in Arabic and English. All the while we were wrapped up like mummies."

"What songs in English? Do you remember?"

"Sure. Some of them. 'America the Beautiful.' 'My Country 'Tis of Thee.' 'Yankee Doodle Dandy.' That one made me laugh."

"Yankee Doodle?"

"Yeah. Yankee Doodle. Do you know it?"

"Unfortunately."

We both laughed.

"Sing it for me."

"No."

"Please. I want to hear your voice."

So I sang it more or less on key in a low baritone. She was delighted. Crane on stage.

After that, we stood up and started across the beach and up the trail and through the gate and into the Mercedes. Where we sat for quite some time. Gloom and doom returned. Adara started the car and rolled down the window so we wouldn't get asphyxiated. More Lana Del Rey. Again, she sang along with the choruses. Then she turned the music down. Spoke low. Almost deadpan. After the hospital encounter, Marguerite and Cole, with backup dressed as UPS drivers, had abducted her and taken her to a cabin in Vermont where they had worked on her for forty-eight hours. Despite all the threats, she had never admitted to conspiring to commit terrorist acts. She had admitted to our little fling.

"They already knew anyway. Marguerite wanted the juicy details. So did Desmond. It was the only way I could get her to keep her filthy hands off me, so I made up a bunch of crap. I had to. I was in a tight spot, Nick."

I laughed. Impressed. This woman. No pushover.

"What did you tell them?"

"Stupid stuff. Foot fetishes. Spankings. Stuff like that." She laughed merrily. "Desmond loved it. He said I have lovely toes. Marguerite pretended to be disgusted. By then, I was pretty sure they weren't going to charge me with anything. I just had to get them to release me."

"And it worked."

"It seemed like it took forever. But they finally drove me back to Boston and dropped me off at The Commons.

"You were damned brave."

"I had to be. Desmond has been really nice to me ever since. I think he's embarrassed. He doesn't have the guts to be a true libertine. I'm glad you're not one."

I laughed. "I barely know what the word means." I reached over, took her in my arms, and kissed her. Then we drove back to the Inn.

Back in Adara's room, we sipped herbal tea to warm up. Then we undressed each other. A little at a time. I had lost a few pounds and she had gained a few. I liked her even better this way. Her hips curved like the moon halfway to its quarter stage.

We waited until morning. She said it would be better that way.

When I woke up, I found her lying on her side, looking at

me. Smiling. Luminous eyes. A feeling I won't forget. Then her long arms entwined me...Afterwards, we lay together in muddled joy. Then she whispered softly, "That wasn't supposed to happen. But it did."

"I'm glad."

"Me too."

Snuggled till it was time to get up. Showered. Out for breakfast. Our eggs over easy with buckwheat pancakes had just arrived and Adara had just taken her first bite when Carrie North walked up and sat down.

Chapter Sixteen

This time Carrie was wearing beige khakis, a pin-striped dress shirt, and a cardigan sweater. Minimal makeup and natural-toned lip gloss.

"So," I said smiling, "I guess now I find out what this is all about."

"You do," she said. Adara, who said nothing, reached out and placed her fingers across my wrist, her eyes calm and expectant.

"Let me start by saying," said Carrie, "that it's very fortunate that no one was killed at the MASA rally in Fond du Lac last night."

"Thank god. I heard some moron set off smoke grenades, and the crowd got a little restive."

"A little restive," said Carrie, "is an understatement. What I found most interesting is the fact that law enforcement was conspicuously absent. In fact, I am told that Marguerite Ferguson personally contacts local law enforcement before each rally and specifically requests no police presence. So far, they've let her get away with it. That will probably change after last night."

I shrugged. "I've heard she's got a lot to hide. But before we go any farther, who are you and which agency are you with?"

Carrie's turn to shrug. "We'll get to that soon enough. Anyway, there's been quite a bit of chatter, but there's nothing illegal about the rallies. Everything is done by the book with the permits in place. And by all reports, up until last night, they'd been rather tame."

Felt the heat. Plunged in. "I hope you're not here to defend her 'cause if you are..."

"Don't get all riled up," said Carrie. "Why don't you just wait and see why I'm here?"

I glared at both women. Adara smiled, half sheepish, half triumphant. A long silence except for my chewing and the chit-chat at the surrounding tables.

"Let me put it like this," said Carrie finally. "My people have received intel from reputable sources stating that Marguerite Ferguson, who goes by various names including Tami Wheat, and an aging blueblood named Desmond Cole, are smuggling Arab nationals into the country to use in terrorist ops. On the day after Christmas, five Saudi and Pakistani illegals were found locked in the back of an abandoned Dodge van in a little California dustbowl town near Bakersfield. The chief of police was smart and called us instead of Homeland Security. We ran it and discovered that three of the Arabs were Guantanamo Bay veterans. It was hard to draw a bead on the other two who stonewalled and generally acted like mental defectives, which I do not believe they are. We finally figured out that they were Pakistanis."

Hmm. Guantanamo Bay veterans. Likely recruited right out of the prison by Marguerite's people. "I don't think you should send them back. You should keep them, start our own domestic Guantanamo. Put it in Branson, Missouri, or make it part of the Epcot Center."

Carrie North laughed. "What a funny fellow you are, Mr. Crane. And such blatant disrespect for—I don't know, for nearly everyone." She smiled merrily. "I would have thought that a few hours with this lovely lady here," reaching toward Adara and squeezing her hand, "would have calmed you down, at least temporarily."

"I am calm. And you can call me Nick." Took a deep breath and smiled at Adara. Turned to Carrie. "Well goddamn, I think I've got it. You're FBI, aren't you? Of course you are..." I shook my head. "All right. Here's the deal. There are only about forty detainees left in the Guantanamo Prison. Very likely the three Saudis cut a deal with Marguerite's people to release them in return for them carrying out domestic terrorist activities right here on American soil. Someone fluent in Arabic must have reached out to them."

Carrie chewed on it. "Funny you should say that. I don't necessarily disagree. We're going to be turning over a lot of dirty laundry before this thing is over. But I'd like to explain something, and I'd appreciate it if you wouldn't bite my head off without hearing me out." I was waiting for this. Her prepared remarks. I sat back and waited, hitching my thumbs into my belt loops.

"Although you believe people like me are the scum of the earth," said Carrie, "there are actually more than a few of us who believe this nation should stand for something besides fucking over the minorities—that we should protect the rights of our citizens and non-citizens alike. That's a fact, Nick. We, and by we, I mean myself and folks like me, are right in the thick of this battle and we're not going anywhere." She smiled. "Tracing the trail of the Saudi nationals is of utmost importance. And just to put your mind at rest, I happen to have agents working on it. Even as we speak." She smiled triumphantly. Didn't blame her. Nailed me.

"I'm impressed, Special Agent North."

"Thank you." Graciously. "Please, call me Carrie. I want you to stop thinking of me as the enemy. We're on the same side here. Marguerite is our target, but she is also the one who will lead us to the source."

"The source?"

"The people who are funding her. Who, we believe, are the same people she's conspiring with…"

Naturally. They wanted a sweeping indictment. Which made sense. Take all these bastards down. Restore the precarious order that was merely teetering in the years prior to POTUS.

Problem was, I didn't have time for a sweeping indictment. I could be killed at any time or, far worse, I could be forced to surrender to Marguerite to save Bobby. I held up my hands. "So you're telling me that you're not only not heartless, but that you and I are on the same side. Hmm." I shrugged nonchalantly, reached for my coffee, and knocked it over. Nerves? I groaned and helped the two women—one classically beautiful with a grace both natural and born of the stage, the other small, gamin-like, a sprightly pain in the ass—wipe up the coffee. We wadded up the napkins and stacked them on the edge of the table.

"What was that?" said Carrie. "Performance art?"

We all laughed. "Bad performance art. But all right. I'll listen to what you have to say. But on my terms and not here in public."

She shook her head. Thirty-something. Perhaps a few years older than Adara. "I want to make something very clear, Nick. I'm not here to investigate you. Nor are any of my people. You've already been thoroughly vetted, and the consensus is that you do more good than harm. So you can stop being so damned paranoid. Frank Constantine clearly had it coming, and his gang has been like a wolf pack snapping at your heels ever since. And as far as any liability on your part goes, your case is closed. Furthermore, if you work with us, during the interim, you are constructively one of us."

Which meant I could be a fibbie too with all the rights and privileges afforded thereto. For a while.

"Law school," I said.

"Yes. University of Minnesota. I barely made it through. That's why I'm a field agent and not some corporate shill." Again, her laugh, a little too strident, could easily imagine her shrieking with joy at high school football games. "Look, Nick, the truth is, I want to nail these bastards. I want to nail 'em bad. Marguerite and her cronies are ripping our nation apart. We are going to take her down. And I believe you can help us take her down...So where do you want to go to talk? I've got an SUV."

Indeed. Full of recording equipment. No dice. We decided on Carrie's motel room, which was three doors down from Adara's.

Adara and I drove back to the inn in the Mercedes. Carrie took her SUV.

"So where did you find Ms. North?"

"My father. I asked him to find someone to help straighten out the mess I got you into."

"Stop right there. I got myself into this. But why this particular agent? I would have expected someone more seasoned."

"Cut it out, Nick. Stop being an ass. My father is a very shrewd man. He is also a generous man. He is eternally grateful for all you've done for us. But do not sell him short, Nick. I would hate that. He researched her thoroughly before deciding to reach out. He does not take this lightly."

I smiled. She was right. I was out of line. We were silent the rest of the way back. But then, just before we got out of the Mercedes, she leaned over and kissed me on the mouth. Women...

Chapter Seventeen

Back at La Quinta Inn, Adara announced that she was driving to Wisconsin Dells for the day to check out a summer stock theater group that she might audition for. Said she'd be back around six.

Carrie and I sat across from each other in the kitchenette drinking herbal tea. I sighed. Stuck here with this cocky fibbie trying to bring justice to a sick world. It hit me. Carrie was like my ex-wife, Cassady, only more conventional. With an idealistic streak and too much respect for authority. Dangerous. But interesting.

How do I distrust you? Let me count the ways. She said she wasn't wired. I asked her if she'd submit to a pat-down search. She was offended. Then she agreed and I declined. But dug in my heels. Going no further with her until she produced and turned off her recording devices. Told her so. Same scenario. She was offended. Then she agreed. Produced a Tile-Tek. I motioned for it. Turned it off. "Continue," I said.

"Continue what?"

"The rest of your devices, please."

She hesitated. Smiled. "Okay, there's only one more." I held out my hand and she handed me an even smaller device that she had clipped on her blouse under her sweater.

"Not that we will ever have a working relationship, but if we did, Special Agent Carrie North, it would have to be based on trust. I generally only work with people I trust."

"Generally?"

"That's what I said."

She surprised me by producing a third device identical to the second. "How'd you know I had it?"

"I didn't. But thank you for disclosing. Do you have a fourth?" She shook her head and we both laughed.

Then we settled down, but I was still reluctant to speak frankly. But good to know I had something of value. Or thought I did. After fifteen fruitless minutes, Carrie slapped the table hard. "Goddamnit, Nick, stop being so evasive. I have the feeling that you're working against the clock. The fact you organized that dangerous, albeit clever, little insurrection at the Fox Theater last night means that you're getting desperate. And that's not your style, my friend." She sat back and folded her hands. I said nothing. "I admit that it was controlled desperation, but it was not a good play."

"I agree," I said. "I'll have to have a talk with that guy." She just smiled. Smug or just knowing? Makes a difference. And she was right. I was working against the clock. Decided to cooperate. To a degree. "It's not that I'm against us working together. And I applaud your goal. If you really want to bring Marguerite and her team of pit vipers to justice. So just listen. I have good intel. Exceptional intel. Better intel than you've ever imagined. But my problem is different from your problem. You want a sweeping indictment. As you should. To take down a large, well-organized group of lethal motherfuckers intent on promoting a Nazi-like criminal domestic terror agenda focused on keeping Muslims and Latinos out of the country. While locking up and/or deporting the ones who are already here. And importing other Arabs to commit strategic terrorist acts that will scare the piss out of us good folks so that we'll all jump on the 'protect our shores' bandwagon. All the while diverting attention from the fact that the real terrorists are ninety percent domestic and of Caucasian extraction."

Carrie clapped her hands in appreciation. "I think that about covers it. But we've both mentioned terrorist acts to be performed by Marguerite's Arabs—first, me at the restaurant and you, just now. I believe every bad actor starts with a single bad act. As in—bad example, I know—you can't be a serial killer without whacking your first victim. If I were Marguerite—"

"—Yes, if you were Marguerite, where would you strike first?"

"Depends on how my little Arab brigade was armed."

"Fair enough. We have to assume the worst case is probably dirty bombs or C4 cartridges. Or both. But most likely C4s."

Carrie shook her head slowly. "This is where I'm stumped. There are so many good targets…"

I got up from the breakfast nook and walked to the refrigerator. No beer. Red wine only. I groaned. "May I?"

"Please do." I found a glass. Sat back down. Swallowed. Grimaced. "Okay," I said. "Maybe we can work together. I won't rule it out. But you've got to give me two things. First, I want complete immunity in writing. And then, you and your people have to help me rescue my partner, Bobby Moore. Marguerite's people kidnapped him on Easter Sunday. If I can't engineer his escape by May 22, they'll ship him off to Scorpion Prison in Cairo…or," long pause, "I turn myself in…in his place…"

"What?" Her mouth fell open. She caught it and clamped it shut. Spoke through clenched teeth, her blue eyes flashing. "You're talking about *the* Bobby Moore, the Vietnam veteran, your partner and best friend, right? The guy who helped you steal Frank Constantine's torture records?" I nodded wearily. "That was ballsy, I admit, but dumb. Really dumb. I don't want you doing anything stupid like that on my watch." Even though she was sitting calmly, I could feel her stamping her foot. Woman used to getting what she wants. We'll see. "But how in hell did they kidnap Bobby?"

I shook my head. Shook it again like I was trying to expel some foul thought. "I don't know. It appears that they ambushed him right in our office. They sent a neighborhood crackhead to

112

the door; someone we've helped out a time or two. My witness said it was six commandos and the crackhead. Whatever they did, it worked."

"And your witness is?"

"A homeless female junky. Bobby and I have been subsidizing her for the last twenty years."

Carrie nodded as if homeless, female junky witnesses were common in her world. "Bastards. But," the words tumbling out, "I think maybe you're missing something."

Huh? I'm always missing something. But amused by Ms. Assertiveness. Just like Cassady. Primed for combat. Women. Always a dilemma. But interesting. And I hadn't gotten nearly enough sleep.

"You tell me...what am I missing?"

"All right. This could be important. Don't you think it's strange that they're giving you so long to surrender?"

Shrugged. Tired of questions. Time for answers. "No, seriously. Why are they giving you so much rope? That's not how this usually works. It's usually either bang, you're dead," she pointed a finger and pretended to fire, "or bang, you're dead." She pointed in the opposite direction.

"Only in this case," I said, "it's bang bang, then hurry up and wait."

She frowned and bit her lower lip. Exhaled. "A lot of loose talk goes on around the water cooler. About certain other agencies and their propensity for...torture."

"Of course, the FBI takes the high road on that issue."

She looked at me. "I wish I could answer in the affirmative with one-hundred-percent certainty. But you're obviously aware that we prefer to help people help themselves." Old news. The FBI and their informants.

Since that horrible Easter Sunday when Bobby was abducted, I'd mostly avoided thinking about what he might be going through. Now it hit me hard. I paled and drank the rest of the wine. Which only made me want to vomit. I slowly gathered myself while she looked on solemnly. I could hardly speak. "The torture is one thing. The other thing is the brainwashing. That's what you're getting at, right? That's the reason for this long delay."

"It's crossed my mind."

We both fell silent. I stood up and began pacing around the room. I would surrender if that's what it took to save Bobby. But what I had on Marguerite was worth at least a dime on a federal kidnapping rap. And I had the smoking gun: the phone conversations that incriminated Marguerite on conspiracy and Cole on aiding and abetting. With our new player Tommy Blank, charismatic man of mystery, smack dab in the middle. Although a kidnapping indictment certainly wouldn't cast as wide a net as conspiracy to commit domestic terrorism, it would be much easier to prosecute.

But wait. Pondering. How did Adara's father Mohammad find Special Agent Carrie North? Someone else had to be involved. Back to the refrigerator. Still no beer. Poured the rest of the wine into my glass. One swallow. Dumped the rest out in the sink. It had to be Agresti. I would've bled out right there on the Charles River Esplanade if Agresti and his Southie Boston PD friends hadn't been there to stanch the flow when Marguerite's boot woman shot me. And that was just part of it. Agresti's Arab clients located Mohammad in the first place, and Agresti set everything up. And arranged for the payoff. Even served as bagman. Agresti had stepped up to the plate.

I filled my glass with tap water. Sat back down and asked Carrie if she knew Anthony Agresti. She looked at me and nodded. Turned out she'd first locked horns with him at trial on a RICO case that ended in a mistrial. Although they worked opposite sides of the aisle, they had become friends. When Mohammad reached out to Agresti, he had contacted SA North.

"And you know what the crazy thing is?" The sun was slanting through the drapes, painting her eyes a brighter blue. "I was already on the case. We were brought in by Boston PD a week or so after you escaped from the hospital. Because of the shooting and your mysterious vanishing act. We interrogated well over fifty people. Marguerite's name came up several times. People didn't seem to like her very much. Desmond Cole's name also came up. So my research guy Tim Swann and I began our usual carpet-bombing approach. He put his whole team on it. But nothing came up."

"What do you mean, nothing came up? They're violent criminals."

"They're right-wing powerbrokers who do incendiary stuff. The fact of the matter is our investigation was derailed by the Thomas Quincey mess."

I shook my head. "What exactly did happen with Quincey?"

She smiled wanly. "I think you already know what happened. There was a very strong desire on the part of the Los Angeles U.S. Attorney's Office to minimize their own involvement."

"And so they spun it."

"Exactly. It was really quite ingenious. The way it was spun," her voice dripping sarcasm, "Javier Fincus manipulated Quincey and was responsible for all the deaths. Not only that, he was also the one bringing Arabs across the border."

"Ridiculous. That theory is so full of holes."

"Of course it is. You of all people should know that. But unless someone like you is willing to testify, ideally you and Bobby Moore, it's been hard to build a case. Quincey gets a slap on the wrist and there's nothing to link Fincus and his crimes to Marguerite or Desmond Cole. So the investigation flagged. Then in early April, I was contacted by Agresti who had been contacted by Mohammad. Agresti told me that if we were interested in Marguerite Ferguson, you probably have intel that could steer us in the right direction. I took that information upstairs. The Boston FBI office has great respect for Agresti..."

"'Cause he's always kicking your ass at trial," I smirked.

"Was that necessary?" She smiled. "Based on his recommendation and my persistent nature, I got the green light to reopen the investigation the day after the five Arabs were found in the Dodge van. Since then, we've been busy little beavers."

It turned out that Carrie's SoCal people had made me in LA. They'd watched me outfitting Bobby's Econoline van on his City Terrace driveway. And slapped a bug on it when I wasn't looking. By the time I'd crossed the Rockies, they were hoping I was heading to Wisconsin to recce Marguerite's rallies. Delighted when it proved true. Less manpower required to keep an eye on both of us.

She and Adara had hit it off from the start. When she told Adara that I was going to be in Wisconsin attending the MASA rallies, Adara had quietly asked to come along, for a single long weekend. "You're a lucky guy, Nick. She wouldn't come right out and say it, but I think she's crazy about you..."

Then her face changed. Her turn to stand up and pace around the room. Refrigerator. Nothing of value. She mouthed a scrap of song. Came back and sat down across from me.

"Listen, Nick, I am really worried about Bobby Moore."

"Me too. What are we going to do about it?"

Carrie shook her head. Looked at me. Surprised to see her eyes were glistening. Just a trace but that was enough. "It won't be easy. Rescuing Bobby at this juncture works against the terrorism case I'm tasked with building. I'm sure you realize this."

Then why in fuck was she acting so damned sympathetic? But reined in my mega-horns and said, "My deal is simple. You get my immunity agreement signed and help me rescue Bobby. Meanwhile, I give you intel. I don't care if you sit on the kidnapping and focus on the terrorism angle. As long as Bobby is released before the deadline. That's my bottom line."

Dropped my gaze. To give her time to think without Crane and his laser-like stare violating her space. She said nothing. For a long time. Maybe too long. But what she finally said was promising. She thought she could get me immunity based on my intel and my past involvement with Quincey and Marguerite.

But rescuing Bobby would be much harder. Obviously. But she understood my terms. She was dead serious and so was I.

Chapter Eighteen

"Do you like her?" said Adara. We were at dinner. Good wine and white tablecloths. Stiff-necked servers. She was having a hearty beef stew with hasty pudding and spring shallots; I had opted for beef stroganoff with asparagus and brown rice.

"Who?"

"The other woman in your life."

I sighed. "You mean SA North."

"Who else?"

"She's all right. I gave her my terms. She listened."

"That's not what I mean." Adara took a bite of her hasty pudding. Chewed. Seemed to measure her words. "I know she listened. She's a professional. But did you like her? As in someone you would like to work with. I think that's important."

I smiled. "I guess I could get used to her. If she gets me written immunity. Which I think she will. She's a live wire."

"She's a regular Energizer Bunny. I think she's cute. And she hates Marguerite almost as much as I do."

Our conversation wandered. Adara said she had a part in a Boston stage production of *Year of the Rooster*. She was playing an aging mother who could not get over the death of her beloved terrier. "It's a good role," said Adara. "The first time I've played somebody old and decrepit. It opens in June at a beautiful little theater-in-the-round near Copley Square."

But then, to my surprise, Adara said she was thinking about

going back into law. She had worked as an immigration lawyer for ICE during her last miserable years with Thomas Quincey. Now, though, she was thinking about reaching out to Agresti, who did investigations for the New England Innocence Project. "Maybe he can get me in. I wouldn't mind cutting my teeth as an investigator."

"The Innocence Project is a noble cause," I said. "And Agresti's the best PI in New England."

But I still felt uneasy. Not about Carrie. Or my striking dinner companion. It was what I had to tell her. Now that Carrie knew about Bobby's plight, I had to tell Adara. I waited until we had finished dinner and were sipping cappuccinos at a Starbucks next to a sushi joint near the airport.

"Listen, Adara, I've got to tell you something. Something important. I won't sugarcoat it. My partner Bobby Moore has been abducted by Marguerite's people. I have to get him back."

"What?" said Adara. She put her cup down. Stared at me accusingly. "Why didn't you tell me?"

"I just did."

"Why did you wait so long?"

"I wanted to talk to Carrie first."

"What did she say?"

"She was horrified. Like everyone else. But listen." I leaned forward. Covered her hand and whispered, "Keep this on the down-low. No one is to know that I'm working with Carrie. Or that Bobby's been kidnapped. Do not tell Desmond Cole anything. Nothing about Carrie and me. Nothing about Bobby. Does Cole know you're here in Wisconsin?"

Adara shook her head. "Desmond doesn't know anything. All he knows is I travel a lot. He doesn't know where I go. I talk to him once a week on the phone. And we go out to dinner every couple of months. Which is fine. It's more boring than anything else."

"What an ass!"

"It's a lot better than when Thomas controlled our money."

She sighed. "And our freedom. But don't worry about me, Nick. I know how to keep my mouth shut."

"Good. I'm counting on you."

"Hey, I appreciate the fact you leveled with me…" She pondered, stirring the dregs of her cappuccino with a wooden stir stick. "I wonder if there's anything I can do?"

"You've already done it. You brought me Carrie. I'm going to need her investigators, and I'll probably need her firepower too."

We fell silent. Drank our cappuccinos and looked around the joint. Solitary souls with laptops drinking coffee. Then Adara spoke, pondering each word. "This is nothing like when Desmond and Marguerite kidnapped me, is it?"

"Correct. Marguerite has no intention of releasing Bobby…unless…"

"Unless what?"

"Unless I turn myself in. 'Cause I'm the one she really wants."

"NO!" It burst out. Practically a shout. Heads turned. Adara started trembling. Rage. And fear. I reached out. Closed my hand over hers. Then she closed her free hand over mine. We sat that way for a long time.

Sometime later, we found ourselves sitting side by side at an outside table in back of a dive bar across the street from the Fox River. Barely ten. Hardly any patrons. Sunday night. They would close soon. The gloom and doom hung heavy. I was drinking whiskey and she stuck to wine. We didn't say much. Mostly looked out over the lights shining on the river. Every so often, she leaned into me and rested her head on my shoulder.

Didn't mind the silence. We both had the blues. In ten short hours, she'd be driving to Milwaukee to catch her flight back to Boston. I started fantasizing about a better world in which Adara and I both worked for the Innocence Project. She had the bar card and would represent our falsely convicted clients. Agresti and I would dig up the exonerating evidence. Together, we would be unstoppable. After a while, she asked me what I was thinking about.

"The Innocence Project."

"That's funny. So was I."

"What were you thinking?"

"I was wondering if Agresti would hire me."

"He would if I put in a good word for you."

"Would you actually do that?"

"Of course I would."

We finished our drinks and drove back to the inn. Our last night together. For a long time. Perhaps forever...

We were sitting in her kitchenette sipping herbal tea. Her laptop was open, and a female singer named Morgan James was looping on YouTube, when she spoke. "I'm not sure how you're going to take this. I like you a lot. Ugh! That sounds terrible. But it's true. I do. But I can't let myself fall in love with you. For all the obvious reasons." She stopped. Her elegant lips curved downward.

She was right. I was twenty-two years older. With a price on my head. We were so different. She was born into culture and class; I was born to run errands for hard rock miners to save money to buy a decent pair of tennis shoes. She read and understood the great poets; I read Ross MacDonald. The three men in her life that I was aware of—her father Mohammad, Quincey, and yours truly—were all in their fifties. Stood to reason that she would want to segue toward guys her own age.

"I understand," I said quietly. "Whatever you decide to do, I'll respect it. You don't even need to explain." I stood up. Walked to the bathroom. Turned on the shower.

When I came out, she was already in bed. Lying on her side, covers pulled up to her waist, wearing a long blue diaphanous nightshirt. She looked at me. Smiled. Very deliberately she rolled over onto her back. Very slowly she pulled her nightshirt all the way up to her elegant throat. A monarch butterfly tattooed above her left breast. The first part of her that I kissed. Not the last. There seemed to be no last...

In the morning, we sat in the kitchenette eating the hotel

continental breakfast and drinking Earl Grey. She kept smiling. Brown eyes the color of the earth before it rains. "This isn't goodbye," she said. "Because we are connected. Connected by pain and desire. That's the problem. We're not good for each other because we tap into each other's sadness."

Felt like a weight and an opening. "That's part of it. Because of these strange circumstances. But that doesn't mean we couldn't tap into each other's joy. And I believe you know that. Otherwise, you wouldn't even be here."

She didn't argue. But she didn't agree. Not in words. But she took me by the hand and started tracing my lifeline. It was still there. I looked into her eyes. A world of unfathomable experience.

We said goodbye in the parking lot. She got in her rented Mercedes, and I got in Bobby's Econoline van. She had to catch her flight to Boston. I was driving to Racine south of Milwaukee, where I would meet Carrie North at eight p.m. at a local steak house.

I had given Carrie an easy but important task to carry out before she left town. And a warning. Do not try to crack the password on Marguerite's phone until after our meeting in Racine. She had raised an eyebrow and promised that she would not.

Chapter Nineteen

Back in Fond du Lac, I retrieved the receiving unit of the ghost transmitter and checked out of my little room across from the Marriott. No sign of the Asian deskman. I drove down county road V toward Campbellsport. Stopped off at Jimmy Sain's farm. Nobody there. Taped a note to his welding rig. Sat there in his barnyard for a long time watching the weather change. A gusting wind came out of the north and the sky grew dark. When it began to rain, I keyed Bobby's ignition and turned on the wipers. Turned around and drove slowly up his driveway to the county road...

Twenty miles north of Racine, a big rig forced me onto the shoulder. I shuddered to a stop. Shivered for a while. Drove on. In Racine, I checked into the downtown Hilton Doubletree. I was scheduled to meet Special Agent North in the hotel bar in four hours.

Read *The Zebra-Striped Hearse*. The Colonel's daughter was eloping with a dangerous young man. Everybody was working against everybody else. I put down the book and turned on the new ghost recordings.

Nothing much on Saturday. Idle chit-chat in the morning and casual discussion of the night's anticipated events. But it got interesting early Sunday morning after the ill-fated MASA rally. First, Quincey told Marguerite that there's nothing better than making love to take your mind off the slings and arrows of outrageous fortune.

"Come again," said Marguerite. "In English, this time."

A long, unctuous sigh. Pure Quincey. "What I just said is English. It's very good English."

"Jesus, Tom, don't be such an ass. Try talking good old American English like our president. Everyday words for everyday people."

"Sure, baby. Let's fuck. It'll take your mind off the bullshit at the rally."

"So that's what you were talking about." I could see her nasty smile, the type where there's just enough lipstick coating the teeth to give them that overcooked look. "Well, I have to admit, it would be fun, and it probably would take my mind off tonight's disaster. But the answer is no. We can't afford to get sidetracked. We've got to keep our eyes on the prize."

Quincey mumbled something inaudible. Then silence. It was six p.m. Two hours till I was due to meet Carrie North. Still nervous about this new arrangement. But written immunity would go a long way.

Then a surprise…

"Twenty questions," said Quincey suddenly. "Where's Bobby Moore?"

"I don't know. I already told you."

"Of course you know. You arranged for the kidnapping. You did the legwork with Tommy Blank."

Right at that moment I realized that the whole brick-through-the-window routine that catapulted me into a black Range Rover heading east farther away from Los Angeles could have been simple misdirection designed to pull me farther from Bobby's orbit when they moved in to abduct him. Which meant that Desmond Cole was definitely one of the conspirators. The fact I shot the three hired guns who tried to stop me? Collateral damage.

"I didn't arrange the kidnapping."

"Who did, then? I probably know him or her."

"Indeed, you do." She hesitated for a moment. "Okay. Why not? It was Jethro Shimanski…"

"Jethro didn't arrange it. He may have helped. You and Tommy Blank arranged it 'cause it's your baby."

"Okay. Suit yourself."

"So how are they treating him?"

"Treating who?"

"Bobby Moore."

"Oh, he's all right. They tell me he's practically a new man. The makeover seems to be doing wonders."

"Oh shit!" said Quincey. Even he was surprised.

Long silence while they moved around their suite, and I silently died inside. A new man. Makeover time. I've lived and died with my rage—best friend and worst enemy—for as long as I can remember. But this time? Nothing. No black anger to bail me out. But so fucking sad. I got up and poured a glass of water. Spilled it. Cursed. Refilled it. Came back and sat down. Couldn't breathe…

"So how is he really?" said Quincey. "I hope your people are treating him decently. Since Crane's the one you really want."

"Precisely. Crane's the one I want. What I'm hearing is that Moore just sits and stares at the wall. Sometimes he mumbles about what Crane's going to do to all of us after he busts him out."

I could breathe again. Barely. Then Quincey surprised me.

"The fact you've been given a status report doesn't mean you know where he is 'cause it's need to know, and you don't really need to know. I don't need to know either, but I do know."

First, she scoffed, then she laughed.

"My dear Marguerite, although I've hit a few bumps along the road, I am not entirely without friends."

Fuck. Quincey was back. I could feel it right through the ghost transmitter. Then a long back-and-forth, different now. Quincey had somehow gained the upper hand.

"Okay, Marguerite, let's make a deal. I'll tell you who my

source is and where he says they're holding Moore. You can check me for accuracy. But only if you sleep with me."

Quincey WAS back. Precisely what I did not need.

Marguerite held out coquettishly. Amiable Quincey said if that was the case, he was going to go to sleep. Quincey won. But after they were finished, his intel was hardly definitive. His source, a man named James Millrose, said that the rumor making the rounds was that Bobby was being held in a decommissioned Titan I missile silo in the middle of nowhere. A loud slap. Quincey yelped. "You little prick," said Marguerite. "That sounds like fake news."

Quincey laughed. "Maybe it is, maybe it isn't." Within three minutes, he was snoring.

They checked out early the next morning. On their way, apparently, to a shooting range near the town of Oconomowoc, Wisconsin. To practice their marksmanship and kill time before the next rally.

I turned off the ghost and called Todd. Asked him if Tommy Blank had said anything about going to Wisconsin or about going to see Marguerite. Todd said he had said something about going out of town but hadn't said where. I told him I needed him to find out everything he could about Tommy Blank's plans for the next few days, especially his travel itinerary. "This is your chance," I said. "I hope you come through."

Then Greg. Told him I needed intel fast on Jethro Shimanski and James Millrose. Along with everything else he was working on. Told him he had till Tuesday morning and that I wanted the information in password-encrypted reports. Everything he could gather but with an emphasis on Millrose, Shimanski, and Blank.

Chapter Twenty

Carrie North was not alone. The man sitting next to her looked like a getaway driver—short, rail thin, big ears, hair plastered across his forehead, goggle eyes blazing hotly. The face of a man fated to haunt libraries and databases. Tim Swann stood up and introduced himself. A handshake, seemingly without forethought. I liked that. I sat down next to Carrie and across from Swann. She nudged me and handed me a two-page document. It appeared that the FBI had just granted Nick Crane complete immunity with respect to any information he might provide concerning a highly confidential investigation of three targets—Marguerite Ferguson, Thomas Quincey aka Miles Amsterdam, and Desmond Cole. I was permitted to investigate other participants and potential witnesses within their orbit. All intel, old and new, was protected. I was to work as a CI under a yet-to-be-determined name. I could still be charged for crimes totally unrelated to the investigation. It was signed by the Assistant Attorney General, U.S. District Court, Boston, Massachusetts...Well...

"Not perfect but it's pretty good," said Carrie. "I managed to get the 'totally' in there to protect you. This agreement gives you broad latitude to do whatever you feel is necessary as long as you keep me informed. So that's your copy. Take it or leave it."

I looked at her. No wiseass. Not jocular. Face a little drawn. Mouth a little tight. Dead earnest. Eyes more sea-green than blue this evening. Striking in that small, earnest face. She needed me. We both knew it. And I needed her.

Made a show of reading it a second time. "Sure, hell yeah, it's decent. More than decent," I added generously. "I'll sign. Got a pen?" She did. And a second copy for me. I signed both copies and folded mine in half. Placed it inside *The Zebra-Striped Hearse.*

A thought. "Based on our agreement, am I allowed to make a citizen's arrest?"

Carrie thought it over. "You have the legal right, I suppose. Just like any private citizen. But better to steer them our way and let us put the clamps on."

I smiled. "Got it. And what's my new name?"

"What do you want it to be?"

My turn to ponder. Came in a flash. "How about Ned Stamper?"

"Ned Stamper?" said Carrie.

"Sure. Why not? I often use Ned when I don't want to reveal my real name."

We ordered steak and lobster. When in Racine…When the food came, we dug in and I casually asked Carrie if she'd retrieved the phone. She had. I told her I'd found a new smoking gun since we'd last talked. To be discussed after dinner. I told Swann a heroic tale about the time I'd played quarterback for the open-pit miners in my Minnesota hometown even though I was only seventeen.

"You are such a man," said Carrie when the tale finally ended. Snot. "But there's something odd here. Why were you playing quarterback for a group of tough-as-nails, open-pit miners in their thirties and forties when you were only seventeen?"

"I was precocious." I laughed and shouldered her in collegial fashion. "But enough about football. My best friend is being turned and Swann and I are babbling about football."

"Best friend is being turned?" said Carrie, in a small voice. "That was our worst fear. What have you learned?"

"New evidence. You'll see when we listen to the tape."

"Being turned?" said Swann. "That's awful."

I looked at them both. Spoke quietly. "It's killing me."

After dinner, we went back to my hotel suite where I gave them the password and we opened up Marguerite's phone. Started with the relevant WhatsApp calls. Tommy Blank and Marguerite. Seven calls, one topic. Abducting Bobby. Tommy's best people, the First Wave, would do the actual taking.

"Okay. That's smoking gun number one," I said after the seventh call. "Swann, did you get most of that?" Swann, who was hunched over his Chromebook typing furiously, nodded.

On to the April 28 call between Marguerite and Cole. Three main topics. Me turning myself in to buy Bobby's release. Marguerite's testicle-removal fantasy. Cole lecturing Marguerite on how to slide Arabs in and out of the country for quick-and-dirty terrorist actions.

"Well then," I said, "this is like a smoking cannon."

Carrie didn't say a word. Sat there. Numb? In shock? It's one thing to go after a bad guy. It's something else to have practically the whole case handed to you. At a very inconvenient time 'cause if she had the grand jury sworn in to indict Marguerite on the kidnapping conspiracy, it would be much harder to build the domestic terrorism case. Which had been approaching critical mass with the Arabs in place in the silo near Weedpatch. And who was managing and organizing the Arabs? At ground level? It obviously wasn't Marguerite. Tommy Blank? Was he that vile? And that powerful? Perhaps. Which brought all of Quincey's sickening violence and cruelty back full force. Truth is, it practically floored me. It was hard to stay rational. Finally, I could speak again. "They're evil. It's disturbing. Let's go on to Exhibit 3."

But before I could speak, Agent North broke her long silence. "I must say, this looks pretty incredible as in clear grounds for an indictment, should we move in that direction, but only if the evidence was gathered legally. So, tell me, where or how did you gain possession of Marguerite's Ferguson's phone?"

I was ready. Smiled and spoke. "I was staking out the lobby of her hotel in Fond du Lac. I found her phone tucked into the corner of a chair near the flat screen. I just happened to see it and assumed she'd left it there by mistake. But as you will see from what I'm about to play for you, she makes a contrary claim."

I turned on the ghost. The first night. Marguerite wakes up. Pissed. She wakes up Quincey. Berates him about his Valium addiction and how she and Cole parlayed his criminal activities into a series of patriotic acts, proving that anything is possible if you have enough money and put the right pawns in place. Then she describes being assaulted and injected with Versed by a low-life Swede who took her phone and money. Mentions that her password is her birthday. Berates Quincey some more—this time for his ill-conceived false flag scheme. I stopped the ghost. "Ironic that in their phone call on WhatsApp, Desmond Cole chides Marguerite for poor execution in her build-up to her recently thwarted terrorist mission. And here she gets on Quincey for the same thing. Seems to be a common thread. Problem is, though, if she's not stopped, she'll find some more Arabs, and sooner or later, she'll make it work. 'Cause she is one determined psychopath."

Back to the ghost. Marguerite talks about how they are the lodestar in support of their leader's reelection campaign. Berates Quincey some more. He discovers he was also robbed. Then they have sex. I turn off the ghost.

"So that's Exhibit 3. Fascinating stuff. I hope you got that all down, Swann." Carrie North was blushing slightly.

I cracked open a Heineken. "There it is, Carrie, Marguerite self-reports that she was strong-armed by a low-life Swede who stole her phone and money. I'm not sure I believe the Versed part. Too coincidental with Quincey already hooked on that shit. She probably made it up 'cause it sounded good. Unless all those pricks are hooked on benzos..." Disingenuous Crane.

"Why would she make that up?" said Carrie. "The Swede

had to incapacitate her somehow. She doesn't strike me as the type who would just lie there and take it."

"Hmm." Frowned and rubbed my forehead. "You know, I hate to admit it, but you're probably right. That's a new one on me. Even my mentor, Frenchy Lefevre, who had seen just about everything, never mentioned the Versed injection incapacitation angle." Throwing her a bone. Subtle change in her body language. A bit more relaxed. Coming along.

"It appears," I said, "that this Swede, for whatever reason, abandoned the phone. I found it and stashed it behind the gas station. Then told you it was there. But after passing through this many hands, I think it constitutes admissible evidence. And because the ghost evidence is inadmissible based on a theory of illegal wiretap, Marguerite's claim that it was stolen by a Swedish mugger is irrelevant."

Special Agent North looked at me. Nodded her head. "It's a close legal call but I'm willing to run with it. I'll consult with our legal experts before swearing out a complaint or going to the grand jury. If we decide to go that route. And you're right. We're dead in the water on the wiretap. That's clear."

Felt a pleasant weariness wash over me. The hell with it. Take the bull by the horns. "I believe, Ms. North, that you have a clear path to use what's on the phone. I will testify that I found it in the armchair, hit the password by accident, and was shocked by what I found. I got scared and stashed it behind the gas station. Then I contacted law enforcement, which turned out to be you. The beautiful thing is there's so much evidence. We have Marguerite and Tommy Blank planning the kidnapping. I have a witness in LA who watched three guys in commando gear drag Bobby out into the street and force him into their van. Todd, the head of Tommy Blank's Second Wave force in Weedpatch, told me that Bobby had been handed off to other soldiers, First Wave guys. I have Todd on retainer right now as a source. He could be useful at trial.

"I think you've got them on conspiracy. For sure, you've got

Marguerite and Tommy Blank. And Desmond Cole for aiding and abetting. And based on their conversation, you practically have Cole and Marguerite on conspiracy to smuggle Arabs into the country to commit acts of domestic terrorism.

"Now I realize that the wiretap clearly cannot be used to indict and would be inadmissible at trial. Which is too bad. But when you hear the rest of the recording, you'll understand why I'm so worried." I fast-forwarded the ghost to the *Where Is Bobby Moore* conversation, complete with Marguerite's ambiguous statements about him being turned. Afterwards, I stood up. "So are they turning him? Is he turned? Is this just a game? What the hell is going on?" I ground my fist into my palm. Then I calmed down and we played that part again:

"So how are they treating him?"

"Treating who?"

"Bobby Moore."

"Oh, he's all right. They tell me he's practically a new man. The makeover seems to be doing wonders."

"Oh shit!"

And then later.

"So how is he really? said Quincey. *"I hope your people are treating him decently. Since Crane's the one you really want."*

"Precisely. Crane's the one I want. What I'm hearing is that Moore just sits and stares at the wall. Sometimes he mumbles about what Crane's going to do to all of us after he busts him out."

They both looked at me. Carrie was pale. Swann, who was naturally pale, looked really sad.

"So, you see why I'm so worried. We don't know what they're doing to him. Could be torture. Could be brainwashing. Or both. All I know is we've got to get him back. Fast." Then it hit me along with a flash of pain in both temples. "I think, Carrie, that in a kind of *sub rosa* manner, you could have your people find Bobby and get him released. If he really is being held at a Titan I missile site. Which is somewhat doubtful. But if he is,

132

you have the manpower and the technology to break him out.
That's the clean, simple way. We get Bobby back, and you
continue your enormously important investigation of the most
dangerous woman in America. And I'll be forever grateful and
will continue to help out your investigation in whatever way I can.
Nick Crane, your faithful servant. Forever. And I mean that."

I sat back down. Give her time to think it through.

Just after midnight, her phone rang. She picked up, stood up,
and walked over to the breakfast nook. Turned her back.
Swann and I exchanged glances. He looked worried. I grimaced
and lay back on the bed and closed my eyes. Until she finished
her call. Then I sat back up.

"Bad news," said Carrie. "They've tracked the phone to me.
Marguerite wants it back."

"That's tough," I said. "But legally, she abandoned it. I'd have
Swann get everything copied. Just in case you can't stonewall it.
You've got your equipment here, right?"

He nodded. Good man. I shut up. Gave Carrie the floor. She
agreed that Swann should get everything copied. Then she threw
me a curve. She wanted to pick Marguerite up and bring her in for
questioning. With Swann present to play the WhatsApp recordings. And she would use the phone evidence as a hammer to put
the pressure on to tell us where Bobby Moore was, or else.

"Or else what?" I said.

Or else she'd swear out a complaint and arrest her for
conspiracy to kidnap Bobby. But if Marguerite released Bobby,
Carrie might just back off, for the time being. Marguerite could
go back to putting on her rallies. And Carrie and her people
would watch her and slowly and methodically build an ironclad
domestic terrorism case.

I listened. Raised an imaginary eyebrow. An art I've mastered.
Knew that what she was not telling me was that Special Agent
Carrie North—thirty-something, green and idealistic—was
enamored with trying to break Marguerite. To turn Marguerite
in the honey-dripping FBI style. One part vinegar, two parts

honey. It was understandable. Even tempting. But it wouldn't work. The black widow was too tough. And she wouldn't say a word until her lawyers arrived. And they would be even tougher. There is a tribe of heartless lawyers all across America who represent powerful, dark-hearted men and women.

Had to drip a little vinegar. "That's a very interesting idea, Ms. North. It could work." I paused, a study in thoughtfulness, then spoke slowly, "Or it could backfire. I'm afraid that you'll bring her in, arrest her—hell, put her in solitary—and she still won't talk. Don't underestimate her. She may believe she's untouchable. Or that the president would pardon her instantly if she was convicted on a kidnapping charge. But a pardon would be much harder to justify if she was convicted of conspiracy to commit acts of domestic terrorism. Also, if you arrest her, or even bring her in for questioning, they'll move Bobby to a new location. Immediately. Which would suck. It's going to be hard enough to find him in the first place. I hate to say it, but I think it's too early to bring in Marguerite. Our emphasis should be on finding and liberating Bobby first." Carrie's cheeks were red. Not smiling. "And Swann's team of technicians should find all the decommissioned Titan I missile silos in the country, at which point we'll narrow down our search."

"You're just like all of them," said Carrie, her cheeks flushing. "Another self-absorbed male who thinks he's the boss. But because I'm a good agent first and foremost, I'm in no hurry to bust your chops. But I will. When the time comes. You can count on it..." She laughed. Very good sign. "All right, then. It's a tough call, but I agree that we have to spring Bobby first...Jim, along with getting the phone copied, have your team find the Titan I installations. Then we'll take a good look at them in the database. I also want you to get everything you can on Jethro Shimanski and James Millrose." Her cheeks were still red, but she was apparently too smart and too decent to not grasp the need to focus on Bobby, my direct manner notwithstanding.

"They're all connected," I said. "Welcome to the principals.

They're connected the way the tentacles of an octopus are connected. They each have their own nasty little brain and they all share the same big nasty central brain. That central brain is the tough one 'cause we don't know if it's even a person. It may just be their creed."

"Which is what?" said Swann, looking up from his screen.

"Some deranged combination of do what thou wilt combined with ultimate greed for money and power. Set against a backdrop of perpetual racism."

"All right," Carrie said. "Don't rub it in. You're the world-class expert on these assholes. That's the reason we're reaching out to you. But listen, there's another angle we need to look at. Don't you think Tommy Blank is a very important part of this?" Good to see she was thinking, not just reacting to me.

"Jesus, North, you're a genius too. Like Swann here." By now Swann was typing and clicking on his keyboard, presumably checking out decommissioned Titan I missile silos. "I agree. Tommy Blank is very important. In fact, he could be the key."

"Thank you. Thank you for listening. I can hardly believe it but just maybe I'm beginning to like you. But don't tell anyone. And naturally, I'd rather start a few notches below Marguerite anyway. Underlings are often much quicker to spill their guts. And it's more effective to climb the tree from the ground up."

I nodded my head. "You're right, North. We've got to find Tommy Blank and bring him in. I bet he'll talk. Based on the little I've heard, he does not sound like a true believer. Which means he has no reason not to sing when you start waving ten years in front of him."

"How do we find him?"

I shrugged. "That's a very good question. But we'll find him. Probably when we least expect it." I pondered. "Maybe even at the next MASA rally."

Chapter Twenty-One

In the morning, Carrie and I met for breakfast at the Douglas Family Diner. We were both starving and packed it away—eggs and bacon and ham and sausages and toast and pancakes and a couple cups of coffee. After a while, Carrie put down her coffee cup. Looked at me and smiled. "Were you always this way?"

"Which way?"

"You know. Heavily armed, lugging around an illegal arsenal, lovely girlfriend, bad manners, and a bullseye the size of Alaska on your back."

"Illegal arsenal?"

"Smoke grenades. They may not be illegal per se but setting them off at the MASA rally certainly was."

"Oh, that again." I smiled. "All right, maybe I did attend the rally. But to answer your question, no, I wasn't always this way. Though maybe the signs were always there. It must have been the Frank Constantine matter that pushed me over the edge. But as for the bullseye on my back, I'd do anything to shed it."

"Would you? I'm not so sure I believe that."

Started to protest but changed my mind. Instead, I nudged the conversation in the direction of brass tacks. How far was she willing to go if we located Bobby but could not spring him due to unforeseen obstacles, and time was running out? Would she stand down if extreme measures were all I had left?

"What kind of extreme measures?"

"Well, that depends..."

She laughed, a bit too merrily. "Give me a worst case."

"Okay, North. Absolute worst. Just the thought of it terrifies me. Second Marines, 6/2 combat team. Desert Storm guys. Six of them. They'd walk through walls to save Bobby. 'Cause they're like him. Damaged. He understands them and because he's smart, he helps them understand their own pain. Bobby's like the sage of pain. I'm not scared of very many people, but these guys terrify me. And they're not cheap. Last fall, the first time Marguerite and Quincey tried to bury me in a Black Site, Bobby paid them five stacks to break me out. And that was a simple job."

"What did they use?"

"Gas and stunners. Fast and decisive. They do not mess around."

"Was anyone killed?" Gave me a searching look.

"Not even close." Glad I didn't have to lie. I drank some coffee and continued. "That job was easy. Nothing like what we have here where we don't know who's involved at the other end. I hope it's just a para outfit that one of the principals hired. That's our best hope. You approach the silo with your HRT crew, tell 'em you're FBI, and that you've come for prisoner Moore. And don't take no for an answer. It will restore Bobby's faith in humanity. Seriously."

"You make it sound easy."

"Could be easy. Could be hard. If we can find the right location, based on the phone evidence, you can swear out an affidavit and get a search warrant. And send your Hostage Rescue Team to serve it. Almost any para outfit would wilt if an HRT crew shows up with a search warrant."

"What if they didn't wilt?"

"Then we'd have a problem."

That's how we left it. Tuesday was for research. We would all reconvene Wednesday afternoon, a few hours before Marguerite's Racine MASA rally.

Chapter Twenty-Two

Greg's reports started rolling in Tuesday morning, one per hour. Jethro Shimanski and James Millrose were not what I expected. No silver spoons in their mouths. No polo ponies cropping grass outside their bedroom windows. Shimanski had been raised by a single mother in a double-wide trailer in the Florida potato fields halfway between Gainesville and the ocean.

"Potato fields?" I said incredulously. "I thought they were in Idaho."

"Dunno," said Greg. "The dark web does not lie, except when it lies." Jethro's father Hank Shimanski pulled a twenty-year state prison bid for soliciting the murder of a business rival. Throughout his childhood, Jethro's mother Ida visited Hank religiously once a month at the Okeechobee Correctional Institution in Miami-Dade County. After the age of ten, Jethro went with her. Hank never wavered. He was innocent and Ida believed him. Brought this "fact" up every night at the dinner table. Said one day God would bring justice. Jethro believed his mother. Pops had been railroaded.

After stomping a rival for the hand of Miss Potato Lady 1978 in the parking lot after his senior prom, Jethro joined the Army to avoid prison. Plodding and persistent, he put in his twenty years, rose to the rank of captain, and took his pension three years before 9-11. Then came several failed business attempts. Laundromats and a hardware store, belly-up. A seafood restaurant, belly-up. Two Chapter 11 bankruptcies. Undeterred, Jethro clawed his way into Detentions, Inc., a private prison company with a footprint stretching from Florida to Texas. Studied accounting at night, earned his degree and eventually his CPA license, which led to his slow rise to CFO. Big salary and even bigger bonuses made him a wealthy man.

Jethro owned houses in South Beach, Memphis, and Chevy Chase. Square-jawed with big shoulders and a formidable gut, he eventually hit the D.C. lobbyist circuit, extolling the virtues of private incarceration. Met Marguerite Ferguson in Georgetown in 2012.

Greg's take was that the principals had taken note of Jethro's bulldog persistence and can-do attitude and—despite his lack of pedigree—had adopted him as one of their own. There's always room for a self-made man...who understands the intricacies of private prison financing.

The private prison bit spooked me badly. I'd never been sold that Bobby was in a Titan I missile site. Based on this new intel, he was more than likely buried in the bowels of some private prison hellhole. And I obviously couldn't use Bobby's Marine buddies to storm a private prison. Even they were unlikely to step over that line. I signed off glumly and fielded Greg's next call thirty minutes later.

Like Jethro, James Millrose's childhood had been no bed of roses. An only child, he was raised in inner city West Oakland. His dad Jim-Bob worked as a janitor and salved his frustrations with alcohol, a fact his long-suffering mother Eleanor vigorously denied. Every Sunday, she would pray for Jim-Bob at the Grace Baptist Church in nearby San Leandro. Jim-Bob had learned to box in the service and passed it on to James so that he could protect himself, no mean skill in his neighborhood. Every time James came home from school reporting that he was suspended again for fighting, Jim-Bob rewarded him by taking him to an Oakland Raiders' game, which meant they could both duck church.

James joined the Navy the day after he graduated from high school (class of '81). Became a master-at-arms. Did his twenty years and took his pension. From there a natural progression to work in the California state prison system. One day it dawned on him that while earning eighty thousand dollars yearly as a prison guard was nothing to sneeze at, he could probably do much better in the private prison industry. He signed on with BP, Inc. (Better Prisons, Incorporated) in San Diego in 2007. Rose through the ranks and eventually became head of Logistics for the entire organization. Compared to Shimanski, Millrose was reclusive. Greg could locate no private residences. Although he wasn't certain, Greg thought that Millrose's main office was in Tempe, Arizona.

It made sense that Marguerite, with her ambition of becoming queen of the private prison industry, would know Shimanski, but I had no idea how Quincey knew Millrose. Greg signed off. Told me he'd get back to me in fifteen minutes after he had organized his notes on Tommy Blank, not that he had much. And that, he'd send me everything in writing later in the day.

Now I was really spooked. Decided to do a little online reconnoitering. Discovered that there were only a few Titan I missile sites. One in Washington, one in Idaho, and two in Colorado. One in South Dakota and three in California. The Titan I sites had housed ICBMs. They were huge. Most of the sites were now held privately. The ones that weren't private were gigantic, rusted, radioactive hulks. Very difficult to access. Closed my laptop, lay down on the bed, and took a deep breath. Counterintuitive to think that Bobby was in one of these. It hit my stomach hard. Bobby was underground, way underground, in a private prison in one of a dozen or more states. Sure, Carrie North could locate Shimanski and Millrose, these twin masters of incarceration capitalism, and lean on them. But with the ghost tape inadmissible, we had very little to go on. If questioned, they would lawyer up immediately.

Just as I'd worked myself up into a lather, Greg rang back.

Excited and for good reason. Tommy Blank was a different animal, his various fake footprints all over the dark web. Man of mystery, master of obfuscation. As someone once said, *they're planting stories in the press.* Greg opined that Tommy was planting them himself but had no proof. I figured it was Marguerite. Hire a couple of hacks. Tell them to make shit up. Sound strategy. No one could decide if Tommy was Buddhist or Christian or Jewish. He wasn't Muslim; I was pretty sure of that.

Instead of solid facts, a portrait emerged of a near-mythical figure. Nearly invincible in any kind of fight and dripping charisma, allegedly kept by Hollywood starlets, including one Malibu maiden. The women were apparently real, well-heeled, and known for their beauty. And Greg had names. That was the important thing.

Tommy owned no residences and had no work history. There were vague claims that he played for pay for a mysterious right-wing power broker. Well, yeah...

I asked Greg to verify Tommy's girlfriends' names and addresses. Signed off. Showered, shaved, and sent out for breakfast. Ate slowly. Quiet mind. Greg phoned back just after eleven with a name and address. Rainey Morgan lived on Malibu Drive near Pepperdine University. She had played the female lead in several moderately successful horror films. I asked Greg to book me a round trip flight from Milwaukee to LAX. I would leave LA Wednesday at noon and be back in plenty of time for Marguerite's Wednesday night MASA rally.

Chapter Twenty-Three

Sharp in a charcoal grey Dolce & Gabbana pin-striped suit, Tony Bott met me at LAX. My best suit, something cheap off the rack at Macy's, was waiting for me in his Jeep Cherokee. Stopped at a gas station where I got changed. I looked like Nick Nolte in *Affliction,* and Tony was one of the best-looking cops in Los Angeles, a cross between Robert Mitchum and Elvis before he got fat.

Rainey Morgan lived in the right-hand side of a tile-roofed, stucco duplex, fronted by a red-brick wall with twin black iron gates. The white sand beach a stone's throw from her rear balcony. Fitting locale for an actress on the way up. Expensive but not cripplingly so. We rang the buzzer at the call box and waited.

"Hullo, who's there?" Sleepy English accent perhaps affected.

"FBI," said Tony, his voice equal parts purr and growl. "We need to have a word with Ms. Rainey Morgan." Nobody intimidates more casually and naturally than Tony Bott. Claims he learned it from his old man, but I suspect it's in his DNA.

A long silence and then the same affected voice. "I'm sorry, sir, but Ms. Morgan is indisposed."

"That's all right," said Tony. "We'll wait. We have reports that Ms. Morgan may be in serious danger. So, I strongly advise you to let us in."

Another long silence. "We don't have all day," his voice a

steel-edged purr. "I'm going to ask you one more time to let us in. Now!"

A much shorter silence. "All right, then. If you insist. I'll buzz you in."

"Damned straight," Tony muttered sotto voce. The machinery whirred and the gate slid open. We followed a flagstone walkway that sloped gently down to the front door, passing a steel blue metal sculpture in the shape of a dolphin and an ornate sundial that looked both ancient and modern. Tony rattled the knocker and the door swung open.

Face-to-face with a peculiar creature, a strikingly handsome, slim young man with pinned brown pupils wearing designer jeans and a Robert Pattinson T-shirt. Arms folded; mouth flared down in a junkie's frown. "Hullo," he said, his accent unchanged. "I'm Jamie. My sister is getting a facial. I trust she'll be done before too long. Let me show you to the parlor." He led us down a short hallway to a large, pleasant room sporting a Warhol—Mick Jagger with long hair and big red lips, green horizontal blotches above his eyes. Tony, a secret art aficionado, walked over to examine it. Now, inside the castle, his bad attitude had evaporated.

"Is that an original?"

"An original lithograph, I believe." Jamie uncrossed his arms and seemed to sink into his nod. Spoke. "It wasn't easy but after a prolonged negotiation, I convinced my sister to buy it."

"Good work," said Tony. "It's a nice piece."

His compliment triggered a brief smile. "Would you gentlemen like something to drink?"

"Sure," I said, "a Pellegrino would be perfect."

"Ditto," said Tony.

Jamie walked casually out of the room and returned with three Pellegrinos on a lacquered serving tray. Once we were settled, him sitting across from us, he took a sip or two and fell into a deep nod.

"Good dope," said Tony.

Header: Patrick H. Moore

We waited till he came out of it and started talking, drawling the words slowly. "I've heard you FBI agents aren't as corrupt as the local police."

"I wouldn't count on it," said Tony. "It depends on if you catch us in a good mood."

And so it went, Jamie, between nods, asking us various questions about different branches of law enforcement and police work in general. He finally dragged himself to his feet and announced he was going to see if his sister could talk to us now. Again, we watched him sashay out of the room. There are ten million stories in Los Angeles County.

Rainey Morgan finally made her entrance wearing a gauzy, floor-length peignoir, her thick blond hair cute in a Rachel. She sat down next to Jamie on the couch and crossed her legs, which were mostly veiled by her wrap.

"Hi there, I don't mean to be rude, but could you please show me some ID." She had that exasperating little girl in a full-grown woman voice. Tony had dug up some dime store FBI shields before meeting me at the airport. I was SA Wayne Donner and he was SA Mike Pasqua. We stood up, walked over, and flashed our shields. Put them away and sat back down.

"I'm sorry for being suspicious," said Rainey, "but Jamie here always tells me I'm too trusting. He's probably right." She had those starlet eyes, bright blue and full of the kind of empty light that stirs the loins and saddens the soul. She smiled and uncrossed and re-crossed her legs, like a guest on a late-night talk show.

"You are too trusting," mumbled Jamie before falling back into his nod.

Rainey leaned forward and spoke softly. "I'm very sorry about my brother." She paused and pulled her peignoir close at her throat. "He's been through a lot, so please, don't think badly of him."

"Why would I?" said genial Tony. "He's a good-looking kid who seems like he has plenty of brains and confidence. Though

144

he obviously needs to get off the dope."

"I know," said Rainey. "He's actually way more talented than his big sister. But don't tell anyone."

"I won't," said Tony. "You have my word."

He fell silent. I followed suit. We waited till she broke. "Okay, officers? What's going on? Why are you here? I hope this isn't about my brother."

"Don't worry," said Tony. "Or maybe you should worry. It's you we're concerned about."

"Me? Why?"

"Here's the thing," I jumped in. "It just so happens that your boyfriend, Tommy Blank, is a target in a high-level federal investigation. We're here for two reasons. First, to convince you to stay away from him at all times. If necessary, we'll help you find safe harbor. Second, to see if you can help us find him." As I spoke, her expression went from surprised to dubious to horrified. For a moment, she lowered her head and held her face in her hands. Jamie came out of his nod.

"You're scaring my sister." Accent apparently forgotten.

"I apologize," said Tony. Still genial. "We do so many terrifying cases that we sometimes forget to be subtle. And my partner here," waving at me casually, "has always lacked a certain couth."

"You both do," said Jamie, suddenly furious. He stood up and started toward us. Caught himself. "I want you both to leave. Now." His sister grabbed him from behind and tried to pull him back. He resisted. Turned. She took him by both hands and led him back to the sofa in an awkward pas de deux.

"Tsk tsk," said Tony, pretending to be angry. "You've just committed an assault on a federal agent. That's a felony, baby. So calm the fuck down. Your sister's not under investigation. We're here to help." Jamie sputtered a bit but managed to control himself.

"Have you ever thought about," I said, casual as hell, "trying to get your brother off the heroin. All he has to do is slam some fentanyl and he'll be your dead brother. You need to get him into a program."

"I only smoke pure stuff," Jamie protested, trying not to nod out. "My source is impeccable, and I never shoot up."

"My ass," said Tony, "or rather your ass. But the point is this, Ms. Morgan, Tommy Blank is a serial killer. Women only. Just your luck. We've got to stop him, but he's damned elusive. And apparently, his work takes him all over the western states. Often in disguise. And he's rumored to have some kind of weird mystique. So, what can you tell us?"

Rainey sat there making a conscious effort to compose herself. Now her hands were trembling. She placed them in her lap. Started to speak, stopped, started again. "He scares me," she said, with just the hint of a quaver. "At first he was wonderful. Like a dream lover. He was so considerate. And so gentle and strong."

"Psychopaths are good at that," I said. "But the mirror always breaks."

She looked at me strangely. "Why did you say that? Tommy hates mirrors."

"Purely accidental. Just a figure of speech."

Tony laughed. "My partner here has a way with words. When you can get him to talk."

Rainey laughed in spite of herself. Then she sighed and took a deep breath. Started to fill us in. She had met Tommy Blank at a party at the Playboy mansion. While everyone else was on parade drinking and snorting coke, Tommy had watched quietly from a neutral corner, nursing a pastel drink. Rainey had spent the evening talking to girlfriends and flirting with various actors and producers. Just another meaningless night on the western shore. Then curiosity overcame her. Several of her girlfriends had commented on the handsome man of mystery in the corner. Armed with sufficient liquid courage and a nose full of excellent coke, she had sashayed over to take a closer look.

He'd been quiet and shy and had explained that he really

should not have come to the mansion that night. He was too depressed. A close friend had just succumbed to pancreatic cancer. A hard, terrible death. He was only forty-one. Tears had filled Tommy's deep brown eyes as he spoke about his friend, his dreams and goals, now utterly gone. With his dreamboat features and sensitive brown eyes, complete with livid scar across his otherwise perfect right cheek, Tommy had penetrated Rainey's defenses in short order. And the fact he loved horror films had made it even better. She was a horror actor and Tommy seemed to have watched every horror flick ever made.

And so it began, but it wasn't long before Rainey started having doubts. Tommy had nightmares and would kick and thrash about in bed. That was the first sign. After about six weeks, on a night when she wasn't in the mood, he'd gotten nasty, and she'd gotten mad and suggested that maybe they weren't right for each other. "Maybe you're right, bitch," he'd said before casually backhanding her across the face. That was the second sign. Nonetheless, she'd given him another chance. A mistake. A few weeks later, when they were about to make love after a pleasant evening out on the town, he'd done a Jekyll and Hyde and raped her brutally. Then, casual as can be, he'd driven her home in his black Range Rover. No Dodge van for this bastard. When they got to her house, he'd pulled over and locked the doors. Flipped on the interior lights. Sat there staring at her for a long time. Finally spoke. Told her she was a good lover but not good enough. Said this was curtains for them, but that he'd be back if he was ever in the mood. Then he'd gotten out of the Rover, locking her in. Came around to her side, unlocked the door and pulled her out. Forced her to buzz the gate open and half-dragged her, half-carried her, down the flagstone walkway. Threw her against the door and watched as she crumpled into a heap. Told her he'd be back when she least expected it and that she better not move away. If he had to search for her, it'd be way worse. And if she lodged a complaint, even if he got arrested, he'd make bail and come after her. And when he found her, he'd cut her up into little pieces. For effect, he'd extracted a long, gleaming hunting knife from under his left pant leg. Crouched down in front of her and held the knife against her throat. Drew just a whisper of blood. Stood up, turned, and walked away. Since then, he hadn't been back.

"You were very lucky," said Tony. "But that's what I'm talking about. That's why we've got to arrest this bastard. Do you know where he lives?"

She did. She'd spent several evenings hanging out at his house where he lived with his aunt and kept his coke stash. Said he didn't like to drive around with drugs in the car.

"He's a dead man," said Jamie contemptuously, coming out of a nod. "If he ever comes around here again."

I raised an eyebrow and Tony suppressed a snicker. Rainey wrote the address down and Tony gave her his cell number. Told her to call him if Tommy ever contacted her. She said she would. Then she and Jamie walked us to the door.

"Listen, Jamie," I said, "you gotta get help with your drug problem. Otherwise, you're going to die. You don't want to die. You're way too young. And way too smart. So c'mon, baby, it's time to wise up." We shook hands. Then we were out of there.

Chapter Twenty-Four

Tommy Blank lived in an ordinary pink stucco house in Mar Vista, just east of Venice. It was raining when we arrived. Tommy's black Range Rover was nowhere in sight. Lights were on in the house. We put our heads together. Some folks just need killing but that wasn't an option. Not yet and maybe never. We needed Tommy to lead us to Bobby, but first we had to find him. "Fuck it," said Tony finally. "Let's just knock on the door and see what happens." Before we got out, he handed me an S&W Bodyguard 380 that I tucked into my side suit pocket.

We knocked on the door. Nothing. Knocked some more. Finally, an old, bloodshot eye peeked through the spyhole, and a high, creaky voice asked us what we wanted. "We're FBI," said Tony loudly. "Special Agents Pasqua and Donner. We're here to see Mr. Tommy Blank. This is very important."

"Mr. Blank is not here. I can take a message." She opened the door as much as the chain lock would allow.

"Unfortunately," said Tony, "the information we have is a matter of life and death. I'm sure you don't want to see Mr. Blank killed."

"What in the world are you talking about?" Indignant old thing. "Mr. Blank is a very popular man. Nobody wants to kill him. I should know. I'm his aunt."

Except maybe his ex-girlfriends, I thought. "I'm sorry to have to tell you this." Quiet Crane. Calm voice. "You see, Tommy works for a group of patriotic men, and certain very evil politicians—who are actually socialists and communists—don't like patriots. They'll stop at nothing to destroy your nephew."

"It's actually kind of an honor," said Tony. "To be so important that those evil SOBs want to kill you."

"Are you trying to scare me?" said the woman. Aggrieved.

"Not at all," said Tony, "We're trying to give you the facts. Now please listen to us. Don't make us arrest you for obstruction of justice. There's nothing I hate more than arresting elderly women who refuse to smell the coffee. These socialists are a cancer eating away at the fabric of our nation. We don't like that. I'm sure Tommy feels the same way. Now can we please come in to talk this over? We need to contact your nephew immediately."

"How do I know you're who you say you are?"

Again, we took out our shields. Handed them in to her one at a time. She took her time looking them over before handing them back. It took more cajoling, but she finally opened the door, a sliver at a time. A slight, elderly woman wearing a Mother Hubbard that came right up to her chin. She led us down the hallway and into a stark living room. Flat-screen TV and moose head with antlers above the fireplace. A few knick-knacks here and there. That was it. The woman gestured for us to sit on the beige leather sofa, which looked brand new.

"I'm Kathy," she said brightly, after she had inspected us carefully. We introduced ourselves and I sat back as Tony took the lead. He explained that we had received a report that Tommy was going to attend a Make America Safe Again rally tomorrow night in Racine, Wisconsin, but that the report had been vague, and we had no time to lose because a domestic terrorist organization was making final preparations to kill him. They were going to take him out of the game. No later than Friday, which meant we had seventy-two hours to find him, warn him, and get him to a safe house. Tony intoned these chilling words with great solemnity, his handsome brown eyes flashing.

Then Tony paused and formed a steeple with his big, capable

hands. Waited. Kathy digested this thoughtfully. Frowning all the while, protruding veins popping out of her hands.

She finally spoke. "You look like a nice gentleman," looking straight at Tony, ignoring me, "and I appreciate your concern, but my nephew has given me strict orders to never reveal his whereabouts to anyone. And I don't know how you found my house."

"That was simple," I said. "We talked to one of his movie star girlfriends."

"Well, they should just keep their big traps shut. But since you seem to know a lot about my Tommy, you probably know that his work is top secret, highly classified. Besides, you already know that he's going to the MASA rally."

"I understand, Ms. Kathy," said Tony, "that operational security is paramount in your nephew's line of work. We're very familiar with that concept. But as I said, the report is vague. We can't afford to fly to Racine only to discover he's somewhere else. We'll run out of time. Boom, Tommy's dead." Tony snapped his fingers. "We can't let that happen. So please, do you know if he's actually going to Wisconsin?"

Kathy looked at me and shook her head in apparent disapproval. Then she turned to Tony and nodded. "That's what he told me. He said he's flying out tomorrow. He didn't tell me which airline."

"Bless you," said Tony. "You're a wise woman. We'll meet him at the rally and build a net around him so tight that they'll never get to him." But then Kathy raised new objections. Said that due to the delicate nature of his work, Tommy was very wary of strangers, even police officers. She was very excited about the rallies and thought that maybe she should come along to introduce us to Tommy. I interrupted explaining that we would have Marguerite Ferguson take care of that. This got Kathy fired up.

"Marguerite Ferguson! Tommy says she's a remarkable woman."

"I couldn't agree more." Crane piping up.

"Ms. Kathy," said Tony, "I appreciate your concern. I truly do. But it's best that we go through Marguerite."

Kathy seemed to accept this. Then she surprised us. "Do you realize, Officer Pasqua, that you and Tommy could be brothers? You've got the same jaw and the same eyes. I can never quite decide which movie star Tommy looks like."

"That's easy," I said. "He's part Elvis and part Robert Mitchum."

"You're right." She clapped her hands as if we'd unearthed one of life's hidden mysteries. Then her mood changed. She said it was after her bedtime but that if Tommy called home, she'd tell him that two FBI agents would meet him at the rally to discuss his safety.

"I don't recommend that," said Tony. "He might get gun shy and decide to stay in California, which will make the killers' job that much easier 'cause their headquarters is out here. So please don't say anything. And thank you for your time, Ms. Kathy; we'll be on our way now." We stood up and moved toward the door. Something creepy about this old woman with her laced-up Mother Hubbard. Glad to be getting out of there. But Kathy stopped us when we reached the door."

"Officer Pasqua," addressing him directly, "do you mind if I ask you a question?"

"Not at all."

"What do you think's going to happen?"

"To Tommy?"

"No, to our nation."

"What does Tommy think?" I asked.

"He thinks we're going to be fine."

"Exactly," said Tony. "Your Tommy knows best."

And then…we got the hell out of there.

Chapter Twenty-Five

With no prompting on my part, Tony decided to fly with me back to Wisconsin.

I moved my reservation up and we caught the last Southwest flight out of LAX to Milwaukee. Before boarding, I phoned Todd from the airport. He was excited. "Listen, Nick, this is important. Tommy really trusts me now. He had me book his flight to Milwaukee. Jet Blue out of Long Beach. Flight 1678. Arrives at—what's that fuckin' airport called—General Mitchell Airport in Milwaukee. His flight arrives at half past three tomorrow afternoon."

We were torn about flying back. Very tempting to abduct Mr. Blank before he got on the plane. Sit him down and have a little talk. Punctuated with love taps. But decided against it. We had to get back to Racine to check in with Carrie and Swann and see what his research had turned up. We touched down in Milwaukee at six a.m. Still dark when we fired up Bobby's van and started down Highway 32 toward Racine.

Tony lapsed into gloom. Why not? After years of exceptional detective work and reasonable propriety, he'd fallen...into the pit with all the other dirty cops...I let him stew. Knew he'd talk but only when he was ready. We were no more than twenty miles from Racine when he sat up straight and stared at me, his brown eyes burning. "Fuck, Nick, the truth is that I liked being on a fucking pad. Roberto gave me one-fourth of all his profits,

153

and I looked the other way. I've got a fraction under four hundred thousand sitting in a storage locker in Pahrump, Nevada. College for my kids, guaranteed as long as I didn't get caught. And I didn't. My goal was half a million. Then I was going to quit, and Roberto was going to stop trafficking and move into real estate. That's what we told ourselves. But I never did quit, did I? Instead, I lost a good friend and am left with a bunch of dirty money. That's a hell of a fucking note. So say something, goddamnit, say something."

Thought it over. Had no answer but had to say something. "You guys were taking down a whole lot of serious traffickers, right?"

"We were. We'd gone through nearly everyone Roberto knew. Javier was the last big guy on his list."

"And he got taken down too."

"That's true. But at such a cost."

"There's always a cost. There's always risk and there's always a cost."

Then we both fell silent. But just as we were turning off the highway, Tony spoke. "The thing is, I fuckin' loved it. I loved the adrenaline. Every damned time. Roberto meeting me at some nowhere bar in La Puente and handing me a big bag of money. And same as always, I wasn't skimming confiscated drug money. Which, as you know, was never my style. This was different. I was receiving a share of Roberto's profits. Like I was a fuckin' trafficker."

"In that case," I said, forcing myself not to laugh, "based on all the arrests, you weren't a dirty cop. You were an excellent cop working with a skilled informant. Meanwhile, you were moonlighting as a coke dealer."

"Shut up, Nick, that's crazy."

"No, it's actually very sane. You were playing a dangerous game and your partner got whacked. And it broke your heart. Now that you've retired from the trade, just go back to being a good cop. And stop beating up on yourself. It's unbecoming in a man."

Another long silence. Tony finally spoke. "I hear what you're saying and it sort of makes sense. But logic is a pile of shit. It's how you feel that matters. Can you go back ten or fifteen years ago before you ever had to kill a man? I don't think so."

The deeper place. "I wish I could, Tony. But I can't. Instead, I seem to move from one narrow corner to the next. But all I can do now is move forward. My job is to rescue Bobby. And I appreciate the fact you're here with me. I appreciate the hell out of it." That's where we left it.

Chapter Twenty-Six

Tony and I checked into a two-room suite at the Hilton Doubletree. Just drifting off to sleep when there came a pounding on the door. And a woman's voice…in some kind of anguish. I stumbled to the door in my boxers. Knew it was Carrie North. I let her in, and she collapsed into my arms. I carried her over to the couch and sat her down. She didn't look injured, but her hair was matted, her little gamin face a mask of pain…

We found Swann in ICU in Ascension All Saints Hospital on Spring Street. He was hooked up to an IV with a breathing tube in his mouth. Carrie had already been there once this morning, but he had been unable to speak. It was no different this time. Carrie told me what she knew. In bits and pieces.

Swann, who would have loved to play football or basketball, was small and had no hand-eye coordination to speak of, so he had turned to running. Years ago, and he had never stopped. He ran on tracks, roads, and beaches. And he liked to get out early. This morning he'd gone for a run on the beach just north of the Doubletree. A determined man. The sand wet and hard packed from recent rain. But this morning, he hadn't run far. A couple of hardy septuagenarians had found him blue and terribly battered, lying half in and half out of the freezing water. He would have died within the hour if the old folks hadn't called 9-1-1. The paramedics had found his FBI ID. They called the local office in Milwaukee who had contacted Carrie.

There was nothing we could do for Swann at the moment. I gently steered Carrie out of ICU and over to the hospital cafeteria, Tony hanging back. To this point, Carrie had barely seemed to notice him. I loaded her up with a basic cafeteria breakfast— scrambled eggs, hash browns, toast, and sausage. She said she couldn't eat but I put a fork in her hand and gently steered egg and potatoes to her mouth. Waited and did it again. A third time. Released her hand and she took over, eating mechanically. Tony and I were starving. We dug in. After a while, she put her fork down. Looked us over. "So, are you going to introduce me to your friend?"

"FBI Special Agent Carrie North, this is Detective Tony Bott. LAPD. His captain has very kindly agreed to lend him to us for a while. He's one of Bobby Moore's best friends."

"Pleased to meet you," said Carrie. "I hope you don't need immunity like Nick. I don't think I can swing another one."

"I don't need immunity," said Tony. "We just need to find Bobby."

At that moment Carrie's phone rang. She listened for a moment. "We'll be right there." She clicked off. "Jim's awake."

Back in ICU, Carrie stood at Swann's bedside leaning over him. The tube was out of his mouth, but he couldn't really talk. Not at first. Finally, his chest heaving from the effort, he started to whisper. Then he whispered for a long time. Sitting in chairs against the wall, Tony and I couldn't make out the words. It reminded me of the two weeks I'd spent in a Boston hospital after Marguerite's boot woman had poured lead into my belly. I'd escaped with help from Bobby and Agresti and had been on the run ever since.

After five minutes or so, Carrie leaned over and kissed Swann on his ashen forehead. Nodded to us and headed to the door. We followed her out to the parking lot and got in Bobby's van. "He needs his computer. Wants to keep working."

Thirty minutes later we were back in the ICU. Swann was asleep, a tube back in his mouth. Carrie set the laptop, complete with charging cable, on his bed next to him.

Afterwards, we reconvened in our suite at the Doubletree. It turned out Swann was even greener than I had thought. Although they were pals, when Carrie was in the field, they usually communicated remotely—Swann in his Maple Street office in the Boston suburb of Chelsea across the river from the Logan Airport. With his research crew down the hall within shouting distance.

"I hadn't planned on him coming," said Carrie, "but he was familiar with the case, and it seemed important to him. I didn't want to say no."

I nodded, trying to look sympathetic. Welcome to Marguerite's world. "So, what actually happened on the beach?"

"Jim said that..." She stopped, swallowed, and wiped her eyes impatiently. "Jim got suckered by a woman with a baby who said her husband was going into convulsions. Down in the rocks at the north end of the beach. When he got there, he was jumped by the alleged husband and his friend. They sandwiched him and beat the shit out of him. Cracked three or four ribs and ruptured his spleen. Then they dragged him down to the water and hit him with a stun baton. They probably didn't know that the tide was starting to go back out. Otherwise, Jim would have drowned because he couldn't move at all." Carrie stopped talking, her lips clamped shut in a hard line.

"This is called sending a message," I said flatly. "They made you at one of the rallies, or maybe even during your earlier investigation in Boston. They recced Swann's habits. Bided their time. Watched him leave the hotel this morning in his jogging clothes. He walked right into it. Which might mean I've also been made."

"Maybe, maybe not," said Tony. "Marguerite may think you're giving her a wide berth. But let me ask you a question, SA North. Did you and Mr. Swann go out in public last night?"

Carrie hesitated. "Oh, shit! Actually, we did. We went to a steak house."

"And?"

"And what?"

"Just this," said Tony gently. "Did you notice any questionable characters? Maybe in a booth or at a table?"

"Hmm..." She hesitated. Finally spoke through clenched teeth. "Why'd you have to ask? The truth is, at that moment I was feeling more like the hunter than the hunted. I guess I was cocky. And I like Jim's company. So maybe I let my guard down."

"Swann's a very likeable guy." Helpful Crane.

"Wait a minute," said Carrie. "There were three guys with short hair sitting a few booths away. Big guys wearing parkas."

"That was them," I said. "Those three guys are Marguerite's bodyguards. They were keeping an eye on you and Swann. They probably followed you back to the Doubletree. Marguerite had them recruit the motherfuckers who attacked Swann. May have brought them in from out of town. A one-time assignment. Paid in cash." I paused. Looked at her. "Swann is lucky to be alive."

Carrie didn't reply. Instead, she just sat there, beside herself. After the attack, Swann had gone into severe shock, from exposure as much as from the beating. But he'd recover. Carrie was the one I was worried about.

I sat there, eyes at half-mast, weary beyond measure. Drifting off when Carrie said sharply, "Wake up, Nick. What did you find out in California? I need to know."

Wrenched myself awake. Too tired to pull any punches. First, I told her what I'd learned about Shimanski and Millrose and how I now believed that Bobby was actually buried alive in a goddamned private prison.

"Okay," said Carrie. "I'll get my people on it and have those two brought in for questioning. No later than noon on Friday. Depending on where they are, I may fly out to see them. And, Nick, I want you with me." A hard glint in her eyes. Shock and hurt morphing into rage. Good. "One more thing," she said. "What about Tommy Blank?"

"Yeah. I was just getting there." I told her everything we'd learned—that Mr. Blank raped actresses for kicks and that one of his victims had corroborated that fact. That he lived with his aunt in Mar Vista just east of Venice, at least some of the time. That he was scheduled to attend Marguerite's Racine rally. I left out the fact he was flying into Milwaukee on Southwest flight 1678 at half past three that afternoon. Because Tony and I were going to jack the sonuvabitch. Simple two-man job.

Carrie started thinking out loud. The best protection is protection. She'd borrow agents from the Milwaukee office. Two guys to protect Swann at the hospital. And two to shadow her both before and during the rally. Meanwhile, her people would scour the country until they located Shimanski and Millrose. I phoned Greg, who was just waking up, and had him tell her everything he knew about their habits and possible locations. At this point, it was probably better to have Carrie spook the private prison guys than Marguerite. I had no illusions about what Shimanski and Millrose would say. They'd deny any knowledge of Bobby Moore or lawyer up first and then deny any knowledge. But I couldn't stonewall forever. I had to let Carrie do her job...The way we left it was Tony and I would attend the rally but would steer clear of Carrie and her people. If the opportunity arose, she and her team would bring Tommy Blank in for questioning. In which case, I would join her to put the screws to the enigmatic Mr. Blank.

Carrie checked out of the Doubletree, and we followed her to a nondescript motel on the edge of Racine where we waited with her until her new security team arrived.

Chapter Twenty-Seven

Tony and I drove to General Mitchell Airport in a rented grey Sonata. He waited at the bottom of the escalator near Baggage while I ate the price of a one-way ticket to Cleveland. Went through security and waited at Gate 17 where Southwest flight 1678 was scheduled to disembark. The flight was on time, and I watched Tommy Blank emerge from the tunnel and stroll casually toward the escalators. He was wearing an expensive black leather jacket. No carry-on. Not as tall as I'd expected but handsome with full lips and thick, dark Hollywood hair, jelled on top, razor cut on the sides.

I fell in behind him, strolling just as casually. He stopped at the first men's room; I stopped too. He matched Rainey Morgan's description—brown eyes and the livid, diagonal scar across his otherwise perfect right cheek. As he turned away from the sink, he looked right at me. Hunger. Gave me a jolt. And a softness in the eyes that I hadn't expected. We exited together. He rejoined the throng and I fell back into the crowd.

Two skywalks led directly from Arrivals to the parking lot. The escalator led downstairs to Baggage. Tommy chose the latter. Tony met him at the bottom of the escalator.

"Excuse me, sir. I'm Special Agent Mike Pasqua, and this is my partner," gesturing as I joined them, "Special Agent Wayne Donner. We have some questions for you. First, we are going to walk you to the exit near Baggage. Don't do anything stupid…"

Tommy stared at us, blinking nervously. Not what I'd expected. We marched him past Baggage and out to the street. By the time we reached our rental car in the back of short-term parking, he seemed near collapse. We yanked off his jacket and patted him down. Nada.

I sat next to him in the back seat while Tony stuck a 9 mm in his face. I took his wallet and cuffed him behind his back. With Siri's help, we then drove to a McDonald's just west of the airport. Navigated the drive thru. Two grilled fish sandwiches for Tommy, burgers for Tony and me. Once we had our food, we parked in a deserted corner of the parking lot.

We took turns examining his driver's license. Tomas Blanc Kovačević. "Ah," said Tony warmly. "French mother, Croatian father, right? I love French women, but they just laugh at me. What kind of women do you like?"

"I d-don't like women very much." High, mildly affected voice. My heart sank. Lodged in the pit of my stomach. Todd had apparently been suckered by the duplicitous Mr. Blank. "How am I going to e-eat with these handcuffs on?"

"Most likely," said Tony, "Officer Donner is going to jam your fish sandwich down your throat unless you tell us..."

"...every fucking thing you know," I said. I produced my drop point hunting knife, which I'd left in the car. Unwrapped one of the fish sandwiches and cut it into eight pieces. "Open your mouth." He hesitated, I repeated myself and slid one of the pieces into his mouth with the tip of the blade. He began to chew. "Where's Bobby Moore?"

He shook his head. Swallowed. I bladed in another piece. "While you're thinking, and I want you to take your time, I'm going to eat my delicious cheeseburger." Five minutes later, I repeated the question. "Where's Bobby Moore?"

He shook his head, looking miserable. "I d-don't know. I've never heard of him." I slapped him hard across the face. His nose started bleeding. I felt bad.

"Okay, shithead. We get it. We're not as stupid as we look.

You're Tommy Blank's body double. He's a smart bastard and you're his patsy. Now, if you tell us everything you know, we're going to cut you loose. So spill. Now." A moment's hesitation and I hit him again but this time it was love taps only. Then I uncuffed his hands and handed him a towel, which he used to stanch the flow of blood. We exited the parking lot and Tony drove slowly till we came to a shopping center. We parked near the street.

It took a while, but our captive, who said his name was William, finally started talking. He'd met the real Tommy Blank in a Castro Street joint. When they spotted each other, they did a double take and started laughing. William was shorter and their scars angled in opposite directions. Other than that, they were carbon copies of each other. Even their muscles were similar because they both worked out. "He had a joyous laugh," said William. "I guess that's what did it." After that, they met every few months when Tommy came to San Francisco. He was polite and passionate and would even go to the opera with William. Before long William had fallen in love. One night in bed together, Tommy asked him to serve as his body double when he traveled to various cities. Starry-eyed, William agreed. Tommy paid him handsomely. Money and meth. He'd made trips to Seattle, Portland, Phoenix, and two trips to Tucson. This was his first trip east.

When I asked what Tommy did on these trips, William stonewalled. I waited, asked again, and started to get mad. "Spill, William, I'm warning you."

"I d-don't know. He doesn't tell me anything. Just s-says I have to do it. Or else." His voice broke. Long silence.

I finally spoke. "What do you think he does?"

I felt like a dentist wielding a jackhammer, but William finally said he thought Tommy was a drug trafficker. Tony got pissed. "If you're helping this bastard deal drugs, William, I don't think I like you anymore." William hung his head. "Where," said Tony, "is your morality?" William's head hung lower.

Almost ready to cut him loose. But not quite. I glared at him and slapped him gently. "Shit. At this rate, I'm going to grow calluses on my hand. So spill." Silence. "Okay, then, I'm going to have to pistol-whip you. You leave me no other option. Officer Pasqua, hand me your gun." Tony handed it over and I wound up dramatically. William broke. Said he didn't believe Tommy was a drug dealer. Said he thought he was an alt-right operative who ran a cell somewhere in California and possibly elsewhere. Admitted Tommy was flying into Milwaukee to attend a political rally.

"Why in hell," said Tony, practically spitting out the words, "do you work for an alt-right operative? Have you no conscience whatsoever?"

"Never mind," I said. "Now listen to me, William, and listen good. Here's what you are going to do…"

The way we left it was that from now on, William had a new job. Unpaid CI for SAs Pasqua and Donner. He would check in with me by phone every time Tommy contacted him, and he would tell me everything he knew. Would inform me every time Tommy asked him to fly somewhere. I checked his phone and wrote down his number. Re-checked his driver's license. He lived near Twin Peaks. Wrote down his license number and his address and gave him a burner number. Told him that if he double-crossed us or breathed a word of this to Tommy or anyone else, or if he tried to disappear, we would track him down and kill him. No torture, no chilling anticipation, just a quick and simple hollow-point bullet into his brain. He said his instructions from Tommy were to fly back to San Francisco as soon as Tommy gave him the green light.

"No," I said. "You're flying back right now."

It cost me more money but there was no way around it. I bought us two tickets on the Southwestern 5:15 flight to SFO. Relieved William of his cell phone. Told him we'd mail it back to his Twin Peaks address when we got back to California. Then I went through security with William and got on the plane with him. Warned him not to borrow someone else's cell phone to call Tommy. Warned him a second time. Got off the plane just before takeoff and waited until it lifted off. I'm sure William was relieved to get out of there.

Chapter Twenty-Eight

We drove to the MASA rally in separate cars—Tony in the Sonata, me in a rented Chevy Malibu. We'd outfitted the Sonata with twenty feet of quarter-inch nylon rope, zip ties, handcuffs and leg irons, and towels for mopping up blood. Bobby's Econoline was collecting dust in a public parking lot a few blocks from the Doubletree. The MASA rally was in the Diamond Auditorium in the Memorial Hall at the Racine Civic Center. Marguerite's people had gone all out. Workmen had erected bleachers that increased the seating capacity to around two thousand. Just outside the auditorium, smaller adjacent rooms, one pillared, the other Danish Modern, were set up with recruitment tables. The crowd was similar to those in Waupun and Fond du Lac with one important difference: This time there were plenty of cops. Real ones in uniforms. Apparently, the city bosses were not going to stand for a repeat of the Fond du Lac debacle. Which was probably a good thing. Tony and I sat in back, in the middle of the top row of the bleachers. Carrie and her team were a few rows down and to the left.

Same routine. Same red-blooded American men and their vibrant, red-blooded women. Plenty of bodies to keep us all warm. The same ominous rumble. My people. You can't help where you come from. Wanted to think that in their personal lives, most of these folks were decent enough. The possibility that they were all suffused with evil was just too sickening.

This time a cover band came on first. They played "Brick House" and "Helter-Skelter" followed by "Rain on the Scarecrow." Then it got grim. Warm-up speakers. Too depressing to describe who they were and what they said but it got to me. Waves of emotion alternating with blind fury. Tony felt it too. We both reached out, placing hands of caution on each other's forearms. Funny in a tragic way. Over the years, we'd both seen many things that no one should ever see. And now this. We had no answers and lapsed into our own personal nightmares. Then Tony muttered, "It could be worse, SA Donner. We could be in the FBI."

Hah! Tony. It's good to have friends. In a world full of creeps like Thomas Quincey and Marguerite Ferguson. Quincey looked good that night if you like tall, lean, thin-lipped bastards with blond hair and blue eyes and a knife-cut instead of a mouth. Sleek and treacherous in a single-breasted Burberry suit, spouting banalities about the dangers posed by undocumented immigrants and the need for all Americans to cherish the freedoms granted us by our Constitution. Still going through the motions but with more zip in his delivery. Life with Marguerite was doing him good. I couldn't listen. Felt for my .38, snug against my left side, closed my eyes...

My country, 'tis of thee,
Sweet land of liberty, of thee I sing...

What the fuck? What was Jimmy Sain doing here? Yet there he was, center stage, wearing torn jeans and a Black Sabbath T-shirt...

Land where my fathers died,
Land of the pilgrims' pride,
From every mountainside let freedom ring!

He finished up. Scratched his belly, a born ham. Blew kisses to the crowd and walked off the stage.

Tony sensed something was awry. Gave me a curious look. But then I got it. My old buddy had decided to go undercover. Freestyling but could be useful...My phone rang. Jimmy whispering, "How'd I do, Nick? Pretty good, right? Don't worry, baby. I'm in the process of infiltrating these bastards." Just as quickly, he was gone.

"That was my old friend." I whispered. "Jimmy Sain. Says he's working UC."

"What?" said Tony. "Is that good or bad?"

"It won't hurt."

The house lights dimmed. Dark shapes crisscrossed the stage. Then the lights came back on. A huge white projector screen at the back of the stage. It hit me—the old familiar freeze. Starts in my chest and rises inch by inch till it settles somewhere behind my eyes.

The screen lit up. A '50s-style diner. Oak booths with red Formica tabletops lining one wall, a trio of old-fashioned pay phones in the back. Fluorescent light fixtures and a zinc counter-top with red leather barstools. A huge American flag on the wall behind the bar and a stainless-steel pie case...Slow, dangerous blues filled the hall. The cold in my brain grew colder.

The door to the diner opened and a stocky, broad-shouldered, clean-shaven man in a dark suit limped in. Head shaved, big face, powerful jaw, deep furrows etched into his forehead and cheeks. The ravages of time. I knew. Even before he came into focus. "Fuck," said Tony softly, "I don't believe it."

Bobby Moore sat down on one of the red leather barstools. His gaze flickered across the menu, then he saluted the flag and snapped his fingers, the sharp crack loud in the darkened auditorium. He swiveled around on his barstool and faced the camera, every feature revealed. The deep lines, the brown eyes schooled by pain. His big plain nose above generous lips screwed into a hard line. And the granite jaw like the rock his father had mined in the Alabama quarries.

For a long time, Bobby just sat there staring into nothingness, the thousand-yard stare of any damaged veteran. Finally, he spoke, soft and easy in his light Southern drawl, like we were all friends in a small room. "Howdy, ladies. Y'all are lookin' good tonight." Ran his tongue contemplatively across his upper lip. "Howdy, gents. How y'all doin'? Hope you got your guns locked and loaded. Mine sure are." He paused, swiveled dramatically in a full circle. Continued. "Now listen up, my friends, I got a little story to tell you. So, if you don't mind, I'll get right to it."

Numb, Tony and me.

"You see, my friends, I served this great nation in Vietnam, and I did it with pride. I was a paratrooper and a sergeant. I led my squad out into the bush every godforsaken day, huntin' Charlie with my tunnel rat buddy, Carlucci. Carlucci from Philly. He and I searched those goddamned tunnels, aka Charlie's goddamned living room. I shot Charlie a time or two down there." He paused, remembering. "And one time I blew him away with a hand grenade. Carlucci, he shot three or four. We were a team, Carlucci and me. Then one day Charlie blew my friend's head off with a hand grenade filled with rusty nails. Down there in the dark. I couldn't hardly recognize him when we dragged him out." Bobby's voice cracked and he cleared his throat two or three times. Continued. "By then my tour of duty was nearly up. I was ready to go home, and I got on the plane, but as soon as we touched down in Okinawa, I turned around and came back. I couldn't leave my brothers over there. So I did two more eleven-month tours. On my last tour, I stepped on a pineapple mine. It blew my leg off just below the knee." He paused, bent down, and pulled up his right pant leg. There it was, the same prosthesis I'd seen a thousand times, pink as a baby's ass.

"Yessir, good people, it messed me up big time. The war ended but it didn't end for me. Now, listen closely, my beautiful patriotic friends: I'm going to tell you something that you Do Not Know. I'll bet my good leg that not a single one of you knows the awful truth 'bout how our government sold our POWS down the river in Vietnam, how they betrayed our brave fighting men. So, I'm gonna tell y'all. This is what came down." He paused, cleared his throat, and rubbed his eyes. Then he laughed, an evil sound that filled the auditorium. When he spoke, his drawl gone, replaced by the hard-clipped cadence of a man in the throes of cold, controlled fury.

"Long after me and my G.I. brothers came back to a country we barely recognized and were treated like shit by the hippie scum, we kept bombing the living crap out of all those communist countries—Cambodia and Laos and North Vietnam. The North Vietnamese army moved their supplies along the Ho Chi Minh trail, so naturally we bombed the shit out of it too, bombed it day and night. There was only one problem." Bobby's cadence slowed. When he spoke, his voice was softer, almost dreamy.

"What happened is Charlie took their American POWs, us brave American fighting men, and put us in shithole makeshift prisons right on the trail next to their supply depots. This meant that if we bombed the supply depots, we would be bombing our own soldiers. So, what do you suppose we did about it?"

Long silence. Undertow of menace. Bobby's face hard as granite. Everybody knew what was coming next; everybody knew it wasn't going to be pretty. "What happened next, you beautiful patriotic ladies and gentlemen, was we just kept bombing the supply depots, which meant we were bombing our own soldiers. Y'all know what friendly fire is, doncha? Of course you do. Well, this time the friendly fire was ordered by WHOEVER THE FUCK was running the show. Some asshole general in the Pentagon or some other West Point sonuvabitch."

In a blind fury, Bobby ripped off his suit jacket. Ripped off his white shirt. A man's man, deep, muscular chest covered by a thick thatch of steel-grey hair, not much belly, impressive in a sixty-eight-year-old man with a prosthesis...

I could hardly bear it. Bobby Moore, my closest compadre for the last thirty years, had been turned. Heard Tony swallow. Fighting back tears. I sucked it up. Turned to Tony who muttered, "Fuck these bastards, Nick. Just fuck 'em."

Then Bobby said that after all these years of being stuck with libtard traitors, we finally had a leader who would NEVER betray our fighting men. Bobby is a clever SOB and—his voice rising and falling, pleading and exhorting—he found half-a-dozen different ways to say it, circling around and returning to his main point. Our president would never betray our fighting men. Then Bobby started chanting, soft at first, then louder and louder...

We will not betray!

We will not betray!

We will not betray!

The crowd joined in. Louder and louder till it was deafening. For at least five minutes. I swear I heard the crack of bullets, maybe fired into the air or maybe it was part of the soundtrack. Then the Boss took over. "Tougher Than the Rest." As Springsteen sang, the camera zoomed in on Bobby's face till it dominated the whole screen. Again, all was revealed. The pores of pain. The iron-grey whiskers that seemed to grow even as we watched. The nostrils mineshafts to the underworld. The lines intersecting lines, a map of his life and mine. The camera moved to his chest. Bobby's muscles. We've pumped iron together for the past thirty years. I'm strong and wiry and you don't want to challenge me to a street fight, but Bobby's like some Herculean demi-god.

And then back to his eyes, huge saucers of pain, his pupils jet-black and dilated, and at that moment I realized they'd dosed him with meth or some other powerful stimulant. It was at least ten years since Bobby had last fallen off the wagon, and now, wherever he was, he was back on the dope. Broke my heart but I stayed strong, kept watching. Willed the camera to stay there tracking his eyes, the eyes I knew so well. Time seemed to hang suspended. Ten, twenty, thirty seconds. Then Bobby winked, his right eye, and ran the edge of his right hand across his forehead, left to right. Tony was my witness. For years, anytime we needed to deflect a dicey situation, one of us would fabricate a cock-and-bull story. Then to make sure we were all on the same wavelength, whoever was speaking would wink, always with the right eye, before running his hand across his forehead.

Bobby's wink was strong and bold. He knew the MASA crowd would think he was winking at them. He also knew that if by some miracle I was watching, I would understand. Relief. Didn't know whether to laugh or cry so I laughed out loud, the strong, harsh laugh of a man with work to do.

The camera finally panned away from Bobby's face. He got dressed slowly, smoothing the wrinkles out of his suit with exaggerated care. When he was dressed, he sat down at the counter and stared into the mirror behind the bar. Then the slow, dangerous blues returned. The camera worked backwards—the pie case, the flag, the menu, the fluorescent lights, the red tabletops, the three phone booths. And back to Bobby, only he was no longer there. Bobby was gone.

Chapter Twenty-Nine

Enough surprises for the night? Not quite. Marguerite had one more trick up her sleeve. Tommy Blank. The genuine article, only he said his name was Timothy Nolan. Dead ringer for William but his carriage was different. Strode rather than strolled to center stage. When he spoke, his voice was low and thrilling, exuding the kind of manly confidence that has hoodwinked suckers forever.

His message was simple. Marguerite Ferguson was the strongest and bravest woman he had ever met, but even she could not change the world without a helping hand. She needed soldiers to spread the message and man the barricades. Nothing Tommy said was striking or creative, but his delivery and manly appearance went over big with the crowd. While he was speaking, Tony and I worked our way down the bleacher stairs and headed to the recruitment rooms. Marguerite was almost certainly due up next, and it was just possible that Tommy would hold court at one of the recruitment tables while waiting for her to finish up. I took the pillared room and Tony took the Danish Modern. Just before we split up, he looked at me and said, "I've got an idea. Just in case Mr. Blank wanders in my direction." Followed by a mysterious smile.

My room had two doors and three tables manned by smooth-faced, nicely dressed lads with close-cropped hair and cold, Quincey-like eyes. Two cops talking on their cell phones, one at each door. The safest I'd felt in a while. I wandered over toward a table marked Foot Soldiers. Took out my phone and called Jimmy. "Don't bother me, Nick. I'm hanging out with these fascists backstage. They seem to like me." Jimmy laughed, the same gleeful chortle that used to ring out on the shores of Lake Bernice when he was fixing to fight two or three big, drunken guys.

"Hey, Jimmy, I'm not Nick. Tonight, I'm Special Agent Wayne Donner. So don't blow my fucking cover."

"Ten-four, Special Agent Donner." Jimmy was suddenly strictly business. I wondered how he'd infiltrated Marguerite's crew, but that could wait.

"Did you watch Bobby's talk?"

"You mean the soldier dude? Scary motherfucker."

"Right, but he's playing these bastards."

"What are you talking about?"

"Trust me, Jimmy. Now listen to me. Has the last speaker, that Timothy Nolan guy, come backstage yet?"

"Wait, I thought his name was Tommy. That's what people were calling him backstage."

"Right, that's his real name. Is he still speaking?"

"I think so. But Marguerite just headed toward the stage, so I think he's about done."

"Okay, good. My other partner, Special Agent Pasqua, and I need to talk to him. But we can't go backstage, or we'll be made. So I need you to shadow Tommy. Go wherever he goes. And keep me updated."

"Jesus, Nick, I was going to have some fun tonight."

"You already have. You sang 'My Country 'Tis of Thee.' And you sounded great."

"I have a good baritone voice," said Jimmy. He sighed. "All right, whatever. I'll do what I can."

Time for some light reading. Found a pamphlet called *How to Subdue and Arrest Criminals*. Simple text and plenty of pictures. There are lots of ways to subdue criminals. Each technique was rated. Krav Maga devastation got five stars, tired old Karate three and a half. A well-executed chokehold was a four, a shank under the ribs four and a half…

I sighed. Folded up the booklet and placed it in my inside jacket pocket. Took out some bills and made a donation. One of the smooth-faced guys smiled. My phone rang. Jimmy. Said Tommy Blank had just walked into the Danish Modern room…

…which was set up differently. Stark. Chairs in a half circle facing a low, empty dais. A single recruitment table with a sign reading Steering Committee at the back of the room. Cops at opposite ends of the half circle. Tony and Tommy Blank were sitting close together at the farthest point from the dais. I sat down midway between Tommy and one of the cops. Took out my *How to Subdue* pamphlet and pretended to read. Occasional glances in Tommy's direction. He and Tony in spirited conversation. I stared at the printed page in front of me. A beefcake guy in a muscle tee was demonstrating a chokehold, his victim a skinny kid with spiky hair and a prominent Adam's apple. I stared at the picture…

There was something about the way Tony was leaning into Tommy Blank. After a while, I stood up and wandered back to the recruitment table. Spent the next five minutes thumbing through Steering Committee literature, which seemed to equate authority with Christianity, which makes sense…if you like authoritarian Christians. I stuffed three booklets in my jacket pocket along with my *How to Subdue* pamphlet and dropped a sawbuck in the donation jar. Stood there for a while longer contemplating nothing and turned around slowly just in time to see Tommy and Tony walk out of the room.

Chapter Thirty

I followed them to the parking lot. They drove off in the Sonata and I surveilled them from the Malibu. A series of left turns and they pulled into the parking lot of a two-story bar called The Brickhouse. Waited five minutes and went inside. They were upstairs sitting side by side with a bottle of Jack propped up on the table. Wandered downstairs. Ordered Pellegrino and drank slowly. The next forty-five minutes proceeded at the slow pace of the moon. I finally sent Tony a text reading, *Save me some Jack.* Just after ten, they came downstairs and went into the restroom. Came back out. Left the premises, Tony staggering slightly. When they reached the Sonata, Tony fingered the fob. The car doors clicked open. Then, very slowly, Tony put his arm around Tommy while I stuck a nine in his back. "Don't move, motherfucker." Tommy flinched but didn't try anything stupid.

"You're a very pretty boy," said Tony. "Now put your hands behind your back very slowly so I don't have to knock your teeth out." Tony opened the driver's door and pulled a set of handcuffs from under the seat. I stepped back and trained the gun on Tommy's chest while Tony snapped the cuffs on. I opened the back door and we shoved Tommy inside. Tony got in the driver's seat. I got in back and kept Tommy covered. Through it all he said not a word.

We drove to the Marcus Renaissance Cinema on the eastside of town. For cover, Tony went inside and bought three tickets for the late showing of *A Dog's Way Home*. I waited until he got back in the car and said to Tommy, "Feel like taking in a movie?"

"It's a good one," said Tony. "*A Dog's Way Home*. Heart-warming. Like Bobby Moore's speech."

"I'll pass," said Tommy in his low, rich voice. "I know the way home. Do you?"

"Oh, a bright boy," I said. "Listen, bright boy, here's what we want. We want to know where your team is holding Bobby Moore."

"Ah, so that's what this is about," said Tommy. "Can't help you there. Next question."

"Oh, shit! Here we go. And to think I was in a good mood." I handed Tony my gun and produced my drop point hunting knife. Cut figure eights in the air in front of Tommy's face. Spoke softly. "It's been a while since I've redesigned anyone's face. Especially a face as pretty as yours. But you know what, Tommy?" Thoughtful Crane. "I trust that won't be necessary. Now I want you to listen to me and listen to me closely. Remember those Arabs you had locked up in the silo in the barn at your Weedpatch house? Of course, you remember them. Well, Tommy, we have it on good authority that you run the crew of misfits that was guarding those Arabs. Which means all we have to do is turn you in, and the FBI will charge you with an 18 U.S.C. Section 2332b, conspiring to commit acts of terrorism transcending national boundaries. We also know that your pal Ms. Marguerite Ferguson and a few of your other so-called friends are planning false flag terrorist attacks to be carried out by the Arab nationals that you are smuggling into our country. The purpose of which is to stir up fear of Muslims and other immigrant groups. All part of Marguerite's master plan to turn this great nation into a fascist cesspool. I have to tell you, Tommy-boy, that's not acceptable. Truth is, it's downright un-American."

I paused to let it sink in. Spoke. "So, what do you say?

Where's Bobby?"

Tommy suddenly sat up straight and said in a voice half silk, half iron, "And if I tell you, what then?"

I looked at Tony and he looked at me. Then he spoke to Tommy. "Let's start with what you know and go from there. We are reasonable men. But please, let's see if we can expedite this. I'm dying to get in there to watch *A Dog's Way Home*."

"And I'm dying to piss on your grave," Tommy said evenly.

"Tch tch tch," said Tony, "your arrogance is unbecoming."

"It's definitely a character flaw," I said mildly. "But that's not the main point. Tell me I'm a fuckin' bleeding heart, but the main point is that Tommy's aunt Kathy is old and frail and it's going to break her heart to have her boy do a dime or more in federal prison on the 2332b. But it can all be avoided if Tommy-boy here pulls his head out of his ass and cooperates like a big dog."

Tommy's right cheek twitched but he said nothing. "Speak to us, Tommy," said Tony. "Much as I hate your arrogance, your silence is even worse. And we're wasting time. Which means Wayne here," gesturing toward me, "is going to have to get busy."

Which I did. Stuck the tip of my knife in the general area of Tommy's thyroid gland. Probed. Just slightly. That did the trick. It usually does. Tommy flinched and jerked his head away. I pulled the knife back, switched hands, and hit Tommy—just a simple basic right to the center of his face. The blood began pouring out of his nose. "Oops, think I hit a gusher. I'm rather good at that." I grabbed a towel and began stanching the flow. Not soon enough. The Budget Car rental people were not going to be pleased.

We sat back and waited. The blood flow slowly diminished. "Shit," said Tony finally. "I don't believe we can take our friend in to see *A Dog's Way Home*. Not with him all bloody. So I'm at a loss. What do you propose, Wayne?"

I shrugged. You never know when a man is going to break,

or if he's going to break at all. Frenchy Lefevre once told me the trick during interrogation is to have absolutely no expectations. To empty your mind and give your target space. On the other hand, getting hit hard in the face can take it out of a man. I was content to wait it out. Tony snapped on the radio, but the local classic rock station got on his nerves, and he turned it off. More silence. I drifted back to the sight of Bobby winking and giving us the sign. Life is hard and there are moments when it feels like all is lost, but then something happens that restores your faith. I sighed deeply. Spoke. "Listen, Tommy, have you ever really loved a man? Not just because you want to sleep with him but because he touches your heart, and you love him like the brother you never had. That's how Mr. Pasqua and I feel about Bobby. It's personal. Therefore, I strongly recommend that you help us out. In honor of the friend you never had. You have nothing to lose and everything to gain." But no expectations. I sat back and waited.

Sometime later, Tommy spoke, neither silk nor iron now. Curious. "So who the fuck are you assholes? If you were law enforcement, you'd have read me my rights and taken me in."

"Hmm," said Tony. "Bright boy is trying to think."

"Tommy, my friend, we are concerned private citizens and we are dangerous. That's all you need to know." As I spoke, I tickled Tommy, whose face was averted, with the tip of my blade in the soft area beneath his right cheekbone. "Just thinking out loud now but I have to say, as a lover of fine art and a born traditionalist, I've always been a stickler for artistic symmetry. And since you already have that beautiful scar on your right cheek, I would be remiss not to carve a separate but equal one on your left cheek. What do you think, Mike?"

"I agree. But not here. 'Cause Tommy is liable to start screaming. Let's go somewhere a little more private."

Forty-five minutes later we came to an abandoned quarry about thirty miles southeast of Racine. We pulled off the road and parked under two elms glowing white under the moonlight.

Tony cut the engine. Spoke. "I feel safe here, Wayne, old buddy. What do you think?"

"Safe is not part of my vocabulary. What I do feel, though, is pissed. Very. And as Mike knows all too well, when I get like this, people get hurt." I slapped Tommy, who had neither moved nor spoken since we'd pulled out of the cinema parking lot, hard across the face. This brought another freshet of blood and this time I made no effort to stanch the flow. But still, no expectations. Truth is my mean gene was kicking in and I just felt like hitting him. Tommy started coughing, choking on his own blood.

"Jesus, baby. You are a fuckin' bleeder. Do us a favor and man up." I held the towel up to his mouth. "Spit the blood into the towel. Gently. And take a few deep breaths." It took a while, but the bleeding finally stopped.

"Okay, Tommy, you have a choice. You can tell us what we need to know, or you can play the fool, in which case we're gonna put a bullet in your brain and throw you into the quarry. I don't think anyone ever comes here. If they ever do find you, it will be ruled death by misadventure. But that's not what we want, Tommy. What we want is very simple. We want you to tell us where Bobby is. If you do and if it checks out, we'll give you the option of disappearing. Back into the underworld that vomited you up in the first place. Simple as that. And you'll be spared ten or twenty meaningless years in federal stir." Tommy said nothing. Refused to even look at me.

"It won't work," said Tony quietly. "Bright boy isn't going to tell us shit. He'd rather act tough and abandon his dear auntie to a lonely old age rather than come to the aid of real patriots like you and me and Bobby Moore. So, here's what I think we should do. We don't need to shoot this bastard. Instead, we gag and hogtie this bastard. Dump him in the quarry. Bye-bye, Monsieur Blanc."

"I hate this shit." Shame-faced Crane. "Why is my partner so smart and I'm so stupid? It was this way in the Special Forces and it's still this way. But before I get the rope, I'm going to give you one more chance."

I leaned in closer and told Tommy that I believed he knew exactly where Bobby Moore was being held and that we were giving him one last chance to come clean. We gave him five minutes to consider. No use. Tommy hung tough. Tony hit the trunk release. I sighed heavily and got out of the car. Returned with the nylon rope and a set of heavy-duty leg irons.

Outside in the dirt, Tony and I trussed up bright boy. When we were done, we stood there looking at our victim. Face down with a gag in his mouth and his wrists and feet lashed painfully together behind his back. Tony rolled Tommy over on his side. "Okay, Tommy," he said. "Last chance. You've got five minutes to think it over. Then we dump you in the quarry."

We got back into the car.

"Who are we kidding?" said Tony. "It doesn't do us any good to kill him. We got to crack him."

"Okay, we'll wait ten more minutes, then we'll try again. If that doesn't work, we come up with Plan B."

"Which is?"

"Damned if I know…"

After ten minutes, we got out and hunkered down on the ground next to Tommy. Tony put him in a half-assed headlock, and I pulled his gag out. The wind was kicking up and his lips were blue, his teeth rattling around in his mouth like marbles in the bottom of a coffee can. We picked him up and tossed him in the back seat. I stuffed the gag back in his mouth and Tony rolled the rear windows halfway down. Then we walked over to the edge of the quarry and stood there, sighting down into the abyss.

"You never met Frenchy Lefevre, did you?"

"Frenchy? You mean that crusty old PI that used to rent space at the Fourth Street Law Office building in Santa Monica?"

"That's the fella…"

"Thought so. I've seen him but I never met him."

"So, listen. One night in a wine bar on Rose Avenue in Venice, he and I started discussing strategy. By then I was fifteen years in the business and Frenchy had at least a hundred under his belt. After a while he says…" Not sure why, maybe 'cause we'd decided to spare Tommy, at least temporarily, but I felt cheerful, almost whimsical. "So Frenchy says in his Frenchified English, '*Monsieur Nickee, there are ze times, very rare, when you have to toss out ze rule book and eemprovise.*' '*I already know that,*' I said. '*No, you don't,*' said Frenchy. '*I mean real eemprovization. Not just reverse psychology and ze bullsheet like that. Thees is ze eemprovisation of a whole deeferent order.*'

"Then he gives me some examples, don't remember what they were, but the essence was you take some fool that you've been leaning on really hard to no avail and begin killing him with kindness, till he can't stand it anymore and finally gives in. So maybe that's what we need to do…"

"What?" said Tony. "We're going to take this piece of shit and kill him with kindness?"

"I think so."

Tony shook his head. "I'm freezing my balls off. Let's get back in the car."

My phone rang. Jimmy Sain.

"Goddamnit, Nick, where the fuck are you?"

"Jimmy! Where are you?"

Turned out he had followed us from the civic center to the bar to the cinema outside of town. Lost us after that. There he was in the middle of nowhere full of patriotic fervor with a quarter tank of gas.

The way we left it was we'd all drive back to Racine and meet in The Brickhouse parking lot.

PART FOUR
Chapter Thirty-One

Eighteen hours later. Six p.m., Thursday, May 9. Tony and Jimmy and I were installed in an isolated two-bedroom fisherman's cabin, complete with old-fashioned radiators, a flat-screen TV, and a CD player, on the shore of Lake Winnebago six miles north of Fond du Lac. Jimmy had talked to his Uncle Eugene who had called around and found the place. We paid for a full week in advance. Tommy Blank was gagged and bound in the trunk of the Sonata, which was parked next to Bobby's Econoline.

Jimmy was in Fond du Lac buying food and fishing tackle, necessities for *bon homme* sportsmen on a holiday. And new clothes for Tommy, who would undoubtedly need them.

Although our cabin was at least two hundred yards away from any neighbors, we weren't taking any chances. Tommy would have to wait until well after dark before we took the chance of extricating him from the trunk and dragging him into the cabin.

At eight o'clock we drove the Econoline into nearby Van Dyne to scare up some dinner. Found a bar and restaurant and ordered grilled salmon, battered cod, and barbeque ribs. A couple of six-packs and a bottle of Jack.

Back at the cabin, we opened the trunk of the Sonata. Tommy lay on his side moaning through his gag. The smell was foul. I leaned in, holding my nose. Whispered. "Don't worry, baby, we'll bring you inside in a few hours. So just hang tough." Closed the trunk.

Driving his flat-black Nissan pickup, Jimmy arrived at nine thirty. We put the food in the refrigerator and placed the fishing gear on shelves in the mudroom. Jimmy and Tony cracked beers and the seal on the Jack and sat down to get acquainted. I went into one of the bedrooms and phoned Carrie North. A task I was not relishing.

She picked up on the second ring. Nearly bit my head off. "Crane, where in the fuck are you?"

"Jesus, Special Agent North, how about a 'how are you' before you kick me in the balls?"

"Nuts to that, Crane. How about telling me where you're going next time before you blow the fucking popsicle stand? I thought we were a team, but maybe I was wrong."

The guilt came over me in waves. She was so damned sincere. Took a deep breath and told her that Tony Bott and I had lost it after seeing an obviously turned Bobby Moore in the video at the MASA rally. That we had spent the night drinking and had woken up in the parking lot of some gin mill. Badly hungover. Told her that it's not pleasant for two grown men to watch each other breaking down every five or ten minutes. Then we'd driven to Fond du Lac where my brother Rafer lives with his wife and twin daughters. The walleye and largemouth bass were running, and we'd spent the day driving around looking for good fishing locations. Caught a few walleyes and stopped at plenty of gin mills along the way. Which hadn't really helped. At least we were calmer now. I paused.

"You really expect me to believe that bullshit?"

"I don't care what you believe. I couldn't just abandon Tony. He was in a bad way."

"Look," she said, a bit more calmly, "I don't believe you, but I don't really care. I admit that watching your friend Bobby speak was heart-wrenching. And just in case you're wondering,

I am determined to bust him out. From wherever they're holding him. Indicting Marguerite will have to wait. Here's the deal. My people have located Jethro Shimanski. He's at a fancy resort near Hilton Head, South Carolina, golfing with his son. I've made reservations for you and me to fly into Savannah-Hilton Head Airport tomorrow. Our flight leaves General Mitchell Airport at eleven thirty a.m. We'll fly back to Milwaukee Saturday morning. Meanwhile, my team is scouring the bushes, looking for James Millrose. And just so you know, Jim Swann is rallying."

"Thank god." I meant it. "I like the guy."

"Funny thing, but it's a mutual admiration society. You made quite an impression on him. He keeps asking about you, and I keep telling him that you're an asshole."

Gee, thanks. I told her I was glad that she wanted me with her when she questioned Shimanski. She said she was torn, but that it felt right. Then she yelled at me some more, and I apologized some more. And told her I'd meet her at the airport at ten thirty a.m. And told her to rest easy. That I wouldn't miss it for the world.

Said good night and walked out into the living room. Tony was looking at pictures of Jimmy's metal sculptures on his phone. Brave on Jack and beer, Tony was proclaiming that metal sculptures were still popular in LA, and that Jimmy's agent should come out to Southern California to pitch them to LAPD.

"I hate to interrupt," I said laughing, "but we need to have a war council." Jimmy closed his phone, and we sat down at the kitchen table. Even half-crocked, Tony can read me. "So, what was that all about, Nick? No, wait, before you answer, pour yourself a drink." I needed little urging. Poured myself a shot of Jack. Knocked it back and began sipping a Heineken.

"I hate like hell to put a damper on our little party, but we've got problems."

"Shit," said Tony genially, "I thought this was purely for pleasure. Fishing and drinking in no particular order. Jimmy tells me there are some wild-ass bars just up the road a piece in Oshkosh."

"So I've heard. But listen, it's not a good idea for Tommy Blank to meet Jimmy unless it's absolutely necessary. Jimmy's on parole. He's already taken too many chances singing at Marguerite's rallies. Second, Carrie North is demanding that I fly with her to South Carolina in the morning to lean on one of the private prison honchos who might be holding Bobby."

Tony looked at me. Raised an eyebrow. Then he shook his head. "Nick, you're not thinking clearly. You better have another drink." Then he explained that you never try to kill a prisoner with kindness without *keeping him blindfolded* at least eighty percent of the time. We just needed to make sure that Tommy was swathed in deepest black whenever Jimmy was around. "'Cause look, with you gone, I'd rather not have to babysit Tommy-boy without backup. Not that I couldn't do it, but remember, this bastard is supposed to be lethal, the world's number one badass."

"Well actually, he's number two. Our friend Jimmy here is *numero uno* in that category." I laughed and clapped Jimmy on the shoulder. "But you're right about Mr. Blank's reputation. We need to be careful. And in a little while, we've got to bring him inside." This sobered us up quickly. Tony capped what was left of the Jack, and I dripped a pot of coffee. Then we slowly sipped the dark brew. At eleven thirty we went outside to extricate Tommy Blank.

It was hell getting the bastard cleaned up. Kept him gagged and blindfolded as we literally cut his shirt into strips so that we could take it off without unlocking his handcuffs. Tommy oozed pecs and triceps and the slim hips of an old-fashioned cowboy movie star, but there's still something pathetic about a bound and gagged naked man smelling like his own shit. I turned the water on in the shower and adjusted the knobs. Tony and I dragged Tommy into the shower and sat him down, still blindfolded. Let the water run for a good fifteen minutes.

Toweled him off, dragged him back into the living room, and chained him to one of the radiators. We unlocked his handcuffs and leg irons, and I held a gun to his head while he pulled on a pair of jeans. At one point, he jerked his head around and I came within a hair's breadth of shooting him. Through the head. Which would not have been a good ending. We trussed him back up, and Jimmy heated up a can of Dinty Moore beef stew. Only then did we ungag him. He held out for a long time, muttering curses and generally acting like an infant till he finally gave in and let Tony feed him.

Then I washed the dishes, and we turned in—Jimmy in one bedroom, Tony in the other, yours truly on the couch. Tommy Blank moaned and grumbled in his sleep, but at least he didn't snore. That was a good thing.

Chapter Thirty-Two

Five thirty, Friday afternoon. Carrie and I driving through the South Carolina Lowcountry on our way to Montage Palmetto Bluff, five miles from Hilton Head Island. Strapped. FBI standard-issue 9 mm Glocks and clip-on tactical flashlights. And a Walther P22 strapped to my ankle. Seventy-two degrees. Humidity already off the charts. The sense of being surrounded by endless water and marshland. No longer wearing my rag of a suit. Jeans and my usual denim shirt. We drove up to security in a rented black Range Rover. Carrie flashed her ID. The woman at security looked surprised and made a phone call. Five minutes later, an unctuously polite, middle-aged man wearing khakis and a red, white, and blue windbreaker drove up in a golf cart. Carrie got out of the vehicle and explained our mission. Took a while but he finally grasped the fact we weren't there to arrest anyone. Wearing a frown, he waved us on through.

Jethro Shimanski and his son were lodged in a charming, two-story cottage a stone's throw from the Wilson Lawn and Racquet Club. We knocked on the door and waited. No sign of our target so we wandered around the grounds. Found our way to the general store where I treated Carrie to coffee and a banana walnut muffin. Strangely, the whole resort had a vaguely California feel.

Still no Shimanski. We motored over to the main hotel and wandered around for a while. Drank a Heineken at the rosewood bar and drove back to the tennis cottage. Bingo. Shimanski and son were standing just outside the tennis courts watching two teenage girls bat a gallon of bright orange tennis balls back and forth across the net. Sun lowering in the western sky. They'd apparently been at it for a while, and one of the girls soon dropped her racquet and clasped her bare arms across her chest. The other girl began gathering up the balls. Her companion stirred herself and pitched in to help. Shimanski and son watched until the girls left the court and started walking back toward the hotel. Man and boy then walked to their cottage and disappeared inside. Five minutes later, we knocked on the door.

"Who's there?"

"FBI. We need to talk to Mr. Shimanski," said Carrie.

Silence. I counted to three. "Well then, I guess you better come in." The door swung open, and we walked inside. He was a big guy. As advertised. Big gut, big thighs, big chest, big shoulders. Big rectangular face, thick lips, close-set pale blue eyes and the short, carefully tonsured hair that politicians and business types favor these days. And two or three days of dirty white scruff. After we introduced ourselves, Jethro told his son Benjamin that we needed privacy.

The boy, who was a younger, thinner version of his father, looked at us. "Why?"

"Why do you think? Use your head. 'Cause we need to talk privately."

"I thought we were going to go to the movies over on the island."

"We are. Later on."

"Screw that," said the kid under his breath. But he shrugged his shoulders and bounced up the stairs to the second floor.

"Spoiled rotten," said Jethro. "We've got a DVD player right here in the cottage. I blame it on his mother but I'm not much better. The little bastard drives me crazy. But that's my problem. So, what can I do for you?"

"Here's the deal," said Carrie almost gently. "We're looking for a man named Bobby Moore. According to our sources, he's being held in one of your prisons…"

"But before we get started on that," I said smiling, "my boss here is too polite to ask, but we're both curious about your industry. Private prisons have been in the news a lot lately. I'm starting to think that maybe I should invest some of my own money."

"You could do a lot worse," said Jethro, fingering his scruff. "Private prisons are one of the fastest growing industries in the whole country…Like most businesses, the job has its good points and bad points. The state people aren't too bad, but the feds are ruthless. They're never satisfied, always want a better deal. My specialty is cost-cutting while still providing the excellent accommodations we're so proud of here at Detentions, Inc. The trick is to find ways to cut fat while never cutting out anything essential." His thick lips curved into a greedy smile. Then he sighed. "Who did you say you're looking for? Bobby something…What is he, a snitch? That's usually why the FBI asks to interview one of our prisoners."

"His name is Bobby Moore," said Carrie. "Robert Joe Moore, to be exact."

"Bobby Moore, Bobby Moore…" He paused, scratched his head. "Just so you understand, as CFO of our corporation, I have little or nothing to do with who gets to enjoy our hospitality. But I'm more than willing to help. Though I can't help wondering why you came all the way down here to talk to me when all you had to do was check the Detentions, Inc. website."

"We did. But nothing came up. Maybe because he hasn't been sentenced yet."

"That shouldn't make a difference." Jethro nodded slowly. "He should be in the system."

"That's interesting," said Carrie, smiling as she spoke. "My people have done a thorough search. Nothing comes up. We've also talked to several of your commanders at several of your facilities. Nothing. Bobby Moore doesn't seem to be in your system. Yet according to a tip from a very highly placed source, he's there all right. Most likely in the SHU somewhere."

"Staring at the toilet bowl," I said brightly. Dumbass Crane.

Jethro nodded glumly. "Well, if you'll give me a minute to fire up my computer, Agent North, I'll check our master database. In the meantime, anybody want a beer? My son and I played eighteen holes today and I'm beyond parched."

"Trials and tribulations of the ruling class," I said. "And I would like a beer."

"Now look here, buddy, that wasn't nice. I worked my tail off to get where I'm at today. It just so happens that I grew up poor with hardly a shirt on my back. Probably more than you can say." He stood up, slow and ponderous. "What about you, Agent North? Want a beer?" She did. Jethro stood up, hitched up his golf shorts and ambled into the kitchen. He took a while. Sound of water running. Drawers opening and closing. Then the refrigerator door. Carrie and I exchanged glances. He finally returned carrying a six-pack of Dead Arm American Pale Ale and a single glass. "Help yourself." Back to the kitchen. Returned with two more glasses. Sat down. Seemed to be in no hurry to check the database. We watched as he poured the clear pale ale into his glass and took a long pull. Made me thirsty. I reached for a beer but didn't open it.

"Just in case you're interested," said Jethro, "they have some great little craft breweries in this state. Nothing I like better than coming here with my boy, playing some golf, and drinking some ale without the wife around to bust my chops."

Several more long pulls, and his glass was empty. He filled it back up. I waited for the click. It came quickly. He sprang to his feet. "Alrighty then. That hits the spot. I'll just go upstairs now and get my computer. And if you don't mind, I have to make a couple of phone calls. Won't take but a minute."

"Take your time," said Carrie.

"Thank you, ma'am." Moving quickly now despite his bulk, he mounted the stairs.

Carrie waited. Whispered, "Do you think he's armed?"

I shrugged. "If he's not, he will be when he comes back downstairs. But I don't think he'll try to shoot us with his boy in the house. I guess we'll find out."

Jethro took his own sweet time. Outside, darkness fell, and the room dimmed. I got up and quickly recced the downstairs. Basic. Well-appointed kitchen and a game room in back. Bathroom off the hallway.

Ten minutes later, Jethro finally came galloping down the stairs, his son trailing behind him. Jethro put his laptop on the table and took out his wallet. Counted out two Jacksons.

Handed them to the boy who grabbed them and stuffed them in his side pocket. Then he was out the door.

"Would you mind turning the lights on?" I said. "It gets dark quickly down here in the tropics."

Jethro didn't mind. Then he sat back and poured himself a third glass of ale. More lip smacking. "So, what's this all about, anyway? And who's this Bobby Moore fella you're looking for? With a name like that, he could be a Southern boy like me, or he could be black." He paused. Drained his glass. Crumpled the empty beer can in his left hand. Put it down and stared at his handiwork. Looked at us. "I always liked doing that. Crushing beer cans. Ever since I turned fourteen and started drinking Regal Select with my pals." He caught himself. "Sorry, Agent North. But you know how that goes. Or maybe you don't…Well. Lemme just take care of this now." He turned on his laptop, connected to Wi-Fi, and started searching. Two or three minutes later, he smiled, ran a blunt hand across his forehead, and poured himself some beer from a fresh can. "Could be a match, my friends. We got two Robert Moores, one Bob Moore, and one Bobby Moore. How old is your fella?"

"He turned sixty-eight recently, April 20 of last year."

Jethro swallowed some beer and stared at his screen. Sighed. "Guess we're shit out of luck then. These guys are all a lot younger."

"Win some, lose some," said Carrie. "By the way, I forgot to mention that the Bobby Moore we're looking for is a highly decorated Vietnam veteran. I have a lot of respect for our fighting men and women. We heard you did twenty years of military service yourself before you went into the private prison business."

Jethro stared at her. Drank. Could feel him thinking. "Now wait a cotton-pickin' minute, ma'am. I thought you were looking for Bobby Moore, but it sounds like you've been investigating me. I'm not sure I like that." He popped the top on a third Dead Arm. Poured but did not drink. "But I guess you don't care what I like, do you?" Squinting at Carrie.

"That depends," said Carrie. "The bottom line is we have got to find Bobby Moore. Maybe if I put it in context, it will help jog your memory. According to my sources, you met Marguerite Ferguson in Washington, D.C. in 2013. You're a private prison executive and she's a large-scale private prison investor. It sounds like a match made in heaven..."

"What in the hell? What does Marguerite Ferguson have to do with this? Maybe you could just talk plain English and tell me what the hell's going on. That way I can decide if maybe I need to call my lawyer." Flushed now, he chugged more beer.

"Why would you need to do that?" said Carrie. "Our standard operating procedure mandates that we do background checks before every formal interview. Unless it's an extreme emergency."

"We know everything about you," I said cheerfully. "Things you probably don't even remember. But by all means, call your lawyer if it makes you feel better. That is your right. Here in our democracy..."

"Look," said Carrie, "you are NOT a target in our investigation. The fact is, we need your help."

"You know what I think?" Confessional Crane. "I bet you're like I am. I bet you're scared of Marguerite. That woman strikes fear in my heart."

Jethro pondered. Chewed his thick lower lip and drank some

beer. "That's bullshit. I'm not afraid of that woman. Why should I be?" Still flushed but relaxing a bit now, spittle forming at the corners of his mouth.

"Mr. Shimanski," said Carrie, "based on our research, we know that you're a fine patriotic American. But the truth is, we're not so sure about Marguerite. If you're interested, I'll tell you why...And if you don't mind, I think I would like a beer." I slung one over to her and she popped the top. Poured.

Then we all drank. I smacked my lips while Carrie merely complimented the ale. The front door opened. Benjamin stuck his head inside and said he was going to walk down to the main lodge. Gone again.

"The thing is," said Carrie, "we believe that Ms. Marguerite is trying to..." She paused. Looked at me. "What's that term that you PIs like to use that describes when one person is trying to falsely implicate another person?"

I smiled. "It's when you try to put someone 'in a cross.' Another way of saying 'nail him to the cross.'"

"What in hell? That friggin' woman? I never did quite trust the..." Caught himself. Paused.

"Here's the skinny," said Carrie. "Bobby Moore is sixty-eight years old. He's a big man like you, Mr. Shimanski. In Vietnam he was a sergeant and a paratrooper. He always took care of his men first. Always. He lost his leg in the jungle, then came home only to be scorned and abused by the anti-war crowd. But he stayed strong and went on with his life. For forty-six long years. Two weeks ago, he was kidnapped right out of his own office in Los Angeles. Based on our sources, we believe Ms. Ferguson and a few of her business associates organized the kidnapping. Obviously, this is a very serious matter. Now listen carefully and I don't want you to overreact, but now I'm going to tell you how Marguerite has tried to 'put you in a cross.'"

Jethro stared at us, sweat beading up on his forehead.

"We procured a tape recording of Ms. Ferguson talking with a gentleman you may know named Thomas Quincey. Also known as Miles Amsterdam. He's a blueblood just like she is. Neither of them grew up in a potato patch, Mr. Shimanski. You can be sure of that. Furthermore..." She paused and looked calmly at Jethro who was fumbling with his glass. Then, to our surprise, he suddenly crashed a big blunt fist down on the table and pushed his glass away.

"All right, goddamnit! I'm not going to waste any more of your time or mine. I'm going to tell you what I know and be done with it. But first I got to take a leak. And I got to make another phone call." He stood up and headed for the stairs, ignoring the restroom in the hall.

I sat back and sipped my pale ale slowly while Carrie fiddled with her phone. Five minutes later, Jethro rumbled down the stairs. He sat down and stared at us in the manner of drunkards from time immemorial.

"Sometime in early April," said Jethro, "Marguerite phoned me with a proposition. For some time, she'd been talking about investing some very serious money in Detentions, Inc., upwards of half a billion dollars. Not chump change. Not hardly. So, she calls me and says she's ready to pull the trigger. There was just one little thing. She needed a favor. She needed me to bury a prisoner in one of our facilities. Off the record and off the books. She didn't even tell me what his name was. She said it would be for only a few weeks. They'd take care of everything. I wouldn't have to lift a finger. You know what I told her?"

"I've got a pretty good idea," I said cheerfully.

"Exactly," said Jethro. "I told her no friggin' way. I haven't worked this hard to throw it all away on some off-the-wall bullshit." Jethro took a deep breath and reached for his glass. No longer flushed. Now he was pale. Had the feeling he just might be telling the truth. Or maybe not. Carrie and I exchanged glances.

"She got hot. Real hot. She told me I could take her half billion dollars and shove it up my keister." He winced. "Excuse my French. That didn't sit well with me. No sirree..." He stopped.

195

"So, what happened next?" I said slowly.

"What happened next is I told her my father did twenty years in prison for a crime he may or may not have committed, and I was damned if I was going to take any chances of following in his footsteps. And then I told her to talk to James Millrose."

"You know James Millrose?" Carrie beat me to the punch.

"Of course, I know him. We all know each other in this business. That doesn't mean I have to like him."

"So did Marguerite contact him?"

"I think that would've been Thomas Quincey's job. I believe they got to know each other when Quincey was doing time in Millrose's Boron, California facility just a few months ago."

I spoke up. "So, did Quincey contact Millrose? After you told Marguerite to take a hike?"

Jethro stared at me. "Could you repeat that?"

"I mean did Quincey contact Millrose after you told Marguerite to take her scheme down the road?"

"That's what I thought you meant. I think he probably did. They would have to put this fella somewhere. And it's easier to hide someone in a private prison than in a regular one. But I don't know what actually happened. I can tell you this, though. If Quincey did contact Millrose, I can pretty much guarantee you that he would have said yes."

"Why?"

"Because he likes to kiss ass."

"I see," said Carrie. "I appreciate your candor. And I think we're pretty much done here. I just have two more questions. First, do you believe the fellow Marguerite was talking about when she phoned you is Bobby Moore? And second, how do we get in touch with Millrose? He's a hard man to find."

"That's a good question," said Jethro. "It could have been Bobby Moore. But then again it could have been somebody else..." He paused. Drained his glass. "As far as getting in touch with Millrose, the best bet is to go through his secretary, Giovanna Tesla. Let me give you her number."

Jethro held the door open for us on our way out. I knew he couldn't wait to get rid of us. I didn't blame him.

Chapter Thirty-Three

Although I wanted to drive, Carrie insisted on piloting the black Range Rover back to the airport in Savannah. The moon had not yet risen over the tree line, and it was very dark. "The deer come out around this time," said Carrie. "We lived in the country till I was twelve. They'd come right into our yard." I was liking her more and more. Woman had feelings. Set my GPS for Highway 46, the road to Pritchardville, the first leg on the way back to Savannah.

"So what do you think?" said Carrie. "About what Jethro said about Marguerite and Millrose?"

"I think he's a sly sonuvabitch. You saw how he claimed Marguerite never mentioned Bobby by name, thus protecting her from any kidnapping charges."

"The bastard," said Carrie. "It was obviously Bobby…You know who else I need positive identification on?"

"Who's that?"

"The last speaker at the Racine rally before Marguerite went on. The guy who said his name was Timothy Nolan. Was he actually Tommy Blank? I have the feeling he was. And then afterwards when we were scouting around, he was nowhere to be seen." She continued, "And where did you guys go? We saw you and your friend Tony leaving the auditorium while Nolan was still speaking."

"Restroom," I said, perhaps too quickly. "We came back

and sat down below while Marguerite was speaking. For as long as we could stand it. Then we bailed."

"There weren't any seats down below."

"There were a few."

"I don't think I believe you. You know what I think?"

"What's that?"

"I think you're feeding me a line. And I don't believe that ridiculous story about catching walleyes with your brother Rafer."

"Whatever." I decided to change the subject. "On a happier note, Agent North, I think you did a helluva fine job interrogating our friend Jethro. But please don't confuse me with the enemy. We're on the same side. You and me and the FBI. But you've got to give me some rope. You take care of finding Millrose, and I'll get my bearings back in Fond du Lac. Then we'll touch base on Monday morning. Wherever you like. Racine, Milwaukee, Boston, you choose."

"You're nuts, Mr. Crane. Monday is the thirteenth of May. You've got to turn yourself in on the twenty-second. Unless we get to Bobby first. It makes no sense that with so little time, you'd just waltz off to go fishing."

I threw up my hands. We were still so far from Bobby and here I was arguing with this impossible woman. And then it happened. A big hulking man in orange camo stepped in front of us, eyes coyote-red in the headlights. Carrie swerved to the left and the hulk dove the other way just as a late-model, three-quarter-ton F-150 came around a curve bearing down on us. Carrie cut the wheel hard right, and we sailed off the shoulder and down an embankment. Our English tank rolled over two or three times on the way down, erasing a thicket of box elder trees like they were little wooden soldiers. The powerful frame held fast, and the airbags deployed. The squeal of brakes up on the road. Waiting. Nothing. No sound. No crash.

The trees slowed us down just enough to keep us from rolling off a ten-foot drop into the river that ran parallel to the road. I think I blacked out. For maybe ten seconds. Woke up choking and coughing. Carrie was moaning. The driver's side of the vehicle was facing straight up. The passenger side was embedded in the underbrush. I grabbed the dashboard with one hand to steady myself, reached up and flipped on the interior lights. "C'mon, Carrie! Unlock the doors. While we still have juice. In case this thing blows." She'd been slumped forward; now she sat up very slowly and turned toward me, her forehead bleeding.

"Wha...What happened? My head..." She reached up, felt her wound, and came away with bloody fingers. "Oh my god, Nick, I'm bleeding."

Her voice rose and I reached out, grabbed her shoulder. "You'll be all right. You just got hit by the airbag. We've got to get out fast. We've been set up. They'll be down here in no time. I need you to unlock the doors. We'll jump out the sliding door in back." I undid my seatbelt and climbed over the back seat, fighting gravity to keep from falling. Grabbed the handgrip above the door. Carrie finally found the switch, and I slid the door open. Flipped on my flashlight and stared at the cold black water, an ebony sheen in the near distance. Then through sheer force of will, I managed to maneuver half-comatose Carrie into the back seat. Worked my legs over the door sill and jumped. Rank smell of weeds and sap and raw gasoline. Landed in a crouch. Pitched forward. Caught myself. Two steps from the cliff.

Her turn to jump. She hit hard, and we fell down together. I tried to stand her back up, but she kept crumpling. Finally, I picked her up and carried her away from the vehicle, upriver or down, I couldn't tell.

Then the sound. Heavy boots thrashing through underbrush. Muted Southern voices. Barking. My blood froze. Dogs. Trackers. I yanked my Glock out of its holster. Roused by the barking, Carrie crawled to the edge of the cliff and disappeared. I waited to hear her hit the water. Nothing.

By now, a sliver of yellow moon had cleared the tree line at the top of the embankment. Flashlight in my left hand, gun in right. Dead brown grass and crushed ferns. Beyond the vehicle to my left, a clearing. Beyond it an ocean of trees...

"Gittem, boy!" Southern voice relaxed, slow and cruel in the cold clear air. The American Staffordshire Terrier was a heat-seeking missile. Didn't want to shoot it. Never hurt a dog before. Waited. Closer. Phenomenal acceleration. $F=MA$. "C'mon, boy! Come the fuck on!" Three yards away the dog leapt toward me in a muscular arc as I dove to safety behind the Rover. Dog's momentum carried it right over the edge of the bank. This time there was a crash, or rather a tremendous splash, followed by frantic barking. Then nothing. On my hands and knees, I looked over the edge of the cliff. A brown mass was being carried downriver. By now smoke was billowing out of the vehicle's engine compartment, then pops and hisses and tongues of flame shooting up into the air.

Crouching low, I darted back toward where Carrie had been before she disappeared. Shocked by their dog's fate and the car fire, the booted Lowcountry gentlemen had halted, seventy or eighty feet away. "Nick, I'm over here." Carrie, a slim, lithe package on a narrow ledge, holding onto a shrub angling out of the bank.

A wave of relief washed over me. At that instant, the Rover exploded in a fireball that lit up the sky. I flattened and covered my face and hair. The heat and light were intense. After thirty seconds or so, I looked around cautiously. Car parts hither and yon. No sign of the booted gentlemen. Figured they were flattened too, waiting till the fire died down. I crawled over to Carrie. Gave her my hand and pulled her up off her ledge. "This way," she said, pointing upriver from where the pit bull had executed its ballsy swan dive into the river. "There's a house a couple hundred yards back down the road. I'm going to call the local FBI office in Hilton Head. They'll need a landmark to find us. We can wait there..."

Woman had spunk. Had to give her that. More explosions

only this time they were pistol shots kicking up divots all around us. I pulled Carrie down behind a scrubby bush, set my flashlight on low power, and pointed it toward where I thought the men were. Could make out dark forms, about six feet apart, crawling slowly toward us. More shots and I had the horrible thought that they were playing with us, trying to force us over the cliff into the river. I motioned upriver toward what looked like woods. Told Carrie to keep low and head for the trees. I'd cover her. Then every twenty yards or so, we'd trade positions.

She stared at me, her eyes bright and fierce in the half-light. Nodded her head. "Okay, Nick. Let's do it." I began to spray bullets toward the boots, and she darted away across the open terrain close to the cliff. Then I burrowed behind the bush, drew a bead on the boots, aimed carefully, and fired three shots at three-second intervals. Give the bastards something to think about. Counting my bullets. Nine down, six to go. Prepared a new clip. By now the fire was dying down and the moonlight was illuminating the slope. Half sand and half earth, a hardscrabble beach extended from the edge of the cliff to the base of the embankment.

Shots from my left, Carrie covering me at two-second intervals. I stayed low and reached her in three or four seconds, enemy bullets whining past me. She had found a depression in the earth that shielded most of her modest form. I was partly exposed and tried to make myself small next to her. She was a lefty. I reached out and squeezed her right hand. "Good work. We're gonna make it. Go time." I sprayed my last six bullets at two-second intervals while she raced to a new resting place. Changed clips. Her turn. While Carrie fired, I raced across a field of smooth white stones the size of sand dollars. The boots were silent. But I knew it wasn't over. No reason to think there weren't many more where those two bastards came from. When I reached Carrie, I played my flashlight across the terrain. The men were walking rapidly back toward the embankment. Clear view. I took careful aim. One boot went down and then the other.

Thought I might have hit one of them. Stay down, boys. Lucky you scumbags are even alive.

Then we ran together in fits and starts across the stones and into a forest of flowering saw palmetto. Single file on a narrow trail through a marshy area leading into close-packed, low-lying Chinese tallow trees draped with Spanish moss. We collapsed trying to catch our breath. "Shush." Carrie held a finger up to her lips. Voices, the hirelings—distant now. "Don't move," I said. "Let's see if they tip their hand." They did. First, a powerful searchlight swept across the tree line, the trees dissolving into vibrant yellows and greens, radiant blood oranges and eerie purples. We hunkered down trying to disappear into the cold damp earth as the light swept back and forth like an unmoored sun.

We allowed ourselves the luxury of watching the light recede as the boots started up the embankment. Of one mind, Carrie and I moved deeper into the trees. When we thought we were sufficiently invisible, we turned our flashlights on, got our bearings, and began threading our way up toward the road.

The Chinese tallow gave way to another palmetto grove. Carrie's feet seemed to glide above the forest floor. We passed maple and sweetgum, dogwood and magnolia...Then we were climbing. Came to a stand of majestic red oak. Carrie stopped. Sighted. A parcel of deer stared back: a buck, a doe, and two younglings, their eyes dark orbs in the silvered moonlight. The buck snorted and shook its antlered head. We watched them dissolve into the trees. Carrie sighed. "They are so beautiful."

She produced her phone and called FBI headquarters in Hilton Head. Identified herself and told the operator to send two rescue teams ASAP to the house on Old Palmetto Bluff Road just east of the May River. She said that when they arrived, we'd walk out of the woods and meet them. Said it was a matter of utmost urgency and that they should bring serious firepower. Thanked the operator. Signed off and put her phone on vibrate only. "Okay," she said. "They'll need fifteen or twenty minutes. This is a good spot. Let's wait here for ten minutes. Then we'll work our way up to the road."

Chapter Thirty-Four

The ten minutes felt like forever. Squatting to stay invisible. Breathing. Listening. Vagrant night breezes rustling the leaves and underbrush. Atavistic fear of wild hogs. Carrie's phone vibrated. They were ten minutes away. Three minutes later we started up through the oaks. Then it happened. The sibilant zip of a semi-automatic rifle. Half-a-dozen slugs plowing the earth in front of us. I pulled Carrie to the ground just as the second wave of bullets buzzed over our heads. We rolled in opposite directions. Our Glocks held fifteen-round clips, decent firepower in a sane world but no match for theirs. We held our fire as scores if not hundreds of rounds violated earth and sky. Then Carrie on the phone. Breathless. Told me we would loop around behind them and arrest them. I told her she was crazy, we had to get up to the road, but she just laughed and said we'd touch base once we were behind them.

So wrong. I'm all for preemptive tactics but only in the right situation. As we moved farther up the hill, two teams of sanctioned FBI badasses were racing to save us. Why risk trying to arrest a heavily armed posse of Lowcountry fellas who were given deer rifles before they learned to wipe their own asses? Way too much uncertainty. I was worried enough about dealing with the FBI. For all we knew, the shooters were their friends.

Few things focus the mind like getting shot at. Problem was the terrain was rough, and the fickle moon had retreated behind the clouds. Suddenly dog-tired, I forced myself to keep moving. One foot in front of the other. Repeat. Again. Tracing a crescent moon through the trees.

My path eased downward through dogwood and magnolia. Feline eyes in the underbrush. I took a deep breath as the trail began to ascend. Again, the red oaks and a clearing to my left. My phone buzzed. "Where are you?" said Carrie.

"Here."

"Where's here?"

"I don't know. Here in these oak trees. There's a clearing on my left."

"I see it too. I'm on the opposite side. I think we've flanked them."

"Maybe. Can you see the house?"

"Not yet. But I'm sure we're getting close."

I told her to forgo any arrests. Said it was too dangerous, and we should just ease our way up to the road. She knew I was right but getting shot at several hundred times was stuck in her craw. I found myself pleading with her.

Then it happened again. A cruel and casual Southern voice. A barrel violated the sanctity of the clearing followed by orange camo—not the big hulking guy up on the road, someone else, short and stocky, wearing a helmet. He nosed into the clearing, sensed Carrie's presence, and headed straight toward her. No more than ten feet away, she shot him twice point blank in the chest. He cursed, stayed upright, and kept walking. I fired low and took his legs out from under him. The half scream, half grunt of the porcine. As he fell—no more than six feet from Carrie, who was kneeling in the underbrush—he fired wildly, and she screamed. No time to think. A mad dash across the clearing. Vaulted onto his back, clubbing him hard in the back of his neck with the butt of my pistol. He fell and our weapons went flying. I grabbed his gun, ejected the magazine, and began clubbing him across the chest and face. Bulletproof vest. As I thought. When he finally lay still, I heaved the rifle into the underbrush and turned to Carrie.

"I'm gonna gut you, mutha." His voice high and shrill, a hawk-faced, shirtless man wielding a pig sticker darted into the clearing and charged me. For a split-second, I was paralyzed. Then I dove low, taking his legs out from under him. He hit the ground, turned a perfect somersault, and came up standing, knife in hand. "That was sweet," said Pigman. "But it's gonna cost you both your eyes." He circled, carving dark shapes with his blade in the half-light of the clearing.

I should have shot him then and there with my P22, but I reached for my drop point instead. Dumb. Pigman was a pro. I'm okay with a blade but no Pigman. To hate is to die a small death every time the feeling blossoms. And I hated this motherfucker. Wanted to take him out on his own terms. But knew I had to be careful. I backed away and circled, first left, then right, while he dodged and feinted. Three kill thrusts. Each time I made myself small and narrow. The first thrust ripped the left sleeve of my windbreaker. The second passed between my side and right arm. The third time I was too slow but angled my upper body backwards just in time. He drew blood, a minor puncture wound, the tip of his pigsticker probing the soft area where my collarbones meet.

Winded, Pigman backed off, surveying me carefully. "Fun," he said. "Fun with a purpose."

This pissed me off. My partner was wounded, and I was bleeding. I came to my senses. Raced to the back of the clearing toward the river, Pigman following, wary now. I ducked back into the trees, pitched to my left, and blitzed back into the clearing, P22 in hand. Pigman's turn to retreat.

By now Carrie had crawled into the clearing, leaving a trail of blood. We fired in unison. Pigman's head exploded (had to be Carrie's Glock with the big burst). Beside myself with fury, I walked over and unloaded. Stopped after three or four shots. Pigman was now pig food.

Carrie was hurt, bleeding steadily from her right arm, and I was dripping blood from my throat. I picked up my Glock and pulled Carrie back into the oaks. Orange Camo's bullet had passed through and through her right bicep. I ripped off my windbreaker and used it as a tourniquet just below her shoulder. Put pressure on my own wound, which was not serious. She was going in and out of shock. She gave me her phone, and I phoned the agent who had called her. Told him Carrie was hit and we needed a medic. And that we were hiding in the underbrush not far from the road near a small clearing between two stands of red oak. "I've got a tracker," said the agent. "He knows this country like the head of his dick. Here, I'll put him on."

I gave the tracker the same information. He chuckled. "I got you covered, ol' son. Hang on and we'll be there faster than green grass through a goose." I signed off. Carrie was ashen, her teeth chattering. I wrapped her up in my arms and told her to hang on.

Fifteen long, wrenching minutes before they found us—two agents, a medic, and a team of riflemen, all wearing standard FBI camo gear and carrying M4 carbines and Remington 870s. "Jesus," said the lead agent, waving his M4 casually, "I'm SA Lew Archer. Where'd those motherfuckers come from?" pointing at Orange Camo, who was lying still as death, and Pigman, who didn't have a brain left.

"They just appeared. They came from the same direction you came from. They're with this fuckin' domestic terrorist group that's trying to kill us."

"How many are there?"

"Dunno. Quite a few. They forced us off the road. At first there were just two down by the cliff above the river. But then the rest arrived. They must have fired off at least two hundred rounds. They're around here somewhere." SA Archer took it in, nodding slowly, while their medic bent over Carrie.

It started with a single shot from down near the Chinese tallow grove. To this day, I wonder how they got all the way down there. They must have flanked us, thinking we'd retreated back toward the river. The battle was on—Alphabet Boys versus the DTs (domestic terrorists). The FBI seemed to have the numbers, but the DTs were determined motherfuckers. An FBI sniper team, wearing vests and firing Remington 700s, set up a perimeter around us. I felt strangely safe and warm huddled down next to the medic and my wounded partner with her chattering teeth there on the forest floor surrounded by these expert marksmen peering through their night goggles. The medic bandaged up Carrie's arm and gave her a shot. Then he popped a piece of sticking plaster over my throat wound. I never purposely do drugs, my alcohol intake is bad enough, but right at that moment, I wanted my own shot like what they'd given me for a solid week in the Boston hospital after Marguerite's boot woman damn near killed me.

I felt guilty 'cause I wasn't helping. Shook it off. They didn't need me and without night goggles and armed with only a Glock, I'd have been useless anyway.

Things finally quieted down. Occasional sporadic shots as the temperature fell. SA Archer finally decided it was time to go mobile. First, he and the tracker and the medic walked over to examine Orange Camo and Pigman. Briefly. Walked back to where Carrie was sitting on the ground. "Goddamn," said SA Archer, "that's Ebenezer Friday's boy, Jeremiah." He pointed toward Pigman. "I thought he was still in the penitentiary."

"Send him back," I said wearily. "Or better yet, feed him to the hogs." We pulled Carrie to her feet, and surrounded by the sniper team, started back up toward the road. Which was no more than thirty yards away. The FBI Humvees had pulled into a turnout just beyond the target house. While we waited for everyone to muster, Carrie, high on morphine, talking slow and rhythmically, told SA Archer everything that had happened in minute detail from the moment Orange Camo number one had stepped in front of our vehicle.

I had no problem with these men. They appreciated the fact I had helped save a sister agent's life. Just as we were about to climb into the back seat of a Humvee to be driven into Savannah, a fibbie wandered up out of the woods and started toward us, loosey-goosey in his regulation camo. Too loosey-goosey. He took a good look at Carrie, turned, and walked back to the edge of the trees, then turned again in one smooth motion, a pistol in his right hand. I shot first, a gut-shot I believe, and he squeezed his trigger as he was falling, missing Carrie and nearly hitting SA Archer, who cursed and spat.

This slowed things down. Considerably. After a headcount, it was determined that one agent, a man named Jerry Clinton, was missing, which led to reinforcements till we must have had every federal agent in the whole county, and half the local police, scouring the hillside. They never did find Jerry, but he found us, finally wandering up out of the woods, wearing only long johns, delirious, with a huge bump on his forehead, but very much alive.

It was after midnight when I was finally able, minus Carrie who spent the night in a Savannah hospital, to check into our suite at the Embassy Suites not far from the airport. I stripped down and got in the shower where I let the spray run over me, cupping my throat so that my bandage would stay dry. I wasn't falling in love with SA North and didn't particularly want to sleep with her—though I might have felt differently if Adara hadn't been her friend and mine—but the truth was, I'd grown fond of her. With the single critical exception of getting carried away and thinking we should try to take the orange camo team into custody, she'd done a fine job from the moment we'd climbed out of the ill-fated Range Rover. Reminded myself to compliment her on her marksmanship next time I saw her. It was hard to get to sleep, but when I did, I kept dreaming of Chinese tallow and dogwood and magnolia and majestic red oaks and a certain gamin-faced woman with a big spirit whose feet seemed to glide across the forest floor.

Chapter Thirty-Five

On Saturday, my flight to Milwaukee touched down just before noon. Two hours later, I parked the rented Sonata next to Bobby's Econoline in front of our lakefront cabin. No sign of Jimmy's Nissan pickup. I knocked on the door and Tony answered. When he realized it was me, his eyes widened. "Hey, Tommy-boy," he called, as I stepped inside, "it's Wayne. I believe the mother-fucker misses you."

"It's true," I said, stepping inside. "I do miss you, Tommy. I could've used some of your martial spirit yesterday." I laughed and both men gave me a curious look. I'd been gone a little over twenty-four hours. Lying on a quilt, his head propped up on pillows with his cuffed hands down at his waist linked to his leg irons, Tommy was still chained to the radiator. No blindfold, though, and his original makeshift gag had been replaced by a breathable ball gag like the fetishists favor.

"Hiya, Tommy. How has Mike been treating you? By the way, I like your gag. Very stylish." I walked over and sat down in a black leather loveseat, my feet a few yards from Tommy's head. I covered Tony, who knelt down next to Tommy and removed his gag. Then Tony sat down next to me. Together, we examined our boy.

"Tommy and I have been getting along pretty good," said Tony after a moment of silence. "Turns out we have a few things in common."

"Fill me in," I said.

"Why sure, buddy. We both like beautiful women. Of any race or ethnicity. Which is a good thing. Though I like Beyoncé while Tommy prefers Nicki Minaj. Admittedly, he's a bit more partial toward muscular men than I am, but nobody said we had to be two peas in a pod."

"Hell, no! You don't want that. Or as I always say, *vive la différence.*"

"*Vive la différence.*"

Tommy snorted in disgust, and I wondered if our best approach might be no approach at all. Just keep up a steady stream of bullshit. Sooner or later, our baby boy would crack.

I stood up. Signaled for Tony to follow me. He popped Tommy's gag back in and followed me to the mudroom, which was quickly attaining conference room status. I sketched out my recent adventures with Jethro Shimanski and the crew of Lowcountry lizards. The big question was obvious. Had Jethro unilaterally called in the camo team, or did he have a little help from Marguerite? I was leaning toward the latter. And they had to have been tipped off in advance. Which meant we'd been surveilled, either getting on the plane in Milwaukee or getting off it in Savannah. And then, when Jethro started making phone calls, Marguerite gave the orders and her Lowcountry cell mobilized with incredible speed.

Tony told me he and Tommy had talked surfing, Hawaii, actors, men, women, music, and dirt bikes. They had also watched *Winter's Bone* and *Thor* on Netflix. But every time Tony brought up Bobby, Tommy had either stonewalled or changed the subject...Jimmy Sain would be back later this afternoon. "He's got something up his sleeve," said Tony. "Your friend is one strange bird."

I walked back into the living room and sat down on the loveseat facing Tommy while Tony went to work in the kitchen whipping up an onion and cheese omelet. For the next fifteen minutes, I sat there staring at Baby Boy who lay there with his eyes closed, facing the radiator. Stare at an object long enough without blinking and it will vanish. Blink and it returns. In Tommy's case, with a vengeance. After he'd vanished and returned four or five times, I tried to imagine a world in which folks like him and Marguerite and Quincey and Desmond Cole didn't even exist. Problem was, given the way I was linked to them, if they vanished, I probably would too. But why was I linked to these scumbags? And what did it say about me? That would be my jumping off point. Took a deep breath. Sat up straight. Spoke.

"Hey, Tommy, open your eyes, baby. I got something interesting to discuss with you." At the slow pace of the moon, Tommy rolled onto his back and then onto his left side, till he was facing me, the radiator chain stretched taut behind him. I waved at him. Smiled. "That doesn't look very comfortable, Tommy. I'd love to let you run free. Like the wild creature you are. Now, here's the deal. I know you're a big picture guy; leaders are always big picture guys. That's why they're leaders. I want to ask you a question, a question with no obvious answer. I know you're smart, take your time and think it through."

Interrupted by Tony who came strolling over carrying a king-sized omelet and spiced and sliced red potatoes. He dished some up for all of us. Then I covered Tony while he fed Tommy, forkful by forkful. Occasionally, Tony put Tommy's fork down and took a few bites with his own. The sound of chewing. Time seemed to pause. Eleven days till I was due to turn myself in or consign Bobby's soul to eternal darkness. Gun in my left hand, I ate slowly with my right.

It's amazing what three grown men can do to an onion and cheese omelet and a pan of red potatoes. Tony finished eating and put down his plate. Sat down next to me. "You know something, Wayne, I'm pretty good at this caregiving bit. Maybe I should give up crime fighting and become a candy striper."

"I was thinking the same thing." Agreeable Crane.

Tony stood up. Collected the dishes. Carried them to the

kitchen and began dripping a fresh pot of coffee.

While waiting for the coffee, I tried to talk sports with Tommy. No dice. He was one of those guys who was good with guns and knives and internal combustion engines but didn't give a damn about our great American team sports. We lapsed into silence. Tony came back with three coffees on a tray. Handed one to me and carefully served Tommy sips of coffee from a plastic cup.

"This is the life, Mike. You're the best," I said, making a show of sipping from my cup and smacking my lips.

Tony finally finished serving Tommy and sat down next to me. "I'm fuckin' *numero uno* in the kitchen, baby. It would make a killer TV series. I play a streetwise fellow who runs a B&B but is actually a fixer, kind of like Ray Donovan, only I've got a lot more class."

I laughed. One of our jokes. Though I could read real books as long as they contained a certain amount of action, I was short on class, while Tony, despite growing up next to a corporation yard in upstate New York, dressed well and could talk intelligently about the works of the Old Masters, not that he could afford anything but cheap reproductions. Made me wonder: Had he actually been on the pad with Roberto to raise cash to purchase good art, which he couldn't afford on a detective's salary while raising four kids? Plausible. I shook it off.

"All right, asshole," said Tommy suddenly. "What the fuck do you want to know?"

"Easy, big dog. You're the one chained up, not me. So chew on this. You and me and my pal Mike here," I elbowed Tony, "have been flung together here in this cozy little fishing lodge with the best company a man could ask for. But here's what I want to know, Tommy. Why are we thrown here together, not from the superficial standpoint of 'cause you motherfuckers abducted me. We need to go deeper. We need to dig. A suitable task for men of our intellect…"

I sat back, crossed my right foot over my left knee, and waited while Tommy presumably reflected. "Okay," he said finally. "I've been thinking about what you asked me. Fuck your 'cozy little fishing lodge and best company a man could ask for' bullshit. What you really want to know is how come people like us end up sucking hind tit in this lousy fucking world, right?"

"Bingo," I said. "It's been eating at me."

"I don't know why you and your feminine friend," smirking at Tony, "are here with me. But what I do know is this. I'm nothing like you pussies. You're both weak. You could have left me there to die in that fucking quarry, but you didn't. 'Cause you didn't have the balls. You're a couple of soft motherfuckers. In fact, whatever brought you here is dead opposite of why I'm here. So listen up. Maybe you can learn something…" Tommy paused, staring straight at me. Eyes got really sad. Misdirection? He shrugged and began to talk. "In…must have been the second grade…I realized that I was the smartest kid. Hands down. There was no competition. I started to experiment with bossing the other kids around. I wasn't heavy-handed like you fools. I was subtle. And they'd do exactly what I wanted 'cause I had brains and edge. I was in charge.

"In the fifth grade, I discovered the little girls would let me kiss them. Hell, they'd let me slobber all over them. All I had to do was talk nice and smile. They were so eager." Tommy's voice dripped sarcasm. "So that they could brag to their friends. I'd already lost faith in men and now I added females to my list. Except for my Aunt Kathy. Then in the sixth grade, I discovered I could talk boys into…" He paused. Ran his tongue deliberately across his lips. Smirked.

The chill. Drunk and violent as my father had been, and bad as it had ended, there had been plenty of wholesome sports stuff when I was young. Boxing, football, and pulling Adam out of the gin mills after work—those were my main pastimes. Except for brief reveries and even briefer conversations, I barely thought about girls till much later on. And when I did think about them, I liked them. Never wanted to hurt them. Cassady often said that despite my self-esteem problems, I actually had a

215

pretty good heart.

"When I was thirteen," said Tommy, "me and my friend Bernie got caught breaking into a warehouse on Sawtelle near 405. We had a driver and a van. We loaded up cartons of Air Jordans, but they pinched us just as we were leaving. By then my father and mother had been dead for years, and I was living with my Aunt Kathy. My case was bad 'cause I was the one carrying the loaded Ruger. It was my first gun. I loved that gun. The judge didn't care. He took my gun away and gave me six months in juvie. Insisted that he was letting me off easy. I saw some bad stuff in there." Tommy winced. "Real bad stuff. I kept a low profile, did my time, and got out. And you know what?" Tommy smiled and looked at me, almost plaintively.

"No, what, Tommy?" I said quietly.

"What do you think, dumbass? Who was most important to me?"

"That's easy," I said slowly. "Your aunt Kathy."

"Exactly." Tommy's brown eyes shining with pride and delight. "I thought she'd turn against me, but she didn't. My aunt Kathy, true blue."

"I could tell. She's a sweetheart."

"Damned straight. After that I kept a low profile till I was old enough to quit school. I knew I was rotten but that the people in charge of this pathetic world were even more rotten. Which in a way made me good. So I worked hard to be like them. My aunt did everything she could to turn me around. She sent me to every kind of shrink, but they all fell in love with me. A psychologist named Janet actually tried to seduce me right there in her office on Santa Monica Boulevard. I could cast a spell, baby. Aunt Kathy made me go to church. I actually liked that pretty well, but then the youth pastor hit on me. The bastard. I hit him so hard my knuckles were sore for a week. He never said a word. The lesson, I concluded, was that everyone has a weak spot, and everyone is scared.

"And that was that, Wayne, whatever the fuck your real

name is and why ever the fuck you're here. I spent the next ten years gettin' by, staying out of trouble. I sold a little coke and weed. If I couldn't make rent, I'd just move back in with Aunt Kathy. I didn't sweat it 'cause I knew my time would come. A lot of people told me so. Then when the president started his campaign, I got interested. 'Cause here was a real sick puppy just like the rest of them, only he was a big dog. People ate his shit up, even though he was lying through his teeth most of the time.

"One night I went to a MASA rally. It was like paradise. Everybody so full of crap, it was wonderful. I don't know if anybody really believed a word Big Dog was saying. Either way, they ate it up. It made no sense. None whatsoever. But Big Dog had juice. That's all that matters—who's got the juice and how does he use it?

"When Big Dog's campaign started picking up speed, I went to another rally and hustled my way into a security job. 'Cause I'm good with guns and weapons and logistics and I get along with law-and-order types. They're my kind of people. That's how it started. It was cake. I was number one with a bullet. But enough about me. I hate talking about myself. You think I'm scared 'cause you've got me chained up, but I'm not scared of you. You could kill me, and I still wouldn't be scared of you. But I do have a bone to pick. You and your gay friend," gesturing at Tony, "messed up my chances with Marguerite. She wanted me to seduce her, or maybe it was the other way around, but you criminals got in the way. So that's my story. What's yours?"

As he spoke, the room fell into shadow. When Tommy was finished talking, I stood up and walked over to the window. Our cabin faced east. Storm clouds massing in the northeast. Bobby seemed farther away than ever. Grabbed my windbreaker and went outside. Our cabin faced the lake. I thought about the fun Bobby and I would have trolling for walleyes if he were here. We would sip beers and laugh. If he was a free man...Meanwhile, Tommy Blank, narcissist, was withholding valuable information. I thought of what Bobby would do if our positions were reversed. Laughed out loud. Bobby could be forceful. I walked halfway down the hill toward the lake, the water gleaming darkly in the near distance. Breathing in the ozone. Turned around and retraced my steps. When I reached the top of the hill, I stood there scanning the horizon. The wind kicked up a notch and the first big raindrops fell. I went back inside. Resumed my post at the window.

After a while, Tony came over and stood next to me. I shook my head, and he shook his. Jimmy driving up in his Nissan broke the spell.

While he waited outside, we gagged and blindfolded Tommy. Left him chained to the radiator and told him we'd be back in a few hours. We spent the early evening drinking Jack and beer in a neighborhood gin mill. Glancing up now and then at the college football on the screen. Talking about everything but our problem.

Compared to Bobby and Tony and me with our embittered idealism and guarded optimism about life, Tommy's degree of negativity was chilling. I knew Tony was thinking the same thing. Jimmy threw a game of eight-ball he could have won. He sat down grinning and started shelling peanuts. Spoke. "One thing I've learned over the years. Maybe the only thing." He paused and sipped some whiskey. Grimaced. Chased it with a peanut. "The thing is, my friends, bullies are always afraid. They always have been and always will be. That's why they're bullies. And our boy Tommy is a bully. And he's afraid. No matter how good he is at fronting. Now I've got an idea. It might work, it might not. The idea is to break down his defenses and make him vulnerable. That's the only way we'll wring a shred of compassion out of the bastard. I should know, baby, I should know."

We drove back to the cabin, the ghost of Frenchy Lefevre riding shotgun in my head.

Chapter Thirty-Six

When we got back to the cabin, we removed Tommy's gag and blindfold and told him that we were going to inject him with a drug that wouldn't kill him but would make him feel very relaxed. He laughed and asked us what it was. We told him that was a trade secret. He grimaced. Screwed his forehead up into a sea of tangled lines as he thought it over. Finally, he nodded resolutely. As if he had a choice. Tony pointed his Beretta at Tommy's head. I wrapped the belt around his left bicep and Jimmy slid the needle into one of his veins.

Sodium Pentothal takes you to a place of no memory in less than thirty seconds. Five minutes later, you stir, first a muscle, then a quadrant. Mind comes last. After ten minutes, you're ready to talk.

Minimally alert, Tommy finally pulled himself to a sitting position. Eyes blank, forehead smooth.

"How are you feeling, Tommy?"

"I feel...like...a bolt...of light-ning...bay-bee," drawling the words in his barbital haze, "a reg-u-lar...bolt...of...light-ning."

"You've got a new lease on life, Tommy. We could have left you to die of exposure in the quarry. *Hasta luego*, baby. But we didn't. So help us out and we'll help you out. And in the process, save your soul. Here's what we need to know. Which prison honcho took Bobby into custody? We know it's either Millrose or Shimanski."

Eyes not quite as blank now, chewing his lower lip rhythmically, Tommy tried to talk. Three failed attempts. Then, success, the deadpan delivery of an inveterate psychopath.

"Oh yeah, bay-bee, I know things. Lots of things. Things you wanna know." He did a neck roll, full three-sixty. Grimaced. "Everybody loves me 'cause I'm so fucking smart." His head slumped forward, and then he lay back down on his mat.

"Rest easy, Tommy. What would you like to talk about?"

Long silence. "I wanna talk about Everlast, baby. *Whitey Ford Sings the Blues.*"

"That's Jimmy's job," I said.

"That's right, baby," said Jimmy. "I know about 'Ends.' But first things first. You need to listen to Nick—"

"—yeah, Tommy. Listen to me. We understand you, Tommy. We know you've had a hard life and you fell in with some bad people..." I paused to give him time to think...then started back up. "We also know you're not all bad. If you were, you probably would have strangled your aunt Kathy long ago when she got on your nerves. But you didn't. You love your aunt Kathy. That's why we're talking to you. That's why we're giving you a chance. You should consider it an honor. You're practically a commander already. You've got the looks and the charisma. Most importantly, you know the score. Of course you do. You're Tommy Blank. The mack daddy. So help us, mack daddy. So that we don't have to get rough. We've been trying like hell not to get rough. You know that. But you get your rocks off pushin' the fuckin' envelope. That's not smart, Tommy-boy. Not with people like us. So where did your people take Bobby? And where did they take him after that? And where did he end up?"

"You...really...wanna...know...don't...you?" Tommy sat back up. Big sarcastic smile. Ran his hand across his mouth as if wiping it off. Replaced by an obnoxious sincere look. I wanted to slap him. "You need to be like me, bay-bee. Roll with it. Make a friend, lose a friend. Take it as it comes..." His head fell forward.

"Hey, look, man!" Jimmy leaned forward, grabbed Tommy under the chin, shoved his head back, and slapped him hard, twice across his scarred right cheek. "You got no standing here, fucker! No fuckin' standing!"

I pulled Jimmy back. Afraid he was going to hurt Tommy. Not what I wanted. Tony was just watching, not saying a word. I turned to him. "Your call, Wayne," he said quietly. Then in a whisper, "This is a tough one."

"Okay," said Tommy suddenly, his big bullshit smile wandering from Tony to me to Jimmy and back to me, his cells adjusting to the narcotic. "You've convinced me. I'm willing to offer you my standard deal." Tommy paused, took a deep breath as the drug caressed his cells. "My standard deal is simple. I show you guys what dumb fucks you truly are. You kiss my ass and grovel for a while, then I give you something in return..." This time a genuine smile, or as close as he could manage. Chipped left upper front tooth.

"Okay, you give us something. You give us what we need, and I will grovel. I don't care. I just need to help my friend." My turn to grin. Maybe this psycho would come through. "So, Tommy, how are we such dumb fucks? Do us a favor and spell it out."

"Ten-four, baby." No more drawl. Didn't take him long to come out of the initial drug haze. I could tell Jimmy was surprised. "So, you fucking dipshits, we're going to play school now. I'm the teacher, you're the students. So, sit down and shut your traps until I tell you to open them."

We sat solemnly in a row on the couch. "And today's lesson plan is..." said Tommy grandly. "Wait! Change of plans. Here we go now. First question is for you, dumbass Wayne. Where did they pinch your boy?"

"LA. You know that."

"Where'd they take him?"

I hesitated. Wasn't sure if under the influence he would connect me to that chaotic night at the Weedpatch farmhouse.

"C'mon, dumbass. Tommy knows everything. Where'd they take him?"

"The farmhouse near Weedpatch."

"Ah! Now we're getting somewhere. Your teacher likes that. But then your fuckin' animal brain hits a concrete wall. It's plain as day, but dumbass Wayne doesn't know how to think backwards. Now think back. When you went all commando at the farmhouse, you didn't know squat about Millrose and Shimanski. How could you? You were just reacting to the disaster. Your boyfriend's been taken. You want him back. So you trailed the operation to Weedpatch. For that you get a pat on the back." Tommy grinned. Pleasantly. "Teacher is pleased. Teacher likes a smart boy. Everyone likes a smart boy. Except the dumb boys. The dumb boys hate the smart boys. They want to kill them. But they don't 'cause they're afraid. The smart boys aren't afraid." He snorted in good-natured disgust. "But they should be. Smart or dumb, it doesn't matter. You should still be afraid..."

Then his manner changed, his version of a pedantic geography teacher. Asked us if we knew where the United States was on a map. Affirmative. In broad strokes, Tony described what the continental United States looked like from east to west. Plenty of details. Said he could include a location for Alaska and Hawaii, but he wasn't going to waste the words. Asked the teacher to get on with the lesson.

Tommy pretended to take offense. He sulked a bit and gnawed on his knuckles, but soon snapped out of it. "I'll hand it to you boys. You're fast learners. Fast learners always get special attention in my classes. I was a fast learner...and I got special attention. Always." Suddenly very stern. "Now then, I want you to visualize this country on a map on the wall just like Mike described it. You know where California is, right? Of course you do. California is one of my favorite places. There's lots to do in California. Now, Wayne, you dumbass, I want you to think. Look at the setup. It's just geography, Wayne. Look at the map in front of you. Southern California is way off on the left. Now then, where is Jethro Shimanski's base of operations, east or west of the Mississippi?"

"East...I get it. And Millrose's base of operations is west of the Mississippi." Probably in Arizona or somewhere. Seems that while I was riding shotgun with Mars, Millrose was being prepped to play a part. I raised my hand.

"Yes, Wayne."

"I think your people handed Bobby off to Millrose. Then Millrose took him somewhere."

"That, Wayne, is a very good observation. Students who make good observations get rewarded in my classroom." He paused. Pondered. Spoke. "No! Wait! Not so fast. First, you got to pay up, 'cause that's the deal. It's humiliation time, bay-bee. Time for you and your feminine friend to grovel. Get down on the floor. Curl up in a ball and confess to how stupid you've been not to see the obvious fact that your Bobby boy was handed over to James Millrose. Then say it over and over again. Rote memorization for you dumb animals. Dumbass Wayne and Pretty Boy Mike. What a pair. Do it! Or else I'm finished."

Tony shrugged. "Bobby would do it for us." I was thinking the same thing. Tony got down on the floor and I followed suit. Did not exactly assume the fetal position. But close enough. Tommy was delighted. For a little while. Then he grimaced. "I want another shot of that stuff. Make it quick. Before this one wears off completely." Jimmy shrugged. Prepared the syringe and found a vein. Again, Tommy went under. "Each shot is less effective," said Jimmy. "Ain't that the way of the world..."

This time it took longer. Tommy barely stirred for ten minutes. It was completely dark now. As I stood looking out the window, Tony unloaded and reloaded his Beretta. An effortless motion like brushing your teeth or riding a bicycle. It took threats and a certain amount of cursing, but we finally coerced Tommy back into consciousness. Once we got him sitting up, he slurped some coffee that Tony held up to his lips. His head kept lolling onto his right shoulder. "Where...the fuck...?"

"Right here, baby. You were telling us a story."

"Oh, yeah," said Tommy. "I was on...a motherfuckin'...roll."

"You were. Now you're back on it...So what did Millrose do with Bobby?"

"Oh shit, Wayne, you're like a..." He paused, apparently racking his memory bank. "You're like a CD that's been all scratched up and pissed on."

"Time's up, Tommy. What did Millrose do with Bobby?"

"Don't...be...such a...hard-ass. We're...getting there..."

Like before, the drug wore off in stages. After a while, Tommy sat up a little straighter. Pouting and grimacing. "Okay," he said finally. "I'm tired of playing school. I'm so damned tired. But you want to know where Millrose took your friend. He could have taken him anywhere, anywhere he fucking wanted...as long as he cleared it with the big boss." Tommy smirked. Wrenched his head around and gazed foggily in our general direction. "You can't ever forget about the big boss."

"Damn straight, Tommy. Where did Millrose take Bobby?"

"Oh, that! You still don't get it. I guess we need to run through the options. Strategically, bay-bee. One step at a time."

I wanted to hit him. Jimmy was seething. Tony was unmoved.

"He had two real options," I said. "He could put Bobby in one of his prisons or he could have handed him off to Jethro Shimanski." Patient Crane.

"Very good, Wayne. Now you see the setup."

"So which did he do?"

"You won't give up, will you?"

"No, Tommy, I won't. Which did he do?"

"We're almost there. But you've got to dig deeper. Who makes the decisions? The big boss, right. Of course it's the big boss. But wait just one motherfuckin' minute. The big boss ain't goin' anywhere near this can of worms. I don't blame him." Tommy was enjoying this immensely. "So who do you think had her nose right in the middle of this?" He waited, sniffed the air.

"I'll tell you who. Marguerite Ferguson."

"Very good, Wayne. Maybe you're not so dumb after all."

The funny thing is, he was right. The setup was kind of obvious, once you knew who the players were. Of course, it was only one of many possible setups. But it made sense. Marguerite would want Bobby somewhere near her center of operations. Cole, who lived the itinerant life of the perennial houseguest, seemed to have no headquarters, and would arrange to be far away. And Cole had never seemed to be the *big boss*. Tentacles of the octopus but where was the head? But for my purposes, the more important question was, which flesh-and-blood principal, or representative of the principals, would hand Bobby—or me—if I was noble enough to come forward—over to the CIA or whoever was chosen to handle the rendition? Not convinced it was Cole...The Lowcountry ambush had come right on the heels of us interrogating Jethro Shimanski. Which could put him right at the center of this. But my instincts told me otherwise. I would have Greg check out the unknown players— Paul Reardon and Elizabeth Octavia Smith. Pronto. And ask Carrie to put Swann on it as soon as we were finished with Tommy. If I knew Swann, he was already back at work.

"Okay, Tommy. Where is Jethro keeping Bobby?"

"Ah," said Tommy. "We're getting close. The loving father smiles. Even on Tommy Blank. Even on you, Wayne. 'Cause we're getting close to the end of our journey. But the end is always the hardest part."

"Where's Bobby?"

"That awful refrain. Jethro doesn't know where Bobby is. Or if he does, we'd never get it out of him. We have to go through his designation person."

"Designation person?"

"Yeah, designation person."

"What's her name?"

"I call her Liz. She's beautiful, but she's out of my league which is rare. It hurts. She's out of your league too. She makes supermodels look like fuckin' crackheads."

"And she does designations for Jethro Shimanski?" I was surprised.

"It's a good job. What are you, a fucking snob?"

"No, I just didn't expect this. So, I guess you're going to introduce me to Ms. Liz."

"Why should I do that?"

"Because I need you to."

"I don't care."

"Okay. We'll just turn you over to the FBI."

"Maybe I'd like that. They got nothing on me."

"Oh yes, they do. They got you for conspiracy to kidnap and conspiracy to commit substantive acts aiding and abetting a domestic terrorism operation. And they got you for raping and beating up Rainey Morgan. That's enough to get you two dimes, Tommy. Two motherfucking dimes. At least. You want to spend twenty years in stir? I don't think so. But if that's what you want, knock yourself out...Jimmy, put the blindfold back on him. And gag him. We'll just let him rot here while we go fishing for a few days. Maybe that will straighten him out." I turned to my *compadres.*

"Jimmy, what should we have for dinner? Saturday night, my friend. We got to hurry up before they close the kitchen...Mike, what are you in the mood for?" We were hungry and nearly out of alcohol. Tony signaled that he wanted to be alone with Tommy. I knew he meant business.

Chapter Thirty-Seven

Jimmy and I drove into Van Dyne. We stuck to the same grilled salmon, battered cod, and barbeque ribs, only this time I had the cod. Jimmy chose the ribs. Salmon to go for Tony. Jimmy and I ate at the bar restaurant and split a couple of games of eight-ball. Neither of us said a word about Tommy Blank. Set your horses free...and they will come back to you...of their own accord.

We decided against another game of eight-ball and ordered a couple of six-packs and a bottle of Jack to go...

Tony met us at the cabin door. Whispering. "Sssh...He's asleep now."

We sidled in and moved some chairs back to the mudroom where we sat in a circle sipping whiskey and conferring in whispers.

"I won't keep you guys in suspense," said Tony. "It didn't take long. He got on his cell phone and stayed on it. It's all set up. Our boy was determined. He's got charisma, even on Sodium Pentothal. Hell, especially on Sodium Pentothal."

"On the phone?" I said quietly. "They'll be able to trace the calls to this location."

"I wouldn't worry," said Tony. "I don't think we'll be here much longer."

"So, who'd he talk to?"

"I'm not really sure. It sounded like a bunch of underlings.

Receptionists and admins, folks like that."

"Yeah? Good. Now, please stop being mysterious. It's making my pulse race."

"Okay, Nick. Just relax. Here's the deal. You and I are meeting Ms. Elizabeth Octavia Smith at the Red State Bar & Grill in Murfreesboro, Tennessee at eight p.m. on Monday. Tommy says she knows exactly where Bobby is. That's Part Two. Part One is almost as good. Tommy has requested an interview with the FBI. He wanted to know if Dumbass Wayne could set it up. I told him I thought you probably could…" Tony trailed off. He shook his head and sipped his whiskey, seemingly in wonder at this turn of events.

"How did you do it?"

"Good question. I didn't really do anything." Then Tony described how after Jimmy and I left, Tommy asked if he could have another shot of Sodium Pentothal. He sulked and grimaced when Tony said there wasn't anymore. He lay back on his yoga mat and closed his eyes but did not sleep. Chewed on his lower lip and thrashed around periodically. Just when Tony thought he was going to have to get tough and move things along, Tommy had sat back up and said he was ready to cooperate. And then began working his phone with a vengeance, finally setting up our interview with Octavia Smith.

"It was astonishing," said Tony. "All the more so 'cause it was Saturday night. He had to keep leaving messages for people to call him back. But they did. Every time his phone rang, he'd roll his eyes and purr into the speaker, 'Tommy here. Who do I have the pleasure of speaking to?' Then he told me he had valuable information and wanted to proffer with the FBI. And that he wanted immunity. I damned near laughed in his face, but stopped myself. This whole thing has been plenty weird. Why the hell not?"

"Indeed," I said. "Why the hell not? But tell me this: Why his change of heart?"

"I think," said Tony, "that us abducting the motherfucker,

hog-tying him, and dumping him out on the edge of the quarry, however briefly, and then chaining him to the radiator for two days," Tony gestured toward the living room, "has shocked the hell out of him. Not that he'll admit it. But keep in mind, if he's even halfway on the level, he hasn't been in any real trouble since he got popped for breaking into the warehouse on Sawtelle when he was thirteen years old."

I nodded. "Makes sense. He's like a virgin when it comes to—"

"—the real rough stuff." Jimmy finished up for me. "It's simple. Tony is right. Let me break it down for you. This might take a minute."

Jimmy had had three drinks in Van Dyne and was feeling fine. Wondered if he hadn't doubled up on his prescription Adderall. "We're listening, buddy, but keep your voice down."

"In the joint," said Jimmy in an elaborate whisper, "you got three levels of dangerous. Level One bastards are so violent and crazy that you just stay the fuck away. The Level Two guys are the shot callers and guys who could be shot callers but don't need the aggravation. I was Level Two." He smiled, a big gaping grin with his two missing teeth. Surprised me with a lightning quick love tap to my left shoulder. It stung. "You're Level Two, baby. Whether you like it or not."

"Now as for you," turning to Tony, "I don't know what level you are." Again, the wide-open grin.

"Neither do I," said Tony. "That's always been a problem for me..." His turn to grin. "What's Level Three?"

"That I can answer. I spent hundreds of nights pondering that very question...I'd say Level Three consists of all your run-of-the-mill tough guys, the guys who like to beat up pacifists and turn out the weak guys in prison but are known for ducking serious combat. Inside, they're green with envy. 'Cause no matter how hard they try, they'll never make Level Two..."

"That doesn't sound like Tommy," said Tony.

"Exactly," said Jimmy. "'Cause Level Three creeps are not leader material. Every single one of them has a big 'F' for Follower tattooed on his chest. But Tommy-boy is a leader. Here on the outside. But on the inside, a shot caller has to be copacetic with all kinds of hideous shit. It goes with the territory. And even though Tommy's seriously Level Two in most respects, he doesn't like to fight. Probably isn't even very good at it. He's been doing it all along with smoke and mirrors, 'cause he's a clever monkey."

I looked at them both. Told Jimmy his decision to use the Sodium Pentothal was sheer genius. Tommy had liked being under the influence. It had made him playful, which, it turned out, was just what we needed. And then I told Tony that his reassuring presence was all it took for Tommy to see the light, or rather to see a light a shade or two brighter than the black sun he'd been living under for so long.

Chapter Thirty-Eight

Three p.m., Sunday, May 12, 2019.

For some reason, we couldn't shake Lake Michigan. The Milwaukee FBI office, a big modern compound consisting of two rectangles and a tower as wide as it is tall, sits on choice lakefront real estate a few miles south of Milwaukee. Strange how we kept going from beach to beach to beach—first the beach in Racine where Swann got jumped; then the sparse and stony Lowcountry beach where Carrie and I had been hunted by the gang of camo-draped miscreants; and now this deluxe parkland, appropriate, of course, to house our illustrious FBI.

Before debriefing Tommy, Carrie and I met in a small private conference room. Sipping a Diet Coke and wearing a sleeveless parka over a Boston University sweatshirt, she was pale and clearly still in pain, her pupils tiny.

"This is good shit," she said, pulling a prescription bottle out of her right jacket pocket and setting it down on the conference room table. I picked it up. Fifteen milligram oxycodone. Thirty-count. Set it back down. Then she told me that it wasn't until she woke up the morning after our Lowcountry adventure that she realized she had helped kill Pigman. Except she didn't call him Pigman. I said it was a shame but that she'd done the right thing. Reached out and covered her left hand with both of mine. For a second or two.

It was time. I told her I knew she was on board to rescue

Bobby, but that she had to stop second-guessing my methods. It might look like I was off chasing crazy chimeras, but my tactics were actually sound and deliberate. Though I was no Frenchy Lefevre, I did have three decades in the trenches. You pick up a thing or two. Call it supplemental knowledge. In this case, it had brought us one Tommy Blank, allegedly ready to talk.

I told her that Tommy had given us a lead on Bobby's whereabouts, and that Tony and I would follow up on it in Tennessee on Monday. And that I was going to need serious backup in the very near future. If the lead panned out. And that in return for her trust and confidence, I would take a back seat when she questioned Tommy. She laughed and told me she'd keep this first meeting casual and exploratory. Asked me what the lead on Bobby was. I told her. She asked if I wanted her to arrange for some discreet backup in Tennessee. I surprised myself. Told her it might be a good idea.

For some reason, I liked Carrie a lot better now. Even though she had insisted that we should arrest the camo people. It seemed funny now, partly because we probably would have been pinned down in the woods anyway, even if Carrie hadn't wanted to jack them. There had been too many of them. And the local FBI had been too slow. Easy for me to laugh. I wasn't the one who had taken a bullet.

"If the lead pans out," I said, "then we've got to figure out the best way to extract Bobby."

"Hmm." She rubbed her chin and slouched further down into her chair. "So, if I'm reading you right, you're telling me we're about to locate Bobby. I seem to remember you asking me if I had the guts to send in a team to forcibly liberate him."

"That's true. When we were thinking they might be holding him in one of the old Titan missile sites. But it's different with a private prison. Private property. You'd need a warrant. The Justice Department would raise holy hell if the corrupt FBI staged an illegal raid on a perfectly legitimate private prison, searching for a man who wasn't even there. 'Cause on the books, he wouldn't be there...By the way, have you given Marguerite's phone back?"

Carrie shook her head. "We're still holding on to it. Her lawyers are screaming bloody hell. I'm not sure how long we can hold out without indicting her for something."

I nodded. "Got it. Okay, here's what I think. Once we locate Bobby, it's going to take some kind of intricate undercover operation to spring him. It won't be easy. And we'll be working against time. But we'll figure it out. Let's go talk to Tommy."

We met Tony outside the interrogation room. He was carrying a two-tiered tray holding five coffees and an assortment of poisonous sugary confections. "Listen, Nick, I'm so damned tired. Do I really need to attend this meeting?"

"You were with me every step of the way with Mr. Blank. In fact, you handled him on your own when I went to South Carolina...on official business." I smiled and turned to Carrie. "Your call, Agent North."

She gave a lazy shrug. "I think Tony should join us." Her phone rang. "Hello. What...you're joking...you're not joking...you better not be joking. Ohmigod! Here you are!"

It was true. Swann. Hobbling with the help of a cane. Five foot nine, one hundred forty-five pounds soaking wet. Same floppy brown hair. Laptop in a carrying case slung over his shoulder. Battered. But far from broken. A survivor. I had to admire him. "I'm in," he said.

The interrogation room was unremarkable. Eight by ten. Cement block walls. Beige, not green. Rectangular zinc-topped table. Room for six chairs. One-way mirrors. Cameras mounted seven feet off the ground. Peachy.

Tony and I had done good. Few men could do better...which meant that this was also a moment of great danger. Arrogance has been the undoing of many an investigator. A single degree of separation divides the natural confidence necessary to succeed and the fatal hubris that leads to destruction.

Carrie and I sat across from Tommy. Tony was to my left on

the end, Swann at the other end. It felt right for him to be there.

Introductions all around. Then Tommy drenched his coffee with sweetener and liquid creamer. Tested it, grimaced, took a bigger sip. Spoke directly to Carrie. "Well then, here we are. What a surprise! Tomas Blanc Kovačević at your service. I'm Tommy to friends. I've just spent three horrible days being abused by your agents here. Unforgivable, the way I've been treated, and don't say they were just doing their jobs."

"They're bounty hunters," said Carrie, speaking slowly and calmly. "Best in the business. And they knew just who to come to." She paused. Smiled at Tommy. "I want you to relax. We're on the same side now. So, let's move forward."

Tommy set his coffee down and ran both hands through his thick black hair. Sat back in his chair and smiled. Miraculously restored. Handsome. Confident. A human vampire. It was uncanny. He hadn't eaten anything all day. Said he was saving his appetite. Said fasting made him think more clearly. Who were we to argue?

"Could you repeat your name, please?" said Carrie. "Just for the record."

"Kovačević. Tomas Blanc Kovačević. But just call me Tomas. My mother was a French whore, and my father was a blacksmith somewhere in the Czech Republic. That's what Kovačević means. Son of a blacksmith. But I prefer Blanc. Biggest mountain in Europe. I like to aim high."

"I agree," said Carrie. "Aim high."

"I'd like," said Tommy, "to work something out similar to what these two assholes," pointing first at me and then at Tony, "have worked out with you. And just so you know, my approach is far less crude than these two thugs. For example, I've already arranged for Mike and Wayne to interview a private prison designation specialist who can lead them to Bobby Moore. If they can act halfway civilized, I'm pretty sure that she'll cooperate."

"I wish the son of a bitch who shot me on Friday night had cooperated and aimed a little higher and a little to my right."

Carrie pointed at her right arm. "It's a good thing I'm left-handed. You wouldn't happen to know that crew in South Carolina, would you, Tomas Blanc? The South Carolina crew that ambushed Wayne and me less than forty-eight hours ago?" She leaned forward. Suddenly wide awake. "'Cause if you do, Tomas, that would help us, and would also help you quite a bit, which is exactly what you need."

"What I need," said Tommy, "is an immunity agreement."

"Perhaps," said Carrie, "but we're not there yet. But I can offer you a Queen for a Day interview. In writing. And I can tell you that you're much more valuable to me as a CI with an untainted reputation than you'd be if you were under indictment." She took two copies of a standard U.S. District Court proffer agreement out of her briefcase. She'd apparently already filled in the blanks.

He read it eagerly, his eyes moving rapidly down the page. Then he read it again. "So then," he said, "if I sign this, nothing I say can be used against me now or at some future date, correct?"

Carrie chuckled throatily. Cheerful when under the influence. And yesterday's Sodium Pentothal had definitely improved Tommy's personality. "Let me explain how this works," she said. "Nothing you tell us today will be used against you. And since you're not indicted and I have no current plans of indicting you, it doesn't matter anyway."

Tommy nodded. He put the proffer down on the table. Tugged his ear. Took a deep breath and grimaced. "Okay, I'll sign. Give me a pen before I change my mind."

Once that was out of the way, Tommy was as good as an encyclopedia, pumping out information faster than Swann could record it. And like an encyclopedia, he had a photographic memory. His domain consisted of a dozen sleeper cells fanned out across the West. From Tucson to Seattle and east to Denver. When asked about the purpose of the sleeper cells, Tommy grinned and said, "You want the real purpose or the official purpose?"

"Keep it real," said Carrie.

"Let's put it this way," said Tommy. "Several of the cells have facilities to sequester fugitives."

"Like the five Muslims at Weedpatch," said Carrie.

Tommy admitted that Marguerite Ferguson was his immediate supervisor and said he believed she was closely connected to Desmond Cole, whom he'd only spoken to a time or two. I asked him who the big boss was. "Oh, that," he said, treating us to his dazzling smile. "The same question I ask myself in quiet moments. It's not Desmond Cole, I know that, and it's not Marguerite Ferguson, but I don't know who it is. It's frustrating as hell 'cause a guy likes to know who he's actually working for."

Tommy claimed to know absolutely nothing about the South Carolina riverfront attack on Carrie and me. And said he knew nothing about the assault on Swann. "You see," he said almost pompously on the heels of his denials, "I'm not a big fan of violence. In fact, I hate it. I was a victim myself until the age of six when my Aunt Kathy rescued me from my brutal mother."

"What do you know about the caravan of paramilitary vehicles that followed Willem Spahn on the way to the Vail Airport back when this began?" said Carrie.

Tommy's most engaging smile. "There was only one paramilitary vehicle, a half-assed one at that, a Humvee. The rest were just vans. It was a shadowing exercise. I was given the order to give that order. It was harmless, like most of what we do. I'd forgotten all about that."

"Have you forgotten about the attempted kidnapping of Willem Spahn later that same day in that little town in New Mexico?"

Tommy frowned and took a bite of a Danish. "That was weird. It pissed me off plenty. Right there in my territory, but I had nothing to do with it. I'm glad I didn't give the order. I would never botch things like that. Unfortunately, my crew down there is worthless. They'll cave for anybody who dangles some Benjamins." Tommy paused, flashed his boyish smile. "Good help is hard to find, but the bottom line is I didn't order that kidnapping."

"What about the two heavies? Down at the end of the block? Who were they?" I asked.

Tommy faced me. Smiled. "Funny you should ask, Wayne. You probably greased their dirty little palms. They're just dumb enforcers. Whoever set this up, and I assume it was based on Marguerite's orders, hired them."

"Which means Marguerite has a whole separate group of soldiers working for her in addition to you, even in the West."

Tommy reached out, palms up, and wrenched his mouth into an exaggerated frown. "They're probably the same people who bring the Arabs across the border...My god, Marguerite is going to be so mad." Tommy's face changed and for a moment he was just a young boy with a big intelligent forehead. "But it's kind of fun to piss her off." He laughed. Back to normal. Handsome. Cocky. Slippery.

When asked about the principals, he said Marguerite and Cole and Quincey were principals, but Jethro Shimanski and James Millrose were not. Nor were Paul Reardon and Elizabeth Octavia Smith. Tommy said he had no idea how the big boss had come to be the boss. To him they were all just rich assholes working hard to fuck up the world.

There were two sticking points. Tommy claimed to know nothing about how the five Arabs had ended up in the silo jail at the Weedpatch farm. Other than that Marguerite's other branch had carried it out. He was insulted that anyone would even think he would do something like that. Said that if Marguerite or someone else was smuggling Arabs into the country, that was on them. He saw no inconsistency in this position even though the Arabs had been housed at a sleeper cell under his control. At that time, he'd been a busy man. First, a quick trip up to the Seattle sleeper cell to deal with a financial problem. Then back to New Mexico to try and sort through the Wagon Mound fiasco. Then a stopover in San Francisco to spend the night with his boyfriend William. They had enjoyed a lovely dinner together before going to the opera. When asked which opera, he said he wasn't sure 'cause opera was William's thing, but that it was pretty good. Said he thought it might have had something to do with a butterfly. Said it got William all turned on. At that juncture, Tommy stared straight at Carrie, his brown eyes sparkling. Then he turned to Swann. "You're lucky it's not you I'm after, little man. Maybe if you wore a uniform. I like men in uniform..." A belt of laughter, suppressed. "Just kidding, baby." Serious now. "Next question."

The other sticking point was Bobby's kidnapping. Tommy said he "wasn't going to put himself in a cross" until he had a signed immunity agreement. Carrie said that was starting to look like a real possibility, but that she believed he was holding back, which was not acceptable.

"Of course, I'm holding back. You've got to give to get, Special Agent North..."

At the end of the proffer, Carrie said she would try to get him immunity. Asked Tommy to stick around for a few days while she expedited the request. She would book him a room at the elegant Pfister Hotel in downtown Milwaukee and put it on the tab. Tommy liked that...

Later, Carrie and Swann and Tony and I went over preparations for our interview with Octavia Smith. It was decided that Carrie would have a team of five or six agents in Nashville waiting for our plane to touch down Monday afternoon. We would be under constant surveillance until we returned to Milwaukee, where Carrie would be hunkered down recovering from her gunshot wound while Tommy's immunity request was either approved or denied.

Chapter Thirty-Nine

Just before Tony and I boarded our Monday midday flight to Nashville, I received a half-breathless call from a still sedated Carrie. Change of plans. Octavia Smith had called Tommy and said that only I would be allowed to attend the interview. No Tony Bott. A slight blow but Tony took it in stride. Said he would stick around until I flew back to Milwaukee Tuesday morning.

When I got to Nashville, the FBI handlers approached me in the airport parking lot and handed me a Glock 19. I drove to Murfreesboro and made my way to the old downtown, a splash of lovely old two and three-story brick buildings with old-fashioned awnings and leaded-glass windows.

Elizabeth Octavia Smith made me wait. I recognized her instantly when she finally sashayed into the restaurant wearing high-heeled alligator-skin boots, pasted-on jeans and a Dolly Parton blouse, knotted just above her belly button. A good-looking woman, her auburn hair was teased up Nashville style. One blue eye and one brown eye. Lines were beginning to form at the corners of her mouth and her voice was high-pitched and slightly shrill.

She refused to talk business during dinner. Said she wanted to get to know me first. We devoured Porterhouse steaks with roasted red potatoes and an array of greens. And drank a bottle of Chateau Montet Bordeaux Superieur Oak. As we ate and drank, I divulged random bits about my random life, keeping it light and amusing, the usual PI stuff closer to a TV series than to real life. And claimed in passing that I was married with three children. Children can come in handy. Even if only one of them actually exists.

Her story was fairly simple. Her ex-husband Larry "Biff" Bensonhurst was a brain surgeon with his own clinic in Nashville. She'd married him seven days after graduating from high school and had divorced him two years ago after fifteen years of loveless marriage. Although she spared me the details, she implied that Biff had bashed her around plenty of times. She had no children but with the help of a clever divorce lawyer named Jerry, with whom she'd had an unfulfilling, albeit convenient, fifteen-month relationship, she'd been awarded their lavish house in nearby Smyrna and a generous alimony settlement. Biff had moved to Nashville.

Just before her divorce was final, Jerry had gotten her a job at Detentions, Inc., where she had quickly worked her way up to manager of their Designations department, a fact she took pride in. Nevertheless, she said, as the alcohol started talking, she was a lonely and unfulfilled woman who now wished she had gone to college, perhaps to study theater arts, instead of marrying right out of high school.

Which brought LA into the mix. She wanted to know if it was as glamorous as the media suggested, and I said glamor is in the eye of the beholder, but that I was pretty sure she'd fit right in. "I wish you hadn't said that. I've always thought that I missed my chance. And now it's too late. I just turned thirty-five. Next thing you know, I'll need a face-lift." I assured her such was not the case.

While working on the first glass of our second bottle of Bordeaux, she started getting salty. First the movie stars and their intimate habits. Then the Kardashians and their NBA boyfriends. Segued into the Hadid sisters. By now she'd slipped off one of her alligator-skin boots and was exploring the outside of my left calf with her right foot. Felt good, but I tried to ignore it.

I asked her why she'd decided that I should meet her alone. "Didn't Tommy Blank tell you?" I shook my head. "Well, it's like this. Tommy and I are real tight. We met on one of the online dating services before I got hired by Detentions, Inc., purely by chance. He's a silver-tongued devil, and for a while I had hopes that he might be the one. But then when we met in person, I knew right away that he wasn't my type. He's way too pretty. I like manly men. But we got along great and have become friends. I understand that he has an important job with some underground patriotic organization. It sounds dangerous, so I keep my nose out of it. Anyway, just on a whim, I asked him which of you boys was better looking. He said that depended on whether I liked them pretty or tall and raw-boned. I said I liked them tall and raw-boned."

"That's me." Inane Crane.

"You've got an interesting face. Do you realize you look like Nick Nolte? Except I don't think he ever smiles."

"I never did either when I was younger. But the good news is, a man can change."

Small talk. The second bottle of Bordeaux was now a dead soldier. I asked for the check, and we got out of there. Knew I had to take control of the play. Wasn't sure how. Octavia took control instead. Said she wanted me to see her house and that after that we'd talk business. Said I should ride with her. I said I'd take my own car, but she insisted. Said I could sleep in her guestroom and ride back to town with her in the morning. I reluctantly agreed, figuring that with my six-man Alphabet Boy escort, not much was likely to go wrong. No choice but to stick with this woman until she divulged.

North-Central Tennessee abounds with waterways. Octavia's house fronted the West Fork Stones River on the outskirts of Smyrna, an old Civil War Railroad Junction, halfway between Nashville and Murfreesboro. After a quick tour of her well-lit acreage, which included a stroll down to the edge of the river where she showed me her Chris-Craft, we settled down in her den with a bottle of one hundred proof Old Forester straight bourbon whiskey. Faith Hill and The Dixie Chicks looping on her sound system.

As we talked and drank, her mood changed from salty and flirtatious to solemn to exhilarated. Then back to solemn and then very solemn, in part, it seemed, because I told her I moonlighted as a youth pastor at the West Los Angeles Cornerstone Church. Told her we were nondenominational and that our Sunday services were heavily scripture-based. She asked me what my favorite part of the Bible was. I told her I loved Revelations and the gospels but kept returning to Romans. And to prove it, I recited solemnly:

For the wages of sin is death, but the gift of God is eternal life in Christ Jesus our Lord.

"Wow," said Octavia, "that's beautiful. I had no idea you were a man of God."

"Neither did I until my forty-sixth birthday, five years ago. Sallie and I had married late in life—my third marriage, if you must know—and she had just given birth to our second child, Benjamin. One day she noticed that the little guy was listless. She took him to his pediatrician. They ran tests and discovered he had hydrocephalus, water on the brain..." I stopped and shook my head sadly.

"Ohmigod!" said Octavia. "Is he okay?"

I stared straight into her blue and brown eyes. "We think so. They had to insert a stent into his brain and drain the fluid out through his chest..." I sighed heavily and drank some Old Forester. "It was touch and go for several weeks. I was beside myself. My friend Jim Tanner insisted I come to church with him and his family. I was raised pretty much without religion and had hardly ever even been in a church. All I can say is it did a number on me. That night I got down on my knees and prayed for the very first time. That was the beginning, dear Octavia, of a beautiful new chapter in the life of this old sinner. Now my kids go to Sunday school every week, and Sallie volunteers with the church recreation department."

"Oh, Wayne! That's so beautiful." Her eyes were glistening. I wondered if the god I ignored would prefer me to impersonate a youth pastor or have drunken sex with a lonely woman I'd probably never see again. Pretty sure I knew the answer. Then I asked her if she went to church. "I did. When I was a young woman. But Biff, that bastard, always laughed at me, called me a Jesus freak, and after a while I stopped going."

"That is so wrong. But so many of us live in darkness. But the good news is, it's never too late. I'm sure Tennessee is full of wonderful churches."

"Of course it is. My girlfriend Tara is constantly asking me to go to services with her at her Free Will Baptist Church. Maybe I'll just take her up on it."

"Oh, that's wonderful." I solemnly drained the rest of my Old Forester. "Bottoms up."

She drained hers. We were drunk and tired. And still nothing about Bobby. It hung in the air. Then came the curveball. "Do you think God would mind awfully much if we slept together just to cuddle a little? No hanky-panky, I promise, just cuddling. I'm so lonely and you seem like such a warm-hearted man."

"Hmm." I considered, scrunching up my forehead and grimacing Ronald Reagan style. Shook my head several times, then nodded and stared into my whiskey glass. "Okay, Octavia. For you. Of course, Sallie can never know about this."

"She never will. I promise, and just to prove it, let me make some coffee and sober up a little. Then we'll find that prisoner you need information on."

At last. I needed no urging, drank a cup, black and steaming, while she drank hers with cream and sugar. Then she led me to her home office where she dove into her databases. Bobby wasn't in the public database, and he wasn't in her private, all-inclusive database. There was no sign of Robert Joe Moore, age sixty-eight, born in Mobile, Alabama. "Well," she said, "this can only mean one thing. Mr. Moore is a very important prisoner, which means I need to check my VIP database." It required several sets of usernames and passwords, but Octavia's fingers flew nimbly across her keyboard, and she finally got in. And there he was, Robert Joe Moore, age sixty-eight. At the firm's Charlesburg, North Carolina facility. On a federal matter. No other information. "We never know what the charges are," she explained. "Just whether the cases are state or federal."

"I know the charges. They're about as serious as a heart attack." At that moment I was overcome by a profound weariness, like I could sleep for days or even weeks.

Octavia kept her word. We slept in her four-poster, king-size bed, she in her bra and panties, me in my boxers, under a mountain of filmy-white quilts and soft linen sheets. It was very comfortable, and it took every ounce of my willpower to keep from taking cuddling to the next logical step. But I stayed strong. First, we faced each other and recited the Lord's Prayer together. Then she rolled over, and I spooned her. Quiet hands. She sighed deeply and soon began to breathe deeply. Slept.

In the morning, Octavia threw on a robe and whipped up some bacon and eggs. We ate together in her sunroom. Seven days and sixteen hours before Bobby's deadline. After breakfast, she drove me into Murfreesboro to pick up my car. Before we parted, she gave me her private cell number and asked me why I was so interested in Robert Joe Moore. I told her it was a matter of great importance to national security. At this her eyes grew big, and she placed her finger vertically across her lips. "One thing this old girl can do, Wayne, is keep her mouth shut. You can count on me." And then just as I was about to get out of her car, she stopped me and said, "I hope that after this is all over, you and I can be friends. You were very sweet and considerate last night. I won't forget it." I told her it was my pleasure and kissed her gently on the forehead. Then I got out of her car and walked over to mine; my backup team invisible in plain sight.

FINAL PART
Chapter Forty

Half past two. Wednesday, May 15, 2019. Charlesburg, North Carolina. I stood in the doorway of my cell on the fourth floor of Charlesburg Corrections & Solutions, Ltd. (CCS). Posing as a prisoner. A converted state prison on the west edge of town, the joint was ancient and crumbling except for the lighting, which was decent. Vertical bars on the cell doors and old-fashioned keyhole locks. Second-generation stainless-steel sinks and toilets. The heat kept going off and on...I had checked in under my official FBI alias, Ned Stamper, to serve a three-year bid on a credit card bust-out scheme that went kaput. Which meant I was housed with the fraudsters. The usual suspects. Mostly white and Asian. Some Armenians. Well-heeled WASPs and refined Jewish guys. A couple of Chinese counterfeiters. The Japanese financial advisor who had no business handling people's money. A single solemn Nigerian. And guys like me who didn't really fit into any category.

Carrie had been dead set against it, but I had stood firm. I was going to go into the fucking prison, and I was going to find Bobby. I would have a man on the inside supplied by Carrie, Special Agent Jeremy Clyde, fronting as my case manager.

Jeremy came highly recommended. An all-American boy with an all-American grimace and the hard edge of a Special

Forces veteran. We understood that there would be no order to abort from above or beyond. The two of us would decide what steps to take and how far to go. Once we had located Bobby, Jeremy would contact Carrie who would have a search warrant sworn out within hours based on the evidence from Marguerite's cell phone and our subsequent investigation. Swann and his team were already writing the affidavit. The key names—Marguerite Ferguson, Thomas Quincey, and possibly Desmond Cole—would be redacted due to the top-secret nature of the play.

But in the real world, if we located Bobby, all bets were off. Based on my ghost transmitter recordings, it appeared that CCS had already been infiltrated by Marguerite's indoctrination team. These scumbags would form a shield around Bobby to protect him from any stray commandos who might magically appear with the intention of busting him out. Which was why our official orders were simply to locate him and let Carrie's people do the rest. She did not want Nick Crane aka Ned Stamper and SA Jeremy Clyde to go commando in a fiery and perhaps doomed attempt to liberate Bobby. I understood. Hell, I respected her position. But knew full well that anything could happen if and when I got to Bobby.

It was remarkable how Carrie and her team and their contacts had opened doors. After rolling an SUV and taking a bullet in the South Carolina Lowcountry, Carrie was now a minor celebrity in FBI circles. The Southern agents respected the way she'd toughed it out without so much as a whimper. People know people who know people, and it was quickly and effectively leaked that the Boston FBI office needed to plant an inmate and a case manager inside CCS as part of their investigation into the Lowcountry attack and related matters of national security. Papers were signed, and I had self-reported earlier that day.

Marguerite, of course, could already have full knowledge of our operation. Somehow, that didn't matter. I figured I was already on a collision course with her indoctrination crew. In fact, I couldn't wait to see the whites of their eyes.

Unrolled my survival kit...socks and underwear and weak-ass soft shoes, skippies the cons call them...and the mean and pathetic toiletries and the pencil stub and toothbrush not much bigger than my little finger. Then I made my bed, fitted sheet and single grey blanket. Stretched out and stared into nothing. Which was peaceful and quiet. Until a con named Ty Hardaway knocked on my cell door. We chatted for a few minutes. Then he asked me if I wanted to join his men's group.

"Is it a Christian men's group, Ty?"

"Most of us are Christians, but that's not our emphasis. We talk about everything—finance, sports, politics—that can get interesting—the books we've read. We try and share our thoughts and feelings, stuff like that."

It sounded okay...if I was actually doing time...I was non-committal, told him I'd think about it...Evening chow came and went, the food tasteless, sucked dry by corporate greed and something else I can't describe, something cold and lifeless that has turned its back on the human race. As the men ate, they became more talkative and the volume rose, the mindless chattering of tree creatures from antediluvian times.

The con who would have been my cellie had been released on Monday. Thus, the comfort of a single man in a two-man cell. Often a good thing, but this time I might have preferred company. I lay there in the three-quarter darkness conjuring up nightmare scenarios...All Marguerite had to do was send some soldiers over to jack me and...I could almost feel the scumbags mustering on the other side of the cell block door. I sat up straight, cupping my ear...Nothing. Just the coughs and snores of men half dead to a murderous world. I lay back down. Reminded myself to breathe. The night seemed to last forever as I fell in and out of uneasy sleep. Got a few decent hours before dawn...

Woke to the sound of bass and snare drums trading places. "Billie Jean" intruding upon our dreams. Then the cheery voices of the early morning DJ team. Kept waiting for an angry voice to shout SHADDUP, but no one did.

After breakfast, I languished in my cell. Dead time. What the fuck was I doing here? And where the hell was Bobby? My plan, which had seemed complex but doable, now felt like trying to climb El Capitan in bedroom slippers. The dayroom and the fourth-floor yard, a large, open-air balcony featuring a basketball court, benches, and pull-up bars, were now open. I slipped back into my skippies. The corridor at the end of my cellblock led past the dayroom out to the yard. The basketball court was empty, but a gaggle of men were working out near the pull-up bars. An old Jewish guy—pushing eighty if a day—and his three ancient buddies were doing pushups, jailhouse style, sets of ten, working up a sweat, oblivious to the cold concrete. With their stringy muscles, comb-overs, and potbellies, some of them would likely die in prison, yet there they were, laughing and grunting and razzing each other.

Inspired, I found a place nearby and did half-a-dozen sets of ten. Exchanged a few jibes with the old guys and went back inside. Was just approaching my cell, which now had a second occupant, when Jeremy Clyde walked up and introduced himself. "Hey, Haunch, I'm Clyde. Jeremy Clyde. Do whatever you need to do and make it quick. I need to escort you to food service down on the third floor."

I stopped. Looked at him. Or rather looked up at him, Clyde being a long drink of water. Plenty of muscles under his tailored uniform. "How come, boss? I was just fixing to meet my new cellie here and see about a card game."

"Not on the agenda, Haunch. You're going to be working as a trustee, and they want you now. So, do me a favor and get your ass in gear." He winked imperceptibly, left eye. I got the picture.

On the way down in the elevator, Clyde slipped me an ankle holster and push-dagger with a five-inch blade. "Hurry the fuck up, Haunch," he said, holding the elevator closed while I got strapped. I needed little urging.

Clyde led me to the food service office. The door was open. We walked in and sat down on hardback chairs facing a cluttered desk. After a while, a civilian employee wearing a monogrammed brown work shirt and an old-fashioned postal clerk's visor, walked in, sighed heavily, and sat down behind the desk. "Hi, gents, I'm Noah Cotton. Sorry to keep you waiting. Nothing but headaches this morning, but that's nothing new."

"Sorry to hear that," said Clyde, treating us to one of his shy smiles. "As you can see," nodding in my direction, "I've brought Inmate Stamper over to meet you. The word is, you need a new trustee to handle the upper floors."

"That's what they tell me," said Noah. He peered at me from under his visor. "So, what's the good word, Inmate Stamper?"

I sat up straight and smiled. "Only that I'm your man, sir. I've never been scared of a little hard work."

"Is that right? We'll see if you change your tune after a week or two." Noah shot me a Mona Lisa smile, reached behind his head, and massaged the back of his neck. "It's not as easy as you might think. It's not the work itself. A well-trained monkey could push the carts around. The problem is the inmates. Especially the wackos on the seventh floor. It don't feel right to serve somebody his lunch and have it come flying back at you." Noah paused, gave me a cool, appraising stare, and nodded his head. "I'm not telling you this to discourage you, Mr. Stamper. But the job is tougher than it looks."

"Don't worry about me, sir. I can handle it."

"Maybe you can. I'm not saying you can't." He paused and pulled his visor down lower over his eyes. "The trustees that last are the average to above average workers. Halfway up the bell curve. Think you can manage that?" I nodded. "Good. The job does come with perks. No random searches of your person or your cell. And free passage wherever your route takes you. You just show your food service ID. And you get a private room for visitation." He paused. "If you're lucky enough to have any visitors. It's a pretty sweet deal. Just don't be too gung-ho. The other trustees won't like it."

Without further ado, Noah pushed two Chromebooks in our direction. Clyde and I fired them up and were treated to a beautiful 3-D tour of the entire prison facility. First floor was intake and reception. Second floor was visiting. Third was food service and housed the old-timers. We fraudsters were on the fourth. Drug offenders on the fifth. Garden-variety sex offenders and admin on the sixth. The seventh and eighth floors were where it got interesting. CCS kept its disturbed and disabled on the seventh floor. The eighth was the SHU (Special Housing Unit) aka PC (Protective Custody). The tour ignored the basement. Interesting...

The video lasted about ten minutes. Seven minutes of tour and three describing the duties of a food service trustee, which consisted mostly of loading your cart and muling food to the top two floors. After the video ended, I sat there nodding my head like I'd just been schooled in some great religion. "Sounds good," I said. "I'll give it a try."

"Glad to hear it," said Noah. "Truth is, the crazies ain't that bad. Most of the time. It's the bastards in the basement who give me the creeps."

"Why's that?" said Clyde in a bored voice.

"That's the hole." Noah lowered his voice confidentially. "People get kind'a nutty down there."

"And the folks who go to the hole tend to be a little crazy to start," said Clyde. Same nerveless, laconic delivery.

I sat up even straighter. Serious Crane. "So, when do I start? And by the way, my Pops didn't raise no wuss. I can work the basement too if you need me to. Anything to help out. What I don't want is to be stuck in the dayroom all day playing cards and listening to people tell lies. I may be in here for fraud, but that doesn't mean I'm proud of it."

From eleven to two thirty, I shadowed a talkative trustee, who looked Italian and said his name was Dante, while he served meals to the mentally challenged and the PC people. Dante told me that there were about two hundred cons on each of the top two floors and four trustees total assigned per meal to each floor. The actual serving went pretty fast, but elevator time and chit-chat time and reloading time ate up the clock. Dante was poetry in motion—if languid tranquility is your idea of style and grace. He stopped constantly. Knew everybody. And did not discriminate between the major depressives and their more extreme cousins, or the PC people on the eighth floor. Just as we were finishing up, I asked him if he ever worked the basement. "Sure," he said slowly. "We all do but nobody likes it."

"Why's that?"

Dante shrugged. "It sucks down there. The lighting is bad, and they keep the cells super dark. And the cons...whew!" Dante put down a tray and blew on his hands. "Those guys are fucked up. They talk to themselves and sometimes they answer back. And then there are the mean bastards who get thrown in the hole for fighting. And the guys who get thrown in for trying to protect themselves against the guys who get thrown in for fighting. Catch-22, baby." He shuddered. "Shit, man, what'd you say your name is?"

"Ned."

"Yeah, Ned, I gots to get myself up out of this place. I ride in the black car, which as you may have noticed, doesn't seem to exist in this prison."

"I feel you, brother." My best sincere look. "I'm in pretty much the same boat. Except I've never had no car black or white."

Another night of terror. Not fear of my own demise this time. Something almost worse, an insistent, cold burn like the prick of an icepick undermining the nervous chatter in my head. Doom and its thousand faces. There are few things worse than the subtle kind of endgame triggered by chance—your plane goes down, a car spins out of control and T-bones you, your building catches on fire...My fear that night was simple. What if I couldn't get to Bobby? What if he wasn't even here? Or he was, but it took too long to find him? Or what if they extracted him, the first step in the dark journey to Scorpion Prison, mere hours or even minutes before Carrie's rescue team, warrant in hand, stormed the joint?

Then I had a thought. And wondered why it hadn't hit me sooner. If Marguerite believed Bobby was turned, she might not be so eager to ship him off to Cairo. Hell, she might want him on stage next to her at her MASA rallies spouting about how this time it would be different and the men and women in uniform would receive the respect they deserve. But even turned, Bobby could get obstreperous. Which worried me. Why would Marguerite want a rabble-rouser, even an intriguing one, acting up at her rallies? Then the hammer. Marguerite didn't need Bobby on tour with her. She already had the diner video, Bobby's command performance.

Marguerite likely had no personal grudge against Bobby. I was the target of her animus.

Much as she might find a fully indoctrinated Bobby an interesting specimen, Marguerite knew that sending him to Scorpion Prison would saddle me with endless, soul-crushing guilt and remorse. The truly evil love to inflict the utmost in pain.

I'd been too intent on seeing Bobby as too mentally strong to be turned. Hadn't considered how Marguerite, thinking he was now on their side, might or might not use him. But as long as there was any chance of Marguerite shipping Bobby to Egypt, I had no choice but to go in and get him. Bad odds. But that's how I like it. The hard way. Or so I told myself.

Chapter Forty-One

Friday morning. May 17, 2019. Five more days. That was all I had. Clyde, spit-and-polished as always, grabbed me right out of the breakfast line.

In the elevator, I said one word. "Guns." He nodded. Then two more words. "Glocks. Standard." This time he gave me a long, serious look. And nodded.

We caught up with Dante who was pushing a double-decker cart marked Basement on his way to the elevator. "I have a recruit for you," said Clyde. "Ned Stamper. I believe you already know him. He's specifically requested basement duty." Clyde shrugged like I probably had a screw loose.

Dante shifted his gaze from Clyde to me and back to Clyde. "Whatever. I've just been filling in down there. His loss is my gain. I'll give him the tour." Dante shook his head like I did have a screw loose.

Clyde peeled off and I followed Dante onto the elevator. We got off at the first floor. Reception to the left, intake to the right. Dante angled his cart to the right and then right again into a second elevator bank. Only one choice. Down to B-1.

I pushed the button and asked, "Is there a B-2?"

Dante nodded slowly.

B-1 was bathed in yellow light streaming from overhead fixtures. High ceilings. Very few cameras. Cells on my left and right formed two rows leading to more cells at the far end. The central area was open. Concrete floor a fading green. A female guard with a round face and tightly curled brown hair climbed down off the guard tower and took out her earplugs. Dante introduced us. Said I would be taking over for him at dinner starting today. He would keep breakfast. Her name was Sylvia. Barely five feet tall. Spunky in her brown uniform. Holster on her hip. "I've got the easy job. Mostly, I just sit here on my big rear end. Nobody comes in except you food people and the cleaning crew. And the guards when they bring folks in. I make my rounds same time you make yours." She beamed, perfectly at home there in the basement.

The cells were individual bunkers made out of concrete block. Six feet wide, eight feet deep. A single forty-watt light bulb. Steel doors and thick plywood ceilings reinforced with steel girders. And a foot of dead air between the top of the bunkers and the ceiling. Like living in a concrete box with a hole in the floor at the far end and a cold-water faucet coming out of the wall. A plastic slop bucket that you could rinse out with water from the faucet. No table. Nothing to set things on. Nothing to set down. No books. Not even comic books. A sleeping pallet with a single blanket along one wall and a trash can near the door to dispose of your food containers. Everything arranged to keep you close to the ground. The same keyhole locks as upstairs on the more civilized floors but no vertical bars here to let in the light...or to stare out of...Still, a step up, perhaps, from life in the hole in many state prisons.

Twenty cells. Twelve were occupied. "They mostly don't stay long," said Sylvia. "Three to five days tops." At each occupied cell, she announced our arrival, addressing the occupant by name and telling him to stand back. After twenty seconds or so, she'd repeat her request. Ten seconds later she put key to lock. The big steel doors were heavy, but Sylvia was strong and swung them open with studied ease. At each bunker, Dante organized a boxed breakfast with coffee and juice on a heavy plastic tray. Sap in hand, gun at her side, Sylvia entered first. She spoke to the cons in a soothing voice. They were usually huddled at the foot of their pallets or standing in the aisle near the back of the cells. Dante put the boxed meals and the drink cartons on the pallets and set the coffee down on the concrete floor. Carefully. All the while keeping an eye on the cons who either mumbled or muttered while averting their eyes or barked out their grievances, their glittering eyeballs bouncing from Dante to Sylvia. I stayed in the background. The folks in the bottom of the jailhouse got better food than we regulars did up on the respectable floors. To keep them pacified, I suppose.

After seven or eight bunkers, Dante had me take over handling the food. I took my time so that I wouldn't screw up. And still almost tipped over two coffees because I was watching the cons, their suffering. With some it was the disease of rage, with others the disease of rage and fear. With some it was only fear. Even worse was the disease of sadness. I tried not to see what I was seeing. The faces, lined and begrimed, covered with sweat and oil and grease, glowing in the dim light. The hunched and broken postures of the stiff-backed rebels loading imaginary guns in their fractured minds. All were damaged. Many would never recover.

And no Bobby. No surprise. If he was here, he was in B-2, the deep hole...Dante was in no hurry and Sylvia liked to chit-chat between stops. The feeding took a long time. The farther back we went, the stronger the smell. Sweat, mold, filth, and something else, call it despair—a cold, dank smell that filled the nostrils.

Once we'd completed the round, Sylvia, who liked Dante blew him a friendly kiss. Then on to B-2, which we accessed from a separate elevator, which meant that unless there was another elevator in the sub-basement leading from B-2 to the first floor, or some other exit, it was impossible to leave the building from B-2 without briefly occupying B-1 before taking the elevator to the first floor. Ingenious way to slow down an escape attempt. While obscuring the fact that there even was a sub-basement.

In virtually every case, you come across clues. The sea is awash with them, and the PI must sift through them with utmost care. There are two clues, however, that scream nascent FUBAR. No security where you would expect it, or over-the-top security in an already secure environment, perhaps the surest signal. I was alert for both.

We got off the elevator and walked down a short, oak-paneled hallway that led to a guardhouse. A young man with a buzz cut and big ears appeared, squinting at Dante. "Hiya, Dante. Who's this you got with you?"

"This is Ned. He's a new trustee. I'm showing him around. He's taking over the dinner shift."

"Oh, really?" He paused, looked me over, and tugged at one of his earlobes. Nodded and spoke. "I'm Officer Wycock. Nice to meet you, Ned. But listen, Dante, after you feed DiGregorio, you need to check back with me. My orders today are to escort food service back to Dr. Fritz in the research bunker."

Dante nodded and my knees buckled. Briefly. "Research bunker." Oh, shit! But not really a surprise. The guard handed Dante a key card in an envelope. The card wanded us through a turnstile and onto a walkway that led to DiGregorio's bunker, which was fairly new and made of molded blue plastic with a flat plastic roof and a steel door.

Security cameras were conspicuously absent.

DiGregorio said to call him Roberto. His bunker was large and comfortable and outfitted with a computer and a flat-screen TV. Roberto did not look Italian or of Latin extraction. More like a John Bull fireplug. Red cheeks and forehead, big gut, and very little hair. A smiler. Good dental work. And his breakfast bordered on the gourmet. He was serving a fourteen-year bid. Some kind of Ponzi scheme.

I asked him why he was down here in this grand bunker, and he laughed nastily. "It's the best of several bad options." He had a prior felony, which meant that without pulling some strings, he'd do the first several years of his double-digit bid in a medium-security federal prison. "No sirree," said Roberto, shaking his head in mock horror. "Being the survivor I am, I would probably get through it with no problem, but why bother? So, I greased a couple of palms with some money I cadged from a sympathetic uncle and here I am. Once I'm down to about seven years, I'm camp eligible, but I'm going to win my appeal before then."

"Good luck," I said.

"You'll win it," said Dante. "I've got a premonition. I've never known anybody to win an appeal, but sooner or later it's bound to happen. You da man. Power of positive thinking and all that crap."

"I'll win it," said Roberto. "In the meantime, what do I lack? Nothing. I've got the internet. I've got a cell phone. I've got television. And subscriptions to Netflix and Amazon Prime. I've even got Hulu."

"You're right," I said. "You do have everything. You're a lucky man."

After that I pushed the cart back to the guardhouse. When he saw us, Wycock came out to escort us to the research bunker, which was accessed through a solid steel door.

Wycock led the way followed by Dante with the cart. I took up the rear. Wycock depressed a buzzer built into the wall and the steel door opened a few seconds later. Just before we entered, Dante turned to me with a look that said, *Be cool, brother.* It was the most serious I'd ever seen him. I nodded grimly and followed him through the door.

We found ourselves in an enclosure with a cheap pine reception desk and four twelve-by-twelve work cubicles. Beyond the cubicles, a wooden barrier with a gate in the middle, which led to what I assumed was Bobby's bunker. The cubicles were empty. A tall beefy man wearing a blue belted jumpsuit and a well-pressed army field jacket sat at the reception desk. Everything about him screamed military—from his lightly gelled buzz cut, clean-shaven cheeks and clipped moustache to his alert grey eyes and his casual yet immaculate uniform. He stood up. At least two inches taller than Clyde. And Clyde was a very tall man.

Details. His uniform bore no resemblance to the uniforms worn by the CCS staff or the civilian workers.

"Good morning, SA Breech," said Wycock.

"Good morning, Officer Wycock," said SA Breech. A moment's chit-chat about another futile season by the Carolina Panthers, then Wycock told Breech who I was.

"So, you'll be handling dinner only, right?" said SA Breech.

"That's right, sir." Humble Crane.

"Very well, then. Our work is usually finished here by four p.m., so I probably won't be seeing you after today. A word of caution, though. Prisoner Ratner is not a well man. When you feed him, we would prefer that you not engage him in conversation. It doesn't take much to get him riled."

"I understand, sir. I'll be in and out in a jiffy."

"Good." He turned to Wycock. "My team is currently working with Prisoner Ratner. They don't want interruptions, so if you don't mind, I'll personally deliver the prisoner his breakfast." Wycock turned to Dante who quickly produced a boxed breakfast that he placed on a tray. Handed it to Wycock who passed it on to SA Breech. And that was that.

Back at the trustee lunchroom next to the kitchen, Dante and I each devoured a basement breakfast with relish, though the coffee was milquetoast.

It was frightening to discover that Bobby really was being brainwashed by a gang of para-criminals in the back bunker in B-2. But not surprising. The fact that Breech called himself SA Breech was a cute touch and insulting to any special agent in any of the real federal agencies.

When I got back to my cell, my new cellie, who seemed like just about the most ordinary lout I'd ever met, was sleeping. I stretched out on my bunk and tried to empty my mind. Not easy but I'm hardly new to this rodeo and after fifteen minutes of steady breathing, I felt first calm and then drowsy. Tried to play it forward, one scenario at a time. A lot depended on Bobby's actual condition. Could he be relied on to handle guns or knives? Normally, of course, there was no question, but these were not normal times. And what about Clyde? How far was he willing to go if I decided to put the blade to the heat?

Chapter Forty-Two

I dozed off, surfaced, went back under, and slept straight through lunch. Woke to a voice telling me I had a visitor. A guard walked me down to the visiting area and ushered me toward a private room. Walked in. Saw her. Her rose-brown hair and elegant cheekbones. It's hard to shock me but I was shocked. My vision blurred. Lost moments in a black-and-white world. Then she came into focus, a slide at a time, like a slowed-down newsreel. I sat down across from her. She was wearing a black Members Only racing jacket, black jeans, and a blue shirt.

"Hi, stranger. I just happened to be in the area," she grinned broadly, "so I thought I'd stop in to see how my good buddy is doing." Hamming for the security cameras.

"He'd be doing better if he wasn't such a jackass."

"Well, I tried to warn you. But you didn't want to hear it. You were just so smug and self-righteous."

"I'm not so smug now. But it might turn out good in the end. I might get religion in this joint."

"Haven't I always told you that's what's missing in your life? You need to get in touch with your higher power."

"Yeah. Yeah." I shook my head ruefully. "But you're right. It was when I stopped going to church that I started screwing up...But enough about me. How are you doing?"

"That," she said, "is a good question. I talked to our friend Agresti..." lowering her voice and whispering his name, "about my new career with the Innocence Project. He wasn't against it, seemed interested, but said he wanted to talk to you about it first. Which is damned inconvenient considering you're in here and I'm itching to get started."

I pondered. Was he passing the buck, or did he just want a reference before putting Adara to work? "Hmm," I said, "I guess I'll have to contact him. I'll get right on it. Just as soon as I can."

Tricky conversational ground. Didn't want to say too much. Instead, I talked about my fourth-floor accommodations and my work as a trustee. Just for show, and in case we were being recorded, I began talking about how defeated I felt. Not for getting caught, I deserved that, but for breaking the law in the first place, for betraying my principles. "'Cause all we have," I said solemnly, "are our principles." Nick Crane, king of contrition. Adara listened, pursed her lips thoughtfully, wrinkled her nose, and said, "You know, I had despaired of you. Now, for the first time, I feel a ray of hope. So don't let me down, baby."

I promised I would not. At one point I stood up, came around the table, and embraced her. Our lips met briefly. A moment's tenderness and I felt something crest inside me. That surging feeling. We stopped. The cameras.

I released her and sat back down.

After that we lightened up. She told me about a long narrative poem she was writing in both English and Iraqi Arabic about her early childhood in Baghdad. I told her about my future goal of opening a small, carpet-cleaning firm. She cautioned me that with all of North America turning to refurbished hardwood or laminate flooring, there might not be that many carpets to clean. "A man's got to do something," I said smiling. "Maybe wall-to-wall carpet will come back in style by the time I get out of here." Adara laughed. Oddly delighted by my foolish game.

Then we stopped talking. Looked...at each other...something was in the air. She leaned forward across the table. Whispered. "Dee Cole knows you're here."

Not unexpected. As such, perhaps manageable. Cole loved, or so I told myself, the spectacle, the jousting between players, the eternal intrigue. I was hardly necessary to his world, but he and Quincey both respected my courage in extremis and seemed to find me entertaining.

"How do you know?" I mouthed the words.

"He phoned me and asked me to check up on you. He was very pleasant. He said you had nothing to worry about but to be careful."

And then he asked you out to dinner, I thought.

"And then he asked me out to dinner."

I held a finger up to my lips. Got up and stood in the doorway. Flagged a guard and asked to move out into the general population visiting area because Adara was feeling claustrophobic.

Resituated, facing each other in folding chairs, with the cons and their visitors talking all around us, she began talking quietly, with very little affect. "Like I told you back in Wisconsin, Dee is my minder and my father's. To a certain degree, we have to cooperate. The fact my father and I have been here for twenty years won't make much difference if either of us is accused of supporting Al-Qaeda Iraq. I never told you—I couldn't have been more than fifteen at the time—one day I was snooping around in my father's papers, and I saw something he'd written about torture chambers in Iraqi prisons. My father is a very good writer; it was an eloquent denunciation of torture based on a conversation he'd had with a relative who got on Saddam's bad side. I had nightmares, Ned. Bad ones. I'd kill myself if I got sent back to Iraq. I don't want to have to keep saying this. I want you to just accept it. The truth is, we're a lot better off with Dee than we were with Thomas." I tried to interrupt…"Wait, Nick. Just listen! Would you?"

No longer smiling. I looked at her. She looked at me. I nodded. "Please proceed." I sat back and folded my hands across my belly.

"So, we go out for a fish dinner at a four-star restaurant in the Back Bay. I think Dee spends a lot of time in Boston now.

That seems to be Willem Spahn's command central these days. Dee was cheerful as always. He insisted that nobody else knows you're here. I don't necessarily believe that. He said he was tipped off by one of his sources. He laughed and asked me, 'Did anybody actually think that I wouldn't find out where Crane is? But I've got to hand it to that son of a bitch.' He said it takes..." she smiled and blew me a kiss, "'balls. To go into a place like this voluntarily.'"

"Either that or stupidity." I returned her airborne kiss. "Did you ask him if Marguerite knows I'm here?"

"I started to, but he answered before I got the words out. He said that so far Marguerite is blind to this important fact, and that he plans on keeping it that way. Then he laughed—in that gleeful way he has that makes you like him even though you don't want to—and asked me if I wanted a second helping of fish." That was Cole. He could definitely be charming...in his glib, obnoxious way.

"What did he say about Bobby?"

"Nothing." She paused, pondered, chewed at her lower lip. "He acted like it was both very dangerous and entirely natural for you to be here. Which means that he knows why you're here."

"Bobby's here." I spoke very softly. "I'm about to make contact."

She nodded. Stared at me. Pensive. Then she burst out, a little loud, a little shrill..."It isn't fair, Ned." Adara on stage. "I'm worried about you. Three years is a long time. And you're not even guilty. That's what's killing me." She threw her hands up in exasperation.

"One day at a time, darling. One day at a time."

Then I stood up and she stood up and we hugged, quickly, and then she was gone. As I sat waiting to be escorted to the elevator, I felt the world shrink around me. Bobby here in this private joint. Tony rising to the occasion. My daughter. Greg. Carrie North. Adara and me, though I wasn't quite sure about her. And a few other bare forked souls treading water, trying to keep from being sucked under.

They say rage conceals the underlying fear and that may be true, but as I got off the elevator and strolled casually down the corridor toward my cell, I felt like a titan among the cowed. Which made me laugh. Knew the feeling wouldn't last.

Never quite made it back to my cell. Clyde intercepted me. "It's your lucky day, Haunch. You got another visitor. Tall black guy with burn marks on his face…" Looked at me quizzically. "Just so all the freedom doesn't go to your head, I think I'll escort you back down."

This time Clyde stopped the elevator between floors. We faced each other. Two serious men. "That's Mars, Willem Spahn's chief of staff. I'll find out what he wants."

Clyde didn't answer. Instead, he handed me a Glock 19 in an ankle holster and two spare clips. Didn't take long to strap it on.

"I've found Bobby. He's in the back bunker in the sub-basement. The indoctrination boys work on him every weekday from eight till around four in the afternoon. I'll talk to him later this afternoon when I drop off his dinner."

Clyde shook his head. "You're blown. We need to abort."

"No. I need to talk to Mars first. I'm bouncing off a lot of factions and the faction that's made me is not the one that wants to hang me." Wishful thinking, perhaps…but it went along with Adara's take.

"Factions? Shit. Sounds like the FBI."

I grinned. "Complex organizations have a lot of pieces. Hey, Jeremy, thanks for the equipment. Now all I need are a couple of smoke grenades and two tasers. And a flashlight just in case the lights go out."

Clyde was too manly to throw up his hands in exasperation, but his annoyance passed across his forehead in a wave. "You ask for a lot, don't you, Stamper? I keep registering this stuff with a clerk in the warden's office as part of our investigation.

No problem so far, but there's a limit."

"I know." Agreeable Crane. "There's always a limit. Speaking of which, here's what I need to know." I eyed him steadily. "How far are you willing to go?"

He looked at me, his eyes a deep shadowy green. "Our orders are to inform SA North as soon as we've located Moore."

"Well, I'll know for sure by tonight. Let's touch base then. Where can we meet?" I stared at him. "Jeremy, don't go wuss on me."

He looked hurt. "Who ya callin' a wuss? I spent the first eighteen years of my life staring up the ass end of my old man's mule. 'Cause we're Amish. Plowing the goddamned fields with a goddamned mule. That took way more grit than this pissant job. With none of the fringe benefits."

I grinned. "Meaning?"

"Meaning, I ain't no wuss. And I'll kick your ass if you ever say it again."

"Okay. Whatever. Your rough childhood is why you're such a force now. And look, this is nothing personal. The truth is, Jeremy, I know you're a goddamned stud. But the bottom line is I have to rescue my friend. And the clock's ticking...Listen, man, I need something else. I need a couple of C-4 cartridges. Just in case." This tickled Clyde's nearly nonexistent funny bone. He guffawed, a loud rasping sound.

"Are you serious?"

"Serious as a megavirus." I felt the cold. From down in the animal brain spreading upwards to where feeling meets thought and your personal propaganda and rationalization squads swing into action...

"I can get you the tasers. I can sell that as a way to avoid more serious violence. And maybe the smoke bombs. But the C-4s? You're out of your fucking mind."

I laughed and offered him my hand. He shook, carefully. Then he said he'd call me down to the kitchen around eight. We could meet in the employee lunchroom.

Mars hadn't changed. Tall and stately, an African prince in a sharp suit complete with elegant cravat. His strong, handsome, disfigured face glowed with health and fortitude. Beside him, I felt like a pipsqueak. We shook hands and I sat down. Composed and deadpan. Instead of talking, he extracted a small spiral notebook from his side suit pocket. Began writing. Wrote for a long time. Then he handed it to me.

The gist was simple. Spahn was grateful because I had saved him from the kidnapping and possibly worse. He was sick of Cole and wanted to shed him. Did not know how. Cole was oily and persistent and threatened to expose Spahn, for what he wasn't sure. All-night poker games? Occasional call girls? Spahn wanted us to get together. As soon as it was humanly possible. To talk turkey.

Mars wrote those exact words. *To talk turkey.* Then he wrote that Spahn didn't trust Cole anymore and that we had to move fast. I said it all sounded kind of crazy. Mars frowned and turned to a new page in his notebook. Wrote. Handed it over. *No crazier than what you got yourself into. Willem says it means an unlimited budget to do whatever we need to do to shed Cole and the principals once and for all.*

Then Mars found a new page and wrote for a long time: *Willem says the decent people of America have to take back the power. Says we probably need to elect a new president. Says he doesn't care if it costs him money. He's got so much money he could stand on the top of the Eiffel Tower and piss liquid gold from here to eternity, and he would still not even dent his treasure chest. Says that although he was a Burgrave, that didn't help him climb the ladder. He did it all on his own. Now he wants to give back. Says the first step is taking the country back from this gang of criminals. That's where you come in. He says you can name your salary.*

When he finally finished, Mars flexed his right hand. Spoke, "I think Willem is scared, Mr. Crane." Mars nodded toward the cameras in the corners of the room. Went back to writing.

Handed it to me. *Willem's like a boy scout with the Midas touch. Barely drinks. Doesn't smoke. Just an everyday guy who has the touch. But he's got no experience with this heavy stuff. Neither do I. We need you.*

I read it two or three times. Nodded. Curtly. "All right. Tell him I'll contact him when I get out. Now I got to get moving. Nice seeing you, Mars. I mean that."

Chapter Forty-Three

I stepped up to the B-1 guard tower at a quarter to five. No one was there. Then a woman with brown hair and regular features walked up to me carrying a clipboard. "Hi, Mr. Stamper. I'm Barbara Finch."

Another working girl making good bank working for the private prison industry. B-1 was uneventful. I was born to serve.

On the B-2 elevator, I said a quick prayer to an absent god.

At first, I thought the guardhouse was empty. Then a woman slowly emerged. Standard CCS uniform. Short hair. Side part. Gamin face, blue eyes, and that determined mouth. Right arm in a sling. Carrie North.

"Hi," she said. "I'm subbing in. Tonight only. Don't look so surprised, Ned. Now listen." She stopped, put her left hand on her hip, and smiled. "I think you should go back there alone. Then if you want me to come back and meet Bobby, I will. You be the judge." Trim in her uniform, her Glock holstered at her side. It hit me hard. Really glad to see her. "Ned," she said quietly, "there's a second exit back there. You need to locate it."

"How do you know?"

"Because I came on at four o'clock. The guy before me, a spick-and-span fellow with big ears, took me back to meet the guy doing security for Marguerite's crew."

"Marguerite's crew?"

"Her indoctrination crew...I saw three guys there all wearing blue jumpsuits. And field jackets. A big guy at the desk and two other guys in cubicles. One of them came out with folders under his arm. Whatever they're doing, Ned, they're tracking it very carefully..."

Shades of Frank Constantine and his *gentler, kinder torture* records. "And they don't look like they're connected to any legitimate agency, right?"

"They look like subcontractors to me."

"Paramilitary working for Marguerite. That's my guess. Same kind of guys who contract with the CIA and NSA."

"No doubt. The point is they're not back there anymore and they didn't come through this way. Which means..."

"Wow!" My turn to smile. "Good detective work. I must say...Okay, just let me feed Mr. DiGregorio first, and then I'll talk to Bobby..."

To my relief, Roberto DiGregorio had shed his earlier talkative mood. Propped up on his bed, he was watching a movie. He waved vaguely toward his card table. "You can leave it there. Thank you, my friend." And that was it.

When I came back out and checked in with Carrie, her cheery mood had vanished. Now her forehead was wrinkled, her blue eyes clouded with concern. She handed me key cards to Bobby's enclosure and bunker. "I'm worried, Nick. I'm just fucking worried." Clamped her lips together and shook her head. "To get through the steel door just press the buzzer. It relays to the main switchboard. You'll be buzzed in immediately. Good luck, Nick."

"Ned."

"I mean Ned."

"Thanks, Officer. I mean that." I saluted her. Pushed my cart toward the steel door.

Bobby's bunker was ringed by workout equipment. Pull-up bars. Weights, long-since banned in public prisons. A portable basketball hoop. And about one hundred square feet of closely cropped putting green, which reminded me of Bobby's goats. I hoped Leo was taking care of them. I thought he probably was. The bunker was about twenty feet wide and eighty feet deep. The back end butted up against the wall.

I walked over to Bobby's door. Announced that dinner had arrived in a strong clear voice. Waited. Nothing. Tried again. Still nothing. Wanded myself in.

The accommodations were similar to DiGregorio's, only larger. Plastic walls painted to look like bricks. Both a living and a sleeping area. An actual couch and bed, a table, and a miniature refrigerator. Stainless-steel vanity with toilet and shower. But no TV and no computer. I arranged Bobby's dinner on a tray and set it on the table. "Bobby, it's me." I tried again. Louder. My voice weird and strained in the empty room.

Stopped. Horrible thought. What if they had moved him this afternoon? But the large male secretary in the blue jumpsuit, SA Breech, would have told Carrie that Bobby was being rolled up. I braced myself against the wall. No. He was here. His condition, not his presence, was the issue. Gun in hand, I moved slowly past the sofa, which was littered with *Military Officer* and *American Veteran* magazines. Made no sense. Bobby was a news junkie but never read military magazines. Recced the sleeping area. No Bobby. His toilet articles were arranged neatly next to the sink. A bar of soap drying on an upside-down plastic soap dish. An unopened package of plastic safety razors lying in wait.

There was a back entrance leading to an enclosed passageway that led to an ordinary wooden door that was held ajar by a rolled-up copy of *American Veteran*. I put my gun away. Swung the door open gently and stepped into the diner stage set. Half expected to find Bobby sitting there at the counter. No luck. My heart quickened. Everything was made out of plastic. Plastic pies in the pie case and even the booths proved to be nothing more than interlocking plastic panels. Walked quickly toward the trio of phone booths at the far end.

Nearing the phones, I stopped. Familiar breathing. He was here. "Hello, Nick." The voice came from off my right shoulder.

I turned very slowly. Bobby. Standing by the plastic cigarette machine. Clean-shaven. Pupils dilated. Shaved head glistening.

"Hi Bobby."

He took one step forward, one step back.

"You are Nick? You better be Nick. You better not fuck with me."

"Don't worry," I said gently. "I'm Nick."

"Don't 'don't worry' me. Not here in Brainfuck City. They just shot me up with this new drug about an hour ago. Pharmaceutical grade bath salts. Right now, you've got spiders crawling all over your face and your eyes look like they're crawling out of their sockets. It's a good thing I'm rock solid. Otherwise, I'd be all the way gone. And you would too." He paused. A shudder ran through him, starting in one cheek and extending down across his powerful jaw before disappearing into his shirt collar. Wearing civvies. Jeans and a denim shirt. Crane attire.

He took one step closer. "Gimme your hand, Nick. Let me see if you're real." I stepped up and we shook. Gingerly. For three or four seconds. He took his hand away. "Okay, you're real. I'm real too except I don't feel real. They've been giving me injections and put a chemical they call Nuphasifine in my food that affects my, what the fuck do you call them, my neurotransmitters. Changes my personality. Makes me long for strong, authoritarian leaders. Every day I feen for Big Brother. It gets worse and worse."

Holy shit. "Why are they doing this, Bobby?"

He shrugged. "Motherfuckers call me Ratner. Prisoner Ratner. Motherfuckers are crazy...wait, Nick, we need to go somewhere where they can't hear us. I'm not paranoid. I mean I am but I'm not. Are you strapped?" I nodded. "Good. C'mon." We walked the length of the diner and Bobby opened the door to the passageway where we powwowed. It made sense. Microphones in the diner. Microphones in the bunker. But in between? Less likely. Bobby was incredible. Still cagey even when sledge-hammered by a drug that made the Sodium Pentothal we gave Tommy

Blank seem like a stroll down the Miracle Mile.

We stood there in the passageway facing each other. "Okay, so...wait! How in the fuck did you get in here? Wait, you must have infiltrated them. Fritz and his crew." He looked puzzled. "But you're not dressed like them."

"No, Bobby, I'm not with Fritz and his crew. I'm not with anyone. I'm here for you. To get you out of here."

"Get me out of here?" he said absently. Then he burst out, "Boy, you look like shit with those spiders crawling all over you, you fucking libtard." He laughed, a chilling sound. "The reason they're doing this to me is because even though I'm mostly turned, they're still not satisfied. They say we've got to be certain. They spend all day working on me and then give me this shot every other afternoon. It comes on fast and hard. Feels like my brain is exploding. I can't describe the fear. It makes me feen for a strong leader. Right when you walked up, I was huddled back there by the cigarette machine praying that Big Brother would come. 'Cause I'm scared. You know me. I'm not scared of much and I can ride out dope rushes that haven't even been invented yet, but I am scared to go to Scorpion Prison. But you see, I don't think they'll actually send me there. 'Cause I'm too valuable as a test subject. You know something, Nick," Bobby couldn't stop talking, his thoughts racing at warp speed, and he kept batting the air in front of me like he was trying to knock the spiders out of the air, "just 'cause I'm turned doesn't mean we can't be tight. I love you, buddy. Which is why I'm leveling with you. But damn, I've been through some crazy shit. I even made a fuckin' propaganda video for Fritz and his team. I was so into my character it was scary. Like a true right-wing patriot. But making that video was a mistake. They like it too much. They want more. The main guys are smart. I think they were with the Company or NSA or some other agency. They're getting paid a lot of money, I think, by...that horrible woman, the one that started this whole mess."

"Marguerite."

"Yeah, Marguerite. So because I was in 'Nam and because they know I've killed some people, they think I'd make a good Manchurian Candidate. The joke's on them. They're the only ones I want to kill. But if they can turn me into the Manchurian Candidate, it's huge for their fuckin' brand. You should hear those fools talk about their brand." Bobby rapped on his shaven head with his knuckles. Resounding solid sound. "They give me these drugs to break down my resistance to surrendering and embracing my role as a professional killer of men. But it won't work 'cause I'm a good person and I'm too strong for them…"

I stepped forward and very gently placed my hands on his shoulders. Released him and stepped back. "Bobby, I'm going to get you out of here. You've only got four more days till they're going to send you to Cairo."

He stepped forward, dilated pupils crowding out the brown of his irises. "You don't get it. Usually, you get it but not this time. Fritz told me he wants me here to continue our work. He told me they'll send someone else in my place. Like they have a torture quota to fill. I feel sorry for the poor bastard."

"That poor bastard is me, Bobby." Thumped my chest lightly with my right fist. "If I don't turn myself in by twelve a.m. May 22, that's Wednesday morning, they'll send you to Scorpion Prison."

"Turn yourself in?" said Bobby, incredulous. Then he laughed but in a puzzled way. "You look like you're already in that fuckin' prison with those spiders crawling all over you. Why would you turn yourself in?"

"To save you from going to the fucking prison. That's their deal. But it's not my deal. My deal is to get us both out of here in the next day or two."

"Does Marguerite know you're in here?"

"I'm not sure about her. Some of them know I'm here. Desmond Cole, for sure. So far he's just watching the movie."

"That's what I've been doing. Watching my own goddamned movie. I don't want to be in my own movie. I want to be in

273

somebody else's movie."

"No, you don't. You just think that way now 'cause you're so badly outnumbered. Do they torture you along with the drugs?"

"No," said Bobby. "They know that doesn't work. People just lie, say anything, to make the torture stop..." He turned away for a moment, turned back, suddenly terrified. "Nick, I got to understand this. Are they really going to send you to Scorpion Prison in my place?"

"I think Marguerite wants to do the torturing herself. At least at first. That's what she says, and I believe her."

"No!" said Bobby, excited like a child. Then he repeated himself several times concluding, "That's no good. No fucking way."

"I agree. The only solution is to get us both out of here and that's what we're going to do."

Bobby stared at me. Then the hard line of his mouth relaxed into a wide smile. Looked twenty years younger. "Well, what if I just want to stick it out here and see what happens?" He giggled nastily. "You know where I fucked up, baby?"

Yeah. Buying into this weak shit. But I didn't say it.

"My mistake was trusting that goddamned homeless crackhead Mitch. After all we've done for him. But I've always been a sucker. My dad was like that. So when Mitch knocked on the door, I made the mistake of treating him like a human being. Fuck...It's embarrassing. I'm slipping, Nick, and now I've let these German bastards turn me. They've got me halfway convinced that being America's new Manchurian Candidate might be just the perfect thing. This year's model. Become a cliché. Go out with a bang."

"It's this environment," I said calmly. "You won't think this way once you're free."

This tickled Bobby. "Goddamned right, buddy. It's this fuckin' environment. And I am terrified of being free." He paused. Raked his right hand across his cheek. Held his fingernails up to the light. No blood. An evil smile. Like some private amusement.

"Okay, then, because these fucking bath salts act like a truth serum, I'm going to give you a little clue." I looked at him. Waited. After a portentous pause, "Fritz and his team usually take the weekend off. Even if some of them are here, they don't do much. Just sit around and go through their paperwork. They pretty much leave me alone. This injection will wear off around dawn. Then I'll sleep. If we were to make a break for it, it has to be tomorrow night or Sunday."

That's more like it. "Where's the exit? At the far end of the diner, right?"

"Right. The door by the phones leads out through the back wall of the diner. I don't know where it goes from there. That's how Fritz and his guys get in and that's how they leave."

"How do they open it?"

"Must be a key card."

"Good. 'Cause I have a key card source."

Bobby looked at me. Thoughts bouncing in and out of his mind. Yet still coherent in his lost soul fashion. That was Bobby... "I bet you do, Nick. I bet you do have a source. So, how the fuck did you get in here?"

I smiled. "That's a story for another day. I've got to get out of here now. Report back to food service. Then back to my cell on the fourth floor. Your dinner's on your table." I opened the door to the bunker. We walked through the bedroom into the common area. Bobby, who had been sifting through these revelations, suddenly cracked up. "Goddamn, Nick. You're the fuckin' waiter. How did you arrange that play? Maybe I am going to have to come back to life just so I can rub elbows with a man of your genius. Hah!"

And then he didn't want me to go. But I had to go. Just before I left, Bobby pulled me close and half-whispered. "You know, baby, they've been planning this for a long time."

"How do you know?"

"Two things. First, Mitch had been coming round for a while. I used to see him hanging around outside and a couple of times I actually saw him walking down the hall on our floor. Bastards were setting me up." He paused.

"And the other thing?"

"The other thing? That's easy. They brought me here less than seventy-two hours after they snatched me. The fucking diner was already built. Just waiting for me to do my red, white, and blue act."

It made sense. We shook hands warmly. Stared at each other. Bobby.

Chapter Forty-Four

As soon as I saw Carrie, I knew what I had to do. "How quickly can you get the warrant sworn out?"

"Monday by noon. I'll have the team standing by. We'll extract Bobby at five p.m. sharp right after Fritz and the goon squad leave."

"What if they decide to move him tomorrow or Sunday?"

"They won't. 'Cause Fritz will want to be right in the middle of it and he's off for the weekend."

"Not necessarily. Bobby just told me they *usually* take the weekend off. But sometimes they come around to finish up their paperwork and shit like that."

Carrie frowned. "Hmm. That's not good. But either way we've got no choice because we can't obtain the warrant until Monday...Look, work with me on this and in return you have the green light to do anything necessary to protect Bobby and yourself in the meantime..." She punched me in the shoulder with her good left hand. "I'll have Clyde work the whole weekend. With orders to check in on Bobby every two hours. And we'll have you deliver all his meals. 'Cause look. It's too dangerous for you and Clyde to try and break Bobby out the back door unless it's life and death. We have no idea what's back there. And I can't have Clyde willfully breaking the law. We need the warrant."

I didn't buy it because Bobby was being held here illegally in the first place. But I didn't fight her. Instead, I insisted that she have Clyde obtain the key card for the B-2 rear exit on both Saturday and Sunday just in case we had to skedaddle quickly. She agreed. I was worried. She could tell. But I had to leave with my cart before anyone missed me. I was scheduled to meet Clyde in food service in about ninety minutes. I'd brief him and she could verify everything with him by phone. She was off duty at eight. She'd drive to Norfolk and catch the red-eye flight back to Milwaukee. She'd call Swann and brief him regarding the additions to the affidavit. Back in Milwaukee, she'd check in with Tommy Blank, who was proving to be an engaging though not entirely reliable witness. She and Swann, affidavit in tow, would fly to Boston on Sunday. Court was Monday morning. It was going to be tight. Very tight. And we had to keep Bobby in one piece until then. I would leave CCS with Bobby and the FBI extraction team. My presence would be all the more valuable if, as anticipated, they injected him with bath salts on Monday as part of a long day of indoctrination.

I whizzed back up to food service. Dropped off my cart. Ate a fine basement dinner while kibitzing with the other trustees. Then returned to my cell and waited. At a quarter to eight, Jeremy Clyde appeared, carrying a briefcase and frowning, his version of a stern case manager. My cellie was off somewhere playing cards. Clyde stepped into my cell and started to open his briefcase. Stopped. Gave me a meaningful look. I nodded. "Wait till we get to food service…or the elevator."

Clyde decided on the elevator. He knelt on the floor and snapped his briefcase open. My eyes lit up like magic lanterns at the sight of two smoke bombs, two tasers, a military-grade flashlight, and to my surprise, two tasty-looking OC canisters. No C-4 cartridges but I'd trade them for the OC anytime. "Here. Gimme your weapons. I can't give you all this crap to take back to your cell, so I reserved a locker for you in the food service dressing room." I gave Clyde the Glock and the clips but insisted on keeping the knife for personal protection.

"So," I said smiling, "I guess you've decided that we're not going to abort."

"That depends." His shy smile. "We're trained to keep all our options open."

I nodded. Clyde snapped his briefcase closed and fired up the elevator. Ten minutes later, I was the proud owner of a food service locker and Clyde was fully briefed. Without prompting, he said that Carrie's schedule for obtaining the search warrant was cutting it too close. I concurred. Clyde said he would obtain the key card to the secret B-2 exit first thing Saturday and Sunday mornings, and that to provide maximum contact with Bobby, based on Carrie's instructions, he would arrange for me to sub in as the basement food delivery guy for breakfast and lunch as well as dinner. Then he escorted me back to my cell.

Nervous. Very. Decided to while away the hours with the fellas in the TV room. The Charlotte Hornets and the Boston Celtics were all knotted up at the end of the third quarter and I had just settled back in my chair to watch the final twelve minutes, when a head-shaved gentleman with black ink sleeves came over and crouched down next to me. "Hey, Stamper." Deep, guttural Armenian whisper. "We want to talk to you."

"Why?" Without turning my head from the screen where the Celtics' point guard was completing an acrobatic three-point play.

"'Cause we want to. Why the fuck else would I be here?"

"Hmm..." Pretended to contemplate. "Okay, friendo. Where?"

"In my cell down at the other end of the cellblock."

"No."

"No? Did I hear you right?"

By now angry cons were telling us to shut up. I rose quickly and walked out of the TV room into the dayroom proper, my new friend following nimbly despite his bulk. I sat down at one of the empty card tables and gestured for him to sit down across from me. He did. So did two other head-shaved Armenians. I sat back and perused my three new friends. Two of them, Friendo included, had thick lips, round faces, and heavy five o'clock shadows. The third looked like he had shaved within the past hour. His lips were thin, almost sculpted, and his skull glistened.

"Well, to what do I owe this pleasure?" I said in a mellow, albeit world weary, manner.

Lips stared at me. He had a ruptured blood vessel under the iris of his left eye, which undermined his otherwise refined appearance. He turned to Friendo. "Would you mind telling this gentleman the facts of life, Robert?"

"Sure, boss...So, listen up, Ned Stamper, or whatever the fuck your name is, you ain't foolin' nobody with your trustee bullshit. We know you're a CI for that tall asshole who keeps calling you out of your cell."

"Thank you, Robert," said Lips. "That's what we believe, which is why we're going to check you. Stoolies don't fly around here. Not in our world. Now, we happen to know that you pulled a three-year bid. I want you to think about that, Mr. Stamper. That's a long time. That's a very long time."

He paused and Friendo stepped into the breach. "What the boss is saying, asshole, is that if you don't get your shit straight, we're going to make your life a living hell."

"Robert is correct," said Lips. "Because we believe in fair play, we're going to give you three choices. Choice number one is we set you up with a patsy and you kick his ass..."

"And I've got just the fish in mind," said Friendo.

"I'm sure we have several good candidates," said Lips. "And after you fuck him up..."

"You got to fuck him up good," Friendo burst in. "Then they'll give you a week in the hole..."

"Robert is correct again," said Lips. "A week in the hole will give you time to seriously reconsider whether you want to be a white rat. So that's option number one. You fuck up a patsy, go to the hole, and get your head straight."

My best friendly smile. Congenial Crane. "I don't like that option. What's number two?"

"Oh, a wise guy," said Lips. "Armen, could you fill Mr. Stamper in on option number two?"

Armen, whose face was even rounder than Robert's, leaned forward and rumbled deep and low. "Option two is you take part in a little blanket party tomorrow night. They'll be six or seven of us. Four of us and two or three Russians. And just one little ol' you…"

"Next," I said cheerfully. Could come up slashing knife in hand in one and a half seconds, which would result in three permanently scarred Armenians. Which would lead to the hole and perhaps much worse, the end of all hope for Bobby and me.

"I'm sure you already know what option three is…and it's not much fun," said Lips. "Unless maybe you like that kind of thing. Tell him, Robert." So Robert did.

"Option three is this big black dude down on the third floor makes you his asshole buddy." Robert grinned nastily. "He'll be keeping you so busy you won't have time to roll on people."

The rage rising. My knife in my right hand just under the table. Took a deep breath. Spoke to Robert. "That nearly cost you your eyes, Friendo. Though actually," turning to Lips, "I think I'll take it out on you instead, you douchebag motherfucker. Now get the fuck out of here before I kill all three of you."

Silence. Robert looked at Lips. Armen looked at Lips. Lips sputtered a bit but couldn't seem to get the words out. Then he stood up. Nodded to his boys who rose to their feet. All three of them then stalked out of the dayroom. I knew they'd be back. Prelims don't mean a thing. I holstered my knife. When I stood up, my hands were shaking.

Walked quickly back into the TV room. Someone had taken my seat. Found another. Game ended. Celtics won. Thirty minutes till lights out. I trooped back to my cell block with the rest of the guys.

My cellie Donald was in a good mood. He had won ten dollars

playing Texas hold'em. We spent the next three hours getting to know each other, which helped keep my mind off my sea of troubles. Finally, Donald got sleepy and fell silent. Took me another hour to get to sleep but I finally went under.

Chapter Forty-Five

There are days when you do not want to wake up. Everyone has had them. I've had more than my share. Saturday morning was bad. Woke up to Prince singing "Let's Go Crazy," which connected somehow with something Frenchy Lefevre told me on the phone in 2017 less than a month before his final stint in the hospital where he coughed his lungs out and expired. Frenchy had said I'd been working the edge for too long and that sooner or later every edge player takes a fall and only a small percentage ever get back up. Frenchy was rarely wrong and this morning I could feel the abyss growling loudly in the pit of my stomach. My thoughts turned to Bobby, and I felt even worse. My oldest friend other than Jimmy Sain and my brother Rafer, whom I rarely see. Not only was Bobby turned, or partly turned, or afraid that he was turned; almost worse, the daily indoctrination combined with the drug regimen had made him mean. I wasn't that worried about getting him to leave with me and the FBI. But very worried about how to get him out if everything went FUBAR, and I had to freestyle before Carrie got the search warrant.

Frowning, Clyde appeared in front of my cell at half past six. As usual he stopped the elevator on our way down. The exit key card changed hands. "I checked. They change it every day. I'll pick up the new one tomorrow." And then he handed me a burner phone. Said he'd already entered his and Carrie's cell numbers under contacts. In case anything got dicey before we made our move. "But listen, I almost forgot. The key card can only be used once. The door stays open for exactly forty-five seconds and then closes automatically. This is to discourage unnecessary use of the emergency exit. The regular basement employees are instructed to use the employee exit on the first floor at all times..." He stared at me, his angular features twisted into his habitual frown, but this time all traces of his usual sly humor were gone. Something was eating at him. "Listen, Jeremy, I can tell something's bothering you. What's up? We're a team. You got to keep me in the loop, baby."

He hesitated. Looked at me. Looked away. Finally spoke. "It's probably nothing. When I checked in with SA North this morning, she told me she was pretty sure that she'd been surveilled getting off the plane in Milwaukee and that she and Tim Swann were going to catch an earlier flight to Boston. She said I should let you know."

I nodded. Worrisome, yes. But pleased by our growing trust. Carrie and me. Beginning to feel almost fraternal. Jeremy said he'd be talking to her again that afternoon.

Slight rigmarole to get me shifted to all the basement weekend shifts but we worked it out with Noah Cotton. Then Clyde left and I watched a kitchen employee load my cart. On the way down, I stopped the B-1 elevator and switched Bobby's breakfast with Roberto DiGregorio's. Just in case they really were messing with his food...

A new woman was perched halfway up the guard tower. Weekend help. Said her name was Perla McGibbon. Half black, half Irish. Very nice teeth. Taller than Sylvia and just as spunky. Same gun, different hip. Her strong voice and take-no-prisoners manner complemented my air of humble servitude, and we made it around the three sides of the rectangle in what for me was record time. Very quiet at this early hour.

One small glitch. Friendo, the pugnacious Armenian from the night before, met Officer McGibbon at his bunker door.

"Stand back, sir," she said. "This trustee," pointing at me, "has to deliver your breakfast." Friendo first glanced my way, then stared. Then he clenched his fists and assumed a half-assed martial arts stance.

"At ease, big guy. I'll just eat it myself." That got to him, and he moved grudgingly toward the back of his bunker where he maintained his stance as I dropped off his food...

Wycock's weekend replacement in the B-2 guardhouse struck me as retired military, no doubt collecting a pension. He barely looked at me, merely grunted as he handed me three key cards—one to Roberto DiGregorio's cell, and two for Bobby's area.

Still in bed, one bare foot sticking out from under his covers, Roberto was even less talkative than the previous evening. I dropped off his breakfast and wheeled my cart over to the steel door leading to the research half of B-2. Buzzed my way in. No sign of Fritz and his crew. I wanded my way through Bobby's gate. Inside the enclosure, I paused and took a deep breath. Rolled my cart over to his door. Knocked. No answer. Of course. He was sleeping. I carded myself in. The place was trashed. A copy of *American Veteran* torn in half. The bath salts must have turned on Bobby after I left. His dinner was mostly untouched. He was stretched diagonally across his bed under a wool blanket, his great head facing the wall.

I smiled. I knew Bobby. When he finally woke up, he would rub his eyes and look around in disbelief. Ten minutes later the bunker would be spick-and-span. I dropped off his breakfast and headed back to food service...

You can never let your guard down in the joint, even a fairly safe one like CCS, and I was glad to run into Ty Hardaway of the Christian men's group in food service just as I was finishing up a delicious basement breakfast. Safety in numbers. We rode the elevator together back up to the fourth floor. Again, he dangled his men's group, which was meeting in an hour. I was almost ready to cave, but it was not to be.

I was barely back in my cell when Clyde appeared again, grimmer than ever. "C'mon, Stamper. They want you downstairs."

For what? Clyde was stone-faced all the way down in the elevators. Destination: B-1. He stopped the basement elevator and turned to me. "You don't scare easy, do you?"

"Hell, I'm always scared."

"Yeah? You could have fooled me." A curious look.

"I've learned to hide it. Most of the time. I feel all the normal emotions."

"You're sure about that?"

Sarcastic bastard. I stared at him. "The only thing I'm sure about is we're going to bust Bobby out of this rat hole. Where are we going?"

His turn to stare. "Don't get your ass in a sling. We're going to meet the brass. They want a progress report. And the captain said something about a problem with some Armenians." He shrugged. "We should just tell them that we'll be out of here by eight o'clock Monday night. Or sooner." Clyde had it sussed.

We met in a pleasant, paneled room with a convenient dumbwaiter, armchairs, and a coffee table. It was hidden behind a plain steel door built into the wall behind one of the B-1 bunkers. Someone's version of clandestine. With coffee and donuts. Gratis. Commander Johnson, a tall man with thinning hair and a perpetually worried look, didn't say much. He let his assistant, Captain Spencer, a cheerful, light-skinned black man wearing a polo shirt and Dockers, take the lead. Their concern was that Clyde and I were sticking out like a pair of oversized thumbs. Tongues were wagging. With just a hint of roguish glee, Captain Spencer noted that he had put the clamps on one of the Armenians, but that it was only for three days. At which point Clyde raised his hand and said three days would work "just fine." Our plan was to wrap things up Monday night. "You do understand," I said, "that if we didn't have to move so quickly, our technique would have been more subtle."

"I understand," said the captain, smiling. "Monday night

will be six days in total since you and your team arrived wrapped in the cloak of mystery. Which we rather enjoy here at CCS. It breaks up the monotony. Commander Johnson and I are very comfortable working with the agencies and their proxies." The word *proxies* rolled off his tongue. "And if I might ask, how is your investigation going?"

Clyde sat up straight and looked nervous. I smiled and stepped into the breach. "We can't give you any concrete details, sir, but I can tell you where things stand in a general sense. We're right at the critical point, like Humpty Dumpty on the wall. It could go either way. Maybe we fall off the wall and the taxpayers' dollars go down the drain. Or maybe it works out and all the politicians are kissing babies and asking for more funds for law enforcement for important missions like ours. Either way, Jeremy and I will know more tomorrow."

Clyde nodded, his long face drawn, and I realized that in forty years he would resemble the commander, who chose that moment to speak. "You men certainly live interesting lives. Somebody should think about making a movie. Because based on my experience, most of the real action takes place underground." He stopped, nodded, and went back to looking worried.

The captain walked us to the elevator. "I want to have a word with you, Mr. Stamper."

"Ned, please."

"Yes, Ned, be careful. Don't underestimate the Armenians. The older guy, Hagop, the one with a face like an axe handle, is an accomplished blade man. He's the only one of them to draw a heavy bid. His boys think he's right up there with Michael Jordan or Jesus H. Christ." Then the surprise. "Now in case they give you any more trouble, here is my private cell number. Don't hesitate to call me. Mr. Clyde already has it." Intriguing. He watched while I entered his number in my contacts list.

Good captain.

Back in my cell, I stretched out on my bunk, knife close at hand. My cellie was in and out, cheery in his unobtrusive manner.

From ten to twelve the radio station played oldies. From ten to eleven thirty I dozed off. Then it was back to food service and down to the basement. B-1 was becoming routine, though Friendo did manage to hiss a few barely audible threats.

When I got to Roberto DiGregorio's bunker, the unpredictable Ponzi-schemer was sitting at his table hunched over a yellow legal pad. He sat up straight and watched as I carefully arranged his box lunch and beverages across the table from him and his writing pad. Then he spoke. "I've been depressed. Maybe you've noticed but I feel better now." He gestured toward his notebook. "These are the arguments I'm developing for my appeal. I believe in being thorough. Write up every reasonable argument and then see what sticks."

"Sounds good," I said, "I would consider all the angles just like you say and then focus on only the best ones. The good news is Dante truly believes that you're the guy who's actually going to win his appeal."

"That's what I tell myself. Every day." He pushed his notebook aside and reached for his food. Crispy brown fried chicken, real mashed potatoes, and fresh frozen peas. Decent. Like a high-end TV dinner.

When I got to Bobby's bunker, he was stretched out on top of his bed snoring. Wearing a USMC sweatshirt and cargo pants. He'd been awake long enough to eat his whole breakfast and half of last night's dinner. The place was still a mess, however, which surprised me. Not the Bobby I was used to. It hit me hard. Mechanically, like a robot, I picked up the magazines. Stacked them up under the TV, which was bolted to the wall. The remote had apparently been thrown against the wall and Bobby's toothbrush was on the floor near the table. The toilet paper had been unrolled and stretched from the bathroom nearly to the front door. I bent to my weary task. Bobby never stirred. When I was finished, I left quietly, scooping up the remainder of last night's dinner on the way out.

Hung around food service for as long as I could. Not sure

why. Dug into my basement lunch. Fried chicken passable but
not superb. Safe for the moment with my back against the wall
in the trustee lunchroom.

Considered phoning or texting Tony. But needed a safe
place. Except for parts of the basement, the prison was well-lit.
We cons were the proverbial fish in a leak-proof barrel. The
best bet was the passageway between Bobby's bunker and the
diner. Decided to call at dinnertime. Might even put Bobby on
the phone. Then the shocker. Clyde looming over my table. Of
course it was Clyde. The large white harbinger of doom.

Knew it was bad. Really bad. And it was. Clyde wouldn't say
a thing until he'd parked us in a small, all-purpose first-floor
office. Even then he checked the room for bugs before he sat
down across from me and hissed, "SA North's in a coma. She
was stabbed. Just an hour ago outside the Boston FBI office in
Chelsea. I got a call from her tech guy, Tim Swann."

Hit me hard does not capture it. Steamrolled me is closer.

"Will she live?"

"Swann said it's fifty-fifty."

Strange but fifty-fifty struck me as good odds. "She'll make
it. That woman's got spunk."

No response from Clyde. Or rather the wrong response.
"You know what this means." More statement than question.

"No, I don't know what this means. So maybe you better tell
me!" First sign of heat.

"It means we won't get the search warrant on Monday. It
means we've got to abort." Said quietly in a voice of regret.

Found a pocket of calm. Gave him a moment. "How do we
abort? What are the logistics?"

"Simple. I call the captain and tell him we're leaving. I go up
to the fourth floor and bring you down to processing. They give
you your clothes and you put them on. Then we walk out together
and are greeted by half-a-dozen FBI agents. I go home and you
go wherever you're going."

I nodded. "Just one thing. We have to take Bobby with us."

"How are we going to do that?"

"We just clear it with our friend Captain Spencer. We say we're taking him out to be debriefed at the FBI office in Raleigh on Sunday morning and that we'll bring him back that evening."

Clyde shook his head. "Captain Spencer will want to clear it with the commander."

"Then that's where it will end." Accusatory Crane. Clyde frowned and again I was reminded of what he would look like in forty years. "It's worth a try. Do it subtly. Just give him a call. Sound him out a little."

"No," said Clyde. "It won't work. Not without the necessary documents."

"C'mon, agents do this all the time."

"'Cause it's written into the agreement. I'm not going to argue about this, Stamper. But just for the record, I will run your idea past the captain. But if it doesn't work, then that's the end of it."

I didn't argue. That afternoon I had to empty my mind. Or go berserk. I hit the court. Waited my turn and played three-on-three. I was old but still had moxie. If you're open, shoot, if you're not, pass. Box out on rebounds and maybe even clog the lane by switching on defense. My team split six games. At four p.m., I bid the players a sweaty adieu and hustled down to food service. Mind racing. Strapped. Gun and knife this time. Had no idea what to tell Bobby. Had to tell him something.

To settle down, I focused grimly on my job. Perla's dinnertime replacement, a spit-and-polish Dominican named Jaeger, dapper in his CCS uniform, executed everything with exaggerated formality. When we reached Friendo's bunker, my nemesis, obstreperous as always, refused to move for at least a ten-count, which exasperated Jaeger, who began to sputter. "It's all right," I said finally. "My orders are to not serve anyone who doesn't want to be served. We can go."

The whining was damned near instantaneous. Friendo kept his distance, and I dropped off the food.

Immersed in *Saturday Night Live* reruns, the old pensioner

was still manning the B-2 guardhouse. "OT?" I said. "Sir?"

"That's right," he said absently, barely looking up as he handed me the trio of key cards.

The fat has been in the fire more than a few times in my thirty-year career. But there comes a time, Frenchy always said, when you get a case that makes every other case seem unimportant. The case you have got to win. The case I was now involved in.

Chapter Forty-Six

Bobby answered my greeting from inside his bunker. "C'mon in, Dinner Boy." Low laughter. Ominous? But when I stepped inside, he was all smiles. Thanked me for cleaning up his happy home and insisted I regale him with a few tales before we got down to brass tacks. So I described my cheery encounter with the three Armenians.

"That's the best thing I've heard since—hell, since the last time I talked to you." Bobby hooted. "I think you were born with a knife in your hand."

"I had to be. Three or four times when I was a kid, I backed down Adam with my drop point. When he was raging at Rafer or me."

Bobby gave me a knowing look. His eyes were normal. I sat there and watched him devour DiGregorio's Salisbury steak with all the fixings. And drink his two cups of coffee, black. A noisy eater and a slurper. You have to know Bobby to love him.

Then things got serious. First, Bobby pointed out that I was working with our mortal enemy, the FBI. Then he added that he had been turned by our other mortal enemy, the far-right money and power people. In short, we were both working with or for the enemy. Clearheaded for a few hours now, Bobby's mind was razor sharp.

"Now, you have to admit, if you're willing to be honest, that the rank-and-file Democrats are also corrupt. Even worse, they're old news, about as effective as the stretched-out dugs on an old sow. The new road is different. It's the hard road of authority."

I told him the world had been down that road before. It was called The Third Reich and we Americans with the help of our allies had whipped them. "We dumped them in the trash, Bobby. Where they belong. Now these new fools want to resurrect that bullshit. Don't fall for it." Incendiary words but in a quiet tone.

"Say what you like," said Bobby. "It doesn't matter. 'Cause it's all fake news..."

I sighed. Shook my head. Got to my feet. "I've got to call Tony. Can I use the back porch?" I gestured toward the back of his bunker.

He stared at me. "You're gonna call Tony? What for?"

"'Cause he's going to meet us when I get you out of here. Which is going to be tomorrow." I sat back down across the table from him, leaned forward, and spoke. "Listen, my fibbie contact on the outside, Agent North, just got stabbed in Boston, right in front of the FBI office. She's in ICU. These fuckers don't play around. That means we're not going to get the search warrant on Monday that we need to go the easy route. But if we don't get out by Monday, you or me or both of us get sent to Cairo. Or you get sent to Cairo and I get handed over to Marguerite, who will take great pleasure in torturing me." I paused.

Bobby shook his head. "I don't get it. Why can't we just go out the front door? Since I'm supposedly being rescued by the FBI."

"My guy Clyde on the inside is exploring that. But I don't think it will work. 'Cause only Agent North could ask for that and she's in ICU. We're going to have to do it the hard way. Clyde might come along for the ride. Or he might not. It might be just you and me. I'll have a key card to get us through the door."

Bobby sat up straight and flared his powerful nostrils. Spoke. "Okay, Nick. Fuck them. Fuck Fritz and his lapdogs. What time tomorrow? Let's call Tony." Bobby was alive. I reached out and pumped his hand. With or without Clyde, I would need him at his warrior best.

Fate was kind and Tony picked up on the second ring. I briefed him at lightning speed. Asked him to put a team together to meet us at street level…him and Agresti, if possible, and whatever FBI agents he could scare up. And said maybe he wanted Swann along for logistics. Told him Bobby and I and maybe a fibbie would be taking the basement exit two floors down. That I didn't know where it surfaced but that Clyde, my agent on the inside, was researching it. And that I'd given Clyde Tony's number. Tony asked me what time and I told him any time tomorrow. He said the dinner hour was probably most realistic. I agreed and told him to look sharp for other operatives when he arrived at the prison, perhaps another team of Alphabet Boys, and possibly some of Marguerite's goons. Men in uniform. Of unknown stripe and dubious persuasion. Asked him if anyone had taken over the reins from Carrie.

"I don't think so. She ran a tight ship. Plenty of foot soldiers but no one close to her in a position of authority. Seems a little odd but I believe she bounces most of her questions off Tim Swann. Though he does seem like a sharp fellow. I think Ms. North's superiors will just let things sit until she recovers."

"Is she going to recover?"

"That girl. Hell, yeah!"

"That's what I thought."

"She's tough. One of the stab wounds stopped two centimeters from her heart."

Then Tony lowered the boom. When Carrie was stabbed, Swann was walking next to her. Tony and Tommy Blank were about six feet behind them. Two assailants had come at her, one from in front, one from behind. "Good thing she's a small target. We were caught off guard. By the time I tackled the main killer, his knife was buried in her abdomen. Swann fought with the other guy who took off running. He did good for a little guy." Tony paused. "And you know what our friend Tommy Blank did?"

"Oh, don't tell me. He scrammed."

"Exactly. He vanished into the crowd, which was practically a mob by the time the FBI and the local PD showed up to arrest the killer, who I had under control."

"So, no sign of Tommy."

"None at all."

"Shit. That means he could have oozed his way back into Marguerite's camp."

"He could be giving you the black spot, buddy."

"He is giving me the black spot. Bobby and I have got to get out of here."

"Pronto. Let me think for a minute." Silence. Then Tony spoke, "On second thought, we better do lunch tomorrow. Before they have time to get organized. You and Bobby on the inside and at least Swann and Agresti and me on the outside. And maybe some fibbies." I thanked him and put Bobby on to say hello.

Then I phoned Agresti, who was not impressed. At first. But too good a PI to not acknowledge the unusual circumstances. But he committed to nothing. Asked him to think it over and gave him Tony's number.

Chapter Forty-Seven

I was making the most of my trustee status. Salisbury steak in a quiet room at six o'clock on a Saturday afternoon. Ten thousand and one worries but used to that. At least Bobby was becoming Bobby again. Just mopping up my gravy with my whole wheat toast when Clyde appeared. Hangdog look. Knew he had struck out with Captain Spencer. He mumbled something. Depressed as always. I tossed my dinner remains and wandered back to the locker room. Wrestling with the thought that the last night is often the deadliest.

Opened my locker and traded in my Glock for two tasers and six darts. Locked up and put the key in my pocket. A dog pricks up its ears. A man has only his sixth sense. Shielding the tasers, I looked out into the lunchroom.

Four of them. Stocky, round-faced Armen and lean, elegant Hagop in front, two bearish cons in back, no doubt the Russians. They advanced, shoving the tables and chairs out of their way. I flipped the locker room light switch off and ducked back into the shadows. Would need to reload each taser once unless Clyde got his ass in gear. "Clyde," I shouted, "bring the Bellini."

"I got you, Stamper." On his way and into the fray. I stepped through the locker room door, and we faced off, two against four, four tasers versus four shivs. Menaced on two flanks, the thugs formed a tight circle, their shaved heads shining like the silver helmets of the armies of antiquity.

"Drop your knives and put your hands on your heads," said Clyde, his lean face impassive. One Russian started to comply but the other charged Clyde while Armen advanced toward me warily, leading with his blade. I welcomed him, stepping back through the doorway into the shadows. Flipped on the light switch, got a clean look, and was about to tase the fool when he shocked me by sliding into me like a base runner hook-sliding into third, with a wicked leg whip at the end that sent me sprawling back into the lockers. Banged the back of my head but managed to hold onto both tasers. Armen charged, I side-stepped. His turn to bang into the lockers. His knife went clattering to the floor. No matter, he spun around, dove, headfirst this time, and caught me around the legs. Tried to drive me toward the open door.

I twisted free just in time to see Hagop staring at me from what seemed like point-blank range. His right arm flashed back, then forward, I ducked and fired. Can't say his knife grazed my skull, but it came real close. My dart caught him in his left pec, heart high. He grabbed his chest, spasmed, and dropped. I turned to Armen who had retrieved his knife. He lunged toward me aiming to drive his knife overhand through whatever part of me he could penetrate.

I tased him left-handed, not a clean shot but enough to slow him down. He staggered and I kicked him hard in the chest, skippies or no skippies. Nearly broke my toes but he went down and lay there moaning.

Reloaded both tasers and bounced back into the fray. Clyde had one of the Russians in a headlock and was punching him in the face. Knife in hand, feinting and weaving, the other Russian was creeping toward him. Easy as flipping a baby, Clyde swung his battered Russian into the other Russian's path.

I watched in wonder. Clyde literally lifted his Russian up in the air in front of him and launched a two-man battering ram into the other Russian. They all went down in a heap. I dragged the other Russian out of the pile and pointed my remaining loaded taser at his head. Clyde punched his Russian—three short rights to the jaw. Then he stood up grinning...

A phalanx of guards led by the night watch commander rumbled into play and things got straightened out pretty quickly. Two Armenians and two Russians were going to the hole. They would be pissed in the morning when I brought them their breakfast. The watch commander's assistant recorded first Clyde's statement and then mine. Standing very tall, with the confidence of a man doing his solemn duty, Clyde explained that he and I were authorized to carry tasers and similar weapons because of the tricky and extremely dangerous nature of our mission. It was all official and signed off on at the front desk. "And you can see why," said Clyde, pointing at our assailants, who were being handcuffed together by a team of guards. "Attempted murder in the first degree." I was more diplomatic. Mumbled something about just trying to do my job. The watch commander didn't seem to care. He was slightly in awe of Clyde. The Alphabet Boys cast a long shadow. Pretty soon, they left us alone.

All the excitement made me hungry again. Clyde felt the same way. We raided the larders but all we could find were cartons of boysenberry yogurt. We each ate two cartons with plastic spoons. I asked Clyde why he chose hand-to-hand combat with the Russians instead of using the darts. He looked at me. Grey eyes alive, roused from battle, but cold as Fairbanks in January. He chuckled. "I knew those bastards weren't that tough and after all this stress, I just wanted to hit somebody."

"Well, you did a good job. Thanks for having my back."

Clyde nearly smiled. Explained that Captain Spencer was not dead set against us taking Bobby out for a proffer, but that the request would have to come from SA North or someone with legal credibility speaking on behalf of SA North. Which did us no good. I looked at him and he looked at me. Questions hung in the air. Neither asked nor answered. Just before Clyde escorted me back to my cell, I swapped out the tasers for my Glock. We agreed to meet at food service half an hour before my morning basement shift. He would bring the requisite key card.

Television. In the half-light with the other cons. The NBA was now on Saturday night. The players swam before my eyes. What was on the other side of the basement exit? Who might we meet there? Had Marguerite been tipped off? She had to know by now. Didn't she?

The game ended and the cons and I walked back to our cells. I lay down on my bunk and closed my eyes. Sleep was elusive and when it did come, I dreamt about our escape route. Marsh grass, brown water, pools of quicksand. Several times I pulled Bobby back as he was about to be sucked under. Then we came to a narrowing trail that dwindled into a quagmire. Bobby hung back but I just kept walking into the heavy, wet sand. When it reached my chest, the now unspeakable fear wrenched my eyes open. Heart pounding, I lay there alone in the silent, brooding cellblock. A cough, a sigh, a gasp from someone's dream world. I lay there listening to the silence.

Chapter Forty-Eight

Woke to the sound of Bill Withers, "Ain't No Sunshine." Splashed some water on my face, checked my weapons and waited. When the time came, I headed down to food service. Clyde, who seemed to be getting thinner by the hour, was sitting at a table in the lunchroom, a small carry-on bag at his feet. I started to sit down, and he stopped me. "Put the bag in your locker. There's a Glock inside for your partner with three clips and more darts. And some other shit." I cached the equipment and sat down across from him. Then he handed me the key card to the basement exit. He looked at me and bit his lower lip, shook his head slightly. Spoke softly and I couldn't catch the words.

"What did you say?"

"I said, which is it, lunchtime, or dinnertime?"

"Lunchtime," I said.

"Okay," said Clyde. "I'll do what I can. It may not be much."

I started to speak. Stopped. Nodded my head.

Clyde insisted on accompanying Perla and me through my B-1 rounds, which was probably a good thing. Everyone seemed strangely antsy and even with our own redoubtable trio—Clyde, me, and pistol-packing Perla—it seemed to take a long time to jockey the cons to the back of their cells so that I could drop off their food.

Clyde shadowed me right up until I was about to push my

cart onto the B-2 elevator. "Okay," he said, "like I said, it may not be much." Then he saluted like any enlisted man, spun around, and walked away.

The pensioner at the gate seemed distracted as always and Roberto DiGregorio had lapsed into one of his funks. Bobby was quiet, too, but showed no signs of wavering or hesitation. He sat down at his table and began eating his breakfast. I walked back to the passageway and phoned Tony. Didn't expect an answer; he was probably en route. He had left a message that said that barring an act of God, he and Tim Swann would arrive in Charlesburg no later than eleven a.m. Per Agresti's request, they would bring him an extra gun.

Then I phoned Agresti. Left a message thanking him in advance for attending our coming out party. Then Bobby and I powwowed. Discussed the weapons we would be carrying, and the help Clyde might or might not bring. Despite the gravitas of the moment, Bobby kept chuckling over the fact that his friend, Nick Crane, the roughneck from Minnesota whom he had known for more than thirty years, was working with and had been given immunity by the FBI. On my way out, we shook hands, firmly, almost formally. Then I clapped him on the shoulder. And departed. Sun Tzu said, *Treat your men as you would your own beloved sons. And they will follow you into the deepest valley.*

This morning's big surprise was a summons to the top brass's private conference room behind the B-1 bunkers.

This time there was no Clyde. No Captain Spencer. Not even the esteemed Commander Johnson. Instead, a dark-skinned man named Mateo with sculpted features and his partner Jake, an older balding fellow with a big nose and a determined look in his light blue eyes.

We got to the gist quickly. For the past three hours, the front desk had been bombarded with phone calls from a company named Debenture Research (DR). DR employed a psychological research and guidance team named Guidance, Inc. headed by a former military psychiatrist named Fritz Ernst. DR explained that Dr. Ernst's team was providing psycho-social guidance to a Prisoner Ratner, a Vietnam veteran. DR had received word that a mental patient with oppositional personality disorder named Nick Crane had infiltrated CCS and was physically and psychologically abusing Prisoner Ratner. Multiple DR people had tag-teamed the receptionist, who following the CCS credo of excellent customer service, had dutifully answered every call. She had been reduced to tears and had finally kicked the calls upstairs until they reached Mateo's desk.

"What did you tell them?" I asked almost casually.

"I said there was no Nick Crane here. They kept digging. A lot of stuff goes on here; this institution works with various private contractors, so I called Captain Spencer to see what he thought. Captain Spencer said there was no Nick Crane here but that there was a man named Ned Stamper engaged in an FBI investigation. He told me to keep that under my hat, if at all possible." Mateo paused for breath.

"Did you keep it under your hat?" Crane so casual today.

"I did, but I know they didn't believe me. Have you ever been the victim of a troll attack?"

I shook my head. "I have," said Jake. "Or rather my nephew has. It was horrible. Thirty foul-mouthed bastards coming at you all at once. Like the goddamned birds in that Hitchcock movie."

"Anyway," said Mateo, "I'd bet my left nut that they're on their way here. Could just be a matter of minutes."

"Okay," I said. "Prisoner Ratner and I will be out of your hair within thirty minutes. Let me call SA Clyde." Clyde had left the prison, ostensibly to lie low, but actually to make final preparations. He was five minutes away. I told him Marguerite's people were on the way and that it was go time. I said that the CCS officers and I would meet him in the food service locker room. He hesitated while I counted to five. Then, begrudgingly, "All right, I don't like it, Crane, but I'm in."

We met in the locker room and carted our weapons and

equipment down to B-2. At some point Mateo winked at me and I realized that through some stroke of genius, either Carrie, presumably prior to the stabbing, or Captain Spencer, had subbed a couple of Alphabet Boys in place of the normal weekend watch commanders. Once we were past the guardhouse, the pensioner indifferent as always, Mateo pulled me aside.

"Listen, Carrie North is conscious. She can barely talk but she's conscious. She knows we're here. And that you and Bobby are going to make a run for it. She says she wishes she could be here to help. I wish we could help, but we'd just get in the way. We're actually just researchers in Tim Swann's department."

I grinned. "Don't worry. You've done plenty already. When did Carrie regain consciousness?"

"Early this morning."

Hmm. "So, somebody gave you orders yesterday to be on duty here today and cleared it with the brass." I stopped. It was obvious. Swann had made the request and Captain Spencer had agreed to it. Maybe he felt guilty for denying our request to take Bobby out for a bogus proffer session. I thanked them and told them to beat it. We shook hands. Then they filed back past the guardhouse, and Clyde and I key carded our way into Bobby's bunker.

Chapter Forty-Nine

Bobby had been busy. His bunker was spotless, his bed a study in military precision. His stainless-steel sink was as unspoiled as the day the workmen bolted it to the wall. The military magazines made two substantial stacks under the flat screen. He was wearing baggy khakis that made him look about three feet wide and an army field jacket over a denim shirt.

No time for more than the briefest of chit-chat. We zipped up our camo jackets and divided up the weapons and supplies. Bobby and I were each carrying a Glock with spare clips, a Taser-X2 (professional grade) with spare cartridges, two smoke bombs, a flashlight, a hunting knife, an OC canister, and ten feet up nylon cord. Our jackets were full of pockets, and they were crammed. No backpacks, they would only slow us down.

Clyde was traveling light—just his hunting knife, a coil of nylon rope, and a Romanian-made AK-47 with a holographic sight, which Bobby, despite all, was eyeing enviously. Knew what he was thinking. Good gun for walking point...But why in hell had Clyde not swapped the semi-automatic for a shotgun? I must've given him a look 'cause he said almost whimsically, "I like it to be sporting."

My phone rang. Mateo. "They're on the elevator coming down. Five big beefy guys."

"Pistols or rifles?"

"Both, I think."

"Body armor?"

"Don't know. They're wearing camo top to bottom."

"Do they have a key card to the basement exit?"

"I don't think so."

"Good."

Go time. Though I'd swear Bobby damned near caved. In the diner. Clyde in front. Me in back. Bobby couldn't seem to make any forward progress. Then we heard them banging around in the bunker. Bobby jerked to life and Clyde wanded the door. Five seconds of agony and it slid open, retracting back into the wall. We sprang through.

Sprinted down sixty feet of well-lit corridor. Overhead fluorescent lighting. Praying for the door to close. It did but not before the five beefy men had stormed through. They started after us. Moving in bursts and staying low. Smart lads. The tunnel jogged first right, then left. Handsome touches, old, think Craftsman. Came to three sets of dilapidated brick arches leading into three corridors. Like a three-pronged spear.

Clyde led us under the left-hand arch. This fork was about half as wide as the main corridor. Badly lit, it broke right after thirty feet. We made the turn and stopped, pressed flat against the wall. So far no sign of Fritz and his crew, which meant nothing. By now, they were surely informed that that there was an escape attempt in progress.

Clyde broke out three maps of the tunnels that led from the back of B-2 into the city. I looked at him quizzically. He tapped his temple with an index finger and smiled. Turned out he and Captain Spencer had met for a covert document exchange earlier that morning at a Starbucks in town. Clyde had made a copy for each of us. He and I sussed the map while Bobby stood guard, casually dangling Clyde's AK-47. The main corridor, which Clyde said was about a quarter of a mile in length, jogged left and right at regular intervals before finally feeding into an unmarked structure. "It's the old guardhouse," said Clyde. "Under the control of Fritz Ernst, I believe. The tunnels point east toward town." There were two main tributaries, the north branch that we were on, and the south branch. After angling away from the central corridor, the branches turned east and ran roughly parallel to the main branch. No apparent structures at the end of the branches. According to Clyde, the corridors rose gradually, and by the time you reached the guardhouse, you were close to street level.

I felt Bobby stiffen. Clyde and I both sensed it. He demanded his rifle back and took up the sentinel position, Bobby staring past him.

"Remember this spot," I said. "This is where we'll rendezvous if we get separated. If we're anywhere close to here." Staring into the subterranean dusk, Bobby and Clyde nodded without looking back.

I studied the map. The underground formed a rough "U" bisected by the curving central passageway. The legs of the "U" were connected to the scoliotic central spine by several connecting branches represented on the map by cross-hatchings. Several dozen little boxes marked "Storage" were drawn adjacent to the north and south branches.

Attack? Surveil? Or simply wait?

At first, we waited. Straining our ears. First their footsteps, cavernous, and then, as they neared, their voices, muffled. The footsteps stopped and started up again, coming straight at us. Bobby and I locked into shooting stances next to Clyde.

For unknown reasons, the camo boys stopped and turned around, apparently heading back toward the main corridor. From there they could turn east toward the guardhouse or take the south branch.

Waited. Their footsteps faded. Then we double-timed east up the north branch, which, we hoped, would spit us out in broad daylight on the edge of town. Once we were close enough for cell service, I would phone Tony.

Clyde paused at the first connecting corridor on our right, which was unmarked and unlit. He looked at me first. Then

Bobby. For the first time, he seemed uncertain. A good spot to duck out of sight, but this was no time to stop. "Listen," I said, "Bobby was a tracker and a tunnel rat in 'Nam. You're our rifleman. Let Bobby lead us out of here."

It was a risk. After the weeks of indoctrination. But I still trusted Bobby more than Clyde with tactical decisions.

Clyde's wide plain mouth flapped down into a frown. Torn but also relieved. Looked at us both and stared into the dark corridor. "Okay," he said finally. "Which way?"

"Straight ahead," said Bobby. He led the way and we walked slowly up the corridor. Thirty yards east of the connecting link the light dimmed, petered out completely, and then returned. Spooky. We came to storage areas, about ten by ten, that had been dug out of the earth on both sides of the corridor. Some showed signs of reinforcement against cave-ins. Others showed signs of human habitation—tattered sleeping bags, cooking pots, the remnants of old fires.

Then we came to the sign. *Restricted Area. No Trespassing.* Rust and flaking yellow paint. All it needed was bullet holes...

"What the fuck?" said Bobby, scratching at the stubble on his chin. A neck and shoulder roll and a grin. Old wolf and respected elder. He considered. "Not a good idea to backtrack. Unless it becomes necessary. In which case, we'll run like hell. But it's an old sign and probably means nothing."

"Hang on," said Clyde. "I forgot." He produced three suppressors. Thus equipped, we moved silently into the half-light.

Then they struck, four tunnel rats, hitting us low and hard. Suddenly, I was rolling around on the ground with a grunting hirsute character. He was cockstrong and kept trying to knee me in the nuts. Hands full, I fought him patiently. Vaguely aware that Bobby had escaped and was running back down the corridor, two assailants in pursuit, while Clyde was running up the corridor in the opposite direction. Rather than pursue Clyde, the fourth rat began cheering on my attacker. "C'mon, Otis. Kill that bad boy. Kill him. Gouge his fuckin' eyes out."

Motion from behind us. Just a blur. Someone jumped on Otis's back and he screamed. I flung him off me. A quick desperate search yielded my gun, which was lodged against the wall. The cheerleader had both his hands wrapped around my defender's throat. She was a young woman with long dark hair. Tall, burnt brick-red, spawn of some earthly demon, the cheerleader was panting as he tightened his grip.

No quarter. Not for this sonuvabitch. I shot him three times—head, neck, and shoulder. He was most likely dead before he hit the ground.

Turned toward Otis, who was lying facedown on the ground. The woman had jammed a knife somewhere in his upper back. Blood was seeping from the wound. Maybe fatal, maybe not. At that moment I didn't really care. I turned toward the woman. She had a broad, pale face and was wearing a long blue smock covering a pair of mud-spattered jeans.

I started toward her. Stopped. She was shivering, rubbing her hands like she was trying to rub away a stain.

"You saved my life," I said softly.

She shuddered, gathered herself, took a deep breath, and let her hands fall to her sides. Began to speak. "Those bastards. They were going to rob and kill you. And gang-rape me if they caught me. I've been following you and your friends for the last little while. I thought maybe you were good people."

"We are good people. And thanks again for saving my neck...Why are you here?"

"I was trying to help my mother. It's too late. She's dead." She stifled a sob. "She didn't wake up yesterday morning. She had a bad heart. All day yesterday I kept watch over her body. I couldn't bring myself to leave. Then today those bastards started coming after me. They know my mother 'cause she's schizo-phrenic and spent a lot of time here. They were her buddies," her voice dripping sarcasm, "because she got a monthly check and was good for beer money. They never bothered me as long as she was alive. But as soon as she was dead..." She stopped, half-gagged, started up again. "They're so disgusting." Another shudder. "I had my knife, and I hid out all day in three or four different dugouts." She gestured up and down the corridor. "I was going to kill them before they raped me. I've studied martial arts. I know the moves. Then I saw you guys and thought you had to be better than the rapists."

I tried to fathom the depths of her pain. "So you were here to help your mother?"

"Yeah. When she had attacks, she would hide in dark places. She knew lots of places around town. And especially this place. I think maybe she came here to die. She had been staying with me in my studio in town for a few days. I don't know where she was before that. She would disappear. I was used to it. But after a day or two at my place, she started acting strange. I watched her, and this time I followed her. We were here for three or four days. I had brought food, so we didn't starve. But I couldn't get her to leave. You know the rest." Misty-eyed, but that was all. She was a strong woman.

She retrieved her knife and wiped it off in the dirt of the dugout where the four antediluvians had been holed up.

I asked her if she knew about the guardhouse.

"I just know it belongs to the prison."

I nodded. "Let's get out of here."

Chapter Fifty

We started back down the corridor toward our rendezvous spot. She said her name was Jenny and I said my name was Ned. She said the only way out was to loop around to the south branch, which led right to the edge of town. Said she had been going to tell us but that she had to trust us first. Then, in the heat of the moment, she had just reacted. "It's going to haunt me," she said quietly.

I told her that he had it coming. And that there were one or more gangs of hired thugs in uniform hunting me and my friends. One gang wearing camo, the other wearing blue jumpsuits. "Human garbage," she said. "I'm so sick of them. Let's get out of here."

We paused when we came to the curve in the shaft where Bobby, Clyde, and I had reconnoitered less than an hour ago. No sign of my crew. Didn't expect to see Clyde, who had been running the other way, but had been hoping that Bobby would be here. I told Jenny I'd see if the coast was clear. Asked her to stay put. Rounded the curve. Moved slowly toward the archway. A few more steps and I could see the far wall of the main corridor. Took a deep breath and eased into it. Well-lit and wide enough to walk three or four abreast. Recced twenty or thirty feet in both directions. Nerve-wracking work. Nothing. No one.

Where the fuck was Bobby? I'd found him and lost him again. I turned back into the north branch and headed for the curve. Didn't hear…what I should have heard…as Jenny walked toward me. A bit sheepish for not having stayed put. I understood. These tunnels were spooky, an agoraphobe's worst nightmare. I smiled when I saw her, but her eyes bulged. "NED!"

I whirled and aimed for the legs. We went down together, and his gun skidded across the hard-packed earth. Another tough motherfucker. One of the five beefy camo boys who'd burst through the door after us when we left the prison. Needed an edge quickly before he wore me down. Managed to thumb his right eye hard just as he was about to overpower me. Then I was on top, firing close range lefts and rights, his bearlike hands parrying the blows. Jenny vaulted over me and began punching him in the face. This got his attention and the split-second was all I needed. Got under his guard with a right uppercut straight into his Adam's apple. That and Jenny's volley of punches did the trick.

She covered him with his own gun, while I stripped him down to his boxers. Let him keep his shoes. Swapped out his flak jacket for mine and cinched up his camo pants so that they wouldn't fall off my hips. Put his cap on my head and pulled it down over my eyes. Cut a length of nylon cord and tied his hands together behind his back in a constrictor knot. Looped two more lengths of cord around him chest-high, locking his arms in place. Secured it with another constrictor knot. Problem was what to do with him. While I was thinking it over, I pointed my Glock at his head and made him say the pledge to the flag. Needed to hear his voice, which was high and tight from pain. Then I herded him, Jenny behind me, back to the connecting tunnel that Clyde had considered taking before we were ambushed. Forced him to turn in at gunpoint and stayed on his ass for the first twenty yards. Told him this tunnel would take him to the main tunnel. Said I didn't care what he did once he got there.

"You fuckin' bastard."

"That's me."

He stood there shivering and kept stalling until I stepped up and stuck my Glock in his ear. Bingo. He ducked his head, turned, and trudged into the darkness.

I turned to Jenny, who was waiting at the entrance to the connecting tunnel. She was shivering and for the first time she seemed really scared. "Thank you," I said. "And don't worry. That's the second time you've saved my life. And I can tell you, these assholes wearing camo are paramilitary and do not go to the police. And do NOT worry about stabbing the rapist back there." I pointed east up the tunnel toward the No Trespassing sign near the dugouts. "He'll survive. The bad ones always do. Now let's go find my friend Bobby."

First, we recced all the way to the No Trespassing sign. Nothing. Just a few more dugouts that we'd missed on our first pass. Then we backtracked to the connecting tunnel. Ducked into it. On a whim. Frenchy Lefevre always said that the most innocuous decisions often loom largest in the end. This was one of those times. We were barely out of sight when the voices began. Loud. Spirited.

The voices grew closer. I was able to pick out Bobby's. He was asking each of the other four camo boys how come they got hit with the ugly stick. And why their mamas hadn't committed suicide in horror the minute they stuck their heads out of the womb. Had them laughing. I shooed Jenny farther down the connecting tunnel away from the north branch. They were still laughing when I stepped into their path, stooping slightly to disguise my height, cap pulled low, stroking my mouth and chin rhythmically, as if thinking, but actually to hide my face.

"Where you boys been?" Trying to imitate the naked man's pledge to the flag voice. "Thought you got lost."

"Shit, Bud," said one of the men. "That's the pot calling the kettle black. You're the one who got lost. But look what we found," pointing at Bobby. "Caught this mothafucka trying to crawl up into his own asshole. We had to pull him back out." He laughed and clapped Bobby on the back.

"All rightee, then. We're on a mothafuckin' roll. I took the other bastard's toys away. He's lying in a pool of his own piss back in that little tunnel." I pointed. "Let's go get him…"

They were all for it. A few quick strides and we were at the connecting tunnel. Two of them turned into it while the other two stayed at the mouth to keep an eye on Bobby, whose hands were cuffed behind his back. I turned to one of the guards very casually and stuck my Glock in his ear while Bobby swung around in an awkward rolling body block and took the other guy down. The sound jarred the two soldiers in the tunnel. They wheeled around, hesitated, and charged. I shot one of them right below his left kneecap. He went down screaming. His partner tripped over him and they were both on the ground. By now, my guy had his gun half out of its holster, so I clubbed him hard, right across the face, pulverizing his nose. Felt sick inside. These boys were second rate. Another prelim. Practice for the main event.

Took a while but we finally got it straightened out. One of the men—under the threat of being stripped naked and forced to walk in the dark—produced the handcuff keys and Jenny unlocked Bobby. We located his weapons, which the camo crew had divvied up. Then Bobby switched clothes with the one closest to him in size.

"All right, fellas," I said, finally. "I don't think anybody's going to bleed to death. Now get your asses moving." I pointed toward the No Trespassing sign. "Keep going in this direction and you'll come out pretty soon. Then your phones will work, and you can call for help. Sorry I can't be more helpful," never cracking a smile, "but if you didn't work for pigs, you wouldn't end up in all this slop." It was either send them away into the arms of any remaining north branch predators or murder them in cold blood, which is what your average psychopath would have done. I've never shot a man except in self-defense or to defend a partner under attack. Bobby killed Vietcong and NVA corps in Vietnam, but never execution-style.

We stood there, Jenny on my left, Bobby on my right,

watching them drag their asses away. Then the three of us hustled down the north branch all the way to the main corridor. Bobby was jacked from battle. I was weary and Jenny was silent.

The south branch was dark. We walked quickly, guided by our flashlights. Ducked into the first connecting tunnel and pored over the map. We could take the connecting tunnel to the main corridor, turn right, and waltz along till we came to the guardhouse. Or take the south branch that Jenny said would spit us out on the edge of Charlesburg. Downside was this meant passing another series of dugouts that Jenny said were inhabited by more riffraff. Or we could zigzag back and forth along the connecting tunnels while working our way east. And still no sign of Clyde...

Time. I folded up the map. Bobby looked at me. Cracked half a smile. He walked point and we kept Jenny between us. After a while, we came to the dugouts. The first few were empty but as we approached the third, a scraggly-haired gentleman bearing black jailhouse tats sprang into our path, his head-shaved boot woman in close formation. Bobby told them to get stuffed, and they backed down, snarling like junkyard dogs. After that we were extra wary. At one point, some desolate pariah lunged at Bobby with a knife. My friend laughed and pointed his Glock at him until he backed down. Another time, I had to brush past Jenny to help Bobby intimidate a cluster of derelicts, but with great care because no sooner had we routed one mangy pride than another closed ranks behind us.

Trudged on. Cannot describe the relief as we gradually left the degenerates in our wake. We ducked into a connecting tunnel and collapsed onto the ground. Jenny started shaking. But not so much as a whimper. Then Bobby shuddered, one of his patented, full-body convulsions. Pulled himself together. Spoke. "You know, old buddy, for a while there, I thought this was maybe even worse than Scorpion fucking prison, but I take that back. We're almost there. What do you say that when this is over, we get a little R&R down on the Florida Keys? Go trolling for marlin."

"Goddamned right, Bobby. You're on."

We were exhausted. Decided to hustle straight up the south branch to where it surfaced. Once we were closer, we would try to phone Tony. Ghosted back into the south branch. Started east. It wasn't far, now. After about thirty yards, we stopped, and I phoned Tony. Nothing. Tried again twenty steps later. Silence. Agony. Then it rang, distantly, but it rang. Caught a second time and a third. Went to voice mail. I wasn't worried. Pretty sure he was near. With reinforcements. Told him where we were and that we were heading for the south exit, which might or might not be patrolled. Signed off.

Fifty yards past the final connecting tunnel, Fritz's people met us coming and going. The same blue jumpsuits. Two teams. They knew it was us. One or more of the camo boys must have surfaced and turned us in. Or maybe they'd just been biding their time, waiting for us, knowing this was the only way out. Disconcerting to have eight AK-47s pointed at us. We were a split-second slow. Did not get our OC canisters out in time. After saving them for just such a moment. But maybe just as well. If we'd been quicker, we might have blinded them, but with so much firepower, they still might have shot us down like a pack of rabid curs. And they might have killed Jenny.

God, how I hated to surrender. I'm sure Bobby felt the same.

Chapter Fifty-One

Back at the guardhouse, Fritz and his goons shook us down for weapons and supplies.

Including our cell phones. Handcuffed us and hustled us down a cement staircase leading into an underground bunker where they sat us down on a low wooden bench against the far wall. Steel rings protruding from the floor between our feet. Uncuffed, Clyde sat on a bench to our right, his expression neutral, hands dangling halfway to the floor.

No sign of Jenny. Figured they'd let her go.

"Wunder hören nie auf!" said a small, clean-shaven middle-aged man with a booming voice and bushy white eyebrows. Had to be Fritz Ernst. Flicking a speck of dust off his immaculate blue jumpsuit, he walked up to us and spoke. "Prisoner Ratner, you have hurt me deeply. Such a betrayal. And to think how I trusted you. Once again, I am reminded of the need for discipline. Prisoner Crane," turning toward me, "I am told that you are a radical who needs to be broken on the wheel, so to speak." He giggled, a disturbing, high-pitched sound. Continued. "This is an area in which I am not without expertise." He paused and ran his fingers through his short, iron-grey hair. "On second thought, I believe I'll let Francis be your minder. Francis has a keen analytical mind and has already expressed interest in your case."

"Go to hell." I thought it and Bobby said it. Fritz responded with a mirthless smile and stepped away to confer with the man

I made for Francis. He was tall and very blond. Short hair. Alert grey eyes. A trace of Quincey, perhaps? Seemed at ease and quite at home here in the bunker. The other three men were of ordinary stature—one dumpy, one thin, and one basic, with a potato-shaped face. I made them for hirelings, not true believers. Subsidiary roles, more cheerleaders than true muscle, or so I hoped. There was no sign of the tall beefy secretary or the other team in blue jumpsuits who had helped Fritz's team pin us down in the south corridor.

Fritz and Francis completed their tête-à-tête. Fritz walked over and told us they were giving us fifteen minutes to introspect before we began the process. He motioned to the skinny fellow, who came over and linked our handcuffs to the steel rings protruding from the floor. Fritz and his crew then skipped up the stairs to the guardhouse.

I looked at Clyde who shook his head and waved his arms like the poles at a railroad crossing. Then he pointed at the wall across from us. Cameras and recording equipment. Of course. Then Clyde spoke. Just loud enough for us to hear. Two words only. "Be ready." Then he said it again, louder. "Be ready." He nodded emphatically, bowed his head, and seemed to doze off. For maybe ten minutes. Then, as if he'd made a decision, he stood up, walked over, and faced us, his back to the camera. Enunciated softly through clenched teeth.

"I've been waiting for you boys ever since they grabbed me. This mission is a motherfucker. Worst I've ever been on." Clyde stretched out his jaw. Drew it back in. "Listen. They're going to inject you with that drug they were giving Bobby. Some kind of test of manhood. I heard them talking. And they have their own party planned for tonight. It's Fritz's birthday or some such bullshit. They're going to be drinking. But don't worry. I'm going to fuck these assholes." He paused and stared at us. "Those bastards ran down the FBI. For no reason. Just to fuck with me. That don't fly with Jeremy Clyde. Not in Missouri and not here in bumfuck North Carolina...They called us 'boy scouts' and 'sobbing sisters.' Then Fritz told me that because I was FBI and because I didn't deserve to get assigned to an asshole like you, Stamper, they wouldn't bother to handcuff me if I'd do 'em a big favor and serve 'em their food and drinks tonight at their party. They said they were sorry but that they had to hold me until they had me checked out to make sure I didn't belong to any left-wing organizations. Said it was contractual and might take a day or two because they were kind of busy. Busy! Huh!" Clyde snorted. "I'll show 'em busy. They pissed me off plenty. But we're taught to recognize opportunities at the Academy. That's right, baby. Those motherfuckers are doomed." He ground his right fist into his left palm. Continued.

"Now listen. In an hour or two, upstairs, there's gonna be a fight. That's when you make your move. I'll make sure the door at the top of the stairs is unlocked. But be ready for anything. This will not be easy." He nodded toward the staircase. "You'll know when." He pulled a MASA cap from his back pocket, studied it, scowled, and placed it on his narrow skull. Crossed the bunker and mounted the stairs.

Bobby and I looked at each other. "We'll know when," he muttered. "Cool." He scratched his head. "That guy's way ahead of us. And I think he's got a little something artificial going on."

"What's his play?"

"I don't know. I guess we'll find out." Bobby nodded wisely. "But he's right. This mission is a motherfucker...The good thing is that lanky old country boy means business...Now listen, Nick, listen to me. You're about to go on one helluva hard ride. The drug will destroy your mind if you let it. The first hour is the worst. It's not as bad after that. You've just got to roll with it. I'm here with you. I won't gouge your eyes out. Not even if I want to." He chuckled grimly. "Just think of me as your brother who you love no matter how much you hate me at the moment. 'Cause the drug will make you hate me unless you can distract yourself."

I nodded. Not good. "The first time I saw you in the diner," said Bobby, "I was deep in the throes. I wanted to rip your head off. But I said a mantra. *Nick is my friend.* I said it over and over to myself until my bloodlust went away. If you thought I was weird when you found me in the diner, that's the reason. It's terrifying. You want help so badly. Any kind of help. That's how they conditioned me to feen for authority."

Bobby's lucidity. Extraordinary after what he'd been through. I needed my own mantra. *Bobby is my friend.*

After a while, they came back downstairs. The skinny fellow came over and unchained us from the floor rings but left us cuffed. Then he sat down on a bench near the stairwell and opened a black case. Began removing drugs and syringes which he spread out carefully on a white cloth. The other underlings fanned out across the bunker. Basic was drinking from a Styrofoam cup and Dumpy was walking the dog with his yo-yo. Francis walked over to me while Fritz waited near the stairwell.

He stood in front of me about a yard away. "How are you, Prisoner Crane?" He smiled, a brief quiver, and rubbed his chin.

"I think you already know the answer to that question." I grimaced. If I were a cowboy, I'd have spat.

"As I expected. You're feeling hostile. It's only natural. But don't worry. We know you have a certain knack. We may have plans for you. But first you need to be disciplined. And it needs to be rough. Dr. Ernst and I believe in tough love. The designer drug that we're going to give you will make you feel like you're in hell. Your own personal hell. I want you to think of it as your punishment for not always being a good patriotic American. And it serves a dual purpose. We need to see if you can ride it out. To see what kind of man you are. And if you pass the test, well then, maybe we can talk." He smiled again. Lips only. Eyes trained on mine. Deep steady stare. "Stewart," he gestured toward the skinny guy, "will inject you. Don't try to resist. If you do, we will tase you. And if you still try to resist, we may shoot you. This is your one and only warning."

"He won't resist," said Bobby who was sitting about a foot away. "Neither will I. I know I've got it coming. I know I fucked up." He winked at me and drew his manacled hands across his forehead.

I waited, the sweat beading up on my forehead. This was my worst fear. Being injected with some kind of awful narcotic.

The underlings walked over and trained their guns on us. Keeping their distance. Francis took out a Colt .45 and blew on the barrel. Fritz just watched. Stewart uncuffed us. Bobby and I could've grabbed him by the throat. Or launched ourselves at Dumpy and Basic. Maybe they would've shot us. Or maybe not. But even if we disarmed them, we would have Francis with his Colt .45 and Fritz to contend with. Ripeness is all and it didn't feel like it was time. I knew Bobby felt the same way. Told myself I had only a finite amount of suffering still in store. We waited.

Stewart took two loaded syringes out of the breast pocket of his jumpsuit. He nodded knowingly at the sight of Bobby's scarred veins and tapped my virgin mainline approvingly. I closed my eyes and waited. First Bobby, then me.

Chapter Fifty-Two

Words are useless but I'll try. First, the intense heat and then, the flashing lights. Drenched in sweat, a clawed animal rabid in my chest, an anaconda wrapped around my throat. Rodents scampering up the walls and across my body. I fell to the floor gasping for air. It only got worse. Tried to burrow into the cold cement like a rat dog seeking prey. When I thought I might be deep enough, I rolled over and looked up. Ceiling infested with warring insect colonies. Then they swarmed me.

I started screaming, or at least I heard my voice, somewhere on the outside, echoing back at me. Then Bobby was leaning over me, his voice a dentist's drill hitting live nerve. "Nick, close your eyes and listen. Ignore what you're seeing. Your only hope is to find your own heart. Which is stronger than all the evil in the world. Close your eyes and find it. Go deep. And face whatever you find. It'll be hell, but it should stop the hallucinations." Then he stood up and disappeared and reappeared in front of our bench, which seemed to enfold him. He bowed his head and shuddered. Carved out of stone by antediluvian bronze chisels.

Find my heart. Absolutely. Anything to keep the dark visions away. The animal was still trying to get out of my chest, but the anaconda and the rodents were gone. I closed my eyes... *After a while, I come to a cavernous, empty space. Then, very slowly, I crawl through a series of valves or hatches. Onto a trail skirting a stand of spruce and fir on the shore of a northern lake.*

Oceans of light are falling out of the sky. A broken window looks into a one-room hunter's cabin. My father Adam sits in a straight-backed chair, his deer rifle across his knees. DTs. Full blown. He's talking about how death comes for everybody...and how he is bringing it. Empty whiskey bottles are strewn about the room. Cords are protruding from his neck, his arms wrinkled and pale, like uncooked chicken flesh.

This is where it begins, the cold that starts in my chest and burns to the top of my skull. Every time I walk into a room or round a corner knowing the devil is on the other side...My father raises his rifle...his voice grows shrill...the room pulses with furry creatures chewing their way across the floor...Adam breaks the spell by spraying bullets, wild shots caroming off the walls. I blow on my freezing hands and lunge at him, knocking him backwards off the chair. His gun falls to the floor. I pick it up and shove the barrel into his chest. I do not pull the trigger. Our eyes lock and all I see is hatred.

When I can finally move, I step back and crack the rifle open. Remove the magazine. Adam never says a word. Just lies there on the plain boards of the wooden floor, staring into his own dark abyss.

Then I'm outside again under the ocean of falling stars running along the trail...

That was the last time I saw my father alive. They found his body six weeks later, down by the lake. The animals had gotten there first. Even though I knew I hadn't killed him, I hadn't done much to keep him alive either. That was the rub. After I graduated from high school, I took the Greyhound to California.

Ever since then when the game gets too rough and the cold overwhelms me, I go for broke. Risk my life to save my life, or somebody else's life. Or something like that. The only way I know to get warm...

Finally opened my eyes. Cautiously. Air still full of flying creatures but not as thick as before. Bobby still carved from stone. I wanted to knock his block off. Started toward him, and the shouting began. Upstairs. We looked at each other, Bobby's face blank and cunning, ancient and immobile.

"Nick," he said urgently, "don't think about how I look. You don't look too good your own self." That set him off and he chortled like a madman. Recovered. "Remember what Clyde said. 'When the fight…'" He didn't finish. Didn't have to. Intense shouting from upstairs. Of one mind, we double-timed toward the stairwell, Bobby leading the way. The staircase teetered like an old cement roller coaster swaying in a gale. I followed Bobby's huge square bulk. The rough cement steps bit hard into the soles of my skippies. Each step a great lifting.

One-third…two-thirds…three-quarters of the way, almost there, the door flew open, and Bobby said "Clyde," who pulled first him, then me, into the guardhouse and steered us down two steps into a nicely appointed dining room connected to a lounge where Fritz and his crew were in a near frenzy, in each other's faces, spitting insults and squaring off, except for Stewart who was standing by himself, half-dressed, staring at the wall, his head cocked to one side.

Clyde whispered something to Bobby and me, and we sidled around the dining room table, me on one side, Bobby and Clyde on the other. Then we army-crawled across the floor and stood on either side of the archway that led into the lounge. The argument was getting louder. Fritz called Francis a cupcake and Francis took a roundhouse swing. Fritz ducked and laughed. "See, you are a cupcake and an asshole too."

Clyde took advantage of the confusion to slip into the lounge. Got behind Dumpy and shoved him hard into Francis, knocking him over. Then he shoved Basic toward Fritz, who dodged nimbly, pulled out his gun, and pointed it at Clyde. Muscle memory and training…the low launch. I hit Fritz hard, thigh high. Felt like he shattered into a million jagged shards. Bobby and Clyde and I formed a thin, wavering line that seemed to stretch from LA to Key West. I managed to plant one foot squarely on Fritz's scrawny wriggling chest while Clyde pointed the German's Glock at Francis. Bewildered, Dumpy and Basic took it out on each other, slap-boxing and screaming insults about degenerate family trees. Only Stewart appeared unmoved, a thin stream of white spittle trickling from his mouth.

As if connected to Clyde by an invisible force field, Bobby sensed what was coming. He moved toward Clyde who under-handed him the Glock. Clyde then used one hand to grab Francis by the scruff of his jump-suited neck. Balled the other into a fist and slugged him hard three times in the face.

Clyde released Francis, who sank to the floor in stages, first to his knees, then a slow and complete collapse. He hit the carpeted floor hard with the left side of his face. Rolled over onto his back and let out a long, low moan. Theatrical. A little too theatrical. I launched myself again slamming into him just as he pulled his Colt from his belt holster. I grabbed his gun hand and banged it hard against the floor, trying to shake the gun loose. He moaned and clenched his teeth but held onto it. I had my hands full. The man could take a beating. He looped his left arm around my neck, but I was slippery with sweat and he couldn't get a good grip.

This seemed to go on for a long time. I finally let out an unearthly scream, let go of his gun hand with one hand, and elbowed him hard in the side of the head. Then a flurry of elbows until I stopped myself. Not dead, but he wouldn't be moving for a while.

I grabbed his gun and stood up. Bobby was on my left, thrashing Dumpy and Basic, while Clyde was bending over the prostrate Fritz who was begging for water. I felt someone behind me and whirled around. Still half-dressed, Stewart lunged at me with a Bowie knife. Caught me somewhere below the ribcage, just a scratch, and I shot him with Francis's gun, a gut shot. My ears rang from the blast. By now, Bobby had disarmed Dumpy and Basic, and Clyde had dragged Francis over to Fritz and was using him as a battering ram, slamming him repeatedly into the fallen doctor.

"That's enough, Jeremy." I tried to stop him. "He's an old man."

"What are you talking about?" Clyde shoved me away, sneering the words. "You just killed a man."

I turned toward Stewart. He was pressing on his abdomen with both hands. Blood was seeping through his fingers. A good medic might save him, just like I was saved when Marguerite's boot woman gut-shot me in October. I looked at Clyde. His eyes were hooded, his mouth a furnace. Still, he compromised by dropping Francis on top of Fritz where they moaned together. I felt sick, turned away. Caught myself. "Jeremy, we got to get out of here."

"Okay. First things first." He gestured toward our captives.

I had no idea how much time had passed, but by now the effects of the drug were lessening. The severe hallucinations were now merely a wobbly, eerie sheen on things. Clyde and I marched Fritz and Francis and Dumpy and Basic down the stairs to the bunker where we handcuffed them to the steel rings protruding from the floor. Bobby, who knows more first aid than I do, heated up some towels in the kitchen and worked to stanch the flow of blood from Stewart's abdomen.

"How is he?" I said to Bobby.

Bobby looked up. He was stacking up the bloody towels neatly. "I think he'll live. But I'm going to have to stay with him until a medic gets here." I shook my head. Compassionate Bobby.

Clyde and I walked over to the table and began helping ourselves to the leftover hors d'oeuvres. "Maybe you've noticed," said Clyde, "that there's no street entrance. We're still underground."

I hadn't noticed, but he was right. No windows. The recessed floor of the dining room gave the illusion of high ceilings, but the guardhouse was actually a squat, square underground structure located at the end of the main corridor, which was apparently shorter than the north and south branches. Unless they also dead-ended, which was too horrible to contemplate.

"The only way out is the way we came in," said Clyde. "The hard way."

"Okay," I said brightly, "we'll just take the first connecting tunnel to the south branch and walk out."

"That easy?" said Clyde.

"A man can dream...You dosed them, didn't you, Jeremy? Probably with the same shit they shot me and Bobby up with. How'd you do it?"

He grinned, his teeth yellow with white patches. "I was trained in pharmaceuticals. Got me a big salary increase right off the bat. I just put the dope in their drinks...But it's not quite the same shit. My shit does more permanent damage." Then he winked.

That's all he would say.

Clyde and I went back down to the bunker. I stood guard. He walked up to Fritz. Demanded to know where the wand to the door was. Fritz refused to answer. Clyde slapped him hard twice and Fritz began to whimper. Disgusted, Clyde turned to Francis, who was resilient beyond all reasonable expectations. My flurry of elbows had broken his jaw but spared his temple. He muttered something about painkillers and said they were in the doctor's case. Clyde demanded to know where the wand was, and Francis shook his head. Grinning, Clyde wound up dramatically to hit him again. No need for a quick direct punch against such a helpless opponent. Francis broke. Whispered. "Stewart...has...it..."

Stewart coughed it up. In his state, he couldn't resist. He also coughed up a set of keys. First, we tested the wand. The door to the main corridor retracted and we stared out into the luminescence that seemed to float like mist. Clyde wanded the door closed. We found a padlocked storage locker in a pantry in the kitchen. I went through the keys methodically. Finally, a match. Our weapons and backpacks had been tossed carelessly into the bottom of the locker along with our cell phones. Next to Clyde's AK-47. Stewart's medical bag was stowed neatly on a shelf.

"Come and get 'em," I said."

"Goddamn," said Clyde. "I clean forgot." He reached into the locker and pulled out his backpack. Rummaged around and produced a first-aid kit. Scissors. Gauze. Q-Tips. Bandages and alcohol.

Bobby began cleaning out Stewart's wound with the same care and concentration Tony had applied to his Beretta in the fisherman's cabin on the shores of Lake Winnebago. Then Bobby folded up a couple yards of gauze and pressed it against the wound. Anchored the gauze in place with surgical tape and ran an Ace bandage around Stewart's back and across the surgical tape. Crude but effective. Or so I hoped.

"Okay," said Bobby. "I'm on board. But we got to get out quick and get the paramedics back here to save this man."

Under Clyde's withering glare, I rooted through Stewart's medical case. Grabbed some Norcos, went down to the bunker, and pressed three into Francis's mouth. Enough to take the edge off, not enough to kill him. Francis chewed them dry and didn't say a word.

I went back upstairs where Bobby was giving Stewart Norco with water. My friend kept a generous handful for himself and suggested that Clyde and I stock up. I complied, just in case, but Clyde resisted. Bobby started laughing. "What are you, some kind of Puritan? You beat guys up for the fun of it but turn up your nose at these lightweight pain pills. What if we get injured? What if we need them?"

Bobby's turn to absorb Clyde's withering glare. The tall man spoke. "What I do is my business. You got that?"

"Whoa," said Bobby. "I get it. You did all this to save our asses." He flung his arms out wide. "We appreciate it..."

At that moment, there was a loud blast that sounded like it came from the south branch. Dynamite, I thought.

We outfitted ourselves much as we had in Bobby's bunker, earlier that morning.

I phoned Tony just before Clyde waved his magic wand.

327

"Thank god, Nick. Where are you?"

"We're just leaving the guardhouse. We just disabled the brainwash boys. We're gonna cut over to the south tunnel and walk out."

"Okay, the gate's open now. It was locked, probably to keep you guys locked in. Had to be Marguerite's people. Swann and Agresti and I have been working on it for hours. We finally got the FBI to convince the mayor to authorize a demolition team to blast it open. That was the blast you might have heard. Tim Swann was indispensable. Agresti and I are coming in to meet you. Swann will wait outside with the fibbies."

"Goddamn, Tony! Good work! But I don't know if you guys should come in. There's still at least one rogue para team running around in blue jumpsuits that is unaccounted for. Or if you insist, bring the FBI with you."

"I tried. They won't. It's just three guys. It's apparently the custom around here that nobody from federal law enforcement goes into the tunnel complex. They don't seem to care if we go in 'cause we're not local and we're not federal."

"Okay," I said reluctantly. "Be careful."

Chapter Fifty-Three

Clyde wanded the door, and we slipped back into the tunnel, three wraiths, one tall, lanky, and raw-boned, one short and powerful, the other somewhere in between. We moved three abreast down the corridor.

We sensed her footsteps before we saw her. Coming toward us. Flattened ourselves against the wall. Waited. Then we saw her in her blue smock, pressed flat against the opposite wall, moving toward us a little at a time. Jeremy got down on one knee and sighted.

"No!" I said. "She's our friend." Jeremy did not move a muscle. Locked in.

"Jeremy," said Bobby, "relax. She's a young woman, and she's our friend."

With great reluctance, Jeremy stood up slowly. "What the hell?" he said.

"She saved my life when we got attacked by those underground creeps. She's good people. I think she wants to leave with us. Fritz and his crew cut her loose when they abducted Bobby and me."

Clyde was still undecided.

"Here, I'll go get her. Just hang tough." I set off down the corridor to meet her. As I neared, she stiffened, then relaxed when she saw it was me. She stepped out into the middle of the corridor, holding her knife in her right hand. Slipped it under her smock, walked up to me, and threw her arms around me.

Met her halfway. Her gaze. Undaunted. Purest admiration. On my part, I can't speak for her. Side by side, we walked back to my team. Bobby greeted her fondly. Clyde nodded but did not speak.

I debriefed her quickly. She'd been patrolling the tunnels for hours, waiting for Bobby and me. Hoping we'd escape. Hiding in the connecting tunnels when not reconnoitering. This was the fourth or fifth time that she'd approached the guardhouse. So glad to see us. I felt the same way about her. She had not seen Fritz's second team, the blue jumpsuit boys, since our arrest. When I asked her why she hadn't gone on without us, she said it was because the south branch gate was locked.

"It's open now. Let's get out of here."

Bobby and Clyde in front, Jenny and me in back, we moved down the corridor. Just as we were approaching the first connecting tunnel, shouts arose in the near distance. Sounds of a struggle.

"OH, SHIT!" shouted Tony, from somewhere in the connecting tunnel.

He sounded close, perhaps no more than forty feet away.

We waited, two Glocks and an AK-47, with Jenny crouching against the wall behind us, fifteen feet from the mouth of the tunnel.

"Get that bayonet out of my back," said a voice. Agresti.

Apparently, the captors were bent on bringing their prey back to the guardhouse. A long minute. Then a stern voice commanded, "Turn right at the opening." Tony came around the corner first. Saw me motioning him to get down. He dropped silently. Then Agresti. Split-second of indecision and he too dropped. Then two men in blue jumpsuits carrying AR-15s with bayonets. Clyde blew them away, the NATO slugs jerking them around like rag dolls. Probably dead before they hit the ground. Could he have aimed low? To disable but not to kill? Maybe. But maybe not. He might have hit my friends.

Like a mad dog, Clyde hurdled Tony and Agresti and

whipped, greyhound-like, into the connecting tunnel where the rest of Fritz's second team was racing back toward the south branch. Clyde sprayed bullets down the tunnel and took off after them.

By now Tony and Agresti were back on their feet. Agresti was understandably shaken, but Tony was laughing. "Goddamn," he said. "That was a close call." He hugged Bobby. Then they were pounding each other on the back. My turn. Introductions. "Anthony Agresti, meet my friend Bobby Moore." They shook hands.

"Damn," said Agresti. "No wonder I wasn't keen on this mission. By the way, who was the human blur with the semi-automatic?"

"Mr. Jeremy Clyde," I said wryly. "FBI. UC. He's kind of refreshing. Being around him makes me realize I'm not the real Manchurian Candidate."

"Never thought you were," said Bobby softly. He looked around in wonder. Rubbed his eyes with his sleeve. Shook hands all around. Then we all shook hands again. Good to have Clyde, a wet blanket for every occasion, off pursuing the blue boys.

"By the way," I said to Agresti, "your FBI friend, Special Agent Carrie North, is pretty damned tough. So far, she's taken a bullet and has suffered life-threatening knife wounds all in the service of our cause."

"She's a good egg," said Agresti, "which is why I recommended her in the first place."

"I'm damned glad you did."

Then we set off down the connecting tunnel, slowly, with great vigilance. Bobby led the way, and we fell in behind him. We paused when we came to the south branch. It may sound funny after all that we'd been through, but we were nervous about looking around the corner. I finally took the bull by the horns. Stuck my head out slowly and sighted in both directions. No one. Told my team Fritz's second team had probably headed west, back toward the prison. They'd probably take the next connecting tunnel back to the main branch and turn right toward the guardhouse. En route, they'd trip over their fallen comrades. Stunned, they'd race to the guardhouse to report it to Fritz, who they knew was there celebrating his birthday. When they got there, they'd discover Fritz and Francis and the other lads in chains in the bunker. They would unchain them. Maybe they would be able to save Stewart; maybe they wouldn't.

We turned left and walked rapidly toward the demolished gate, looking over our shoulders at every third step.

Chapter Fifty-Four

Swann met us outside, thrilled but also pissed because he wasn't part of the "boots on the ground" rescue team. He filled us in quickly. Clyde had left by himself. Seemed highly agitated. Refused to say much. Just that he was flying to Boston to be debriefed by Carrie. Had to laugh at the thought of the tall man at Carrie's bedside, his long arms dangling, trying to be solicitous.

We had an obligatory drink with the local special agents, a soft-spoken, hard-jawed lot. I marveled at how Swann had talked them into pulling weight with the mayor to get the gate demolished. The fact they already knew about Carrie's Lowcountry exploits had worked in our favor. As the Kentucky bourbon began to loosen their tongues, one of the agents, a man named Mason, said the only reason Clyde could go into the tunnel complex was because he was UC, which meant no one would ever know. Custom was king down here and he and his colleagues honored the local desire to keep the Alphabet Boys strictly above ground. "Not that we want to go in there," said an older agent with a regulation military moustache. He sighed. "Sometimes, I think I don't understand the human race. Other times, I know I don't."

"It'll only get better," I said.

"I surely hope so."

Bottoms up and it was time to go.

We had the agents escort us to Tony's vehicle, a blue Navigator, and they very kindly shadowed us while we drove Jenny to her apartment. Bobby and I went inside with her. Everything in order. No sign of intruders. Still, in an abundance of caution, we convinced her to lie low for a few weeks in a downtown hotel. Tony put it on his AMEX card. Then he and Swann each gave her two hundred dollars for expenses. Tony had already phoned the local police and explained that there was a dead body, female, in the north tunnel near the No Trespassing sign. Jenny's mother. Heartbreaking. But time to go. I gave Jenny a big hug and insisted we exchange phone numbers. Something about that girl. Not that I expected to ever see her again.

Then the hard-jawed agents very kindly shadowed us out of town and onto the highway to Raleigh. After a few miles, they buzzed us and turned off at the next exit.

Tony and Bobby sat up front. Agresti, Swann, and me in the back, Swann in the middle.

"You saved our lives," I said to Swann. "By making that connection with Captain Spencer. Back in October, Agresti here saved my life. This time it was you. I can never thank you enough. How did you do it? Word was that the captain wouldn't grant any outrageous favors without talking directly with Carrie. What are you? Some kind of hypnotist?" I clapped him on the back. Was surprised that he suddenly seemed embarrassed.

"I might as well come clean," he said, after a long pause, "I'm good at doing voices. I do actors, athletes, politicians, you know...I was racking my brain. Carrie was still full of tubes. And slipping in and out of consciousness. She could not get on the phone. Then the light bulb came on. I could do a woman's voice..."

"Brilliant," said Agresti. "Just fucking brilliant."

"Swann is brilliant," I said elbowing him. "Not only that, I think Special Agent North has the hots for him."

"Aw, c'mon," said Swann. "It wasn't that hard. 'Cause I didn't have to do Carrie's exact voice. Just something fairly close. She had only spoken to Captain Spencer a few times. I was so nervous, my palms were sweating."

We all laughed. Swann, the nonpareil.

When we got to Raleigh, we stopped at a BevMo to stock up. Checked into two suites and one single at the Renaissance Raleigh. Bobby was telling Tony about life with Fritz and Guidance, Inc., so they shared one suite. Swann and Agresti were already thick as thieves talking sports and crime detection. They shared the other.

I was glad to have the single. Took a quick shower, dried off, and sat down on the bed. Just after two a.m. Not out of the woods. Not hardly. Marguerite was still out there. Desmond Cole was still a snake in the grass. Quincey was making his way back into the high life. Plus, the feeling that Fritz's assistant Francis and I might meet again one day. I had wrecked his all-American face. He would not take that lightly.

But Bobby was safe. At least for now. We were all safe. For the moment. One of my most challenging campaigns. I uncorked a bottle of Pinot Noir. Drank and thought about Adara.

Fell asleep. Woke back up. Adrift...

We flew out in the morning—Tony to LA, the rest of us to Boston. Before Tony embarked, I walked him to his gate. He told me he had decided that this whole escapade was his penance for going on the pad. I told him in that case he was now off probation. And that without him, there would have been no rescue. Which was true and made him feel good. It had been one helluva ride...

In Boston, Agresti and Swann and I took turns visiting Carrie at Massachusetts General Hospital. She was in pain and on drugs, but she would live. In fact, she was recovering quickly. Spunky woman. That was the good thing. The bad thing was her fondness for her morphine drip. Swann was worried.

Carrie was furious about missing the action and damned glad that we had sprung Bobby. She had debriefed Clyde and given him leave for some R&R. She agreed that Bobby should be given immunity. And couldn't wait to get back to work. Now that Bobby had been delivered, she could focus on building her domestic terrorism case against Marguerite...and Quincey...and Cole...and, unless he had a helluva good explanation for disappearing, Tommy Blank.

Agresti went back to work interviewing witnesses on a cold case on the island of Nantucket. Bobby spent his time inhaling historical Boston. I drank coffee in a North End café. Watched the people and looked out at the street. Laid off the sauce. I do that now and then.

Thought about Marguerite and her crew. Knew they wouldn't quit. Neither would I. Bobby told me that was the difference between me and the pantywaists who were too cowardly to stand up to the fascists. I would fight to the bitter end.

I said I had no choice.

"Of course, you had a choice," Bobby said cheerfully. "No one twisted your arm and forced you to go underground at CCS."

I looked at him. "You know better than that. You would have done the same thing."

He thought it over. Looked away. Looked back at me. Smiled. "I guess maybe I would have."

Chapter Fifty-Five

The following Tuesday at around nine p.m., I was just settling down with *The Zebra-Striped Hearse*, which I still hadn't quite finished, when one of my cell phones rang.

"Hey, stranger."

My heart jolted. Adara. Tried to play it cool. Couldn't. She asked me to meet her at the Champion's Sports Bar on Copley Place.

I rushed over. With extreme care. Had the cab driver run counter-surveillance for a good ten minutes. Saw nothing out of the ordinary. I gave the driver two Jacksons. Keep the change.

Walked into the bar and nearly had a heart attack. Desmond Cole stood near the door talking to a young male companion. I staggered. Literally. Caught myself, stepped aside, and stared. It wasn't Cole. But could certainly have been his body double.

Took a deep breath. Greatly relieved. Calm down, boy. Then the stern "don't get involved" part of my psyche tried to take over. Adara was a fine woman but...She was too young. From a different social class. Out of my league. Et cetera...She spotted me and walked over. Vast confusion.

"There you are." She smiled. Her sculpted lips. Light cascading from her almond-shaped eyes. Hair long and natural. Expensive leather jacket. Purple blouse. Tight jeans. Strappy black sandals with heels that added to her height. She grabbed me by the hand and pulled me to a table in the corner. Two vodka gimlets waiting.

"Drink. Quickly," she said. "We have to leave. Did you see him? With that kid near the door?" she asked.

"You mean Cole's body double? At first, I thought it was him."

"Greasepaint can do wonders. Dee is such a fucking voyeur. He knows you're in town. The young guy is a PI. Dee sent his double along as a reminder..."

"That he still has power over you."

"Exactly. The bastard. Go ahead. Tell me I was wrong. I thought he'd outgrown this. They've been watching me ever since you arrived back in town. He's going to regret this."

She paused, took a big drink. Put it down. Reached out and grabbed my hand with both of hers. Sweet voltage.

"Don't worry, Nick. I'm prepared for this."

Twenty minutes later, slouched in the corner under the awning of a nearby Courtyard by Marriott, I watched as she hobbled, bent-backed, through the door out into the drop-off area. Wearing a train conductor's uniform and plain black shoes, her hair under her conductor's cap, she looked thirty years older. At least. Greasepaint. She'd already arranged things with the concierge and our specially selected taxi screamed into traffic on three wheels. Had the driver take Highway One north toward Chelsea before doubling back into Cambridge. He dropped us off in front of an immaculately kept Victorian B&B in back of Harvard Square. I gave him a Franklin.

Certain that we hadn't been followed.

Our room was large. High ceilings. Overstuffed couch and chairs. Walnut coffee table. Old-fashioned radiators gurgling gently. Unseasonably crisp that spring night. Two bottles of champagne cooling in an ice bucket.

Unstrapped myself while Adara changed out of her disguise. Two guns and a hunting knife. Popped the cork on one of the champagne bottles. Glad I'd only drunk one vodka gimlet. Almost like a fresh start.

We talked about this and that. Her father, who had been

asking about me. And who said he wanted to get together for dinner, sometime soon. Her play, *Year of the Rooster*, was opening in a few days. "I love playing the poor old mother. But what I really want to do is start working with the Innocence Project."

"I haven't forgotten. In fact, I already spoke with Agresti. He said he'll be contacting you as soon as the dust settles. He's a cautious fellow."

"While you're Mr. Tweak-the-Tiger and see what happens." She smiled merrily and licked a bubble of champagne from the corner of her mouth.

I rose to the bait. "Some might say that. Others might say I'm the soul of discretion. Which is why I'm glad we're sequestered here in this out of the way but utterly charming B&B." Champagne loosening my tongue. I put down my glass. She put down hers.

At first our kisses were gentle. It grew slowly. But it grew. Kiss by delicious kiss. And then we were devouring each other. Tonight, she meant it. I could tell. Didn't know what it meant. Maybe nothing. Did my best to stay in the moment.

It was different in the morning. Gentle and tender. Then we went back to sleep. When we woke up, we groaned and got moving. She had a rehearsal at one o'clock and I had a flight to catch.

Goodbyes are rarely easy. We stood near the door talking and embracing. "Don't be a stranger, Nick." She arched her long, graceful neck and kissed me on the forehead. And then a column of descending kisses down across my nose until she came to my mouth.

She left first, and I followed ten minutes later. Waved to the other guests and got in the cab that was double-parked in front. Back to my hotel where I met Bobby. We flew from Boston to Milwaukee. Took a taxi to Jimmy Sain's farm where we had cached Bobby's Econoline. Jimmy wasn't there. I left a long note of thanks under his doormat. Then we drove west across this great land. Across the plains and across the mountains. We didn't talk much about what we had just been through. Bobby said nothing about his weeks of brainwashing, and I didn't prompt him. When we did talk, it was mostly about the good times past and gone and the future good times we hoped to experience. Although we both suspected that before long, we would once again be locked in mortal combat with Marguerite and her gang of terrorists.

At around nine p.m. on Saturday, June 1, we arrived at Bobby's house in City Terrace. Where we were greeted by his goats. Inside, sipping Heinekens, we talked about everything except what would come next. There would be time for that. But for the moment, we were simply glad to be home.

Later that night, lying alone in Bobby's guestroom, I breathed deep and slow. To quiet my racing mind. I thought about how Swann had impersonated Carrie North at our time of deepest need. How Jeremy Clyde had gone out on a limb for us. How Jimmy Sain had found a way to get Tommy Blank to talk. How Tony Bott had been there by my side. And how Adara felt in my arms. I was moved. Friends and lovers. Here in this world. Finally, I slept.

ACKNOWLEDGMENTS

I would like to thank all of my friends who supported me throughout the writing of *27 Days*. Special thanks to Ellie Eich, my friend and early editor, who read and commented upon the manuscript countless times before I submitted it for publication, and to Peter Hoffman, who schooled me in the art of thriller writing and helped me discover the joy of writing in the first person. I also want to thank crime novelist Charles Salzberg for recommending this book to Down & Out Books and being unfailingly supportive since the day I met him on my crime blog back in 2014. Special thanks also to Eric Campbell and Lance Wright at Down & Out Books for very kindly agreeing to publish my work and to my editor Chris Rhatigan for helping to improve it. I also want to thank my cover designer Margo Nauert for her intriguing cover design and my boss John Brown for his unfailing good humor while teaching me the nuts-and-bolts of private investigation. Finally, I would like to thank my late friend, Vietnam veteran Warren Larry Foster, for whom I feel the greatest affection.

PATRICK H. MOORE is a Los Angeles based private investigator and sentencing mitigation specialist. Since 2003, he has worked on over five hundred drug trafficking, sex crime, violent crime, and white-collar fraud cases.

Patrick started All Things Crime Blog in 2013. For several years it was one of the most popular crime blogs in America and currently has over three million views.

Patrick studied English Literature and Creative Writing at San Francisco State University.

While in college, he published numerous short stories and novel excerpts. More recently, in 2014, he indie published his first thriller, *Cicero's Dead,* which sold well and was a finalist in the thriller category in the Beverly Hills Book Award Contest.

27 Days is Patrick's first traditionally published novel.

On the following pages are a few
more great titles from the
Down & Out Books publishing family.

For a complete list of books and to
sign up for our newsletter,
go to DownAndOutBooks.com.

Getting Dunn
Tom Schreck

Down & Out Books
November 2022
978-1-64396-287-0

Discharged from the army and back in the States and unable to cope, TJ Dunn spirals into an emotional daze, spending her days working at a suicide hotline and her evenings moonlighting as an exotic dancer. Her only outlet for her anger is a punching bag at the local boxing ring where she works out with a handsome trainer, Duffy.

Just when she thinks she's reached her limit, an anonymous phone call shocks her back to life and gives her a new mission, justice for those she loves and she won't stop at anything to do it.

Edgar & Shamus Go Golden
Twelve Tales of Murder, Mystery, and Master Detection
from the Golden Age of Mystery and Beyond
Gay Toltl Kinman and Andrew McAleer, editors

Down & Out Books
December 2022
978-1-64396-278-8

Edgar & Shamus welcomes mystery connoisseurs to the Golden Age of Mystery and Murder—Twelve original tales of mystery and suspense written exclusively by Edgar Allan Poe Award and Shamus Award-winning authors.

As if picking up where Sir Arthur Conan Doyle, Dame Agatha Christie, and Dorothy Sayers left off, the who-dun-it, why-dun-it, how-dun-it, and unshakable alibi are all afoot in *Edgar & Shamus*. Travel back in time with an all-star cast of some today's leading experts in the art of crime fiction.

Mickey Finn: 21ˢᵗ Century Noir
Volume 3
Michael Bracken, editor

Down & Out Books
December 2022
978-1-64396-279-5

Mickey Finn: 21st Century Noir, Volume 3, the latest entry of this hard-hitting series, is another crime-fiction cocktail that will knock readers into a literary stupor.

Contributors push hard against the boundaries of crime fiction, driving their work into places short crime fiction doesn't often go, into a world where the mean streets seem gentrified by comparison and happy endings are the exception, not the rule.

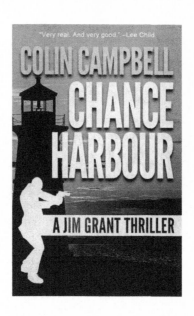

Chance Harbour
A Jim Grant Thriller
Colin Campbell

Down & Out Books
December 2022
978-1-64396-277-1

Dementia is robbing the old man in the ICU of any coherent thoughts until his face finally clears. "Okay. I know what happened. I need you to call my son. He's with the Boston Police at Jamaica Plain."

But Jim Grant isn't at Jamaica Plain; he is getting over being resurrected. Until he gets a call to say his father is seriously ill. But Grant arrives too late. His father has been abducted. A bomb has exploded outside a diner. And the FBI wants to know how his father knows a Russian oligarch who is even older than he is. For father and son it could be the last chance to reconcile their differences. It might also be the last chance for everything.